UNBELIEVABLE

UNBELIEVABLE

JENN LESSMANN

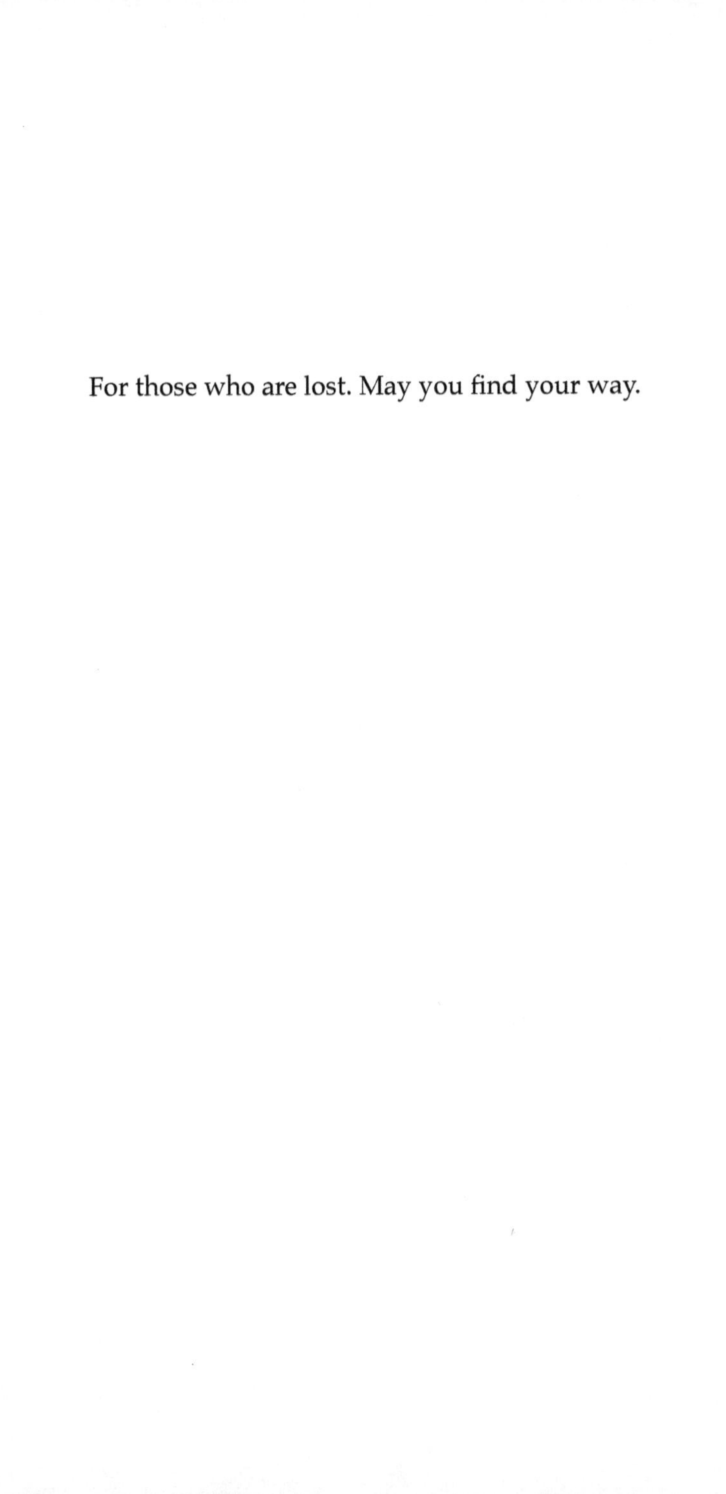

For those who are lost. May you find your way.

Previously…

The world has changed. There, I said it. Things have to be different now, and not just for me. What we did is going to affect everyone. You can't bring down a mystical Gate that stood for centuries and not expect consequences.

Goddess, I hate consequences.

My hometown, Queen's Creek, was founded by refugees. Women and men who fled persecution during the witch trials. Not the ones you're thinking of. The good people of Virginia hanged convicted witches over a one-hundred-year period, spanning many years before and after what happened in Salem. Not all of them bore the Gift.

The first Gatekeeper did. Mary's magic came from an affinity for water, as did many of the others. The witches of Queen's Creek manipulate energy, directing it toward their intentions, and those blessed with Gifts can strengthen their powers by drawing on the elements. When the hunters came —like they always do—Mary sacrificed herself to create the boundary spell that protected the town. It lasted almost three hundred years.

Until I broke it.

To be fair, it was failing on its own. Magic was glitching all over the place, strange storms, charms gone wrong. The will-o'-the-wisps that usually confined themselves to the banks of the Creek, munching on excess magical energy, somehow managed to break through to the mundane forest on the other side.

My father and older brothers studied the problem. The Speaker of the covens asked them to develop the elixir of life. She hoped to extend Alice's term as Gatekeeper while she trained a replacement. Any young witch should have been honored to take the position, but the Gatekeeper's successor had to accept the role. It would have been a reasonable request if it hadn't amounted to a death sentence. Murder by isolation. A life term of imprisonment disguised as service to the community.

I could have followed in Mary's footsteps and those of the other three Gatekeepers who took their turns feeding the spell. I was chosen, after all. But the town had grown beyond the capacity of the boundary spell to keep it hidden. No young life would have balanced the energy.

Especially one bound since childhood. I didn't even know I had a Gift until the blackouts started. My parents' efforts to protect me felt as misguided as the elders' dependence on a boundary spell developed by their great-grandparents to hide a settlement that was never intended to be permanent. Magic was never meant to be contained.

So I let it out, broke my bind, released the energy of Queen's Creek into the world.

And attracted the hunters to my home.

When I went back to school, I thought I'd saved us all from a magical apocalypse. The energy built up inside the boundary would have destroyed us. It had to go somewhere.

But like attracts like, and the witches who lived outside our bubble suddenly found themselves with more energy than they'd ever accessed before. They didn't know what to do with it, and some of them pushed at the edges of wisdom.

They tried bigger and bigger spells, risked more complicated workings, performed their magic where mundanes could see it.

Tori built a coven of sorority girls. The bonfire must have shone across campus like a lighthouse, drawing dangerous attention. Even if two of the girls she'd chosen hadn't had a hunter for an uncle.

Daniel Wesson. The man who burned the apartment building where Tori's sister lived while Grace hid under a bed. Two witches died that night. One to the fire. One to the smoke.

More flames lit the magic shop when he tracked our movements to my brother's temporary home and business. Thomas's wards slowed the flames, and we dragged ourselves down the fire escape. When we returned hours later, bruised and exhausted, the building still stood, a testament to the Chicago Fire Department more than Thomas's magical security system.

We couldn't let it happen again. To anyone. But we'd released the boundary around Queen's Creek that held in our people and our magic, and we couldn't go back to the way it used to be.

Magic is energy plus intention. The energy comes from the elements, from life and love, and everything that grows. The intention comes from the witches. Our people. We're stronger together.

But how could we maintain that strength without giving up our freedom? The answer took me back to the beginning. A binding spell. This time, we bound the individual members of our community to each other, creating a net that linked us all, no matter where we stood in the physical world. Witches of Queen's Creek could draw on the strength of their friends and family. We hadn't tested the distance yet, but so far, it worked.

The fact that a few weeks ago, I'd planned to finish my Wakening on the mundane side of the Creek and live a permanently unmagical life felt almost unbelievable.

1

The mug should have shattered into a million jagged pieces. A rain of stoneware or an explosion of earthenware. I used to know the difference. Not that it mattered once it slipped from my fingers. Now, it was redefining hand-thrown pottery on its way to the stone floor of the café. *I swear to Athena-with-all-her-skills, it was an accident.*

A stronger curse escaped my lips as I reached for the falling mug, and I summoned my Gift with faster reflexes than I was physically capable of. My skin tingled with magical energy.

"You got that, Cate?" my twin brother called from across the café. He didn't even look up from the stack of papers in front of him. If anyone asked, he would tell them he was working on inventory for the magic shop and suggest they mind their own business. The suggestion would probably be strengthened by his Gift for influence. So far, no one had asked. Mostly because no one else was in the café. We didn't get a lot of foot traffic at 2pm on a weekday.

That didn't mean I could use magic risk-free. Mark, the store manager, sat in the back room actually doing inventory.

And there was a new barista around here somewhere, but she'd gone to clean the restrooms twenty-five minutes ago and hadn't returned. Still had that new-employee dedication to quality.

I frowned, hand extended above the arrested disaster. A gray-streaked mug hovered less than a foot from the ground, a splash of coffee drooling from its tilted mouth, frozen in midair before a drop kissed the floor. The time bubble was one of the smallest I'd ever created, just large enough to contain the spill. My fingers curled, a twisting motion beckoning the cup and its contents back to me. Time reversed direction, the mug righting itself and flying up to the counter as if someone hit rewind on the café's glitchy security camera recording. As if it had never happened. As far as the mug was concerned, it hadn't.

I released a tight breath and glanced up at the dark glass ball that hid the camera in the corner of the ceiling. No blinking red light. Somehow, using magic always seemed to disrupt the Wi-Fi. I counted to five before releasing the energy that had called the mug back to me. Without the magical interference, the camera blinked back to life.

"Tah Dah!" I called, spreading my arms wide in celebration. A little too wide, as it turned out. The back of my hand brushed the mug, and this time, its destruction was assured. Ceramic shards exploded against the floor, splashing lukewarm coffee on the other side of the counter.

"Hex it all!" I blew a strand of purple hair out of my face and resisted stomping my foot on the sticky rubber mats.

Thomas turned a page, keeping his head down. "You alright over there?"

If I hadn't been almost one hundred percent certain it would end in catastrophe, I'd have held out my hand again and called the broom from its home in a little nook by the bathrooms. Make it dance all Sorcerer's Apprentice-style. The daydreams I had before spring break felt closer these days, verging on possible. But even though I'd become more adept at using my Gift—like reversing time to bring the cup back to its original position—the more casual forms of magic Thomas and the rest of my family used still eluded me.

How long would it take me to master the basic telekinesis the kids from Queen's Creek used growing up? My parents' bind had saved me from my destiny as the Gatekeeper but set me back about twenty years of practice.

Grabbing the broom and dustpan the mundane way, I shoved a roll of paper towels under my arm for good measure.

"Time to cut back on the coffee, I think," Thomas said, still flipping pages that had nothing to do with the magic shop he'd taken over while the owners were away.

"The coffee is not the problem," I said, although caffeine jitters no doubt contributed to my lack of coordination. Probably should have quit after my third cup. Kneeling on the floor, I sopped up the offending beverage with a handful of paper towels.

Thomas looked up. Seeing my expression, he sighed with more drama than the situation required and walked slowly up to the front of the café. Crossing his arms and leaning back against the counter, he said, "So, what is the problem?"

I pushed up my glasses and tucked my hair behind my ears, suddenly embarrassed. Usually, I was the calm, responsible twin. I chewed my lip. "When does it get easier?"

He tilted his head, and an unruly wave of blond hair flopped across his forehead. Taking the broom from where I'd leaned it against the counter, he twirled it like a baton. "It's just like anything else. What do they say? Ten thousand hours to become an expert? You're at what? Five hundred or so since you broke the bind? Maybe give yourself a break."

"I don't have time." As soon as the words were out, I

wished I could pull them back. I stood, taking the broom from him.

Thomas dropped his head, but it didn't hide the smirk.

"Ha. Ha. So funny. My Gift is time manipulation, and I can't keep up." I rolled my eyes. "I'm not kidding. What am I supposed to do? Freeze the whole world while I take Advanced Studies in Magic?"

Where would I even find a class like that? Did Nora have a secret curriculum outside the college catalog? Something like that should have come up in an academic advisory meeting if your advisor was a witch. But she'd hidden her arcane roots from me for most of my college career—what else was she holding back? Maybe I could have been enrolled in Herbalism or Astrology this whole time. Was it too late to change my major?

Thomas's eyes softened. "What makes you think you need to keep up?"

I tapped the broom on the floor. "Are you kidding? I—"

My brother put his hand on the broom handle. "No. Shut up and listen to me for once. I love you. Your friends love you. Adam—"

"Adam has done so much already. I can't ask him to make up for my weaknesses anymore." The former Guardian of the Gate cared for me, but our history still felt like a story I once read rather than something I experienced firsthand. Adam and I should have sat down and talked things out days ago, but I didn't know where to start. Or how I wanted that conversation to end.

I swept the broken bits of ceramic into a pile at my feet and reached for the dustpan.

Thomas pulled it from my hand. He held my eyes for a moment, then kneeled in front of me, setting the pan against my pile. "I know you don't want anybody to take care of you, but that doesn't mean you have to do everything yourself."

It was easy for him to say with a Gift that soothed every interaction. He'd never had anything to prove.

We got the mess cleaned up just in time for the afternoon mini-rush as students stopped in after classes. Despite their chatter, the café felt quiet without Brian's constant humming. The new barista returned from cleaning duty right as the doorbell rang. But she never once used a dramatic slide to cross behind me or flipped the shaker like a Hollywood bartender. She just stood at her register, smiling as she passed me cups like taking complicated coffee orders fulfilled a lifelong dream of hers.

Must remember to check the schedule on my next break. I could have sworn Brian was working today. But my days had gotten a little mixed up in the aftermath of the hunters' attack.

What if he didn't turn up for his next shift, either? Maybe he left school after his near-death experience. No one would blame him.

Except.

I kind of liked having a mundane friend who knew about my magic.

And I needed his help working out this whole time-space-continuum problem. Somehow, my Gift, my father's work, and the Time Stream that formerly bordered Queen's Creek were all related. If we could figure out how, we might be able to bring him back. Maybe even undo what had happened to Elspeth and give her back her youth.

Adam, Thomas, and I had access to an ancestral grimoire and a community full of witches to help us understand the magic. The alchemy was holding us back. That stack of papers Thomas kept carrying around may as well have been written in a foreign language instead of our father's cramped handwriting. The science outstripped anything they taught at the general education level in college, and the guys hadn't matriculated after graduating from secondary school in Queen's Creek. None of us studied Physics.

That was where Brian came in, but he hadn't actually come into the café in days, and he wasn't answering my texts. I was starting to worry, but I covered it with frustration.

I didn't want to find a new physics tutor. How would I explain what I needed to learn and why I needed to learn it to some random TA?

Maybe they wouldn't care as long as I paid for their time. *Ugh.* How many coffee hours was that going to take?

Marking the next cup with a Sharpie, New Girl paused. "Cate? We're getting a line over here. Should I call Mark to expedite?"

Nobody wants that. I shook my head to clear it and took a breath, checking her notes on the cups. "Sorry, Isa. Brain freeze. I'm good."

2

After work, Thomas and I walked over to his apartment above the magic shop, where we'd set up a nightly study session. He tried to explain what he'd read at the café on the way there, but I didn't get the impression he understood much of it. Giving up, he stuffed the papers into his messenger bag as he walked. "Maybe Adam found something."

When I pushed through the beaded curtain into Thomas's apartment, I nearly tripped. Thomas used to confine his hoarding to the fire escape balcony, a couple of bookshelves, and an overflowing dresser. But now the studio space looked more like one of the frat houses after a party.

He blamed his new roommate. Adam left Queen's Creek with only a satchel and an oversized duffle bag, but he must have charmed them to be bigger on the inside because Mary Poppins couldn't have unloaded as much crap from her carpetbag. When Thomas had first come to the café, he complained that the space felt claustrophobic now that he had to share it.

Still, those were Thomas's t-shirts draped over the back of the futon and my brother's shoes piled up next to Adam's boots in the corner by the door. Mugs of cold tea that couldn't all be attributed to his houseguest sat abandoned on nearly every flat surface. Thomas's milk crate coffee table disappeared under a cascade of papers and notepads. A stack of old books teetered beside it. So, not exactly like a frat.

At the sound of the jangling beads, Adam looked up from his spot on the futon. His concentration broke when he saw me, a wide grin replacing a deep frown. He dropped the papers from his hands and crossed the room in the time it took me to say, "Hey, Adam. What did you—"

His hands cupped my face, pulling me in for a warm kiss.

My breath caught as much from the surprise as the kiss itself. We saw each other yesterday, but he acted as if we'd been apart for years.

In some ways, we had. My Wakening lasted three years. Apparently, I wasn't the only one who felt the lost time. How long would it take Adam to feel caught up? It wasn't that the kisses weren't good or that his embrace didn't fill something inside me. But he'd been thinking of this moment, of me and our relationship, since the day he left on his own Wakening. For me, our past felt like a dream. As much as I didn't want to wake up, it didn't feel real. I liked him, felt safer when he was around, missed him when he wasn't…but it felt as if he wanted more. He gave more. His whole heart lay open in front of me, and I was afraid to break it. So I kissed him back, promising myself that we would talk later.

Thomas pushed past us and added his stack of papers to the pile on the coffee table. He cleared his throat. "Your phone's ringing."

I lifted my hands to Adam's chest and gently pushed him away.

As I pulled out the phone, Thomas set out his kettle and started making tea. "Chamomile?"

I nodded, remembering my resolution to cut back on

caffeine.

"Sounds good." Adam settled back on the futon.

That settled, I answered the phone without checking the ID. "Hello?"

"You have to help me." The voice on the phone shook.

I shivered. The hairs on my arms stood up, responding to her energy, even from the other side of the city. Getting used to our connection was going to take more time. "What's wrong?"

I hadn't heard from Tori in a few weeks. Not since she took the job at the public library. Her hours kept her so busy she hadn't come into the magic shop or stopped by the café. When she wasn't in class, she was there, down in a basement reading room, translating rare occult texts from Latin for mundane readers. And I was good with that.

We hadn't talked about what happened last time she'd come to the magic shop with us. After we escaped the hunter and turned him over to her parents, we'd gone our separate ways. Nora told me she was staying out of trouble, and I believed her. Forgiveness was easier at a distance.

I had to keep reminding myself she hadn't meant to hurt me. The hunter killed her sister, and he would have killed us.

It almost justified the pain she'd caused me. The betrayal of her attack. She did what she felt she needed to do to save herself. To stop him.

Even so, I'd probably never fully recover from it. Never completely trust her. She'd chosen revenge over my safety, over the safety of all of us. Thomas and Adam had almost died fighting the hunter, and she'd made it more dangerous. I wrapped my free arm around my waist, willing myself to stay calm until I could figure out what had Tori so upset now.

"I think I hexed it all up. They're going to fire me for sure. Nora's going to kill me," Tori's breathy voice rose an octave with her anxiety. If she didn't bring it down a notch, only dogs would be able to hear her.

"Breathe," I said. "If Nora was going to kill you for something, she would have done it when you made her sit through that hearing."

Our witchy academic advisor had never enjoyed the administrative responsibilities of her professorship. But recently, she'd needed to unravel more than a little red tape on Tori's behalf. When Tori broke the school code of conduct and the witches' covenant of secrecy, the subsequent disciplinary hearing forced Nora to balance mitigating the mundane consequences with protecting us all from the witch hunter who attended under the guise of supervising Tori's accusers. Afterward, Nora made Tori promise to abandon the potions business that got her into it.

"You didn't see her face when she got me this job, Cate. This was my last chance. She's going to send me back to Salem for sure. And then my parents—" she cut herself off with a squeak as if she couldn't bear to imagine their response.

I pursed my lips. The Walshes gave me the willies. Honest-to-goddess, tingles-up-my-spine, sour-stomach creeps. They'd done nothing but show up exactly when we needed them, threatening anyone who posed a danger to us, and offering to take care of the hunter after we defeated him at the theater. But there was something in Mr. Walsh's tone when he said, "He will meet justice." I didn't know how he and his wife intended to "handle him," and I wasn't sure I wanted to.

"It can't be that bad." Even though every interaction I'd ever had with Tori indicated the opposite.

"What's Wednesday done this time?" Thomas set my tea on the counter and physically smoothed the hairs on his arms.

Should I be comforted or concerned that he felt the effects of her energy as much as I did? We still didn't know enough about the spell we'd cast to bind everyone in Queen's Creek. It should make us stronger—all of us able to draw on the energy of the whole community—but what else would this connection do?

Adam looked up. Raising an eyebrow, he mouthed, "What's going on?"

I put my phone on speaker and laid it on the counter next to my tea cup. "Tori, can you start over? What happened? What makes you think you're getting fired?"

"Crowley's balls, Cate! I don't *think* I'm getting fired. I'm getting fired for sure. They just don't know it yet. They told me what would happen if I—No, it isn't your fault. They won't do anything to you—You have to help me. Maybe they won't find out." Tori's words tumbled over each other, fading in and out. Something shuffled in the background. Someone sniffled.

Adam pressed his hands into the back of a bar stool. "Is someone else there with you?"

My eyes widened. *Shit.* I replayed the conversation in my mind. Had we said anything that would give us away? No, right? Just us normal mundanes talking a normal, mundane friend off a ledge. She had a unique choice of expletives, but that didn't mean anything.

"What? Oh, yeah. But don't worry about her. She's a friend. Actually. Wait. Do worry about her since you clearly aren't worried about me," Tori huffed.

Thomas rolled his eyes. "Girl, if you don't start talking…"

The temperature increased around my brother. Usually, I wouldn't approve of using his Gift to encourage another witch to talk, but Tori never behaved like any other witch.

Still, I tilted my head, giving him my responsible twin look.

"What?" he asked, shaking out his wrists. The temperature dropped back to normal.

I sipped my tea. It needed honey.

"What's going on, Tori? Who's with you, and why are you getting fired?" Adam asked.

More scuffling and low voices. Then Tori said, "So, guys, this is Noemi. She's the librarian in charge of the Reference section. She's been supervising my work because they want to put some of these in circulation. Even though I told her most of it's just shopping lists and attendance records. Mundanes are not going to care about Goody Osborne's groceries if she wasn't using them to hex her neighbors."

"Some people will find that fascinating. You never know where someone's research will take them," came an authoritative woman's voice.

"They can hear you," Tori said. "Maybe start with *Hi*."

The woman cleared her throat. "Excuse me. Sorry. Hi. My name is Noemi Alvarez. Reference librarian."

"Witch," added Tori for clarification, her tone leading Noemi to continue.

"Witch," Noemi agreed. "Well, vampire-witch. Vegan vampire-witch."

I put my cup down and backed away, my hand on my mouth. *I just...what? Vampire? Like...for real?* The past few weeks had shown me stranger and stranger things—magic and danger beyond what I'd imagined, despite growing up in an enchanted village. But vampires?

Adam frowned down at the phone before raising his eyes to meet mine, then Thomas's.

My brother burst out laughing.

"Thomas," I said.

He doubled over and completely lost it.

Adam shrugged, suppressing his own laugh. "A *vegan* vampire?"

"I'm sorry. We need a minute." I hit the mute button on my phone. "Can you get it together?"

Thomas grabbed the counter, steadying himself. "I'm sorry.

I'm sorry. But...come on. A vegan vampire? What even is that? Does she like, suck the juice out of produce?"

Adam slapped my brother's back as another round of laughter set him off, almost choking when he tried to breathe. Adam smirked, avoiding my eyes.

"Not you, too." I shook my head but couldn't hold in the giggle that bubbled up when I saw how hard he was trying not to laugh.

"Cate? Thomas? You guys still there?" Tori's voice cut through the noise.

I held up my hands, gathering myself.

Thomas straightened, knocking on a wooden cutting board as he took a deep breath.

I glanced at Adam. "You good?"

He held up one hand, turned to cough over his shoulder, turned back, and nodded. "Good. Go ahead."

I unmuted the phone. "Sorry. We just...Adam had a cough."

Adam cleared his throat. "Yeah, you know, my allergies..."

"It's okay," Noemi said. "You can laugh. I know my lifestyle is not exactly...normal."

Tori snorted. "I mean, whose is? You don't owe anybody anything. I called them for help, but if they're going to be supernatural bigots about it, we'll...we'll just...I don't know. Can you guys not be jerks for, like, five minutes? We have a big problem, and I'm not sure we can solve it on our own."

I looked at the guys, both now shamed into better, if not their best behavior. "What's wrong, Tori? We're listening. I'm sorry."

Tori and Noemi whispered something unintelligible back and forth.

Thomas leaned his elbows on the counter, looking down at Tori's avatar on the phone. "Spill it, ladies. My tea's getting cold."

"Okay, so, the problem is…" Tori swallowed. "We lost a book."

I almost laughed again. Libraries lose books all the time. They'd probably charge her for it, but I couldn't see them firing her.

Adam raised an eyebrow, the same thought likely crossing his mind. "Do you need help with the fee?"

"Guys, be serious. I'm not working the kids' desk here," Tori said.

"What kind of book is going to get you fired?" Thomas asked. "Are we talking a rare first edition? One of those antiques with the arsenic dyes?"

One of the cabinets in the shop downstairs held a set of books like those. Emerald green cloth covers lined a high shelf behind a locked glass door. Holloway's Charms had one of the largest and most unique collections of rare occult books in the States, thanks to Rune Holloway's interest in archaic texts. They belonged in a museum, but they were safer behind my brother's wards. The Holloway brothers had no idea how lucky they were to have accidentally hired a real witch to look over their magic shop while they explored pagan monuments abroad.

"No," said Noemi, her tone a command as much as a response. "It's much more dangerous than that."

3

I climbed onto a barstool, and Adam sat on the one beside me.

"It's a grimoire," Tori said. "An old one. It might be charmed. I'm not sure. It vibrates with trapped energy."

"It belonged to a Gifted witch from the dark times," Noemi said. "It came in as part of an estate sale, mixed in with antique novels, folios, and reference texts written at least two generations ago. I've been sorting through them for weeks. Tori is cataloging the ones written in Latin."

"She can read Latin?" Adam whispered.

"It's a dead language," Thomas said, smirking. "Must be a prereq for Goth 101."

I rolled my eyes. "Or it was recommended by her high school because she's pre-med."

Tori's indignant response—a string of Latin words I didn't understand in a tone I didn't have to interpret—almost brought the language back to life.

"Where's the book now?" Adam asked.

"That's the problem," Noemi said. "We don't know."

"I'm sure it's there somewhere," I said. "It didn't just walk out of the library on its own."

"Not on its own," Tori said.

"What did you do?" asked Thomas.

Tori scoffed. "Oh, sure, it had to be me. Didn't it? I was trying to help Noemi and—"

Noemi interrupted. "I took it home."

"Say again?" Thomas said.

"You took an antique, potentially dangerous and enchanted book out of what I have to assume was a restricted section or private collection at a mundane civil center and brought it home with you?" Adam rubbed his face.

"It is a public library," said Tori. "Just because mundanes currently run the government doesn't mean they're the only ones who use our services. The fact that all of the occult books are kept behind lock and key is—"

"Yes. I needed more time with it," Noemi said. "I figured it was safer with me anyway."

Adam, Thomas, and I exchanged glances. How dedicated was this vampire to her vegan lifestyle? Would she break her diet in self-defense?

"Okay," I said, swallowing. "So, it's probably still there. Have you searched your house…?"

"It's a bungalow," Noemi said. "Barely over a thousand square feet. If the book was still here, I'd be tripping over it by now."

"How long has it been missing?" Adam asked.

Tori and Noemi answered at the same time.

"A few days."

"About a week."

I looked at Adam.

His fingers traced a circle on his temple, accessing his Gift for sensing the truth. "It's closer to a week, but they're estimating, not lying."

The idea of a book with that kind of power lost in the world made me sick to my stomach. The sorority girls at school were able to draw enough magical energy to hex each other after watching a YouTube video. What would they do with an ancient textbook? Goddess, the hunters nearly killed us using mundane weapons and a charmed amulet. How dangerous would they be if they had access to more powerful sigils?

"Has anyone else been to your place?" Adam asked. It was the most logical question, but I'd been too distracted to think of it. Those last few weeks taking over as commander of the Watch really honed his investigative instincts.

"My nephew, Lalo. He lives with me." Noemi hesitated. "And my book club."

"Your book club?" Thomas dropped his face into his hands, leaning on the counter.

"Just a few other women. My friend Emily from high school, her stepdaughter, my neighbor, and one of Emily's friends from the PTA," Noemi said.

"There are five of you?" Thomas's head tilted in his hands. *Five women. Five witches? The points of a pentacle.*

"What kind of books has the club been reading?" I asked.

"Oh, we take turns choosing the book," Noemi said. "We're pretty eclectic. A little historical fiction, biographies. Emily likes romcoms. We've read a few of Reese's picks. You know, I think she has better taste than Oprah. This last one was—"

"Do any of them seem interested in the Craft?" Adam asked.

Noemi hummed. "Well, we sometimes have a project going for the meetings. Just something to do with our hands. Meredith brings those little jewel painting kits. The ones with the tiny sequin things?"

"He means witchcraft," Tori said, sighing audibly.

"Oh! Yes, of course. Sorry. I'm out of practice. My parents wanted to mainstream us, you know? No magic in front of mundanes. And we're always around mundanes, so…no. We don't do magic at book club. Unless you count Emily's margaritas!" Noemi laughed, but the sound petered out when no one joined her. "Sorry. No. They're not witches."

"Are you sure?" My academic advisor had surprised me by coming out of the broom closet a few weeks ago. Three years after we started meeting about my college and career plans.

"Oh, I think I would know," Noemi said. "Especially lately. Have you noticed the increase in magical energy? It's like everybody got an upgrade."

You're welcome. Had Tori told her about us? It didn't sound like she knew anything about our contribution to the wave of magical energy that recently swept across the country. But she had to have said something to explain why she thought we could help.

"We're pretty sure they're mundanes," Tori said.

"Pretty sure?" Thomas mouthed.

Better and better.

"Did you show them the book?" Adam asked. "Was it out where they could see it?"

"So, I didn't intend to. I left it on my desk in the back bedroom where I'd been studying it. Tori's translations have been so helpful, but she didn't do the whole book, you know? Just the headlines. Enough for us to know what was in there." Her tone shifted as she addressed Tori. "I really do think it might have exactly what we need. I'm so grateful you brought it to me. It's going to change our lives."

"What did you mean, you didn't intend to?" Thomas said.

"Sorry. Yes. I mean, no. I didn't intend for any of them to see it. That's why I left it back there. But Mama Lily spilled her wine, and Lalo was in the hall bathroom. So I told her she could use the ensuite in my room. She had such a lovely blouse on. I hope she got the stain out."

"So, this Lily person was alone in your room with the book?" Adam asked.

"Well, yes. But not for long. You know, Emily had an idea to use vinegar, but I thought baking soda was better with stains. So we brought her both. And then Emily's stepdaughter came in. She's a teenager—she followed us because she wanted Emily to drive her to some club. I think she was meeting a boy, but she's not my daughter..."

"Are you saying the whole book club saw the grimoire?" I asked.

"And her nephew, probably. Since he lives there," Adam mumbled.

"No, I don't think...No. Definitely not the whole club. Meredith stayed in the living room. The wine spilled on her jewel tray, I think. She was cleaning it up."

Thomas closed his hands over his face, muffling his words. "Oh, thank the goddess. That really narrows it down."

"Do you think you can help us? I can't get fired. I don't want to go back to Salem. They'll never let me out again." Tori's breathy voice caught.

"What do you think we can do?" *Please suggest something I can do from a distance.* "I mean...I'm not saying we won't do whatever we can. But we don't know any of these people, and your Gift—"

Is stronger than mine. Is more practiced than mine. Is more active than mine.

Scares me.

"I can't do a locator spell," Tori whispered.

"What?" Thomas's head popped up. A locator spell was beginner stuff. Elementary witchcraft. Literally one of the first things they taught you in elementary school. Little witches were always losing things.

"It's why I couldn't find the hunter who killed Grace. I went down there. To the apartment. I thought I could use Dr.

Bear. But it didn't work. I've never been able to track energy until you gave me that compass."

"But your Gift—" I said.

"I know. It's ironic, right? I can manipulate energy and draw it out. And since I merged my Gift with Grace's, I can amplify it. But I can't find it if I don't know where to look. I can't sense it without some kind of tool to help me."

"Are you calling us tools?" Thomas frowned in mock offense.

I rolled my eyes. "You want to borrow Thomas's compass?"

"And Adam's map, if that's okay," Tori said.

"Will that work?" I asked Adam. My older brothers had designed the compass—they called it a kynigolabe—to track witch hunters, an early warning system for attacks. We'd used it to follow two hunters on campus after they set the magic shop on fire.

Adam ran his hands through his curly hair, pressing them against the base of his skull as he thought about it. "We could ask Gabriel. But wouldn't it be easier to use a pendulum or a dowsing rod? Those things are actually designed for this."

"She said she can't do a locator spell," Thomas said.

But Tori wasn't the only witch over there. Mainstreamed or not, the vegan vamp must have some basic skills. "You're sure Noemi can't…"

"She doesn't know how," Tori said. "And you could be here in the time it would take me to teach her."

"Please hurry. The club is coming back tonight, and if one of them didn't take it, I want to find it before they get here," Noemi said.

"And if they do have it?" I wasn't sure I wanted the answer.

Tori spoke with confidence, which had the opposite effect on my nerves. "We'll get it back."

4

I t's a bad idea," Adam said after I hung up.

"It's a terrible idea." Thomas poured fresh hot water over his tea. "A vegan vampire? You know Wednesday's leaving something out. If the book's that dangerous, what was this librarian doing bringing it home? And what was that about *it could change their lives*?"

"Somebody has to go over there," I said. "They called us for help. No way Tori would do that if she wasn't desperate."

"That's exactly why I don't think you should go," Adam said. "I don't trust her when she's calm. We definitely can't trust her when she's desperate."

"Well, I'm not going over there," Thomas grumbled over his tea.

Adam spread his hands on the counter. "None of us should go."

Wrapping my finger around my teacup, I stared into the translucent liquid, searching my mind for clues I was unlikely to find. I didn't want to discount Adam's Gift. If he said she couldn't be trusted, he was probably right. How could I ever put any trust in her after the way she'd abused it when the hunter came after us?

I swirled the tea, and the particles tracing the bottom of the cup formed a circle. Could I come around? She'd helped us bind the community of Queen's Creek, so I should probably give her some benefit of the doubt. But did one selfless act of kindness balance out the hurt she'd caused? Even if it was Kindness on a grand scale? How long would she have gone on using those girls for their energy if I hadn't stepped into her circle? What would have happened to me at Thomas's if the hunter had made it upstairs after she took my energy?

But what would happen if we didn't help? What would she do next? Tori's strength made her a great ally against the hunters, but her actions were never predictable. Her friendship was risky enough. I didn't want her as an enemy.

Thomas watched me sip my tea. He narrowed his eyes. "You're going anyway. Aren't you?"

"I don't think I have a choice." I drank the last of it and set the empty cup on the counter.

Adam put a hand on the back of my chair. "You always have a choice."

Even if it's not the one you'd make?

I didn't think he'd try to stop me, but his hand behind me made it clear he didn't want me going anywhere. "I'll take the compass and the map. They'll tell me if anyone is looking for us, even if they don't help me find the book. If anything looks sketchy, I'll call you."

His lips tightened, and he looked down. "I don't like it."

Thomas dumped the dregs of my tea over a paper towel and left the cup sitting upside down. "Shall we take a look?"

I raised an eyebrow. Tasseography was an elective back home, but I didn't think Thomas had read the leaves in years.

"Couldn't hurt," Adam said. He straightened, stepping closer to the counter and rubbing my back.

I pursed my lips. "Sure, but I've had a lot more practice with this."

Pulling Nora's tarot card out of my back pocket, I dropped it on the counter next to the tea cup.

Thomas looked at Adam. "Both?"

Adam nodded. "Might as well."

Sighing, I put my hand over the card and closed my eyes, setting my intention. *What is the best course of action for me in this moment? What should I do? How should I respond to Tori's call for help?*

The card warmed under my fingers, as it had every time I'd asked for guidance. Energy shifted around me. When I lifted my hand, the image had changed. Where the Queen of Wands had sat on her throne, a younger woman stood. The black cat that guarded the queen transformed into a wild lion whose unruly mane mingled with the woman's curls. The vibe was the same. Courage. Confidence. Determination.

But Strength was a card from the major arcana. The lesson was bigger. Life changing.

I'd been ready to go. Maybe I was a little nervous about seeing Tori again, but how hard could it be to find a misplaced book? Now, with the card doubling down on the need for courage, for inner strength and self-control, I worried that the fears I'd been suppressing might have justification after all.

Thomas smacked his lips, flipping the cup in front of him. We all leaned over it to see what shapes the leaves would form.

The dark clusters held no meaning for me.

"Is that an X?" Adam pointed to a blob near the middle.

"What does an X mean again?" I asked.

Thomas frowned. "Bad stuff. Trouble, delay…death."

I turned the cup to get a different angle on it. "I think it's an umbrella. Or maybe a palm tree?"

"What does that mean?" Thomas mumbled into his fist, his elbows resting on the counter.

"I don't know," I said. "This was your idea."

"I think that's a sun," Thomas said, pointing to a different glob of sediment. "That's got to be good, right?"

Adam lifted the cup and tilted it to one side. "Maybe it's a wheel."

Thomas straightened, tapping the counter. "A wheel is definitely good. Progress. Forward movement. Like the Chariot in tarot."

I sat back on my stool. "I think I'm going with the card on this one. It's going to be fine. We just need to be brave."

But I didn't feel brave. My stomach burned, acid surely melting the lining even as we sat there. The fact that I hadn't already developed an ulcer from the stress of saving the world was probably a magical feat in itself.

Was I really going to walk into the house of a vampire on the word of a witch who'd previously been ambivalent at best when it came to my survival? On the phone, Noemi had a sweet, gentle voice with a warmer tone than Tori's, but she couldn't be like that in person. She was probably tall, dark-haired, with sunken red eyes and prominent canines. Her cold, dead skin would refuse to warm, even in the height of summer, while she skulked in the shadows to avoid the sun.

Or maybe she would shimmer in the sunlight, putting Thomas's sparkle to shame.

What is a vegan vampire, anyway?

"Message me when you get there," Adam said. "And once an hour afterwards. Or we're coming in to get you."

"We are?" Thomas paled.

Adam's concerned expression morphed into something more fitting of the Guardian at the Gate. Unquestionable and impassable.

Thomas bobbed his head. "We are. Of course, we are. So make sure to text, or we're storming the castle."

"Thanks, guys," I said, pocketing Nora's tarot card. I didn't want to admit it, but it felt good to know they could be there in a blink.

5

oo bad I couldn't be there in a blink. Travel hadn't been at the top of my To Learn list when I unbound my Gift. The guys could have delivered me to Noemi's doorstep, but I didn't like the idea of making any sudden moves on a vampire's territory. Better to approach slowly and get the lay of the land.

So I made my own way to Noemi's house, taking the red line to a bus and walking four blocks. With each step, I pushed away reasons to turn around. Setting aside my discomfort with seeing Tori again, what I came here to do should be quick. Easy in, easy out. I almost believed it. *I might convince myself by the time I find the house.* There was nothing to fear. My Gift had grown, and I wouldn't let Tori take advantage of it. Eventually, my confidence would match my strength.

A locator spell was just craft, really. Get a pendulum, any slightly heavy thing on a string, hang it over a map, and ask it where to go. Tori's heavy ankh necklace would probably have worked if her Gift wasn't getting in the way. Like a lot of forms of divination, dowsing could be explained away as letting your subconscious lead you. Maybe your hand twitched a certain way. Maybe you felt drawn toward a place you recognized. Your brain connected pieces together behind the scenes. All the little details you picked up without even realizing it.

But wasn't that magic, anyway? Witches used all of their senses, even the ones that didn't get as much credit. And if you pushed some magical energy behind it to make the direction less subtle, wasn't that just as natural?

Maybe that was Tori's problem. She had too much energy. It'd be like trying to read a compass by setting it on top of a magnet.

As soon as I turned the last corner, I could sense another problem. The suburban bungalow sat in the middle of a block that dead-ended at an elementary school. Twenty or so kids ran around the blacktop and hung from the playground equipment, yelling and squealing with a sense of chaotic joy only found after the last bell rang. Across the street, one of the neighbors pushed a gas-powered lawn mower that kept puttering out and needing to be restarted.

A locator spell called for quiet magic.

The sun hung low in the sky, lending a sense of urgency to the last hour of daylight. But I stood frozen at the end of a cracked sidewalk. It led up to an unassuming single-story brick house with a dormer window popping out of the roof. A suburban standard. Mundane as all the others.

My feet refused to go further. *Courage.*

The lawn had been mowed recently and the bushes against the front of the house were trimmed. But the grass fought back against the imposed order, sprouting up through the cracks in the sidewalk and refusing to grow under the ancient oak tree that shadowed the side of the yard.

I tapped a thumbs-up emoji on my phone and sent it to Adam to mark my arrival.

He sent back a happy face.

Swallowing hard, I walked up the path, avoiding a root that had broken through the pavement. A kid's scooter leaned against the iron railing that lined one side of the poured cement stairs and more toys—a soccer ball and some action figures—lay abandoned on the porch. When I got to the front door, electronic explosions told me the toys' owner had found a different game to play.

The door swung open, and Tori's pale face hovered in the darkened foyer, like some kind of spirit fighting its way through the veil. Her black-rimmed eyes lowered as the setting sun sent a streak of light between the houses across the street.

I stepped back with an embarrassing squeak. It struck me that I might be facing more than one vampire in this house. *What if she's been turned? Would I even be able to tell? She always kind of dressed like one anyway.* Muscles tensed all the way up to my neck. But before I could deal with the complicated emotions that arose from Tori's potential death and return as a creature of the night, she reached out of the shadow to grab my arm. I took comfort in the fact that her hand didn't immediately catch flame.

"Oh, praise be! You're here!" She released me once I crossed the threshold. The light from the kitchen made her glow around the edges, a paper silhouette come to life. She wore the same chunky black boots I'd come to associate with her, the silver buckles flashing when the light caught them.

"Is that her?" another voice called from the back of the house. "Bring her back here. Ven!"

Tori grabbed my arm again, dragging me out of the dark foyer, through a cozy living room and a wide dining room lined with built-in bookcases, to the narrow kitchen at the back of the house. She came more into focus the farther we got into the house, where her black pants, black tee, and dark gray sweater didn't blend in with the shadows. She'd pulled her straight black hair into an uncharacteristically perky high pony, but when she glanced back to make sure I was still following, her new dangly silver skull earrings explained the choice. "Coming, Noemi. I told you she'd do it."

A curvy Latina woman who looked around thirty stood at the stove, stirring something that smelled amazing. She wore a pink flowered blouse with high-waisted jeans that hugged her hips. Long brown hair with blonde highlights fell over her shoulder in soft waves. When I walked in, she tapped the wooden spoon on the side of the pot and set it in a sunflower-shaped spoon cradle, pushing a stack of library books to the corner of the counter. Reaching out her hands for me, she smiled a welcome that would have lit her foyer despite the dark circles under her eyes.

"Ahh, Cate," she said, grasping my hands. "Thank you for coming to our rescue."

Her calloused fingers warmed my perpetually frozen hands. The heat radiated up my arms, relaxing my neck and shoulders. Any fears I had about meeting a vampire melted with the tension in my muscles. I smiled down at her. Noemi stood three or four inches shorter than me, but the low ceilings of the bungalow made her look perfectly proportioned to her home.

"I'll do what I can," I said, wondering again how much she knew about what happened between Tori and me. Tori hung back, and I tried to focus on Noemi's warm energy, so much different than everything I'd ever heard about vampires. "Like I told her, there's not a lot I can do. Where did you last see the book?"

"Yes, of course. This way." She turned off the stove and led me back through the dining room. An alcove I'd missed before led to two bedrooms. The electronic game noises came from the one on the left. She cracked the door, waving at me to wait. "Oye, Lalo! Turn it down, mijo."

A little boy's voice grumbled on the other side of the door.

I didn't understand the next words she said, but the game volume lowered dramatically.

Noemi closed the door behind her. "Sorry, my nephew is testing me. It was in here. In my room."

She flicked the light switch and ushered me into the primary bedroom. A soft glow flooded the space from two large table lamps on either side of the bed. A beautiful quilt covered in roses and vines lay over a queen-sized bed with low wooden posts. The headboard was hidden by a stack of pillows in different pastel shades. Noemi stepped around the bed to show me the antique desk against the wall on the opposite side. It had been painted white with delicate gold details. A vase of pink roses sat at the corner of a leather desk mat next to a porcelain cup filled with pens. Books on magic, gardening, and herbalism fanned out to one side. Noemi tapped the empty space in the middle of the mat. "Here. It was just here. And now gone."

I stared at the spot like it would reveal its secrets to me just from the force of my concentration. Nothing. But then something flickered. My fingers tingled, and the hair stood up on the back of my neck as my Gift called on the energy of the space. It wasn't what I'd planned, but maybe...

I need to see what happened here.

"Let me just try something." I reached for the desk and flattened my hand against the spot where she'd last seen the grimoire.

Noemi raised an eyebrow, but Tori stepped back, sitting on the bed.

Activating my Gift, I imagined clocks rolling back, visualized the sun rising backwards through the sky, turning back east.

Noemi froze. Then she stepped forward again, tapping the mat as she had before, stepping backwards around the bed.

Tori stood, backing up behind Noemi to the doorway. Not shadows or doubles, like when I'd used a replay to see what Luke had been up to at the real estate office (back before I knew he was actually Duncan behind a glamour). Not a vision of the future, like when I'd foreseen the path of Wesson's bullet. They actually moved back in time, like the mug I'd dropped at the café.

This was so much bigger than freezing things in place.

My headache returned in full force. *Too much.* I released the energy, and time ran forward again. Noemi stepped up and tapped the mat. "Here. It was just here. And now gone."

My breath came out in a rush, and I grabbed the edge of the desk for balance.

"Are you alright, niña?" Noemi rubbed my back. "Maybe you should sit down."

She pulled the chair out from the desk, and I sank into it.

Tori's eyes widened. "What did you do? That was a lot of energy. Did you see what happened?"

I shook my head. *Mistake. Dizzy.* "It was different. Not like the visions I had before. I think I actually reversed time."

Noemi sank onto the bed. "This is quite a Gift. You have been blessed."

"You're getting stronger," Tori said.

"But I still can't control it. I didn't mean to go back. I just wanted to see it." When I'd tried this before, the past had overlapped my vision of the room, like some kind of virtual reality hologram. A video playing on top of the scene. Double exposure. And no headache.

"You're pulling too much energy." Tori leaned back against the desk, crossing her arms.

I rubbed my face. "I think so. It's like there's no volume switch. When I call my Gift, it's just on or off."

Tori frowned. "I have an idea. But you're not going to like it."

My chest tightened. My skin prickled at her presence so close to me. My fingers sparked. What was I doing here? I should never have agreed to help her.

6

We can do it together," she said. "And I'll stop when you say."

This is a mistake. I wish Adam were here.

"Really? Do you promise?" I didn't try to hide the doubt in my voice. Sitting back in the chair, I crossed my arms, mirroring her pose. She had to know I didn't trust her.

"I'm sorry." Tori looked down, avoiding my eyes. Her voice trembled.

"Is that supposed to fix this? You're sorry? And what? Now, I'm just going to forgive you for siphoning off my magic. For stealing my energy and leaving me helpless on the floor?" My fingers dug into my arms, and I winced at the little shocks the sparks of my rising energy left. *Careful. Don't want to burn holes in your sweater.*

Noemi sucked in a breath.

"Oh, she didn't tell you about that? I bet she left a few things out when she suggested you call me for help. Your colleague almost killed me." I glared at Tori, whose dark eyes focused on the floor. "Twice."

"It must have been an accident," Noemi said, but she pulled her feet up on the bed, putting a little more space between herself and Tori.

"It wasn't," Tori whispered.

"No," I said. "It wasn't."

"But you came anyway. I called you for help, and you came. What are you doing here if you don't trust me?" Tori twisted her ankh necklace between two fingers, absently tightening the chain around her neck.

Good question. Maybe I was getting too used to being the Chosen One. Getting a bit of a savior complex. *I shouldn't be here. This is her problem…*

But what if she can't handle it? "You lost an ancestral grimoire. It could be in mundane hands. That might not have mattered a few weeks ago, but you know things are different now."

The necklace rasped against the chain. "And whose fault is that, Cate? While we're casting judgment here, who released a burst of magical energy that had been safely contained for centuries? I'm not the one upsetting the ecosystem and throwing the whole magical world out of balance."

"It wasn't safely contained, and it's not going to affect the whole magical world." *I hope.*

"Isn't it?" Her eyebrow jumped.

Noemi leaned forward. "Wait. Are you the reason for the energy storm?"

We both turned to the bed.

"What storm?" I asked.

"You felt that?" Tori dropped her charm, letting the ankh fall against her chest. She gripped the desk on either side of her hips.

Noemi looked back and forth between us. "A few weeks ago. The electrical storm. But it wasn't just lightning. I felt it in my bones. Even Lalo felt it."

She climbed off the bed and went to the closet, pulling a glass jar from a shelf. "I collected rainwater that night. I thought the energy might help with my…condition. But it's too potent. Makes my spells implode."

The liquid in the jar looked like regular rainwater, so clear it was almost invisible. But the energy it held pulled at me. The sensation was familiar. The way it called me to come closer. To dance. A smile turned up my lips, and I had to grit my teeth to keep from laughing. Memories flashed through my mind, and I could almost feel the sand under my feet. I'd been caught in so many storms since spring break, but only one had made me feel powerful, connected me with a community of young women in celebration. Before Tori pulled it all away, and I had to stop her.

I could do it again. "Put that back, please."

Noemi tilted her head, looking from me to the jar. "This was you? The storm? The burst of energy that came before it? You are the reason magic is stronger?"

"It's a long story," I said.

Tori arched an eyebrow. "Oh, I think we have TIME. Don't we, Cate?"

I sighed. "What have you already told her?"

"Nothing. I swear. I've been good. Sworn to secrecy and all that. But she's a witch. The covenant is meant to keep mundanes from learning about magic. Don't you think witches have a right to know why their magic is suddenly six times as strong and ten times less reliable? It's a safety hazard for goddess-sake."

"I wasn't the one calling the quarters on a public beach with a bunch of uninitiated sorority girls. You raised the energy that fed that storm."

"It was a private beach, first of all. Belonging to a Jesuit college. Practically holy ground."

"You're so lucky no one was in that church."

Noemi sank back on the bed, cradling the jar in her hands. "You did this at a church?"

A gold cross winked on her collarbone, hanging from a delicate chain that had been mostly hidden by her shirt collar. I bit my lip. Although I'd heard of Christian witches, most of the spiritual members of my community back in Queen's Creek were polytheists, worshiping an eclectic combination of deities brought in by the early refugees. Norse gods, Hellenistic goddesses, and Celtic figures often sat side by side on home altars. Elspeth and Duncan left offerings for Ahone and Okee, as their ancestors had before mine even set foot on this continent.

But the Puritans had used Christ to drive us out, to justify murdering our people. It was hard to imagine calling on Him for blessings or honoring His work when His followers tried to destroy us.

Also, she's a vampire. How does that work?

Tori faced her colleague. *Friend?* "It was nothing. I promise. And I only did it once. I'm reformed. For the love of Minerva, I work at the library now."

Noemi shook her head. "I don't understand. You caused the storm? But you said that she—"

"Look, the storm was already happening. It had been coming on for weeks. All I did was try to direct some of that energy," Tori said.

"You weren't taking energy from the storm. You took it from those girls. You took it from me. And you did it again at the magic shop. You drained me and left me to burn while the hunter attacked Adam and Thomas downstairs. You left us and ran back to the beach to do it all over again. What would have happened to those girls if we hadn't bound you?"

"They would have been fine. A little hungover, maybe. If I'd had their energy, things might have gone differently at the theater. You want to talk about putting others at risk? You bound my Gift until it was convenient for you. When I confronted the hunter, he had a gun. What did I have? Your useless brother—"

"He was trying to protect you! He went after you, knowing Wesson's sigil would paralyze his Gift. We bound your magic to keep Wesson from taking it. How long would you have lasted if he'd negated all the energy you stole?"

"You are unbelievable! That Chosen One thing has really gone to your head. You always think you know best. You're the only one who can solve any problem."

"Isn't that why I'm here? You asked for my help."

"Your help. Not your judgment. You opened that Gate and upset the balance. I'm the one who helped you protect your people. *For through her strength shall others rise.* That prophecy was about me."

"You're so strong. What do you need me for?"

A small voice interrupted. "Tia?"

7

A skinny ten-year-old boy in a red hoodie stood in the doorway holding a tablet. He'd put earbuds on at some point, so the game sounds I'd heard when I came in were all but inaudible. He kept his eyes on the screen. "Tia? I'm hungry. Can I have a snack?"

Noemi moved so quickly she might have blinked to the doorway. Only a slight breeze caused by the air she displaced said otherwise. She bent over the boy, pulling his earbuds down around his neck and smoothing the waves of his dark hair. "Lalo, mijo, I asked you to stay in your room while I have visitors. It's almost dinnertime anyway."

He tilted his head back, raising his eyes from the screen at the last moment to look past her. His long lashes made his eyes seem too big for his small face, and dark circles like Noemi's stood out against his light brown skin. He leaned to the side to get a better look at us. "Who're they?"

"Just some friends. Why don't you go ahead to the kitchen, and I'll come help you in a minute?"

Lalo squared his shoulders, frowning at her. "I can do it myself."

Noemi nodded. "Go ahead then. Just stay out of the chips,

or we won't have enough for dinner."

She gave him a little push to get him moving toward the door. He resisted, twisting back to whisper something to Noemi.

"No, definitely not." She pushed him a little harder this time, and he grumbled but headed out to the kitchen.

She called after him, "And we're going to talk about that game later. I don't like the way it's influencing you."

His muffled response made her roll her eyes, shutting the bedroom door behind him.

"Please excuse my nephew," she said. "He's been through a lot. We're still working some things out."

"He lives with you?" I asked.

"Yes. My brother and his wife…they passed last year. An accident. I'm his guardian now." She looked over her shoulder as if she could watch him through the door.

"That must be hard," I said. Everyone in that room knew what it was like to lose someone.

Noemi smiled. Her nails clicked together as she picked at the cuticles. "It was. It is. But it's what you do for family, right? He needs me. And I didn't know it before, but I need him."

It was a cheesy thing to say. Something you only heard in Hallmark movies. But when I thought about everything my family had been through since we lost my dad and the way we continued trying to be there for each other, even when we weren't all in Queen's Creek, my eyes started to itch a little. I almost embarrassed myself, but then Tori spoke.

"And now we need you," she said. "Look, I'm sorry. I know you don't trust me, and you probably shouldn't. But I can help you manage the energy if you let me."

"What's to stop you from—"

"Draining you? Goddess, Cate. I'm not—Noemi's the vampire. Are you afraid of what *she* can do?"

"I would never do that," Noemi said.

"What?" I rubbed my eyes. It had been a long day, and I was tired of worrying about other people's motives.

"Drain you. I would never. I've never taken so much as a sip. We're not...I don't do that." Noemi's face looked a little green.

"Wait...we?" I looked from her to Tori, who shook her head. *More than one vampire? Not Tori. Then who?* "Are you saying the kid—"

"I'm not saying anything. Let's focus on the book. That's why you came. We have to find the book." Something about the way she said it, with her cheerful voice trembling and her fingernails still clicking against each other, made me stop.

This is bigger than library late fees. "What's in this book? Why is it so important?"

She took a short breath. "What do you mean? It's an heirloom grimoire. It's historically relevant to at least three fields of study. It's worth—"

If she didn't leave her nails alone, they were going to start bleeding. A whole new list of concerns flooded my brain. Vegan or not, vampires and open wounds couldn't be a good combination. But if it's her own blood...

Stop it. One fear at a time. "But what do *you* want with it? Why did you bring it home in the first place? I thought Tori was doing the translations?"

"I am. I was. But she...Why *did* you bring it home?" Tori asked.

Noemi sat back on the bed. "It's supposed to have the cure."

"The cure." An hour ago, I hadn't known vampires existed. Now, I'd been invited to the home of a vegan vampire who wore a cross around her neck and had custody of what I had to assume was a child vampire—if he was still a child. He looked like a child and acted like a child. Did vampires age?

Could someone be born a vampire? If she made garlic bread for dinner, I was going to have to reevaluate my unconscious biases. Modern media got so much wrong about witchcraft. Why had I assumed anything I knew about vampires would be true? I'd never met one before, so I'd assumed they didn't exist. But if there was a cure, maybe they didn't? Not in any noticeable numbers, anyway.

"There's a cure?" Tori asked. "Why didn't you tell me?"

"I didn't want to get my hopes up. It's only mentioned in a few of my sources, some old journals...but they say the *Ichoriad* holds the key. The recipe for the elixir of life."

"You're looking for the elixir of life?" I leaned forward, my eyes wide.

Noemi frowned. "You've heard of it?"

"I thought it was a myth," Tori said.

"It's not a myth." It might have been, once. Some of Dad's colleagues had certainly thought so. A waste of his time, misuse of funds. Corey's Folly. But I'd read his notes. Years of research cited primary sources going back centuries. The recipe was lost, but someone had written it. And someone could find it.

Maybe Noemi already had. Until someone took it.

"We have to find that book." I stood, turning back to the desk as if the book might reappear.

"Oh, so now you want to help?" Tori crossed her arms, arching an eyebrow.

My fingers curled around the back of the chair. I ignored the faint buzz of energy. "Look, I'm not going to say I'm sorry for being hesitant to risk my life and magic on someone who energetically assaulted me and left me for dead. But if that grimoire has information on the elixir of life, it might save more than one."

Noemi sucked in her bottom lip and took a breath through her nose. "Okay. Umm. I need to get Lalo his dinner and get some snacks ready before the ladies get here for book club. You don't have to tell me what's going on. But before you do magic together, you might want to clear the air." She lit a stick of incense from a box by the bed, blew it out, and waved the smoke in a circle above her head before setting it into a ceramic stand. She left silently, closing the door behind her. A sweet, woody scent spun out from the incense.

I watched the ribbon of smoke unwind, afraid to speak before it had a chance to do its work.

8

I'm sorry," Tori mumbled.

"Excuse me?" *Did she just apologize? Like that's supposed to make everything better?*

"You heard me. I'm sorry, okay? I was so close to getting justice for Grace. I couldn't let you stand in my way." Tori looked down, picking at a loose thread in her fishnet sleeve.

So, not so much an apology as an excuse. "What happens next time I'm in your way?"

She shrugged. Her eyelashes fluttered before she looked up at me. "I guess we'll see."

Cool. Not ominous at all.

I held her gaze, taking a breath of the warm, piney air. The incense reminded me of the trees around Queen's Creek. I couldn't ignore the chance to finish my father's work. Especially if it might also help me find him.

And who knows? Maybe it really will cure vampirism, and we'll all win some kind of supernatural Nobel Prize. I didn't know if such a thing existed, but it was about as likely as vampires existing in the first place.

"I'll help you find the book, but once we finish this spell, I want you to promise you'll help me learn to control my Gift. I refuse to have my Gift dependent on yours to keep from setting off fireworks every time I want to use it." I held out my hand.

Tori eyed it, her black lips quirked to the side as she made a show of considering it. "Aww, what a sweet proposal. I'd love to mentor you. It'll be a nice change of pace if you can hold back that judgmental attitude."

I pulled my hand back, shoving it in my pocket. "You're really not going to make this easy, are you?"

Tori smiled. "You promise to listen to me?"

"Promise not to kill me?" I said, only half joking. *Maybe less than half.*

She stood in front of me, stepping so close we shared the same air. Staring into my eyes, she recited an oath I'd never heard before in a tone that made my skin vibrate: "By breath and blaze, by sand and sea, this do I swear to thee."

Her hand came up between us, pinky extended.

I raised an eyebrow.

She grabbed my hand, hooking our pinkies together, and shook hard. "Satisfied?"

"Did you just pinky promise not to murder me?"

"An oath is an oath," she said. "Unless you want to do it in blood?"

"No, no. This is good." All I needed was to be bloodbound to this psycho. "Let's get this done."

I turned back to face the desk, only cringing a little when Tori stepped behind me. She put her hands gently on my shoulders, and I felt something click into place. My fingers tingled, shooting sparks across the desk. The air in the room stopped moving. Tori stepped back, reversing the last move she'd made. But before she broke the connection, static charge zipped from her fingers to my shoulders. I gasped. Time stopped again, ending the reversal. The energy I'd raised receded from my hands, gathering in my chest. My lungs expanded with the warmth of it. A pinch in my shoulders set it moving again, and the energy chased its way out of my body into Tori's. Her breath caught, but she stepped closer, drawing off the excess energy before it sparked again.

I forced myself to concentrate on the empty space in front of me. *Show me what happened here.* I could almost see the shadow of the book on the desk mat. It solidified as a ghostly hand laid the book down. With Tori funneling away the energy that had built since spring break, my Gift behaved as it had done before, a vision instead of actual time travel. It was like walking through a living picture.

The book opened, pages flipping past, one after another. They moved too quickly for me to catch more than a glimpse of their contents, but it was enough to know, without a doubt, that this book held mysteries I'd never seen before. Illustrations shimmered with gold flakes. Scripted text in blue, black, and green ink crawled across the paper. Lists, recipes, narratives. Whoever had written this book intended it to pass on the collected knowledge of many generations.

The translucent hands stopped, spreading the leaves to reveal a sacred inscription. Tiny sparks floated above the page like lost will-o'-the-wisps. They sparked and flashed, casting light on the spell.

I leaned forward, struggling to make out the words. These pages had been written in elaborate calligraphy, words almost becoming illustrations themselves. But my time walk continued, following the path those hands had taken. I tried to turn to see the face of the person who had spent so much time with the book, but Tori's fingers gripped my shoulders. I was afraid to break our concentration by speaking.

The pages flipped again, turning back towards the front of the book until the cover closed over them. The hands caressed the leather binding as if it were a treasure they'd sought for centuries. Maybe they had. I still couldn't tell who they belonged to.

I focused on the hands instead of the book, trying to glean any clues about the kind of person we were watching. But they remained ghostly. Had the person used some kind of glamour? If they'd disguised themself, made themself invisible or something, that would explain why Noemi hadn't caught them.

I needed to try a different angle. I released the energy I'd been directing to the time walk, and it faded from view. Without the excess draw, the energy Tori pulled from me made me feel weak. My head dropped to my chest, suddenly aching as if I'd run for hours without water. I groaned.

Behind me, Tori jumped. She pulled her hands away. Then she put them back, and a surge of energy filled me.

My head cleared, my heart raced, and my skin glowed. I blinked.

Tori released me slower this time. "Are you okay? I didn't know you were going to stop. I didn't mean to—"

I turned in the chair, resting my hands on the back as I looked up at her. "It's fine. It wasn't your fault. We need to come up with some kind of cue to let you know when I'm ready to come out of it next time."

She tilted her head. "Next time? So, you want to do this again?"

"I don't think we learned what we needed this time. I couldn't see anything but some ghostly arms. Did you see the person? Could you tell who it was?"

Tori shook her head. "I saw some shadows, but I couldn't make them out."

"I think I need to stand farther back. Find an angle that lets me see who comes in the door and goes to the desk."

Tori looked around the room. There wasn't much space around the furniture. "Let's sit on the bed. You can sit at the edge, and I'll sit behind you. That way, if anything goes wrong, at least we'll have a soft place to land."

We arranged ourselves on the bed, and I took a breath, holding my hands out in front of me. Tori rested her hands on my shoulders again. This time, I placed one of mine over hers. "When I squeeze, let go."

"Okay. Are you ready?"

"Now." I called the energy. My fingers tingled, but no sparks flew. The magic flowed steadily but slowly, funneled through Tori's Gift. The light in the room shifted, and the replay began. Our shadows stood up from the bed and walked backwards to the desk. My double sat in the chair while Tori stepped up behind her. Sparks lit my double's fingers.

From the bed, I leaned forward, waiting for the translucent figure whose hands I'd seen before to appear. The vision blurred and reformed, figures at the desk disappearing, something else taking our place. The book rose into view, fuzzy around the edges. I pulled more energy, but the vision didn't take on any more details than it had the first time. My neck itched, tiny shocks marking my skin above where Tori's fingers rested on my shoulders. Her hands tensed as I pulled more energy. I wasn't ready to give up, but each time I increased my draw on the energy, she increased hers, maintaining a steady level. This was never going to work. I needed to be able to modulate my own Gift. I squeezed her hand.

Tori's fingers grew colder as she released her control on the energy. The power of it flooded my senses, making me dizzy. My ears rang. I pushed the energy into my vision, demanding the images to clear. A figure came into focus at the desk, overlapping my own like a double exposure. She stood over the book, a dark silhouette. Not a shadow this time, a girl dressed all in black.

I flinched.

Tori's hands tightened on my shoulders. The vision blurred as she pulled back some of the energy. "What did you see?"

I shook my head, squeezing her hand again. She kept her grip, but the tension in her fingers relaxed a little.

Concentrate. I kept my breath steady, drawing the energy back to focus on the images in front of me.

The dark figure regained her shape, leaning over the book. Her unnaturally black hair fanned forward, obscuring her face as she flipped the pages. The edges of the figure firmed up, revealing a tight black tank top, torn black jeans, and huge chunky boots. A noise in the hall interrupted her, and the figure froze. She flipped the book closed, stepping away from the desk. I knew who she was before she turned, but my breath still caught when the Tori of the vision faced the door to the bedroom.

The door opened. Light streamed in from the hall, obscuring the new arrival. I blinked and the vision thinned. The door stayed open.

Noemi gasped. The librarian stepped into the room, looking back and forth between the vision of Tori at the desk and our physical bodies sitting on the bed. It took me a minute to process her presence. Vision Tori held up a hand, saying something that I couldn't hear. My head whipped back to the door, but Noemi was not part of the vision. She was really and truly in the room with us.

I released the energy, and the vision faded, Tori's double dissolving into ether, leaving the desk and its chair empty.

"What did you do?" Noemi said.

I jumped off the bed and faced Tori. "Did you take the book? Goddess, what is going on here?"

Tori balled her fists on her knees. "Of course not. I didn't know the book was here, did I? I should have taken it, though." She glared at Noemi. "You snuck it out of the library, and I would have been blamed for it."

Noemi knelt beside her. "Did you take it back? Tell me it's safe in the stacks, and I've been panicking for nothing?"

"Don't you think I would have told you if I had it? I didn't want to call Cate for help, but that book is dangerous, and we're the ones everybody's going to come for if Chicago explodes in a surge of black magic." Tori hugged her knees to her chest, shrinking in on herself.

Noemi slid her hand along the bed but stopped short of touching her.

I reviewed the vision in my head. Tori stood at the desk, flipping the pages of the book. Something startled her. A noise. She turned toward the door. "Then what happened next? Who came in while you were looking at it? The door opened, and you turned…"

Tori sucked in her lips and closed her eyes. When she opened them, there was an apology behind her lashes. She reached for Noemi's hand. "It was Lalo."

9

Noemi shook her head. "He knows better than—"

The doorbell cut off whatever defense she would have offered.

Noemi's nephew answered the door. "Buenas! Tia and the brujas are in the bedroom, but you should come through to the kitchen. That's where the food is."

"Lalo!" Noemi charged to the front door. Feminine voices laughed and a muffled conversation drifted back from the foyer. *So much for finding the grimoire before the book club came over.*

The kid called a half-hearted "Sorry, Tia!" before he started over, dramatically welcoming whoever was at the door. "Saludos. Welcome to my aunt's completely normal, boring book club. Please come to the kitchen to share snacks and stories."

Tori and I arrived just in time to see him swing the door wide with a dramatic bow, one hand extended in the direction of the kitchen. Lalo peeked up at me to check how his performance went over.

He was trouble for sure. But I wasn't convinced he'd taken the book, even though this ridiculous quest would resolve much faster if it turned out to have been under his bed the whole time. I gave him a thumbs up, setting off a toothy grin that revealed a dimple in his cheek. He stood to attention, facing his guests.

Time to meet the suspects.

A teenager stepped through the door and winked at him, then dropped a quick curtsy. "Thank you for the kind welcome, sir." The girl wore a red lace dress with bell sleeves and a sweetheart neckline filled with crystal pendants of varying lengths. Her short, choppy hair was tucked behind her ears with bright red sections peeking out from under the natural dark brown. Something about her was familiar, but I couldn't place it.

A blond woman came in behind her, sipping an iced coffee from a large plastic cup with a siren logo on the side. She looked older than Tori and me, probably somewhere in her mid-thirties. The woman laughed, engrossed in her own story about something she heard at the coffee shop.

Noemi switched on the hallway light, smiling and nodding in response, but she didn't take her eyes off Lalo.

The boy bounced in place until the ladies entered, then slammed the front door shut behind them. He pointed toward the kitchen and took off for his room. "It's that way. Okay, bye!"

The pings of his video game started up as soon as his bedroom door closed.

Drawing a breath through her nose, Noemi hesitated, but the blonde kept walking, following Lalo's instructions. The girl's long lashes fluttered when she saw me, but she shrugged her narrow shoulders and went after her.

Noemi shook herself. "Sorry. Yes, come into the kitchen, everyone. Let me get you something to drink."

Tori started to follow her down the hall.

"Don't you think we should…" I gestured to Lalo's door.

Just to be sure.

"You really want to search the kid's room with normies in the house?" she whispered. "We're trying to keep them from finding it, aren't we?"

"Maybe he didn't take it." *Nothing to see, nothing to hide.*

"All the more reason for you to come meet the book club. If he didn't take it, one of them must have. We might need you to put a stop to things if…" Instead of finishing her sentence, Tori held up her hands in a mock casting and backed down the hall.

So much for easy in, easy out.

I texted Adam another thumbs-up to let him know I was still alive and waited for a space of two breaths before following her. In the kitchen, Noemi stood at the sink, rinsing off Lalo's dinner plate. She looked up and grabbed a dish towel as I walked in. She forced a smile. "Cate. This is Emily Garcia. Emily, you've met Tori."

"Hey." The blonde waved. Her oversized t-shirt was loosely tucked into the front of her gray joggers, and a long pastel cardigan hung past her butt. The kind of white woman Nyla would call *basic.* I could imagine her in an ad for expensive athletic gear or a restaurant with really good salads. *This is her friend from high school?* Her skin radiated health—no tell-tale dark circles like Noemi's. And I didn't sense any magical energy from her, but witches have other interests. They must have *something* in common.

"Nice to meet you." I smiled, reaching out for magical energy again and still coming up empty. Sensing energy was more Tori's thing than mine, but I thought I'd gotten better at it as my Gift grew stronger. I took a breath. There was something there. Not Emily, but just past her. I stepped to the side to get a better view of the back of the kitchen.

Tori sat at a built-in banquette at the end of the counter, facing the teenager. Tori's magic wasn't active, but I felt it like a distant hum, ready to break into song at the slightest cue. Her vibration wasn't hard to pick out since the other girl at the table felt as mundane as the blonde despite her witchy style.

"And that's her stepdaughter..." Noemi gestured to the girl.

"Hey." The girl repeated Emily's greeting, barely looking up from her bedazzled phone. I couldn't let go of the feeling that I knew her somehow. Her makeup was certainly memorable enough. Red smudged eyeshadow stood out against her olive skin. Fake lashes and winged liner brought out her hooded eyes, and her lips were stained a dark berry. Not a popular style among my classmates, who often showed up to classes in t-shirts and pajama bottoms. She was too young to be in college anyway.

I struggled to remember if she'd ever been in the café when Tori came in. I could almost see the two of them hanging out. Different flavors, same vibes. But Tori promised to stop indoctrinating mundane girls and using them as energy sources after what happened with the hunters, and I wasn't sure she knew any other way to relate to them.

So, where do I know her from? I almost wrote it off as déjà vu, but the crescent moon nose ring identified her. I held back the urge to snap my fingers when it finally slipped into place.

"Isa," I said. "We've met."

The new barista at the café. The makeup had thrown me off. She couldn't wear it like that at work—her whimsigoth style didn't meet the uniform requirements. But it was her. She didn't seem like the type to volunteer for mother-daughter activities, much less a suburban book club. *What is she doing here?*

"What are you doing here?" Isa echoed my thought, her already-arched eyebrow raised dramatically.

Picking up the library's battered copy of Practical Magic

from the stack Noemi had left on the counter, I recited the cover story we'd agreed on. "I'm here for book club. Tori told me you guys were having some interesting conversations about witchcraft."

Isa smirked.

Her stepmother pursed her lips. "When you say it like that, you make it sound like we're in here doing spells or something. I know my makeup's good, but I promise I'm not hiding green skin and warts under here."

She waved her hand in front of her face with a photogenic smile. Her color palette was a practiced neutral, and I might not have noticed she had any makeup on if she hadn't mentioned it.

Tori caught my eye behind Emily's back and shook her head. Either Emily had a background in performance, or she was as mundane as they came.

"Sorry, I only meant you were talking about the way the author uses magic. You know, metaphorically, or whatever." I set the book on the counter.

"Emily's only interested in the romance and the garden," Isa said. "She wants to figure out how to grow giant lilacs like they did."

"That garden was so beautiful." Emily sighed. "I'd just love to get results like that…you know, without having to murder your father for fertilizer."

She laughed awkwardly, sipping her iced coffee until the straw scraped against the ice. Rattling the cup, she set it on the counter but kept fidgeting with the straw.

Noemi refilled it from a pitcher in the fridge.

"Bless you," Emily murmured.

The front door creaked open. "Hello? Can I come in?"

Lalo's head stuck out from his room down the hall. "Mama Lily's here!"

Noemi raised her eyes to the ceiling, her mouth a thin line

as she tried not to laugh. "Gracias, mijo."

The kid disappeared back into his room.

Tori sat up straighter, facing the doorway to the front of the house.

"Come on back," Noemi called, wiping her hands on her pants. "We're in the kitchen."

She pulled a metal filter from a drawer and set it into the mug, filling it with a few spoonfuls of tea from a mason jar.

The door closed, and footsteps sounded from the foyer. An older Latina woman came through the living room wearing cowboy boots under a long patterned skirt. Several layers draped from her shoulders: a loose tunic with wide three-quarter sleeves and slits up the sides, an embroidered vest, and a knit shawl, all in contrasting colors. A necklace of wooden beads peeked out from between the layers, dangling almost to her waist. Her silver hair was twisted up in a messy bun with a single narrow braid holding it in place. She looked like a lost art teacher. She was definitely a witch.

But Noemi had said the book club members were all mundanes. I felt like I'd been given a test, and I hadn't studied for it.

Tori tilted her head in what she probably meant to be a subtle instruction to pay attention, but I didn't need the hint. Isa sucked her lower lip between her teeth, eyes darting from Tori to me to the door. She couldn't know what we were thinking, but the shift in energy that Lily brought with her was undeniable. Even if Isa turned out to be as mundane as her mother.

When Lily stepped through the door, a wave of magical energy washed over me, so strong that I grabbed the counter for balance. Noemi's eyes fluttered. Behind me, Tori inhaled deeply, covering it with a yawn.

Interesting. Had opening my Gift for the time walk made me more sensitive to magic, or had the other witches grown accustomed to the strength of her energy from their previous meetings?

Emily appeared not to notice anything strange, but she looked up from her coffee when she heard the woman come down the hall.

"Well, hello, dear." The witch paused in the doorway. "Who is our new guest?"

My skin tingled with her intent. Her magic reached out to mine, almost like the scan Adam had done when I was still bound.

Noemi poured hot water into the mug and handed it to the new arrival with a slight bow of her head. "Welcome back. I missed you this week."

Turning, she presented the woman to me with a smile. "This is Lily Vallaria. She was a close friend of my grandmother back in Puerto Rico. Mama Lily, this is Cate Corey. Cate is a friend of Tori's. We asked her to join us."

"Did you, now?" Lily wrapped her finger around the mug and inhaled the steam.

Noemi pulled a new mug from a cabinet and made her own tea, answering Lily without looking at her. "We didn't think you'd mind."

Lily's gray eyes considered me over her mug. The energy tightened around me. Then it released, gone as suddenly as it began. She smiled. "Certainly not. The more, the merrier. Welcome to our little club, Cate. Blessed be."

10

When everyone who wanted one had a beverage, Noemi led us back to the den, her book under her arm and a big bowl of popcorn in both hands. She set it on a coffee table and settled into an overstuffed armchair. Isa curled up in a corner of the couch, tucking her legs underneath her. She pulled the bedazzled phone back out of her bag and half hid it between the folds of her skirt. The ruse would never have fooled a teacher, but her stepmom either didn't notice or chose to ignore it. Emily sat beside her, one leg crossed over the other. She leaned forward to grab a handful of popcorn and put her iced coffee on a magazine. Lily pulled a large pillow from the floor by the couch and laid it on the brick fireplace. She somehow seemed perfectly at ease on the hearth, even with no cozy fire burning behind her. Tori and I pulled chairs from the kitchen table and added them to the circle.

An awkward silence lasted for about three breaths before Lily broke it. "Shall we get started?"

Emily looked toward the door. "Aren't we waiting for Meredith?"

"I don't think she's planning to participate anymore."

Noemi stirred her tea, making soft clinking sounds against the cup. *One. Two. Three.*

"Oh really?" Emily frowned.

"It wasn't her thing." Noemi sipped the tea, watching Emily over the mug.

"I'm not surprised." Lily's long fingers drummed across her lips as she considered her next words.

Emily flipped some popcorn into her mouth. Covering her chews with a raised hand, she asked, "What do you mean?"

Lily interlaced her fingers and hooked them over her knee. "Put off by the witchcraft, you know. Imagined things a little more chocolate frogs and a little less bury-your-ex-in-the-garden."

"That wasn't witchcraft. That was murder," Emily said. She pulled the straw out of her cup and ran it across her lips.

Isa looked up from the faint glow of her phone. "That was self-defense. And she didn't mean to kill him."

Emily tapped her straw against the plastic lid. "The way the flowers grew over him was witchcraft."

"And the potion." Tori stood to grab a handful of popcorn, catching my eye over the table.

It'd been a while since I'd read the book, but no doubt Tori would have remembered everything from the dose of belladonna to the recipe for midnight margaritas.

"Was it a potion? Or was it just poison?" Isa's eyebrow went up, but she smiled immediately, breaking the effect.

"Is there a difference?" Emily asked.

"If you intend one, there is." Noemi tapped her spoon against her mug again.

"Okay, but Gillian was…" Isa started.

Emily cut her off. "I don't think Sandy meant to kill him."

Sandy? What book did she read? The sisters in Practical Magic were named Gillian and Sally. Tori shot Noemi a look, but the hostess just shrugged. Lily smiled as Emily continued.

"Don't you think? She was protecting her sister, and he drank too much anyway. And honestly, I really think he deserved it after what he did…He was going to wreck that car for sure—"

"Emily—" Isa frowned, dropping her phone and flipping through her copy of the book.

Emily rattled the ice in her cup. "I mean, don't get me wrong. He was hot, but that was not a healthy relationship."

I held back a laugh. *Some book club.* I vaguely remembered the description of Gillian's abusive boyfriend in the novel, but if Emily was defending Sandra Bullock, that wasn't the version she was picturing. His movie character didn't even have the same name.

Her stepdaughter looked up, her lips a tight line. She dropped the book in her lap, glaring at Emily. If she'd been a witch, the blonde would have caught fire right there in Noemi's living room.

Our host noticed the vibe change immediately, even if Emily remained oblivious. Noemi shifted in her seat, glancing between them. Her spoon tapped the mug again. The air in the room dropped a degree or two, energy unwinding. Probably unnecessary, but with the way magic had been acting lately, it couldn't hurt. She cleared her throat. "Well, no. Of course not. But he's not meant to be, is he? He's there to show how badly things are going for Gillian. He's not really a character on his own. He's a sign of how low Gillian's own self-worth has fallen. That she's constantly getting into this string of terrible relationships."

"But that was the family curse. Anyone they love dies, so why would she want to fall in love? Doesn't mean she has to be a nun." Emily stuck the straw back in her cup and slurped the melted ice.

"Emily—" Isa's light skin started to pink under her makeup.

Noemi leaned forward, speaking softly like she did with Lalo. "Sure, but don't you think it comes back to the sisters' sense of self? And how they both, in different ways, are constantly running away from—"

Take the hint, lady.

She plowed on, completely missing the off-ramp Noemi provided. "How could anybody run away from that house? It's so gorgeous. I'd kill for a kitchen like that."

I couldn't look at her. Blinking, I forced an interest in something else. The rug. The stack of books under the table (all fantasy novels, except one—a farmer's almanac). The arm of the chair, where the varnish was almost worn away.

Tori groaned.

I caught her eye and shook my head.

"Awk-ward," she mouthed.

Lily put two fingers to her lips to stop a laugh. Her eyes gave her away.

Isa stood, slamming her book on the table in front of Emily. "Did you even read the book?"

Emily jumped. Her cup fell over, but the lid restrained the last bits of ice. "What? Of course, I did!"

"Why are you lying?" Isa righted the plastic cup and stepped back from the table. Her hands shook, and she balled them into fists. *No sparks.* Her eyebrows knit together. "The whole point of this stupid exercise was to share the experience. If you weren't going to read it, what are we even doing here? We could have just watched the movie instead of dragging me to hang out with your boring friends."

She gestured around the room.

I raised an eyebrow. *Hey, I don't want to be here either.*

"No offense," she added as an afterthought.

"None taken." Noemi sat back in her chair, apparently done protecting Emily.

"Oh, no. Offense definitely taken," Tori said, crossing her

legs and picking at one of the holes in her dark jeans.

Lily smiled, apparently owning the accusation.

Emily reached a hand toward Isa, but neither of them moved any closer. "The doctor said we needed a shared hobby…"

"Watching movies is a hobby!" Isa pulled out her phone, frantically texting.

Emily slapped her hands on her lap. "I thought you liked this stuff. Isn't this what you're doing when you stomp up to your room after school? It looks like an occult bookshop in there."

I wonder if she's been to Holloway's Charms? Might need to check Thomas's accounting.

Isa's eye-roll was the kind mothers always say will make them stick that way, or fall out, or something equally gruesome. "There's barely any magic in this book. The title is totally misleading. Which you would know. If you had actually read the book."

"Fine. I'm sorry. I didn't read it." She looked at Noemi, raising her eyebrows and tilting her head to the side. "I know this is one of your favorites, Noe, but I just couldn't get into it."

Noemi shrugged. "It's fine. That's why we take turns. Everyone's not going to love every book."

"Not if they don't read it." Isa tapped out a final message before she dropped the phone back in her bag. "Zaze is coming to get me. I'll wait on the porch."

Emily stood. "You are not going anywhere with that boy."

I nearly applauded Emily's dramatic interpretation of an involved parent. She looked pretty proud of the performance.

"At least he doesn't have to lie about our shared interests." Isa stomped out of the room.

"You better not be sharing more than interests," Emily called after her. She stepped around the table and then stopped. Facing the group, she closed her eyes and put her hands together in front of her. An apology or a prayer. Opening them again, she flashed her palms at us, wiggling her gel nails show-choir style. "This is not how this was supposed to go. She knows…our therapist said…well, you know teenagers…"

Tori snorted.

Emily blushed, probably realizing half her audience was closer to her stepdaughter's age than hers.

"It's okay, Em," said Noemi. "Kids are…unpredictable."

"Exactly. A month ago she was all pink bows and ponies. Now, it's all occult symbols and crystals. She dresses like she's auditioning for an Anne Rice remake and dates a guy who goes by Azazel. How am I supposed to keep up?" She paused as if we might actually have an answer.

The front door slammed.

I'll have to check the schedule at the café. If we don't find the book in Lalo's room, Isa and I may need to have a talk about her new hobby.

"Perhaps start by following her out." Lily smiled to soften the dismissal. "We'll choose something more aligned to your interests next month. Gardening, maybe. You can try growing your own lilac and wisteria."

Emily nodded. "Thank you for understanding. I think I will just see if I can catch her before that boy…" Her voice trailed off as she disappeared down the hall. At the door, she called back, "Thanks for having us, Noe! Call you later!"

11

The room exhaled as though all of the negative energy slipped out the door with Emily. The air pressure shift almost made me dizzy.

Noemi set her mug on a ceramic tile on her coffee table, letting the spoon clatter to the side. The spell she'd been working during the meeting released. The temperature rose with the returning energy. If she'd wanted to keep the meeting peaceful, she'd failed.

"Well. How long do you intend to keep up this little social experiment?" Lily twisted a large ring on her index finger. "Is it going the way you expected?"

Noemi settled back into her chair, cupping a handful of popcorn as she made herself more comfortable. "What? No. I really thought she would read the book. You read it, didn't you?"

"Honestly, dear." Lily looked up, interlacing her fingers. "What do you hope to gain from continuing to meet with these…people?"

Noemi sighed. "You're the one who said I needed to build a community. Get out there. Meet people. For Lalo."

"A coven, not a coterie. I'm sorry, but this club was

doomed from the beginning. You need people with power." She looked me up and down with pursed lips. "This one might do. Where did you say you found her?"

Noemi gestured to Tori. "Tori recommended her. They go to school together."

I'm missing something here. Lily is a witch. She recognizes that I have power. Why did Noemi lie about all of the book club members being mundane?

Lily untangled her fingers, twisting the ring on her third finger this time. I felt a tug somewhere in the back of my mind. Pressure. The witch watched me with glittering eyes. "Friends from school? You're not from Salem, then?"

I didn't know what this lady had against Tori's hometown, but something in her tone made me glad I'd never been to Massachusetts. The pressure in my mind increased. I had to say something to release it. Something true...

"She's from Queen's Creek," Tori announced.

The pressure released so quickly that my head swam. *What just happened?*

Noemi smiled, and for a moment, I felt like nothing could be as bad as it seemed. The feeling passed when I looked away.

My stomach tightened. The covenant of secrecy was still in place, as obsolete as it might be. Even though I'd recognized Lily's energy the instant she'd walked in, and she must have recognized mine, I was unprepared for an open conversation with a witch I'd just met.

It's fine. This is how witches get to know one another without the covenant forcing them apart. Still, to just say it out like that—I felt exposed more than relieved.

Tori leaned back in the chair, bracing her hands on the back of the seat. The posture made her shoulders hunch. Her long legs stuck out in front of her, crossed at the ankle. She stared at the toes of her chunky boots.

Why do I feel like I've been delivered to a buyer?

"It's a small town in Virginia—" I started.

"Oh, I know exactly where it is." Lily licked her chapped lips. Her fingers kept moving, now spinning the ring on her pinkie. "So, you're the one we have to thank."

I looked at Tori, but she avoided my eyes. "Excuse me?"

Lily chuckled. "For setting things in motion. It was you who freed magic."

My breath caught. That was exaggerating things a little, wasn't it? Freed Queen's Creek's magic, maybe. Okay, definitely released the magic that had been contained in Queen's Creek. I could own that. And it had spread, giving witches outside a temporary boost. But the energy was already balancing out, wasn't it? Just settling to a new, slightly higher level?

"I'm not sure what you mean," I hedged.

Tori chuckled. "Oh sure, now she's modest."

"Weren't you the one bragging about how much better witches had it in Salem?" The kitchen chair creaked as I turned to face her.

Tori rolled her head to the side. "Please. Chosen One. Don't pretend you weren't the subject of a prophecy that altered the magical world as we know it."

"So were you." I crossed my arms. "As you made a point of reminding me."

She flexed her feet, making the spikes on her ankles click together. "Doesn't seem to matter as much."

"I'm sure what you did matters a great deal to the people of Cate's community." Noemi patted Tori's knee. Then she looked at me. "Doesn't it?"

She used the mom voice that had convinced Lalo to go to his room despite the lure of snacks and strangers in the kitchen.

"Yeah," I said, as if I would give any other answer.

"Everybody in Queen's Creek is protected now. No matter where they go. They have you to thank for that."

"I'm sure they're very grateful." Lily smiled as if Tori had claimed credit for rescuing a litter of kittens.

Tori huffed and leaned her head on the back of the chair, finding something interesting in the textured ceiling.

"But you." Lily clapped her hands together. "You changed the world. And for that, all of us owe you our thanks."

"Umm…you're welcome. For sure. But I think you're overstating things. What I did changed Queen's Creek. The rest of the world already had magic." I looked to Noemi and Tori to back me up.

Noemi smiled.

I almost expected someone to pop up and yell, "Surprise!" *Was the missing book some kind of ruse to get me here? What did this woman want?*

"Every revolution requires a match to light the flames." Lily's voice started low but built as she continued, her eyes alight. "You released a source of hidden energy and now there is no reason for any of us to cower in the shadows. Just you wait. Queen's Creek may have been the first secret community to drop their cloak, but they will not be the last. And as each one opens their Gates, more magic will enter the world. Witches will regain their strength and take their rightful place."

Should I applaud or follow Isa and Emily out the door? The older woman radiated a warm glow, her energy rising with the enthusiasm of her speech.

"Mama Lily's never been a fan of the covenant," Noemi explained as if this powerful witch were an eccentric grandmother reminiscing about the good old days instead of calling for radical change.

"The covenant be damned." Lily slammed a fist on her knee. "It was insane to think that women of our abilities could remain hidden. Our lights will not be dimmed. It's time for our coming out party. And you've sent the invitations."

"I—I didn't mean to." Would it be awesome for witches to practice openly without fear of persecution? Absolutely. But after what Tori and I went through with Jasmine and the hunter, I didn't see how it was possible.

"I told you she wasn't ready," Tori mumbled.

"You talked about me?"

"Only hypothetically," Noemi said. "We didn't know if you would even come and meet with us."

"Is that what this is all about? You lured me here, to what? Help you start some kind of witch rebellion? Is the book even really missing?" My heart beat so hard I felt it in my ears.

Tori and Noemi exchanged a glance and then Noemi shot an embarrassed look at Lily.

"What is she talking about?" Lily asked. "That grimoire you were hiding in your bedroom? You haven't lost it, have you?"

An innocent question that implied the complete opposite.

Was it a mistake? Admitting she'd seen the book? Or does she not care if we know? I could already sense the strength of her power. If she wanted it, she could take it anytime. She didn't need to hide.

Tori narrowed her eyes at the old woman as if she'd caught her.

They could have told me they suspected her. What was the point of telling me they were all mundanes?

"So, you admit you saw it," Tori said.

Lily waved a hand, setting all of her rings sparkling. "Of course I did. All of us did. It was right out there on the desk. You're lucky Emily felt so guilty about knocking over the wine. She was so focused on getting the stain out of my blouse, she wouldn't have noticed if you'd called the quarters right there in the bathroom."

She shook her head at the ceiling and then leaned conspiratorially to me, "Such a mundane. Why do we even bother?"

"Bother?" My brother looked down on mundanes. Tori didn't hide her disdain for them. But everything Lily said warned of deeper prejudice. That, combined with her talk of revolution, worried me.

She looked disappointed in my response. That worried me more.

Sighing, she continued, "Trying to pretend they're our equals. She wouldn't have known the first thing about what to do with that book, even if she'd noticed it sitting there. The thing practically glowed with untapped energy, and she walked right by it. *Try this vinegar. I saw something on TikTok where…*" Lily's voice shifted up an octave. The impression mimicked Emily perfectly.

She wouldn't have known what to do with it. But Lily would.

I chewed my lip. It was a risk, but I had to know. "What did you do with the book?"

Her mouth opened and closed. *Gotcha.*

She twisted her rings with frantic energy. The room felt smaller. Pressure. A push this time instead of a pull. I'd made a mistake. She wanted what was best for all of us. Lily smiled benevolently. "I'm sure I don't know what you're talking about?"

She shouldn't have said that. It was a step too far. Unbelievable. This woman would never admit ignorance.

"She wouldn't…" Noemi frowned. She rubbed her eyes as if she were just waking up. "Wait? Did you? Why? Why wouldn't you just ask me for it?"

Lily's face darkened. Like, actually rejected the light in the room, as if a living gloom passed over her. Her eyes widened. The sparks I'd seen earlier completely vanished, replaced by something else. Fear.

But then it was gone. The shadow and the fear both faded. Her eyes glittered like they had when she'd questioned me. Back in control, she said, "I will not stay here and face these accusations."

She stood, sweeping her shawl over her shoulder like a cape. The lights flickered, casting angled shadows across her face. The bulb in the ceiling fan popped, and the room plunged into semi-darkness.

By the time Noemi switched on a lamp in the hall, Lily was gone.

<h1 style="text-align:center">12</h1>

I took a breath. Closed my eyes. Counted down from ten. *Goddess, why do you try me so?* Everything always spun out of control when Tori was involved. Three. Two. One. I glared at her. "You told me they were all mundanes."

She backed up, catching herself on the edge of the couch. "I didn't. I only met them once. She—"

"They are mundane," Noemi said. "Mostly. Mama Lily's a green witch. It's basically gardening. Practically academic. She's still in the broom closet. I promised not to tell."

"What are you talking about?" Tori said, gripping the couch with both hands. "That was not the same woman who came to the last meeting. Her energy is…double, maybe triple what I've ever felt from her before. And all that stuff about revolution? There's no closet big enough."

"If she was ever in the closet, it doesn't sound like she intends to stay there." I crossed my arms to hide the energy at my fingertips. *Breathe.*

Noemi's eyebrows pinched. She brought her fingers to her lips, shook her head. "That was strange. She's usually such a quiet presence. Peaceful, you know? She's been a huge help since Lalo came to live with me. Like the abuela he never had.

I was thinking about asking for her help with the elixir…once we get the book back." She looked up at the busted bulb in the fan and sighed. "I hope she's okay."

"That was strange?" What was wrong with her? Noemi's entire personality had changed when Lily arrived. I thought it was respect for an elder, but this level of denial…

"You could have told me you knew who took it," I said, watching her walk into the kitchen. "Would have saved us a lot of time and trouble."

Tori sat on the arm of the couch. "You really think she has it?"

"Are you kidding me?" Were they both blind?

"But why?" Noemi pulled a folded step ladder from behind the door to her pantry. "Why would she steal it? She's usually the one sharing ancestral knowledge with me. What does she need with an old grimoire? I mean, it's historically interesting, but we haven't found anything in there that hasn't been passed down…"

Oh, I don't know. Maybe because it's supposed to have the recipe for the elixir of life?

Noemi's behavior didn't make sense. Why was she protecting the older woman? Out of deference or out of fear? She tried to dismiss Lily's power and ambition when it was obvious to anyone with any kind of sensitivity to magical energy. Then she tried to downplay the importance of the book, but she'd already told me it could change her life. Did she want help or not?

Maybe Lily was influencing her in some way. I remembered the tug when she'd asked about where I came from. The way I'd felt compelled to tell her the truth. Could it have been some kind of charm to make people trust her? Those bulky rings on her fingers might serve more than fashion.

Noemi avoided my eyes.

Does she know what Lily can do? Does she accept it? It could be hard to stand up to the people you cared about. Where would Noemi draw the line? Or was she so far under her mentor's influence that she didn't see it needed to be drawn?

She shook as she opened the ladder under the fan.

Not totally in denial then. I stepped around the coffee table and steadied it for her. "Maybe she wants it for the same reason you do."

She climbed the ladder and tapped the dead bulb. Looking down, she said, "She's not a vampire. Tori, could you bring me a new bulb? I left it in the pantry. Second shelf."

Tori went to the kitchen.

Noemi sat on the top step of the ladder, resting her head against the handlebar. She spoke without looking at me. "I know this might be difficult to accept. The whole vampires exist thing. It makes you question—Tori didn't know either. Hell, I didn't know until the accident—"

"The accident that killed Lalo's parents?" I asked. *Was it an accident? Or an attack?* If that was how they'd become vampires…only a year ago…it would explain why she still held out hope that their condition could be reversed.

She turned back to face me. "What I mean is…they exist, but you don't need to panic about them. They're not that common. And I would know if Lily had been turned. She's not a vampire."

Small comforts. "If that book contains the recipe for the elixir of life, it could do a lot more than cure vampirism. You said she was powerful. After the things said…What if she wants more?"

Noemi unscrewed the bulb and handed it to me. "Mama Lily has been a friend of my family for years. She's one of the only ones who stood by us. She would never steal from us."

"Are you sure?" Tori pulled the new bulb from a pack and passed it to Noemi. "Cause I don't have a lot of time for mundanes and their fake mystical bullshit, but what that witch said about them was wild."

I quirked an eyebrow.

Tori played at taking offense. "What? I'm reformed. Mandatory counseling with Nora once a week. Fish are Friends, Not Food. Or whatever."

Hopefully, Nora's guidance could undo some of the prejudices she'd grown up with in Salem. *Fingers crossed.*

"Maybe it was Isa," Noemi said. She replaced the bulb and climbed back down. "Did you hear what Emily said about her occult interests?"

Tori hooked her thumbs in her back pockets and stepped back. "Yeah, maybe she's trying to impress the boyfriend. What was his name, Azazel? Who names their kid after a demon?"

"I doubt it's his real name. It's a costume. Like her makeup and the outfit. I don't think she'd have any idea what to do with a real book of magic. Besides, could she even read it? You said it's in Latin." I collapsed the ladder and handed it back to Noemi.

"I just don't think Mama Lily would steal from us." She shook her head and carried the ladder back to the pantry.

"Well, it certainly wasn't Emily." Tori snorted.

I tried to picture the blonde stirring intention into her iced coffee or tracing runes into her moisturizer. *Unlikely.* My bet was still on Lily, but the faint electronic pings coming from down the hall reminded me of another unfinished conversation.

"What about Lalo?"

"He saw me with the book, Noe." Tori joined Noemi in the kitchen.

I glanced at Noemi, wondering if she'd told him her plan when she brought it home. I didn't have to ask. Noemi closed the pantry door and leaned on it. "I didn't hide it from him.

He knows why I brought it home. It's as much for him as it is for me."

So, he had a vested interest in keeping it safe. Even from Tori. "What happened after he came in?"

"He asked what I was doing. I said I recognized the book from the library. I wondered what it was doing here." She looked for a response from Noemi, but the other woman looked down at the floor.

"Did he have an answer?" I asked.

"He said I shouldn't be in there," Tori said. She touched Noemi's arm. "Very defensive kid you've got. I thought he was going to fight me over it."

That got to her. Noemi looked up, her cheeks pinking. "He wouldn't..."

Tori shrugged. "I don't know. His face got all dark...but then the doorbell rang. Just like today. The book club ladies showed up, so we went to let them in. And you know, he went back to his room. At least, I thought he did."

Excellent timing, that club. No rehearsal I've ever run has been so punctual.

"He didn't take it then," I said. "Because it was still there during the meeting when they spilled the wine."

"He could have gone back after." Tori rocked back on her heels. Her eyes drifted down the hall to where the light was still on in Lalo's room.

"He didn't." Noemi's eyes flashed.

I didn't want to upset her. What happened when you made a vampire mad? Did she Hulk out? Fangs and nails and red eyes? Did her forehead do that thing like on Buffy? Okay, maybe I did want to upset her. Just a little. To see what would happen. "Can you be sure, though? If he's had it this whole time..."

"He would have told me." She straightened, stepping away from the support of the pantry door.

No sign of a monstrous transition yet. Probably for the best. "Look, I get he's your kid, and you want to protect him. But isn't that exactly the reason you should make absolutely certain he isn't hiding a dangerous magical book under his bed?"

"Who's hiding a what?"

13

L alo stepped into the kitchen, barely taking his eyes off the tablet cradled along his arm and propped against his belly.

Got to put some kind of alarm on that kid. They put bells on cats, right?

He pulled his giant headphones off one ear and a high-pitched voice squealed something unintelligible.

Those are way better than the earbuds. Kid has some nice tech.

"Mijo, what are you doing up? Are you still hungry?" Noemi opened the fridge.

"Nah, nah…" He waved a hand at her, letting the headphones fall back into place. Louder, he said, "My battery's about to die. I need your charger."

Noemi swung the fridge shut, facing her nephew with her hands on her hips. "I think that's a sign, don't you? You need a screen break. It's almost bedtime, anyway. That thing is not good for your eyes."

Lalo dropped the tablet—now with a black screen—to his side and pulled the headphones down around his neck. "Tiaaaaaaaaaa. I was in the middle of a show."

"YouTube will still be there in the morning." She put her

hands on his shoulders and turned him around. "Back to your room and read a book."

Lalo groaned but headed back to his room.

"What are you reading, kiddo?" Tori called after him.

Noemi shot her a look over her shoulder.

Lalo stopped and turned around but didn't answer. Suddenly shy, he looked down at the blank tablet and snapped the elastic on the case.

Tori took a tentative step forward, ignoring Noemi's protective stance. "I used to love reading about Greek mythology when I was your age. Do you like Percy Jackson?"

He shook his head, making his dark curls bounce.

She tried again. Another step, another question. "Maybe graphic novels? I've got a little cousin who's really into Dog Man."

"I survived," he said.

"Umm. Yeah. You did." Tori looked back at me, her dark-rimmed eyes wide.

Mine probably matched. The room felt cold again.

I'm not sure I'm ready to hear a first-person account of a vampire attack if that's where this is going.

I swallowed. "Do you...do you want to talk about it?"

The kid looked from me to Tori. He wrinkled his nose, and I could practically see the wheels turning. He'd been confused, but now he was up to something. He leaned around Tori to catch Noemi's eye. "Can I show them?"

"Sure. Go get the book. But then it's bedtime." She rubbed her head and went back to the couch as Lalo tore down the hall.

Tori spun around. "Wait. The book? Like, THE Book?"

Noemi yawned. "What? No! The book he's reading. It's a series. They're graphic novels about major catastrophes. Nonfiction. They're called *I Survived*. I don't know why he likes them so much. Seems kind of morbid to me."

Morbid. To the vampire.

"So when he said *I survived*, he wasn't talking about his own experience…" I sat in the armchair across from Noemi.

"No. Believe me. I would love for him to come out of his shell more and talk about what he went through. What we're going through now. But he's not ready. I'm hoping some of these books will show him, you know, you can come through something terrible." She tucked her legs up under her and patted the spot beside her as Lalo came back from his room. "Sit here, mijo. You can tell us all about this one."

Tori sat in the chair she'd used during the meeting. "What's the book about?"

Lalo held up a slim paperback with an illustration of a young girl climbing a tree to escape an enormous bear. "It's a grizzly attack."

I gulped. "Cool. I mean. Wow. That looks scary."

Lalo shrugged.

Noemi nudged him. "You came out here for a reason. Tell us about your book."

"So, this girl is on vacation with her family in a national park, and grizzly bears attack them."

"That sounds terrifying," Tori said, crossing her leg and letting her foot bounce.

Lalo nodded. "It's pretty scary, 'cause the girl, she's only eleven. And I think her mom is already dead, so…"

"So, she's kind of alone out there, huh?" I said.

He nodded again.

Noemi squeezed his arm. "But she survived, right? It's right there in the title. So we know she's going to be alright. Even though it's scary at the time."

Lalo straightened a little. "Yeah. Yeah, she's definitely going to survive it. They always survive. That's what the books are about."

"Have you read a lot of those books?" Tori asked.

More nods, a little more enthusiastic this time. "The librarian at my school, she knows all the best ones. And she knows I only want the graphic novels, so sometimes she holds them for me. And then I can get it the next time my class goes to the library."

"That's nice of her." Noemi seemed conflicted about her colleague's kindness.

"Yeah, she knows I can read hard books. I don't get scared." He grinned.

A kid who prides himself on reading challenging books might be extra intrigued by a book his aunt kept hidden. Especially a book written in cursive and Latin. It was practically encoded. Was he up to it?

"You're very brave." Noemi pulled him in for a hug.

Lalo accepted it for about a three-count, then pulled away and waved to us before he took off back down the hall. "Okay, I'm going to go read this now. Good-night!"

What are the odds that's the only scary book he's got in there?

My phone pinged before I could suggest an inventory of the kid's bookcase.

A text from Adam with a single character: ?

Oops. Between the sudden end to Book Club, the unexpected revelations from Lily, and story time with the kid, I'd completely lost track of time. I sent Adam a thumbs-up.

Then added: sorry. leaving now. I'm OK. don't blink!

I made my excuses and got out of there.

With any luck, Lalo stashed the book somewhere in his room, Noemi would talk him into giving it back, and this whole terrible day could be forgotten.

Well, the missing grimoire part, anyway.

Lily made me a little nervous. If Lalo didn't have the book squirreled away somewhere, she definitely did. And I didn't love the idea of a collection of potentially world-altering spells in the hands of an apparently mobilized radical feminist with plans to magically disrupt mundane society. What was all that about *witches taking our rightful place* and *women of our abilities*? Queen's Creek had been founded by a woman, but it had taken witches of all genders to build a successful community.

Noemi didn't seem to take Lily's talk of revolution seriously, and she knew her better than I did. But the steel behind that woman's eyes belied her grandmotherly appearance. We shouldn't dismiss her as a threat.

The bus back to campus dropped me in front of the college library. From there, I could walk back to the dorm or go up to the L and catch a train to the magic shop. The trip out to Noemi's already felt like the journey of a thousand miles. My bed called my name, but my mini fridge couldn't compete with Thomas's fully-stocked kitchenette. I needed to recharge my energy from any source, and my stomach rumbled in agreement. Plus, Adam would probably keep texting me until I gave a full report.

I sent Thomas a train emoji, followed by an array of food emojis.

When I arrived, the magic shop smelled like pepperoni. I followed the scent up the stairs to Thomas's apartment and gratefully accepted two slices on a paper plate. The guys looked like they hadn't moved since we got Tori's call. After I filled them in on the book club meeting—complete with time-walking, my ongoing trust issues with Tori, and my concerns about Lily—they agreed to hold off on storming the green witch's bungalow until we knew for sure the kid hadn't taken the grimoire to his room. Occam's razor and all that.

It was the logical thing to do, but that didn't make the wait-and-see approach any easier.

The guys didn't have any new updates for me, so once the pizza hit my bloodstream, we dove back into Dad's notes. Thomas sat cross-legged on the floor beside the coffee table, papers spread in a fan around him. He passed them to me a few at a time, sometimes adding his own notes on multicolored post-its. I sat on the futon beside Adam and picked through them, pen in hand, in case I had anything to add. It clicked under my thumb.

We'd seen them all before, but somehow, Dad's scrawls seemed less chaotic after my conversations with the librarian. We had something specific to look for now. The elixir was real. He might have been closer than we'd thought to discovering it. Had he known about the *Ichoriad*? Maybe if we found Noemi's book, we could find a way to bring him home. For the first time since we'd started trying to decipher his words, I felt something like hope.

14

Welcome to Lakeshore Lattes. What can we make for you today?" Isa chirped.

Brian had better show up for his next shift. The new barista might have been defiant during her mandated attendance at book club yesterday, but she brought fresh-faced enthusiasm to her work at the café. She was starting to make me look bad.

Despite the fact that our store manager had told her—on at least three occasions I knew of—that shift managers must hold a high school degree, the sixteen-year-old insisted that her consistently superior customer service and efficiency in completing side work would force him to recognize her capabilities and make an exception.

I didn't know how to tell her a promotion was less than unlikely. She'd skipped the eyeliner and worn light pink chapstick, but even if she took out the nose ring that made our conservative manager's eye twitch, he would probably hire the exiled Morgan back and promote her before making a teenager shift manager.

Assuming Morgan wanted to come back and hadn't found another way to earn her car money. Maybe she could share

Madison's ride. The twins seemed to have made up. After all, the backstage drama ended when the show closed.

My phone pinged, and I turned my back to the bar to check the message.

Tori: Lalo didn't have it

Great. It had to be Lily, then. I didn't know what kind of hold she had over Noemi, but something told me getting the grimoire back from her would be more challenging than cleaning out the kid's room.

Someone knocked on the pass-through counter where I should have been handing off drinks, and I shoved my phone back into my pocket. A familiar voice called, "Hey, where's my matcha latte?"

"Umm…coming up. One minute." I lifted each cup in the growing train, looking for the one marked for the impatient customer. Three cups back. A matcha latte. Iced. Soy. Inexplicably topped with caramel drizzle. *Wait.*

I smiled, looking up from the cups at my roommate on the other side of the counter. She narrowed her eyes in her best impression of one of our patrons. I stuck out my tongue. Her dirty look faltered, but she recovered.

"Girl, you better get it together. Keeping people waiting out here." She tapped her acrylic nails on the counter for emphasis. Behind her, an older woman glared at me, and I could see her mentally cheering on Nyla's angry customer character.

"I will kill you in your sleep," I whispered.

Nyla smirked.

Lifting out the next order and leaving it on the counter, I called, "Triple shot white chocolate mocha!"

"Oh, is that mine?" Nyla feigned confusion, reaching for the hot drink.

I rolled my eyes, pouring espresso over foam for the next customer. "You are going to get me fired."

"Not if you get my drink up here," she countered. "Then I'll leave you alone."

I dumped matcha powder on top of the ice and set the shaker back on the counter. "You're going to have to wait your turn, just like everybody else."

She crossed her arms, leaning against the counter. The angry woman reached past her to grab the white mocha and disappeared out the door.

"Have a great day!" I called after her.

She ignored me.

I shook my head.

"Hope that kicks in before she gets where she's going," Nyla said. "Lady was tense. Her whole vibe was stressing me out."

I considered a snarky response about her own contribution to the vibe of the café but swallowed it in favor of knocking out a few more orders to clear the line.

"Doppio affogato!" I barely had the cup across the counter when a middle-aged man wearing earbuds took it from my hand.

He pulled one earbud out and held up the cup. "This is my doppio?"

"Doppio affogato." *How would I know if it's yours or not?*

He nodded, shoving the earbud back and knocking against Nyla's hip in his hurry to be on his way. He glanced at her but didn't stop to make eye contact as he said, "Excuse me."

"No excuse for him," she grumbled.

"Here's your matcha, ma'am," I said, handing over the green drink.

"Bout time." She held out her hand.

I pulled the cup back to the bar. "Sorry, did you say extra caramel?"

She squinted suspiciously. "You know I did."

Grabbing the caramel bottle, I lifted the lid and lined it

with sticky syrup. I poured enough over the floating ice to raise the level of the drink to the edge of the cup. Surface tension be damned. Nyla's eyes went wide. This time, when I set the cup in front of her, all she said was, "Thank you."

"You going to practice tonight?" I asked, not looking at her while I completed the next three drinks.

"Canceled. Team captain has Covid." She sighed.

No wonder she's so cranky. Nyla used dance team like therapy. She said she needed the sweat to *exercise her demons.* Pun one-hundred-per-cent intended. Free time never relaxed her. The only time I ever saw her sit still was when she perched at the top of a ladder, painting the drop for a show. And even then, she had to be engaging some major muscle groups to keep her balance.

Wait. The captain has Covid? Jasmine was the captain of the dance team. Nyla introduced her to Brian.

Is that why Brian's not here? Jasmine gave him Covid? Or is it something else? If she told the team she had the plague, she was planning to disappear for a while. An excuse like that... *that's not missing one practice. That's at least two weeks off duty.* You could do a lot in two weeks. Especially if you weren't planning on coming back.

That would be okay if it were just Jasmine. *Please, goddess, let him come back.*

"Oh, umm. That's rough," I said. "How long has she been out?"

Nyla sipped her matcha, her eyes combing the ceiling as she thought about it. "Umm...well, she missed practice last week, but Berkley covered for her. I think she twisted her ankle or something in that gas leak at the theater. Remember how they had to evacuate everybody on opening night? That was crazy. Anyway, that's probably how she got it. At the hospital, you know? Nobody wears masks in the emergency room, and they're all coughing all over the place."

Honestly, if somebody was going to get Covid, the auditorium of the theater was just as likely. But Jasmine hadn't been there to see *Kiss Me Kate*. She'd come to the theater to poison my academic advisor. While other students were setting up internships with local businesses, Jasmine had apprenticed herself to a witch hunter. Murdering Nora was probably her first assignment.

Brian would know. *Ugh*. This whole not being able to just ask Brian thing was really going to be a problem. I needed to find him.

"So you guys are taking the night off?" I asked, reaching past Nyla to hand off a mocha latte.

"Well, yeah. I mean. We're supposed to be learning a new routine this week, but Berkley doesn't know the steps." Nyla's disappointment in the team's junior captain dripped from her words.

"Why don't you take over?" I punched the button for espresso and loaded the machine with the next cup.

"Girl, I do not need that responsibility. I dance for joy. It is a release. I'm not about to get put in charge and have to care what other people are doing." She eyed the customers waiting for their drinks as if any of them might spontaneously combust at any moment.

"You saying you don't care what Jasmine is up to?" I gave her a side eye while I poured steamed milk over the espresso. "Because she definitely does not have Covid."

I could practically see Nyla's gossip antenna go up. She turned back to me so fast that one of her red box braids swung around and caught on her straw. "What do you know?"

I shrugged, shoving a cup under the hot water dispenser. "Something happened between her and Brian at the theater. I got the feeling…I don't know. I was going to ask him what's going on with them today, but…" I let her follow my gaze to where Isa stood at the register.

"Maybe he took the day off to take care of her. You know your boy's sweet like that." Nyla waited for me to counter her hypothesis.

"I don't know. Maybe you could check on her. Ask for the notes on the routine. Bring her dinner or something. Just to be sure she's covered." I passed out the next cup. "Grande hot tea!"

Nyla sipped her green drink. "Hmm. Maybe I will. Just to make sure she's okay. For the good of the team."

Wow. Nyla really was mad at Jasmine for missing practice. The girl was making enemies all over campus. "Let me know what you find out."

"You closing tonight?"

"Yeah." I wiped down the steamer wands. "And then I think I'm going to go to the library for a while. I am so not ready for exams."

The semester had gone by fast. For all the time I'd put in trying to understand Dad's work, I'd barely glanced at the notes for my classes. I was so close to graduation. I couldn't let my family drama get in the way. Even if my family had recently expanded to include a nerdy mundane who was dating a witch hunter and an unstable witch who'd befriended a vampire.

15

Frosted glass separated the Quiet Room from the rest of the library. Outside, shadows and muffled voices marked the annual transition from regular academic use to exam prep. The usually empty carrels and banks of computers in the main space housed stressed students who'd coasted through their courses only to panic in the face of potentially grade-destroying finals. It was already dark outside, but they'd probably be here well into the night. I practically had to hold my breath, walking through the haze of anxiety to get to the safety of the study space. Only half the tables were occupied. An introvert oasis.

I pulled my eyes away from the glass, remembering why I'd come here. Theater History: Modern and Contemporary. *Prepare to identify and analyze the cultural, political, and economic context of three plays between mid-18th century Europe and the present.* The professor provided a list of potential plays, but we were on our own to research their historical background. I made my choices and started highlighting my notes from her lectures. My eyes glazed over.

The things I wanted to learn right now wouldn't appear on any of my exams. I gave up after ten minutes. With my laptop open in front of me, I logged into my school account and opened a new document in the cloud drive. Physics of Time Travel. Enter. Enter. Enter. Insert Table. Source. Notes. I pulled a heavy textbook from the stacks and brought it back to the study room, flipping to the index to look for anything on the science of time, the Higgs Boson particle, or Einstein's special theory of relativity.

"Cate?" Brian's voice hovered just above a whisper in deference to the Quiet Room rules mounted on the back wall and taped to every study table. He pulled the screen of my laptop down a little to catch my eye over the computer.

Some day, I was going to finish a thought before somebody interrupted it.

Shit. Brian?

I shoved my chair back and jumped up. "Goddess of Grace and Mercy! You're okay! Where have you been?"

He looked…fine. Not at all like someone recovering from several days of suffering from the plague or torture.

"Shhh!" somebody hissed. Several of the Quiet Room denizens abandoned their intense exam prep to openly stare at us.

"Sorry!" I whispered.

Brian laughed. He came around the table for a hug, then pulled out the chair beside mine, gesturing for me to sit with him. He kept his voice down to avoid further annoying the small study crowd. "Sorry about going no contact. I've been dealing with…well, you know. Trying to get my head straight."

Did I know? Was he really saying I hadn't heard from him since the hunter attack because he was processing the trauma?

I matched his tone. "But you're alright? You're not sick or anything?"

He leaned back in the chair, opening his arms to my

inspection. "No permanent damage. Just a little confused."

The other students satisfied that our conversation would not provide an entertaining distraction, went back to their books.

"Do you want to talk about it?"

"I'd rather get back to normal, if we can," he said. "What are you working on?"

I crossed my arms, considering. *Normal? Never heard of it.* I could press my luck on why he missed work. Or ask about Jasmine. Didn't seem like that would go well, though. The library didn't exactly invite potentially combative conversations. He clearly didn't want to tell me where he'd been or what he'd been doing, and I couldn't exactly pry it out of him in public. Not here. Not now.

Fine. If we weren't going to be honest with each other, at least I could get something out of this. My research could use some direction, and hadn't I been wishing for exactly this opportunity? What had Thomas said? "I know you don't want anybody to take care of you, but that doesn't mean you have to do everything yourself."

I'd asked everyone in Queen's Creek to trust and depend on each other.

"We're stronger together," we told them. Tori and I effectively modeled the principle by depending on Thomas's popularity and Adam's reputation to convince our elders that we were no longer children who could be ignored. Returning from a Wakening was supposed to indicate our readiness to accept the adult roles our community demanded of us. It was because we'd left that we now understood the danger that would require a community bond.

But I'd spent so much of my life trying to prove that I could handle things on my own that it felt next to impossible to ask for help. And I needed help if I wanted to find my father.

Time to live the message.

I turned the laptop so Brian could see my empty chart with the ambitious title.

"Still trying to understand your Gift?" he asked. "Are you leaning toward a Sliders alternate-Earths vortex or the Back to the Future split-timeline model?"

"Hey, where'd you go?"

"Sorry. What were you saying?" I kept my response low. *Ugh.* Brian's tutoring made the science more accessible in theory, but we'd gotten into specific models, and the numbers made my head swim. I had trouble maintaining focus. Why was I like this? I did the hard thing. I asked him for help. The very least I could do was show him respect while he tried to do me this favor.

"Maybe we should take a break." Without waiting for a response, he pushed his laptop closed. "Are you working tomorrow?"

"Yeah, I asked Mark to put me on closing for the rest of the week since the show's over." The end of the theater season always gave me an energetic hangover, but at least it freed up my evenings. I needed to replace the savings I'd spent on that unplanned flight to Virginia over spring break. The last few trips home were cheaper—Adam and Thomas blinked us across the country in seconds—so hopefully, I'd have enough to cover room and board for the last quarter. Thomas offered to let me stay with him, but the studio over the shop felt a little crowded now that it housed both my brother and my boyfriend. Plus, how would I avoid having The Talk if we lived together?

"Okay, I'm going to send you some notes you can look over on your break. There's a YouTube video in here that explains this stuff better than I do." He tapped the laptop.

"You've been amazing." I meant it, but I never knew how to express genuine appreciation in a way that didn't sound awkward. So, I leaned into it, lacing my words with saccharine. "Are you sure you aren't going to be a professor? Seriously, you're much better than the TA I had for lab."

"You sound like Jasmine." His smile dropped as soon as the name slipped out. He looked away.

What? My breath stopped, and I had to consciously remind myself to accept oxygen before I passed out. Scent memory flooded my nostrils with salt and peanut oil. Poisoned French fries. Was he actually carrying on a romantic relationship with someone who'd tried to murder our favorite professor? It had to be some kind of mistake. Nothing else made sense. I leaned forward, pushing my laptop to the side. The effort to keep my tone hushed scraped my throat. "You are *not* still seeing her, are you?"

He looked down at his fingers, at his laptop, anywhere but into my eyes. "It's complicated."

I threw myself back, rocking the chair. The legs screeched on the tile, and a few students studying at the next table shot me dirty looks. I waved an apology. My hand became a fist as I lowered it to the table. *It's complicated?* Anger replaced my initial confusion and panic, a cold line running down my back.

I pursed my lips, unable to put my thoughts into words. Afraid of which ones might escape.

"You have to understand—" Brian started.

"I understand," I hissed, barely above a whisper. "Do you?"

My nails bit into my palms, and I ground my fists into my knees to keep them from shaking. How could he associate himself with her after what she'd done? Much less date her. What excuse could possibly make up for that?

Nyla would have made a crass comment about which of his body parts was doing the thinking, but I'd always thought Brian was above that sort of thing. Apparently, he was no more enlightened than the high school boys who snuck on campus for the parties.

He looked miserable.

"She's going through some things." His voice carried none of the conviction it had when he defined physics terms.

I swallowed against the acid fighting its way into my throat. "She. *She's* going through? She tried to murder Nora! She was working with the hunter who killed Tori's sister. *He tried to shoot you*. He almost killed—"

Brian grabbed my hand, looking around to see if anyone heard me. "Let's talk about this somewhere else."

I pulled my hand back as if it burned. I'd trusted Brian with my secret. With my life. He'd witnessed my magical breakthrough and still waited for me to be ready before asking me to explain. And even then, he'd been supportive and curious instead of frightened or angry.

I should have known it was too good to be true.

My neck tightened, tension from my jaw spreading around the back of my head. I felt sick as a new idea pushed its way to the surface.

If he'd accepted my secret life, why wouldn't he protect hers, too? "Did you know? Did she tell you what she was before you started dating?"

"Not here. Please." The last word was soft but urgent. He stood, dropping his laptop into his backpack and looking over his shoulder. People were staring. The muscles in his neck stood out. He didn't look at me.

Why couldn't he have just said, "No"? No is easy, only two letters. I'd have believed him. But "not here." As if I could willingly follow him anywhere now. This one conversation had already recategorized friend to foe. Or at least friend to potential danger. And I didn't know if we could go back.

I gripped the edge of the table, my eyes widening. "She did. You were in a relationship with a killer, and you knew what she was doing."

"Cate—"

"Stop talking." I threw my hands up without thinking. After years of focusing all of my intent to direct even a hint of magical energy, now my unbound power manifested with the slightest encouragement. I didn't even consciously call it this time.

A wave of energy vibrated between us. Spots floated in front of my eyes, and my hands shook. My magic rippled out, expanding from my fingertips, breakers rolling over the table, the chairs, the other students in the study room, and crashing into the wall. My ears throbbed with the silence.

Breathe.

16

I gasped, my chest heaving with the effort. *What am I doing?*

In front of me, Brian stood frozen with one hand on the table, the other pinning his backpack to his shoulder. His wide lips pulled into a thin line, and his dark brown eyes glistened. His pained expression almost broke me. But his regret didn't make up for his guilt. It was there in his eyes, too. He knew he'd betrayed me. I needed to know how badly.

My breath came in short, audible bursts through my nose as I sat there, chewing my lip and planning my next move. I didn't mean to call my Gift, but here it was, as big as anything I'd ever done on purpose. *Now what?* Even with my recent power boost, I couldn't hold the entire study room in a time bubble much longer. For one thing, anybody could come through the door at any moment. Then how would I explain the living statues? *Oh, it's a performance piece, you know, a project for Contemporary Theater 319. Something about the inertia of the modern education system.*

Ugh. They'd already heard too much. I couldn't face the questions. The whispers.

Go back.

I'd reversed time for the mug at the café. Just a little thing, but it had nearly broken and then returned to safety. At Noemi's house, I'd controlled the whole bedroom for a few seconds. Actually moved two people back in time. The energy had overwhelmed me. What if I didn't let it go? What if I used it?

My fingers twitched, curling in on themselves. Brian's hand slid back, lowering his bag. In the corner of my eye, someone else moved, shifting in their chair with the same slow-motion movement. I froze, and they did too. I opened my hand again, extending my fingers to the room. Brian's bag came back up to his shoulder.

In.

Out.

Backwards.

Forwards.

Rewind.

Fast Forward.

I suppressed a cackle. My fingers tingled with the energy my Gift pulled from the air in my lungs, from my intention, from my own spirit. *I'm a Spirit Witch. My intention* is *the energy.* Smiling, I curved my fingers again, pulling, winding time back on itself until Brian sat back at the table.

"You have to under—" he said again.

Nope. Not interested in understanding anything right now. This is definitely a Later-When-I'm-Not-So-Mad conversation. Possibly a Never-Ever-Not-If-I-Can-Help-It conversation.

My fingers curled slowly this time. Where was it safe to stop? How much time did I have to erase to make believe this never happened?

He never told me. I don't want to know.

Maybe just another minute or so.

"You sound like—"

No.

I pulled back a little further, blinking against my growing headache.

"Are you working tomorrow?"

"Yeah."

Everything is normal. That conversation never happened.

The library woke. Everyone shifted back to whatever they'd been doing before I panic-froze the room. The tiny sounds of students trying to be quiet echoed through the space. No more statues. My ears buzzed with the released energy. I tilted my phone to check the time.

"Actually, I should go. I have an early class in the morning." I closed my laptop and dropped it in my bag, along with any potential consequences of the conversation we never had.

Tomorrow problems.

Brian mirrored my movements. "Okay, I'm going to send you some notes you can look over. There's a YouTube video in here that explains this stuff better than I do."

Standing, I waited for him to look up. I could hardly bear to look at him. I had to get out of there. My headache pounded, making me dizzy. "Thanks."

"It's no problem. I want to help." He pushed out his chair and shouldered his bag, ready to walk me out as usual.

"I'll see you tomorrow," I said and strode out of the library, willing myself to keep my balance even though my vision was obscured by dots of light. It cleared after a moment or two, leaving me with just a dull pain behind my eyes.

My heart raced, and I struggled to keep from checking behind me. Brian didn't follow, even though that exit probably raised some questions. My eyes burned, and I honestly couldn't have said whether my unshed tears came from anger or regret.

I couldn't catch my breath. The energy I pulled in the library stayed with me, and it wanted something to do.

Hadn't I done enough? I practically remote-controlled a whole roomful of people.

Turning the corner in front of my dorm, I glanced up at my window and then back over my shoulder. The streetlights cast a warm glow over the sidewalk, but right now, neither my mundane housing nor the friendship I'd just walked away from felt safe. I kept walking, rounding the next corner and ducking into a small courtyard. Five concrete picnic tables dotted the space, circling a brick-bordered island of mulch where a tree that was probably older than the college stood, lit by post lights in the landscaping. Large, flat umbrellas made from hard plastic protected each table from the weather.

Students sat around a few of them, eating and talking. A boy sitting alone tapped on his laptop, stopping only to slurp from an energy drink. Two identical cans sat on the table behind his screen. A couple of girls sat on the bricks under the tree, laughing over something on their phones.

I dropped my backpack on an empty table toward the back of the courtyard and sat with my back to the building. From here, I could see both the path where I'd come in and the door that led inside the dorm.

Not that I was paranoid.

Much.

One of the girls laughed, and it echoed against the stone building. My hands shook. *Cool. Are we going to panic about everyone we pass? Or just the people I've called friends?*

I took a breath. Should probably eat something. I hadn't had anything but coffee and stale pastries since I got up this morning. Caffeine probably contributed to my anxiety. Having thus logicked away a panic attack, I unzipped my bag and pulled out the snacks I'd packed for the library. A pack of crackers with peanut butter, a bag of popcorn with sea salt, an apple with only one small bruise. My water bottle was trapped in the bottom under my notebooks. As I dragged it out, a few loose papers came with it. They drifted off the table.

Ugh.

Frustration replaced fear.

I had to get on my hands and knees to retrieve a page that slid under the table. When I grabbed it, something else fell. I bumped my head, trying to catch it. "Ouch!"

I smacked the underside of the table with my hand in self-defense and immediately regretted it when I sliced my pinky on the rough cement.

I stuck my finger in my mouth and peeked out from under the table, prepared for an audience of curious mundanes. But clumsy college students didn't draw attention. Literally nothing of interest to see here.

No one cares what you're doing.

My breath finally released.

Leaning forward, I found the smaller paper that had fallen from my notes. Not a paper. Nora's tarot card. How'd it get in there? I thought I'd left it in my desk drawer, unsure if I needed it anymore, now that I could access my Gift without the conduit.

It warmed to my touch, sending a comforting heat up my arms. *I could use some guidance. Help me figure out what to do. Can I trust Brian?*

The card shivered, settling into a new image. A path leading far into the distance under a full moon. Two towers on either side. A dog and a wolf. Doubles. Duplicity. The moon is not as bright as the sun. It casts shadows. Illusions. Things are not as they seem.

The Moon card reflects your own fear and uncertainty. But it also warns of something hidden.

What more is Brian hiding from me?

I should have talked to him. I should have listened. *But*

what if he tells me something I don't want to know?

My phone pinged on the table above me. I crawled out, avoiding any new injuries.

A message from Adam: We found something. Are you coming over?

I shoved Nora's card into my back pocket, stuffed everything back in my bag, and slung it over my shoulder. None of the other students reacted to my hasty exit. The safety of my anonymity felt cold. Texting a quick response to Adam, I put distance between myself and the unmagical life I thought I wanted.

17

A dull ache clung to the back of my head as I climbed the stairs to my brother's apartment, reactivated by the jingling bell on the magic shop's door. I had to find a way to access my Gift without knocking myself out afterward. Maybe I should contact Elspeth or my mom. This couldn't be normal. No one else I knew suffered from using their magic.

Thomas met me at the top of the stairs, bouncing on his toes. "You're here! Check this out. It's so cool."

I dropped my bag by the entrance. "What did you find?"

He stood beside the coffee table, spreading his arms like a game show presenter.

Adam smacked his hand out of his face. "Take a look."

I sat beside him on the futon. The papers mostly came from Dad's notes. I'd seen them all before. A lot of different colored pen strokes scrawled in every direction, overlapping and mostly illegible. Only now, they stood up, folded like origami triangles.

I raised an eyebrow and gestured to the pyramids of paper. "What are you building here?"

Thomas knelt beside me, taking two of the pages and

aligning them along the folds. "Look. What do you see?"

My brother in two-day-old pajamas making cootie catchers out of our father's life's work. Maybe it wasn't fair, but between my anxiety about Brian and our collective failures over the past few days, I didn't have a lot of patience for Show and Tell. "Umm. Let's jump ahead to the part where you acknowledge the fact that I wasn't here when you made this great discovery and skip the guessing games, okay?"

He rocked back on his heels and squinted at me.

Might have been a poor choice of words, given the fact that I actually could skip ahead if I wanted to now.

Thomas didn't like the implication, unintentional though it may have been. "You're not going to do that, are you?"

I crossed my arms, considering.

As much as using one's Gift against a fellow witch was frowned upon in Queen's Creek, this wouldn't be the first time one Corey sibling cast a spell on another. Thomas's influence was the reason I'd forgotten my relationship with Adam in the first place. Things would be much less awkward between us if we didn't have such different memories of what we meant to each other.

Sparks twinkled at my fingertips.

"She's not going to use her Gift on you," Adam said. When I sat back and gave him a look I usually reserved for Thomas, he put his hand on my knee and added, "Not that I would blame her."

I took a breath, reminding myself that Thomas hadn't meant to do it. That he wouldn't have been able to do it if, on some level, I hadn't wanted to forget. My Gift settled just below the surface. *Clearly going to need some kind of practice montage to get control. Over my magic and my emotions.*

The guys waited.

"Just tell me what I'm looking at," I said.

"Look at the green one first." Thomas leaned forward

again, fitting the two pages together. The lines on one paper continued onto the other. I squinted, trying to focus only on the words written in green ink. They were hard to make out, might not even have been English, but the pattern was there. If you followed the shape of the words, they formed the beginning of an image.

Adam lifted another page, folding it along an old crease. He held it next to the two Thomas already had, fitting it like a puzzle. The image continued.

"How big is it?" I asked. "What's the final image when you get it all together?"

"It's a sigil." Thomas tilted the combined pages. "But I don't know what it is. I've never seen it before."

Adam put his pages down and pulled a notepad out of the pile. He'd sketched a diagram across the page. It kind of looked like a tree.

"What do you think it means?"

"That's just the beginning." Adam handed me the notepad so he could pick up more folded pages. He turned them differently this time. "Watch the blue."

The lines written in blue ink undulated over the pages, flowing in curves and curlicues. I flipped the page in the notepad and saw a corresponding sigil drawn. Concentric waves, like a stone dropping into a pond. Or a distorted bullseye. The next page in the notepad was blank. I set it beside me and took the pages Adam offered.

I played with the papers, turning them backwards and forwards, trying to match up the colored writing. "Are there more?"

"That's what's weird," Thomas said. "Yes, but no."

I matched up a few lines of purple ink across three pages.

Adam added a fourth, following the lines with a finger. "See it here? It's the same as the green one, but if you do this..." He flipped the pages, folding them along a different crease.

I tilted my head to follow the new pattern. "It matches the blue one."

Adam nodded. "These same two sigils come out no matter which colors you follow. I tried to make different ones, but they don't match up. You end up with leftover pieces that don't connect. Or they overlap, and then you can't see the whole thing."

"These two sigils meant something to Dad," Thomas said. *What did that mean for us?* "Any guesses?"

"We've got nothing if you don't recognize them." Thomas flattened the pages out, and the sigils disappeared.

I took the notepad where they had drawn them and flipped back and forth between the images. They looked familiar, but I couldn't place them. I shook my head.

Thomas sat back, dropping the pages on the pile.

I closed my eyes. The sigils glowed on the inside of my eyelids. Where had I seen them before? I shuffled through memories, trying to place them in every book I'd ever read, every paper I'd ever seen. In the graffiti under the train tracks across the street from the shop. Nothing fit.

"What did Brian say?" Adam asked.

My eyes popped open, and I let the papers fall. "What?"

"Your text earlier. You said you found Brian and you were going to get him to talk about quantum dynamics. Did he have an answer on the gravitational pull of time thing?" Adam's elbows rested on his knees, his hands clasped together.

I focused on his hands, the square nails, the freckles on the backs, anything to keep from looking him in the eye. *He's not like Caleb. He can't read your mind. But he can sense the truth. And I'm afraid.* Not of him. But maybe Brian. Maybe myself. "Ummm…yes."

His thumb rubbed against his other hand. *Anxious? Or just*

an itch? "And?"

I don't want to tell them we might have another enemy. Someone we thought we could trust. And what if I'm wrong? What if I overreacted in a roomful of mundanes and somebody noticed? What if I'm the one putting us at risk?

Thomas frowned. "Why are you being weird?"

Adam reached out, lifting my head with a hand along my jaw. Meeting my eyes. "Did something happen at the library?"

Gold streaks swirled in his brown eyes. He'd used his Gift to read me at the Gatehouse when I came home to look for Dad. Could he compel me to tell the truth now? The way Lily had tugged at my mind turned my stomach. Adam would never do that to me. *I can trust him. He should be able to trust me.* "Okay, so this is going to going to sound crazy…"

"Oh good, more fun." Thomas sighed and went to the kitchen to refill his cup. He added a tea bag to his mug and poured hot water from the kettle over it, filling the room with the scent of peppermint.

While he stirred, I tried to explain. "But really, it might not be that bad. I mean…some of it's bad, but some of it's actually really cool."

As much as I thought I'd given up magic when I left for college, I hadn't really had another option. Now that the bind was broken, my control of the energy grew stronger every day. The choice I made three years ago didn't have to be permanent if I didn't want it to be. It was up to me how I wanted to live my life.

Adam rubbed his forehead. "Cate, you're not making any sense."

"Did we miss something? Did you jump forward? Is this what it feels like when you skip ahead?" Thomas tapped his spoon on the side of his cup and dropped it into the sink, letting it clatter against the porcelain.

Adam's eyebrows shot up.

I held up my hands. "No. No, I told you I wouldn't. I didn't. I mean, I did, but not here. Not just now."

The guys looked at each other. Thomas shrugged.

Adam put his hand back on my knee. "What did you do?"

18

I turned to Thomas. "Okay, so remember what I did with the mug yesterday?"

He smirked. "When you blatantly used your Gift in public? In front of the security cameras and everything?"

Adam looked back and forth between Thomas and me. "She didn't. You did that?"

I glared at my brother. *So petty. Just because I'd warned him that using magic at the café came with risks...Alright, I was a hypocrite. He didn't have to call me out on it.* "Oh, but it's fine when he does it. The cameras went out anyway."

"Cate." Adam leaned back into the futon and crossed his legs, resting one foot on the opposite knee. He rubbed his eyes.

I stood. "There was no one else there. Can you just listen? Yesterday. I dropped the mug, but then I used my Gift to freeze time around it before it hit the floor. I isolated a time bubble that only affected the mug and the coffee inside it. And then I reversed time and it fell up instead of down, back onto the counter, like it never happened."

Adam looked to Thomas for confirmation.

Thomas nodded.

Adam smiled. "Wow. That's…wow. That's amazing. But what does it have to do with Brian?" He leaned forward and squeezed my hand. The cut on my pinky stung.

I looked down at my hand in Adam's, grounding myself in his stability. "So, what I did with the mug…I did sort of the same thing at the library…but with the whole room. And the people in it."

"You cast a time bubble in the library?" Thomas set his mug on the counter.

"Yes." *Here it comes.*

Adam ran his thumb over my knuckles. "I thought we said you weren't going to do that again until you had more practice. We were going to start small: inanimate objects, animate objects, small animals, maybe a squirrel or a cat."

Pulling my hand back, I stepped away from the futon. They used to look to me for what to do. Chosen One. Gatekeeper. I never wanted the mantle, but now we had to talk about how I used my Gift? I asked for help, not supervision. What happened to my impetuous Knight of Cups? Had he traded them in for Pentacles? "I think I've practiced enough."

"So, you did it on purpose." Thomas pushed off the counter and stepped toward me. "In front of mundanes."

"A few? Okay, yes, like six or seven people were working in the study room. But that's what I'm trying to tell you." My hands started moving as I talked, demonstrating what I'd done. "I cast a time bubble on the whole room. They all froze. And then I manipulated time in the bubble. Backward and forward. And backward again. They undid whatever they'd done in those minutes and then picked back up where they started. And when I released it, nobody noticed."

"Nobody noticed? How can you be sure? What if one of those students has memories of whatever you undid?" Adam leaned forward again, dropping his foot to the ground.

"They don't." I flexed my fingers, half wishing I could skip to when we'd already had this conversation. But my Gift had never worked that way. If I wanted to participate in it, I had to live through it. "After I froze them, I controlled the rewind. I took it back to a specific moment and released it exactly where I wanted."

I took a breath. "I think I'm getting better at controlling my Gift. Stronger. I couldn't change time before, only watch it go by." *And now I've done it twice! Three times, if you count the glitch at Noemi's when I reversed time accidentally, before Tori helped me tone it down.*

"Nice!" My brother held up his hand for a high five.

I slapped his hand and turned to Adam, who hadn't moved from the futon.

Adam brought his clasped hands to his chin, thinking. When he came to some kind of conclusion, he looked up. "Congratulations, that's a big deal, and I'm proud of you."

He didn't sound proud. He sounded like his next words might hurt more than the little cut on my finger.

"But can we talk about why you chose to freeze your friend while he was giving you a physics lesson?" he asked.

Thomas nodded and climbed onto one of his barstools, sitting backwards and resting his arms on the back of the seat.

Okay, so not too painful. A fully justified question, actually. Still, the back of my neck tensed. I ran a hand under my hair. *Now or never. Saying it doesn't make it real. It was already real.* "He's still dating Jasmine."

My brother nearly fell off the stool. "He's what?"

Adam stood. "Why would he do that? He almost got shot."

"That's what I said!" I threw my hands up. Maybe I'd done the right thing after all.

"What did he say?" Adam asked.

Thomas straightened on his stool. "Is she blackmailing him or something? Threatening him?"

I hadn't thought of that. I pictured Brian's face, searching for clues that he'd been under duress. His expression had been pained, but I'd thought it was guilt. "I don't know."

"What do you mean?" Adam crossed his arms again.

Thomas twisted the stool back and forth, a nervous fidget that explained why all of his furniture was mobile. "Why hasn't she been arrested? Didn't she try to murder your professor?"

All very good questions I probably could have asked instead of panic-freezing a whole room of people. "I don't know"

"What?" Thomas locked his feet into the frame of the stool, holding himself in place.

I needed something to throw at him, but none of the folded notes was particularly aerodynamic. "I don't know! I didn't see her after we got away from Wesson. The police went with him to the hospital, remember? And when the EMTs took Jasmine and Brian to get checked out, you blinked us back to the Creek. This was the first time I'd seen him since we came back."

Adam raised an eyebrow. "And you didn't know they were still together?"

I should have guessed. I could have assumed. It didn't occur to me. "How would I know that? I'm not stalking his social media for status updates."

If she really had gone into hiding, he wasn't exactly going to be posting selfies of the two of them in her safe house. Or quarantine, or whatever. I still wasn't sure where Jasmine actually was.

"What did he say when you got there? You guys didn't catch up? Didn't he want to know where you'd been?" Adam took a step toward me, his tone lowering with suspicion.

Every word we'd said to each other replayed. Duplicity. Double meanings. No. We hadn't been speaking in code.

Nothing felt off until he told me. But he'd known the whole time. He hid it for over an hour while we studied. Was he laughing at me while he dropped hints that went over my head?

Imagining Brian as a spy for the hunters made my stomach flip. Were they watching us? Did they see what I did? My throat burned as acid shot up from the whirlpool in my digestive system. It couldn't be true. "I told him I went home. He knows about what happened with the boundary and Dad's notes. He knows I was bound, and I'm trying to learn more about my Gift. He's fascinated by magic and wants to understand how it works."

Adam frowned, looking at the floor and rubbing the back of his neck. "He's fascinated by magic, but he's dating a hunter who wants to destroy it. What is he thinking?"

No one had an answer. We fell silent for a moment as we all considered Brian's motivations and the potential consequences of losing him to the hunters.

Thomas climbed down from the stool and came to stand beside us. "He knows too much about us. About Queen's Creek. What if he's told her about what we're working on? It's bad enough the hunters know Queen's Creek exists. What would they do if they knew about the time stream or how close we are to the elixir of life?"

Adam looked into my eyes. "You have to find out what's going on there. We need to know what side he's on. "

"He's on our side." *I hope.*

Adam nodded, still holding my attention with his gaze. He pulled my phone from my back pocket and handed it to me. "Call him."

The phone lit up, and for a second, I thought it was Brian. That would have been real spy behavior.

But the phone didn't ring. Instead, a text banner slid across my lock screen.

Tori: Need you at Noemi's. Come now!

I held it up to show the guys.

Thomas sucked his teeth. "Well, that can't be good."

Adam's eyebrows raised.

I texted her back: What's going on?

Tori: Come NOW!!!

Brian will have to wait. Remind me to thank Tori for delaying that impossible conversation. "Guess I better go…"

"You want company?" Adam asked.

My mind shuffled through seven or eight possible outcomes of showing up alone at a vampire's doorstep after dark. *One-hundred-percent. Yes.*

But hadn't I just finished telling them I'd gotten stronger? Surely, I could survive a second visit to the suburbs.

"No. I can handle Tori. Maybe they found the book."

"Same deal as last time," Adam said.

"Fine." I waved my phone before tucking it in my pocket and heading out. Once through Thomas's beaded curtain, I jogged down the stairs.

Holy Hera, let this not be the emergency it sounds like. This knight rides to the rescue on the red line.

19

Thirty-five minutes later, I hopped off the second bus and walked up the block to Noemi's. The empty swings on the school playground creaked. As I came up her sidewalk, a dog barked. The sound wouldn't have been out of place except that I hadn't seen anyone walking a dog, and none of her neighbors kept animals behind the iron fences that surrounded their property. It barked again, louder this time. As I stepped on the porch, there was no question. The sound was coming from inside the house.

I didn't remember seeing any dog bowls or toys last time I was there. Did Noemi get a dog today? What super weird timing with all that was going on.

I knocked at the door, and it swung open. *Someone left it unlatched.* "Hello?"

"Close the door!" Tori's voice came from the back of the bungalow.

"Quick! Don't let him get out!" Noemi called. Something crashed. Scrabbling sounds on the wood floor followed a series of unusual noises and some words I couldn't translate.

"What's going on?" I stepped inside, avoiding a pile of

shoes on the mat by the door.

"The door!" Tori yelled just as a large animal barreled around the corner through the living room.

Instinctively, I backed up, tripping on the shoes and falling back against the door, effectively following her instruction. The animal skidded as it reached the end of the area rug, sliding on the hallway runner so that it bunched up between us. It looked like a dog, but it could have been a coyote or wolf, with a long snout and oversized pointed ears. *But oh, what big teeth you have, Grandma.* There was something feral in its yellow eyes.

My heart beat outside of my chest. The vibrations sent shivers down my arms.

The animal froze in front of me.

I hadn't even realized I did it, but yes, those were my hands out in front of me. Those sparks at the ends of my fingertips came from my energy, from whatever I had left after my experiment at the library.

"Tori?" I braced one foot against the threshold and pressed against the door to straighten my stance. "Noemi? Why is there a wild animal in your house?"

Tori and Noemi rushed out of the back, panting as if they'd just finished a workout. Tori leaned one hand on the wall in the entryway, the other gripping her ankh necklace. Between breaths, she said, "Oh, good. You caught him."

Noemi didn't stop until she reached the animal. She threw herself to her knees, wrapping her arms around the frozen creature. "Mijo, what did you do to yourself?"

I flinched. *Mijo? Wait…this isn't… can't be…*

As I came to my realization, Noemi noticed the fact that her newly transformed nephew had become a statue. "He's not moving. What did you do?"

Her eyes went red and the veins in her face stood out as if all the blood from her skin had been redirected. Moving faster than my eyes could track, she released the dog-boy and shoved me hard against the door. Her nails dug into my skin like claws.

I closed my eyes and turned my head away from her, wondering if real vampires had hypnotic abilities like the ones on TV. Too late, it occurred to me that in avoiding potential mind control, I'd basically offered her my neck.

"Noemi, wait! Stop!" Tori took a couple of steps toward us, then thought better of it and stopped out of reach. "He's okay. Look. It's her Gift. He's fine. He's just…"

"Not moving," Noemi growled. Her face had lost almost all of its color, and her pupils darkened her eyes.

"It's okay. It's okay. She's not hurting him. She just stopped him. It's a time bubble. Look." Tori picked up a leaf that had blown in through the open door and held it just above Lalo's head.

Noemi turned slightly, but her grip didn't loosen.

Tori dropped the leaf, and it floated down toward the animal's pointed ears. A few inches above his head, it stopped, suspended in the time bubble.

"What—what is that? What's happening to him?" Noemi's voice softened.

Tori stepped back. "Let him go, Cate. He's not going to hurt you. But she will."

My hands shook. Controlling my magic was hard enough without my concentration split between the fear of what would happen if I released the hound and what would happen if I didn't. The sparks tickled my fingertips. I flicked them away.

The leaf brushed the dog's snout, and he shook his head, huffing at it.

Noemi collapsed in front of him, and I could breathe again. "Aye, mijo. What did you do? You could have just talked to me."

I rubbed my shoulder where Noemi's nails had drawn red lines in my skin.

Tori grimaced. "Sorry? I didn't know who else to call."

Trapped against the door, I gestured to the insanity on the floor in front of me. "What is going on? Is that Lalo? Why is he a wolf?"

"He's a German Shepherd, actually. And I'm not sure why he chose that form. Couldn't have been something sweet and fuzzy, like a golden retriever? Maybe a doodle thing? Those are cute." Tori wrapped one arm around herself and twisted her necklace around the fingers of her other hand.

"Why is he an animal at all?" I directed my question to Noemi, but she ignored me, soothing her nephew with ear scritches.

Tori knelt, still keeping her distance but getting a better angle on the boy-turned-puppy.

"Not sure. I think it's his Gift, maybe? Apparently, he's been experimenting with transmutation, you know: milk to pop, earbuds to headphones, preteen to pet..." She gestured to the animal.

Lalo sat up, panting with his tongue lolling out between some very sharp canines.

"Is he a shifter?" *Do those exist? I mean, if there are vampires...*

Tori shook her head. "No. If he was a shifter, he could change back. But it seems like he's stuck that way. He's just a witch."

"And a vampire." *Because apparently, you can be both.*

"Isn't that enough?" The bail on Tori's necklace rasped against the chain.

Slowly, on the balls of my feet, I stepped around Lalo and Noemi. Putting Tori between me and the increasingly fang-tastic family, I tried to process what had happened since I'd left last night. They were just supposed to talk to the kid, maybe walk around his room and see if anything grimoire-shaped stuck out. Tori had texted that they didn't find anything. How did a follow-up on DogMan and Percy Jackson result in an actual dog child?

In this form, the kid couldn't tell us much, even if he knew anything.

Noemi wasn't going to let anybody near him anyway.

I took another step back. From there I could see down the hall, through the kitchen, a straight shot to the back door. I considered my options. Tori called me for help, but none of this felt like my skill set. Or Adam's or Thomas's, either, honestly.

When I turned back to make an excuse and book it out the back door, Tori's dark eyes trapped me. I sighed. "Okay, let's just start over. How did we get here?"

Tori stood, leaving Noemi to tend to Lalo. "So, last night, after you left, we decided it would be best if Noemi talked to him on her own. You know, no accusations, just kind of *Hey, kid, read any good books lately?* So I went back to the dorm and got caught up on my Chem notes because that exam is going to kill me. But, like, it's also useful? Because, you know, potions and herbs are just a bunch of natural chemical compounds, so…"

I rubbed my eyes, suddenly very aware of how late it was getting. "How long has the kid been a dog?"

"Not long, like ten minutes before I texted you? I came over after dinner, and oh shit! What time is it?" Tori pulled her phone out of her boot, tapping the screen. When it blinked to life, her eyebrows jumped.

"Tori—" *Don't you dare leave me here with someone scarier than you.*

"No, really. I have to be back in the dorm by 10pm. I can't miss check-in. It's part of my probation. Shit. I'm calling an Uber." She stepped over the pile of shoes and put a hand on the doorknob, her other hand already opening the ride-share app. "Text me when he can talk again, okay?"

The dog grumbled and made a lunge for the door as she cracked open. "Lalo, stay. Good boy."

She winked and then ducked out.

I pushed the door closed behind her before the dog-boy could escape.

Great. Alone with the vampire. The supposedly vegan vampire who definitely would have slit my throat if Tori hadn't talked her down. And a really big dog. A super friendly, slobber-monster dog who nonetheless has very sharp teeth and questionable self-control.

I knelt where I was, showing my hands. "I'm here to help. Please. If you want me to."

Noemi's teary-eyed face surfaced from the dog's thick fur. "I do. Did I hurt you? I didn't mean to. But he's my responsibility now. I can't let anything happen to him. I can't..."

She looked back at her nephew, to whom something had most definitely happened, and her face crumpled into tears again. She whispered something that sounded like an apology into the side of his neck.

"Noemi..." I inched toward them. "Can you get him back to his room?"

She didn't respond.

I reached for the dog, pressing soft hands down his back. "It's going to be okay."

Noemi nodded, sniffling. "It will. I know it will. But I don't know what to do."

"Let's start by getting him somewhere safe. Where we don't have to worry about chasing him down the street."

"I can try, but he's not exactly cooperative in his human form." Noemi wrapped one arm around his neck and the other across his chest, behind his front legs. He licked her face.

Eww.

The kid has front legs and back legs now. The kid has paws.

Human Lalo seemed like a pretty agreeable kid to me, but my experience was limited. I held out my arms, blocking the door, not that he could open it. Noemi wrestled the animal, trying to find a better way to hold on to him. It wasn't like he was wearing a collar.

I never had a dog, but how hard could it be to get an animal down the hall and into the bedroom? I just had to figure out what he wanted. "Noemi, let him go a minute. The door's closed. He can't get out. Let's try something else."

She stood, letting him wriggle away, but he stayed close to her, weaving back and forth behind her legs. She frowned. "Alright. What do you want to do?"

"Hey, Lalo," I called, backing down the hallway, patting my legs. "Come here, boy."

"I could have done that," Noemi grumbled. She sniffed and wiped a tear.

Lalo trotted to the front door and lay down on the mat. Basically, the opposite of *come here*.

He liked video games and graphic novels. What did he eat last night? Chips. Popcorn. She made him dinner, and I remembered something on the stove that smelled amazing. The kitchen still smelled amazing.

"Hey, Lalo, you had a busy day, huh? Did you have dinner yet? You hungry?" The linoleum creaked as I crossed into the kitchen. A glass of milk sat on the banquette table with a small plate. A roll and some meat with rice and cut vegetables. A matching plate rested on the counter next to a glass of water.

I pulled the roll from the plate on the table and stepped back into the hall. Tearing off a few pieces, I tossed one toward the dog. "I bet you're hungry, huh? Your dinner is still warm. Come and get it..."

The dog stood, sniffing the floor between himself and the toast piece. Noemi backed down the hall toward me. "Yes, mijo, look…you didn't get a chance to eat dinner. Your tummy must be grumbling."

Lalo scurried forward to snap up the bread, but he backed up again to eat it.

"Good boy," I said. "Come on. Get some more."

20

It took three pieces of bread and both plates of meat to lure Lalo back into his bedroom. Belly full, he jumped up onto his bed and curled around, circling six times before he settled. We stepped out quietly, closing the bedroom door and returning to the kitchen.

"Was Mama Lily right? Are you the one we have to thank?" Noemi asked. "I guess I do. For this. For today. You've come twice when we called for help. Tori is lucky to have you as a friend."

"We're not friends." I sank into the bench seat at the banquette.

Noemi dumped her water glass and got out two coffee mugs. "If you say so."

"It's complicated," I said. "We needed each other."

"You don't have to explain. Do you want some? The pot is still warm." She poured the coffee without waiting for a response.

"Yes, please." *I need coffee more than life.*

"Good." She set it in front of me with a small carton of cream and a ceramic sugar bowl.

"Thank you."

"I owe you an explanation," she said, pouring her own cup.

I didn't argue.

We both sipped our brew while she prepared herself to tell the story. She sighed, inhaling the delicious steam. "Lalo's Gift started to emerge a few months ago. I wasn't sure he would have one. You know, not everyone does."

Oh, I know. I nodded, remembering the early years of my bind when I didn't know my Gift had been hidden from me. Knowing something was wrong but unable to explain. I couldn't identify the problem. I just knew I wasn't like everyone else.

"Honestly, after what happened…he hasn't aged, physically, since the accident. I don't think anyone's noticed. It wasn't so long ago. But his friends all had growth spurts, and he's…still small. But he's still maturing. He's still learning. He's always trying new things. I didn't want to tell him that he might never discover his Gift. That I didn't know if he could still be a witch." She looked up at me for support.

I'd never had a kid. I couldn't imagine the responsibility. And Lalo wasn't even hers. It wasn't like she'd planned for him. Even if you could plan for a kid like him. There might not be any other kid like him. Suddenly, I questioned the way I'd judged my parents' choices. Maybe they weren't as diabolical as they'd seemed. They'd only wanted to protect me.

Noemi waited for my response, some indication of sympathy or understanding.

"It must have been hard." *Thank you, Captain Obvious.* But it was the best I had.

It was enough.

Noemi smiled. "Yes. You know, my brother and I, we left our parents back in Puerto Rico to come here for college. We put ourselves through school. That was hard. Being away from our family. Supporting ourselves. Finding our place. When he got married, I was alone."

I fought the urge to tell her about leaving Queen's Creek and coming back, only to find out how my parents had betrayed me. Or how hard it had been to decide which side of the Gate I wanted to spend my life on. Fighting with Thomas. Our stories weren't as different as she might think. But I didn't interrupt.

She stirred cream into her coffee, watching it swirl. "His Gift surfaced a few weeks ago. He's aligned with water like my brother was."

I had a brother whose affinity was with water. Benjamin. His Gift enhanced his vision, as if everything were clearer to him than to anyone else. Elspeth's empathic Gift also came from an affinity with water.

Noemi sipped her coffee, inhaling deeply. The mug clicked softly on the table when she set it down. "He senses the flow of matter, and can change it, rearrange the pieces that make it what it is, make it something new. But it's hard to train him when I have a different affinity. We've only just started to try little things. Change the color of this pen. Make a peach from an apple. Nothing that would affect him. I'd never want him to change who he is for anything."

And they said I had potential. "Wow. That's…advanced. I mean, a Gift like that could…"

Could be dangerous.

Could change the world.

Noemi seemed to understand my amazement. "I thought it was impossible after his change. But here we are. As long as he has a good source of energy, he can use it to manipulate things. The energy is the problem. How much do you know about vampires?"

I coughed. *Okay, so we are just going to talk about it. And why not? She told me what she was in our first phone conversation.*

Noemi's openness would take getting used to. "Umm. Just what you see on TV. Nocturnal. Blood drinkers. Antagonistic relationship to the church. But I'm starting to see that's all wrong. I mean, you don't even sparkle."

Noemi laughed. "Only when I get the glitter coat on my nails."

"Okay, but then…garlic? Silver?" These legends had to come from somewhere.

"Think of it like a disease," she said. "In fact, when Lalo first came to me, he was weak, pale. He would get these headaches. The doctors thought it was sickle cell. He didn't have enough iron. His white blood cell count was off."

"I mean…that sounds like a blood disorder." *Are you sure he's not just sick?*

"We don't breathe."

"Oh."

"Our hearts don't beat."

"Okay, but wouldn't that kind of be a red flag for the doctors? Why isn't he locked up in a lab somewhere?" *Why aren't you both?*

"I convinced them it wasn't necessary as long as we came in for regular transfusions." She held my gaze a moment, conveying something more than words. We'd never discussed her Gift.

I pictured one of those vampire TV shows where the hot creature of the night breaks into the blood bank and drinks blood out of a bag like a juice box. That would take some convincing. Our interaction at the door left me no doubt she could terrify people into submission. But somehow, I didn't see a doctor doing their best work under that kind of duress. Besides, they'd have to report an attack like that, wouldn't they? She could have a Gift like Thomas's or my mom's, but muses and sirens still allowed free will. And, again, the whole, *why wouldn't they report it immediately afterwards* question? Had the movies gotten something right? I asked the question I'd wanted to know since she had me trapped against the door. "So, can you…like…hypnotize people to make them do what you want?"

"Hmmm." She took a deep drink of her coffee. "Not the way you're thinking."

"In what way then?" My fingers tightened around my mug. Not that it would make an optimal weapon against a potentially mind-controlling vampire in her own home.

"I use my Gift. From before. I'm still a witch, aligned with the element of air. My voice carries weight. My energy settles over people like a warm breeze." As she spoke, the temperature in the room rose almost imperceptibly.

My skin tingled as if a breeze brushed the hairs on my arms. I felt wrapped in a warm blanket, cozy and comfortable.

"It's soothing," Noemi said.

Like a spiderweb. I pushed through the peaceful net and came up for air, blinking, although the kitchen lights weren't bright.

Noemi released her energy and the temperature fell back to normal, the space around me expanding.

"So, you sedated them into compliance?" A few more minutes under Noemi's influence, and I might have agreed to almost anything just to float in that warm cocoon.

"I kept them from panicking and guided them to making the best medical decisions for their new patients. Including upholding their own standards of privacy." Noemi finished her coffee and crossed her hands on the table.

"They thought he had sickle cell. What about you?"

"Well, I had them test me, too. I mean, my brother must have been a carrier, right? So, I was probably also a carrier. But I'd been getting a lot of infections and joint pain…" She paused.

"You told the doctors you had symptoms."

"Not until I actually had them. But by then, of course, I knew they'd gotten his diagnosis wrong." Again, she waited.

I appreciated that she didn't raise her energy again. She just let me spiral as I processed how she knew Lalo didn't have a blood disorder. *Because you read a lot of stuff about sickle cell at the library. Because you got a second opinion. Because you Googled...*

"Because he bit me."

Of course he did. Because he was a vampire first. And as peaceful as she makes me feel, I'm sitting across from a vampire who was turned by the child in the other room. Her Gift makes her more dangerous by making her seem less so. Lalo is a sweet kid and a cute puppy, but he and his aunt are predators. Neither of them should be taken for granted.

He bit her before he was a dog. Will he control himself now? What will she do if I'm not helpful enough? If I can't change him back?

Why did I sit on the banquette with my back to the wall? It felt safe at the time, but now I couldn't get to the back door without edging past Noemi.

She raised her hands, and I gasped, expecting to feel her energy cocooning me. But she pushed no intention through the gesture. Instead, she defended his attack on her. "He didn't mean to. He was just so hungry. And we hadn't started the treatment yet. He would never do that now."

I stared at her. "He's a dog now! Would he even know what he was doing?"

She bit her lip.

"Noemi. Why hasn't he changed back?"

She shook her head, tears glistening in her eyes. "I don't know. He's never transformed himself before."

"Never?"

"I thought about it. Of course, I thought about it. With a

Gift like that? What if he could transform himself back to human?"

"He might be able to change you, too."

Her head dropped to her hands. "Yes. Oh, gods. I didn't want to pressure him. I don't want him to think I blame him for what we are. It wasn't his fault. We're lucky, really, that he survived that night. His parents didn't. But living like this… it's…"

"Hard."

"Yeah."

"But you never suggested it to him…?"

"No! I was…I wanted…he's only had the Gift for a little while, you know? I was going to build up to it."

It sounded so much like Adam's plan for me. But I hadn't been that patient. Maybe Lalo had gotten tired of being a patient.

"Meanwhile, how often are you taking him to the hospital to get stuck with needles?"

"Once a month."

"On the full moon?"

"We're stronger then. It might be a coincidence. It was a full moon when he turned. It was full when I took him for his first transfusion."

"Cool. Cool." *Remind me to check my moon phase app later.* "How does he feel about those appointments?"

She shrugged. "He hates them, but he knows it's necessary. He doesn't want to hurt anybody."

"German Shepherd is an interesting choice, then."

Puppy Lalo must have weighed at least seventy pounds, almost more than Human Child Lalo. If he grew into his floppy puppy feet, he was going to be a big dog.

Noemi sipped her coffee. "They're not dangerous animals unless you provoke them."

21

id you see how he did it?" Maybe we could reverse the spell. Knock over a totem and break the illusion. He didn't feel like an illusion.

"No." She chewed her lip.

"No?" I didn't want to question her parenting skills, but Lalo seemed to spend a lot of time on his own. Did she have any idea how he spent it?

Her nails clicked against each other. "Well, he was still mad at me about last night."

Right. The interrogation. "Tori said you talked to him about the book last night?"

She took a deep breath. "You know, he's been living here for a while now, but in some ways, we're still feeling each other out. I didn't want to accuse him of anything, but we had to know…and Tori said he was interested in it."

"What happened?"

She spread her fingers on the table. The effort to stop fidgeting was clear. "I went in after you both left. He was already in bed, so I sat beside him. I asked him about his day. He told me about that game he's been playing. But he could tell I wasn't paying enough attention. I was looking around his room. He asked me what I was looking for. So I told him. I said, 'I brought a very important book home from the library, and now I can't find it. I was wondering if you'd…' I was going to say *borrowed*, but he jumped up. He thought I was accusing him of stealing. He kicked me out."

I raised an eyebrow. "He kicked you out?"

"Yeah, he didn't want me in there anymore," she said. "He told me to get out of his room."

"And you just left?" *My mother would never…*

Noemi shrugged. "Yes. I'm not his mother. I can't…I'm trying to respect his boundaries."

Honorable. Ill-advised but honorable. "He's ten, a newly turned vampire with an insane Gift, and he had access to a powerful grimoire. I think we're beyond his personal boundaries."

Her face flushed. "His boundaries are keeping that bedroom door between him and us at the moment. You can't choose when you acknowledge a person's boundaries. They protect both of us."

"You think he's changed himself back?" *Cause otherwise, I don't see how he's coming out of there. The doorknob is protecting us more than that kid's boundaries.*

She tilted her head, listening. "It's been very quiet in there for a long time. Do you think we should check on him?"

"If we go in there, and he's still a dog, what are we going to do?" I genuinely had no idea.

"Come back out, I guess? I don't know how to fix this if he can't do it himself. I can keep him calm, but I can't turn him back…wait." She looked me up and down. "Can you turn him back?"

"What? I don't know anything about transmutation." I'd need a spell and probably some herbs, maybe a few crystals. The missing grimoire would really come in handy right now.

She stood. "No, turn it all back. That's your Gift, right? You can turn back time? Turn it back to before he changed, and then we'll stop him from doing it in the first place."

"I don't know." Not that I hadn't thought about it, but this was bigger than pushing back the clock a few minutes. He'd been a dog for over an hour.

She gripped the back of the chair. "Just try, won't you? And if it doesn't work, we'll find some other way."

Half of me hoped the Beast Boy would revert to his original form before we went in there. But the other half wondered if I could do what she asked. Hadn't I basically done it in the library? I pulled back time to before Brian's admission, effectively erasing what he'd said as if it never happened.

Maybe I was the one people should be afraid of.

"Let's just see how he is first," I said.

She reached across the table for my mug. I hadn't finished the coffee, but sharing time was clearly over. Noemi dropped the mugs off beside the sink and led me back down the hallway to Lalo's room. We both took a steady breath before she opened it.

Inside, the tawny fur of the German Shepherd rose and fell with the deep breaths the animal took in slumber. He'd fallen asleep in a pile of quilts.

Noemi tiptoed farther into the room and knelt by the bed. "He's snoring."

The soft rumble of his snores lifted the hairs on my arms. *He's snoring.*

Lalo doesn't breathe. His heart doesn't beat.

He wanted to change, to adapt his form away from what happened to him. And he succeeded. He wasn't a vampire anymore. He was just a dog.

Just a puppy.

I reached out for his magical energy, but I didn't feel anything stronger than I had when I tested Emily. He wasn't a witch anymore.

No wonder he can't change back. He doesn't have the human brain to form his intention. He doesn't have the energetic Gift that aligns his energy with the elements.

He's an animal.

Noemi fell back on her heels, one hand coming to her mouth. When she turned, the tears that had threatened to fall earlier trailed down her cheeks. "You have to turn him back."

"Are you sure?"

She nodded, though it seemed like the opposite of what she wanted.

"He's not a vampire anymore," I said. "Maybe there's another way."

I scanned the room. Noemi and Tori hadn't wanted to search it, but if we could find the grimoire…could the elixir of life give Lalo his life back? There had to be something in that book that could help us. A grimoire that old with a recipe like that? No way was that the only trick it was hiding.

"It's not here." Noemi stood, stopping me from lifting the trailing sheets to look under the bed. "We'll find it, but he doesn't have it. I should have believed him. Take us back so I can make a better choice this time. He wouldn't have done this if I hadn't made him feel like there was something wrong with him."

"There was something wrong with him." I slammed my hand over my mouth, but the words were already out. *Shouldn't have said that.*

Noemi's eyes flashed, and the pupils dilated. Her face changed in ways I hadn't noticed last time: her cheeks sinking in, her mouth widening.

I backed against the door, holding up my hands in front of me. "I'm sorry. I'm sorry. I didn't mean it like that."

She didn't move, but it wasn't because I stopped her. A low growl emanated from the back of her throat.

My fingers sparked as I called the energy back to me. I didn't want to freeze her. It wouldn't solve anything. She'd still be mad when I released the time bubble.

But I could go back.

"Take him back. Use your Gift and put him back the way he used to be." Her voice dropped an octave, rumbling and deep.

"Okay. I'll try, just…don't eat me." I held my breath, trying to become one with the door. How did I keep getting trapped against doors that only swung in?

Noemi gasped. She shrank back, her brown eyes wide with embarrassment instead of hunger. "What? No. I don't…I'm sorry."

"I don't know if this is going to work. I can't promise you —"

"Just try. Please."

"Where were you when he changed? It's probably easiest if you just go there now. Things are all going to shift around." Nothing in the room looked out of place. He had stuff on the floor, but none of it looked like it had fallen dramatically during his transformation. Still, I stayed by the door. In the library, I'd seen what happened before I reversed time. Here, I had no idea what path anything would take.

"I wasn't in the room when he did it. But when I found him…" Noemi moved only a foot or two from where she'd been standing, then turned to face the middle of the room. "He wasn't in bed. He was over there, by the closet."

I closed my eyes, thinking of the control I'd had when Tori siphoned my energy. Those time walks didn't change anything, though. They just showed me the shadow of what happened, like a recording on a security tape. What Noemi wanted me to do would require more energy—to actually move us back through the timeline and reset things.

My breath became deeper. I rolled my head, loosening my

neck. I called the energy, and it warmed the blood in my veins. Strength spread through my body.

Opening my eyes, I focused on Lalo. He'd woken at some point in our less-than-comfortable visit, and he lifted his head from the covers. Maybe he sensed the energy changing around him. He yawned.

Lalo's head tilted to the side, watching me with curious eyes. Well, slightly interested eyes, anyway. My skin vibrated.

Back up.

Time reversed, slowly at first. Lalo's head dropped back down again, and his eyes drifted shut. Noemi moved, following a reverse path around the room. Her vamp face was even scarier in slow motion.

Keep going. Back up. Back up.

The air in the room swirled around me, lifting my hair from my shoulders. The reversal sped up. The house moved around me, forcing me to follow the path I'd come instead of showing me what happened in the room before I got there. It was different than when I'd watched the replay with Tori. I hadn't been in the room at all when she'd looked at the book. The time walk had just shown me what happened there. When I reversed time in the library, I didn't move...but I'd only gone back a few minutes. I'd been sitting at that table for hours.

I should stop. Tell her it isn't going to work. I don't know what I'm doing.

Her face when I said something was wrong with him. What would she do if I failed? She'd asked for my help. Nicely. *Please* and everything. But I'd seen how quickly she could change.

My fingers itched. *Keep going.* We were back in the kitchen. I could almost reach my unfinished coffee. *What would the caffeine do for me in this state?* But it was gone, and we were back in Lalo's room. The dog stood on his bed, backed around in six circles and jumped backwards to the floor. He backed up toward me.

The reversed time sped up. The door opened, and we raced backwards down the hall. The tension in my neck returned. Just a little further. Back to the front door. Tori returned.

Noemi slammed me against the door. The force of it knocked my head back. I felt her claws on my skin. And then she was gone again, kneeling with Lalo on the floor. My head ached.

Keep going.

Noemi and Tori disappeared back down the hall. Lalo lay down, then slid back as the rug unfurled beneath him. Time dragged him back to his room, leaving me at the door.

This is where I came in.

How long did Tori say he'd been changed? Ten minutes before she called?

Ten minutes ago, I was on the bus. Before she called, I was at the magic shop.

I won't be here to warn them. He'll change again, just like he did before.

Don't panic.

I froze, holding the time bubble in place. A thousand possibilities competed for my attention. They hammered against my skull. The pain forced me to my knees.

I only need one that works.

My breath exploded from my lungs, knocking me forward. *Uno Reverse.* Time flipped, and I flew forward back through everything I'd already seen and done. I staggered to my feet just in time to hit the present like an unexpected speed bump. It slammed into me, and I fell backwards.

Back into the door.

Back in Lalo's room.

The dog on the bed tilted his head at me.

Noemi pointed at the middle of the room. "...By the closet."

My legs gave out. I slid down the door, blacking out before I hit the floor.

22

Thomas's futon was becoming far too familiar. The ratty blanket he'd thrown over me smelled like ash and candy. Rolling over, I pushed it away, not ready to question the origin of those scents. I sat upright for almost thirty seconds before catching my head in my hands and letting it sink to my knees. *Ugh. Magic hangovers are the worst.*

My brother looked up from his recliner, dropping a book onto the floor beside him. "Ah, Sleeping Beauty awakens. Welcome back to the Land of the Living, dear sister."

"How did I get here?" *That black blur on the coffee table must be my glasses.* I reached for them and managed not to throw up in the process. Clearing my vision knocked the headache back a few levels but didn't completely resolve it.

"Your new friend Noemi went through your contacts. You really have me listed as your emergency contact? I'm touched." He threw a hand over his heart.

"Don't get excited. I didn't know anybody else outside the Gate when I bought the phone." My brother was the most logical In Case of Emergency contact anyway. If I'd needed someone to call Thomas back then, it'd have to have been an emergency. I groaned.

"Should I grab the trashcan, or are you gonna hold it together over there?" He raised an eyebrow.

"I'm fine." I clearly wasn't.

He pulled a trashcan from under the kitchen cabinet and tucked it between me and the coffee table. "Yeah, not that I don't believe you, but…aim for this, okay?"

I hugged it.

Thomas stood on the other side of the table with his hands on his hips, considering me. "You don't look injured, and you don't smell like beer. If this wasn't a hunter attack or a frat party…what'd you do, burn through all the magic in the Chicagoland area?"

I scowled. "When was the last time you saw me at a frat party?"

He shrugged. "You're missing out. Free drinks and a crowd of mundanes practically begging to use *under the influence* as an excuse for all kinds of hijinks."

"I doubt they mean under your influence."

"They'll never know, will they?" He winked.

It wasn't exactly "Witches will take their rightful place," but Thomas's sense of superiority came from the same place. If Lily started a revolution to put down mundanes, which side would Thomas fall on? "Why do you do that?"

"Do what?"

"Act like you're better than them. Just because you can manipulate magical energy that they can't even sense. You have a Gift, not a mandate."

"But we are better. Empirically. We're more evolved. It's just science."

"It's just magic. And I couldn't access it before Spring Break, so I don't know how you're so ready to dismiss them."

"They're not like you. We always knew you had a Gift."

"Did we? I didn't."

He started to say something, but I held up a hand, still rubbing my forehead with the other.

"Don't start talking about the prophecy and our family legacy and *the odds were always in our favor.* I couldn't float a feather. For years. When I left for my Wakening, I had no intention of ever coming back. I know what it feels like to take the long way around. To depend on others for things they can do without thinking. We can't treat them as if they're less-than, just because we were privileged enough to be born with more."

"I don't treat them like they're—"

I glared at him.

"Well, not to their face."

"Don't you see how that's just as bad?"

He frowned.

I didn't know how to explain it to him. What had he been doing out here for the last three years while I was in college? My memory of our youth still had some holes in it, but we went to school together in Queen's Creek. Did he forget all his history lessons? "Like…morally? Ethically? Supremacy, in general, is not a good thing?"

"That's not what this is. Don't make me the bad guy because I made a joke." His face reddened.

Oh, now you're offended?

I took a breath. A lot of witches felt the way he did. They didn't see the problem with a little casual prejudice. But if we kept letting those jokes go, it only encouraged the more radical among us. Witches like Lily. We had to course correct before it was too late. But Thomas's emotions were all wrapped up in it now. He wasn't going to hear me if he thought I was accusing him of something. Threatening his hometown pride. His ancestral identity.

"You're not a bad guy." I rubbed my eyes and adjusted my glasses, sitting up straighter. "But you can't say things like that. Even as a joke."

Thomas rocked back on his heels. He looked from me to the back balcony, where Adam often hung out when he needed air. Chicago's skyline didn't live up to the stars over Queen's Creek.

My brother crossed his arms. "What happened to you? You're acting like you're going to run for office or something. When did you go all political? Is it that vampire's book club? Are you in some kind of cult?"

There had to be something here I could throw at him.

But the coffee table still sank under the pile of Dad's notes, and none of the folded pages were particularly aerodynamic. Maybe the pencil. I picked it up, twisting it between my fingers.

Thomas's face fell. He bent cautiously in front of me and slipped it from my hand, setting it on the kitchen counter, well out of reach.

I had to try something else.

How about logic? How about safety?

"We have to change the way we do things, the way we talk about people. More witches are going to come out into the world. More magic. But we're still outnumbered by mundanes. How do you think they're going to react if there's suddenly a powerful minority coming into their spaces and treating them like they're somehow unworthy?"

Thomas stepped closer. "Is this about the hunters? Did you see Brian again? Is Jasmine—"

I waved him off. "No. I don't know. I don't know what the hunters are doing. Not Wesson, or Jasmine, or any of the others we haven't met yet. But there are more. Hunters. And scions. And who knows how many allies they have among frightened mundanes."

"Paranoid mundanes, you mean." He turned away.

"Maybe not."

Leaning on the kitchen counter, he looked over his shoulder. "The descendants of witch hunters who killed our kin for healing them are not paranoid?"

I swallowed. This headache was not going away. "I met someone yesterday. Noemi's book club isn't as mundane as she led us to believe. There's at least one very powerful witch in the group, and the things she said…weren't that far off from the jokes you've made. She wants to start a revolution."

Thomas smacked the counter and turned to face me. "There's a militant witch in your suburban book club, and I'm the problem?"

I spread my hands out. "It's all connected."

"Sure. Okay." He sat backwards on one of his bar stools, throwing one leg over it like a cowboy. "Is this freedom fighter the reason I had to drag you half-dead from a bungalow last night, and you never once texted for help? You know, there are easier ways to get excused from your morning classes. I bet they don't even take attendance."

I laughed, closing my eyes against the pain. "Since when do you care if I make it to class?"

He rubbed the back of his neck. "It's not like you to disappear. And Adam—"

"Where is he?" I wasn't looking forward to his lecture about missing the hourly check-ins I'd agreed to, but at least he hadn't blinked in to rescue me. *Why didn't he blink in to rescue me?*

Thomas leaned forward, bracing his elbows on the back of the stool. "You should have seen him when I got the call. I've never seen someone so conflicted. I think he feels guilty about letting you go alone. But he's also pretty mad at you."

I deserved his anger. I'd been stupid. I should have called him from Noemi's, texted the A-OK sign like I'd promised. I should have talked with him days ago. So much could have been resolved if I'd just told him the truth about how I felt.

I'd put off that talk for too long.

"Where is he?" My voice cracked. *Should probably drink some water. All the energy I burned through for no reason…*

"He needed some space. I think he went back to the Creek."

I dropped my head back between my knees. Counted down from ten. Counted back up. Lost track of the time with my eyes closed and my ragged breath cooling the beads of sweat dripping down my face.

"Drink this."

I twisted my head to the side. A mug thunked down on the table in front of me.

My whole head is going to crack open.

"Hey." He kicked my foot. "Drink."

I mumbled my gratitude and dragged the mug to my lips.

The tea helped. Sleep would help more. I leaned back into the futon, cradling the mug. Maybe another nap. And then we could talk some more. I hadn't even told him about Lalo. Thomas would love that story.

I took a breath and blew across the surface of the tea, imbuing it with my intent. *Heal me.*

The next sip lit every nerve from my lips to my stomach. A cooling sensation I felt all the way down made me aware of my self and connected me back to my body. It wasn't energy, but it rejuvenated me anyway. I blinked as my brain started working again, waking up through the fog of exhaustion.

The room should have been brighter. Thomas's sliding door had no curtains, and the balcony faced east. Cloud cover should move, casting watery shadows on the floor. Not this faintly golden glow. *I missed my classes. How long did I sleep?*

"What time is it?"

23

By the time I arrived back at the dorm, I was ready to collapse on my college-issue extra-long bunk and disappear under the covers until graduation. But I'd already missed my classes, and I couldn't afford to miss my shift at the café. If I didn't change fast and get over there, I might end up moving in with Thomas after all. I still had a payment due for the last quarter's room and board.

A poster at the top of the stairs reminded us to practice self-care during exam week. A helpful message from the RA. How could I be expected to care about exams when my magic was growing faster than I could master it, and the only person strong enough to help me manage it had once stolen it and left me for dead? A powerful book of spells was, at best, unprotected and, at worst, in the hands of a magical revolutionary. My best friend might have betrayed me to a shadow organization bent on exterminating people like me, and my boyfriend had gone back home because I pushed him away.

The door swung open as I stuck my key in the lock. Nyla flung the door wide, sending my keys flying into the room.

"Girl! Where have you been?"

"I was—woah. What is going on?" Before I could think of a reasonable explanation for my disappearance all night, she waved me into the room and slammed the door shut behind me.

"You are not going to believe what I found out." Nyla's eyes danced with unshared gossip.

I grabbed my keys from the floor and dropped them on my desk, mentally preparing for a romantic update on one of the show's former cast members or a scandal from the dance team. Leaning on my desk, I kicked off my shoes.

Nyla paced in front of me, waiting for my full attention. When I looked up, she said, "First of all, Jasmine does not have Covid."

Isn't that what I said? Wait…how does she know for sure?

Nyla continued, so invested in her story she didn't notice it took me a minute to catch up. "Her roommate says she hasn't been back in days. And I was like, 'What do you mean?' Because who takes a vacation at the end of the semester, with exams coming up? And if she was going to drop the dance team, you'd think she would have told somebody instead of leaving us guessing about when we were going to practice for our next competition. The LAST competition for some of us? Who does that? But of course, her roomie is all 'shrug' and 'it's none of my business.' And I'm like, 'What? I mean, you live with this girl, and you're telling me you don't know where she is or when she's coming back?'"

Nyla paused to give me a side-eye as I tore off my t-shirt and grabbed my work polo.

"Sorry," I said from inside the shirt. That reasonable explanation still hadn't come to me.

When my head popped through the collar, Nyla waved away the apology and went on with her story, too concerned with Jasmine's drama to ask about mine. "And she goes off on me, talking about 'I'm not her mother. If she wants to go off with her boyfriend and not tell anybody, that's on her.'"

I never met Jasmine's roommate, but I had no doubt Nyla's impression was dead-on. *That last line though…*

"She went off somewhere with Brian?" It didn't make sense.

Nyla threw her hands up. "That's what I'm trying to tell you. You said he wasn't at work yesterday, right?"

I shook my head. "No, but he's still here. I saw him at the library. He didn't say anything about Jasmine."

Well, he did. But I stopped him from explaining himself. Would he have told me about this if I'd let him? Was he hiding her somewhere? Why?

"So either she ditched him and went off somewhere on her own, or it's more of a stay-cation, and she's holed up someplace nearby waiting for him when he goes out for classes." Her tone made it clear she suspected the first option, and I had to admit it sounded a lot more plausible.

Not that either option made much sense. I pulled down my ripped jeans and tossed them in the hamper. "But why would she do that?"

Nyla tossed her braids over her shoulder, making the beads clink against each other. "I don't know. The roommate said Jasmine's been acting all kinds of weird for a while. Like, get this, she thinks she might have been cheating on Brian with some old white guy."

"What?" Jasmine had done a lot of crazy shit in the last few weeks, but her loyalty to Brian had been the one constant. She'd turned against the hunter at the last minute to protect him.

Nyla popped a hip to the side and braced one hand on it, gesturing with the other. "For real. This girl says she minds her business, but you get her talking, and she doesn't miss a thing. She says this guy is like, old enough to be her father, but I get the impression she kind of wants to call him daddy herself, you know what I mean?"

"Eww." I could think of one older white man who would have reason to meet with Jasmine. But the idea of Jasmine or her roommate hooking up with the hunter made my skin crawl. I shook the wrinkles out of the khakis I'd worn to work yesterday.

"Hey, to each their own. I'm not here to judge. But I'm not about to let that girl do Brian like that." She fanned her fingers and pulled them into a fist. "Mm-kay?"

The vision of Nyla taking on Jasmine was more satisfying than it should have been. But none of these theories helped me narrow down where I could find her. I might need to talk to the roommate myself. Maybe after my shift, assuming I still had one when I got there. I pulled on my work pants and tucked in my shirt. "She really thinks Jasmine's cheating on him?"

Nyla shrugged, dropping her hands to her sides. "I mean...yes? She didn't actually catch them doing anything. But she says he showed up all kinds of hours and picked her up. Let her drive his truck. And then he just stopped coming around."

"When?" I asked, even though I had a pretty good idea.

"A week or so ago." Nyla snapped her fingers. "Round about when that thing happened at the theater, actually. You think he was the guy they took away in the ambulance? I heard somebody got knocked out in the stampede, and he's in a coma now."

"Nobody's in a coma." *I don't think. Who knows what Tori's parents did with the hunter after I stopped him from getting his horror movie revenge?* I bent to tie the laces of my ugly black work shoes. They smelled like rotten cheese from a milk spill last week, but I wasn't going to waste my laundry quarters running them through the machine.

"You sure about that?" Nyla sat on my bunk, leaning

forward to avoid hitting her head on the frame.

I looked up from my shoes. "No? But I feel like there would have been…I don't know, announcements or vigils or something?" *Unless they covered it up.*

Nyla ignored my attempt at logic in the face of drama. "Anyway. He disappeared, and Jasmine was acting weirder than usual. Really nervous, apparently. Looking over her shoulder and all that. And then Brian came over, and they had a fight."

"They what?" *Brian's always been so…mellow.*

"Yeah, roomie says she went to the lounge to give them some privacy, but she could hear them down the hall. Something about 'Don't you understand?' and 'I can't do this anymore.' Says she thought they were breaking up for sure, but then out walks Brian, and Jasmine's right there beside him, hand in hand and her head on his shoulder." Nyla raised her eyebrows.

"They left together?" My hand hovered over a new hair tie on my desk.

"And she was never seen again." Nyla hummed the theme to one of those old mystery shows, wiggling her fingers in the air.

I rolled my eyes, pulling my hair back. "Don't say it like that."

"Like what?" She grinned, leaning back on my bed and propping herself up on her elbows.

"Like you think he's going to turn up in a true crime documentary or something."

"Maybe he is. We don't know what happened after that." Nyla sighed and stared up at her bunk. "They left together. She disappeared, but he's been going to classes like nothing happened. Apparently."

She sat up again. "I mean, you saw him yesterday. Did he say or do anything that made you suspect something was up?"

The way he caught himself after he said her name. The way he wouldn't look me in the eyes. "He said she was going through some things." I grabbed my hat and pulled the ponytail through the hole in the back.

She smirked. "I'll bet she was. She went through the woods and into a hole in the ground."

I crossed my arms. "You are not seriously suggesting that our friend murdered his girlfriend."

She looked disappointed. "No. But come on, wouldn't that be more interesting than she had to quarantine because she got Covid from a slightly suspicious, albeit very attractive older family friend, and Brian drove her back to her parents' house to recover?"

"He drove her back to her parents'." Much more plausible than an illicit affair.

"I mean. Probably? Don't they live in Skokie or Evanston or some shit? What good is having a boyfriend with a car if you can't get a free Uber when you're too sick to face the CTA?" She had a point.

Can it really be that simple? Just this once? Please, goddess?

24

ark's going to fire me.
I hustled down the sidewalk, ducking my head to keep from losing my hat in the wind. Twenty minutes late was bad. Showing up missing the health department required accessories would be worse.

"It's about time," my manager boomed from the bar as I crashed through the café door.

Great. He hates the espresso machine. How long has he been stuck making lattes?

"I'm sorry. I—" *Umm…overslept? Missed my train? Got mugged? How much sympathy did I need to keep my job?*

"Later." Mark waved a cup at me. "Just clock in and take over for me. I have to get the order in."

He should have put the order in while the shift supervisor handled the morning duties, and he had more staff in to take care of customers. But he'd probably spent that time hovering and gossiping with the security guard under the guise of *managing the customer experience.*

Coming around the counter, I silently prayed for anyone but Brian to be on the register. I'd lost track of my friend's shift schedule, trying to forget what he hadn't told me. He was going to ask if I'd checked out the links he sent me. Maybe want to know why I hadn't messaged him about our next study session.

The barista behind the register looked up, her mouth a straight line and her eyebrows low. Her nose ring glinted.

Maiden-mother-and-crone. Clearly, I was not specific enough about the acceptable alternatives to my friend with the missing hunter girlfriend. I used to have normal coworkers. What happened to the mundane college kids and local artists who needed a side gig?

It's for the best. Imagine working together, knowing he might meet up with Jasmine later. My stomach twisted at the memory of his admission. Three years of friendship was apparently nothing compared to the love of an apprentice hunter. How long had he known what she was? Did that explain why he wasn't shocked by what I could do? Did he know what she was here to do? If so…

Maybe she was using him. But if that were so, why would she stay with him now that I knew her secret and she knew mine? It wasn't like he had other witchy connections to betray. My brain spiraled into more and more complicated conspiracy theories while the cups stacked up at the bar. Mark wasn't moving fast enough.

I nodded at Isa and ducked into the back room to hang up my coat and grab an apron. The office was empty. No one on break, and the store manager on bar. The shift was understaffed, even without my tardiness. *Everybody's going to be in a great mood today.*

Mark pulled off his hat as I walked around the corner, leaving me with a row of marked cups and a hissing milk steamer. I swiped the screen on the second register to officially get on the clock and stepped behind the big machine without a word.

Fifteen minutes later, the line died down, and I called the

last order from the handoff counter. I plunged a plastic cup into the ice bin, topped it off with cold water, and shoved the straw in my mouth. Leaning back against the counter, I closed my eyes. My head throbbed dully. This kind of pain should have come with better memories.

"Sorry about my stepmother." Isa turned her back to the register, resting her shoulder against the pastry case.

I held the cold cup against my temple. "She wasn't so bad. A lot of people love that movie."

"She promised me she would read the book." Isa slid open the pastry case and pulled out a chocolate croissant without using the tongs.

I winced. *Goddess, help us if Mark sees her do that. Or one of the customers.*

"How did you get involved in that book club anyway? It doesn't seem like your...style."

She looked down at her clothes, the standard black pants and company polo under a green apron with her name tag. The only hints of her other life—besides the nose ring—were perfectly drawn wings at the corners of her eyes and red lace edging around her white socks. "The guidance department at school did a whole unit on code-switching, so I'm experimenting with my alternate identity. *Look how normal I can be in a corporate setting.* And all that. But our therapist says I should be myself around Emily, and she's supposed to be taking steps to meet me halfway. I picked books. She found the club. Noemi actually has good taste. I mean, it's not romantasy but Gillian really got into some dark shit. Forget morally gray."

She picked at the croissant, pulling off tiny bites at a time.

"What book would you have picked?" *Maybe something a little older? Something with handwritten pages? In Latin?*

Isa dug a hunk of chocolate out of the pastry and chewed while she considered. "I don't know. Maybe one of those A

Court of Something and Whatever books. I heard those are good. Something with magic and sex."

I smiled. Another tick in the Mundane as Her Mother column. Not that witches didn't read for fun, but when you understood how real magic worked, those novels could get frustrating. It'd be like a hospital resident watching Grey's Anatomy in her limited free time. There'd be a lot of things to overlook. Suspension of disbelief was easier if you didn't have years of study on the subject.

A customer dropped her purse on the counter and stared up at the menu behind us.

"We'll be right with you," I said, covering for Isa while she shoved the rest of her croissant into a pasty bag and tucked it on the shelf under the counter next to my water. "Do you know what you're having?"

The woman chewed her lip, her eyes still focused above my head. "Umm...I'm craving one of those peppermint things you guys have at Christmas. With the chocolate and those little crunchy things on top?"

"We can do that. It's not on the menu right now because it's seasonal, but we have all the ingredients." I started to show Isa how to build a peppermint mocha in the order screen, since the direct order button wouldn't appear until late fall, but she already had it.

Without looking at the screen, she wiped the crumbs from her lips and opened the order. She smiled at the customer, her fingers hovering over a button on the tap screen that definitely shouldn't have been there. *Did I imagine it, or did that button glow a little brighter than the others?* "One peppermint mocha coming up. What size would you like?"

"The medium, please. Can I get that decaf? Nonfat." The woman dug through her purse.

"Whipped cream?"

"Oh yes. That's the whole point." The woman smiled,

pulling out her wallet.

"Sure thing." Isa tapped the unseasonable peppermint mocha button, then put in the size and modifications as if there was nothing unusual about her screen. "Decaf medium nonfat peppermint mocha."

Maybe Mark updated the system early? Like, several months ahead of schedule? *Because that sounds like something our manager would do.* A few months ago, Mark forgot to proof the weekly order, and we ran out of lids. I had to go borrow a few sleeves from our sister store down the street.

Isa took the customer's payment and stepped back behind the pastry display to finish her croissant. Her screen went blank.

"Umm, where do I pick up my drink?" The customer finally looked me in the eye.

Crap. I pulled a cup and shoved it under the espresso machine. "Sorry. It'll be on the side bar in just a minute."

Once I'd finished her wintery special with whipped cream and chocolate slivers, I passed it over the counter and signed into the second register.

"Show me how you did that."

"Did what?" Isa crumbled her pastry bag and dropped it in the trash.

I scrolled through the regular daily offerings. No sign of the peppermint mocha. "Where did you find the holiday menu?"

She stepped up to her own register, tapping the screen to wake it up. "It wasn't on the holiday menu. It was just right... there."

I leaned over to compare her screen to mine. Same options: drip coffee, lattes, specials, teas, bottles. No holiday drinks.

Isa shifted her weight, tapping one foot on the floor behind her. "Huh. That's weird. It was there a minute ago. Maybe it was under specials?"

It wouldn't be, but I tapped her screen anyway. Strawberries and Cream. Lavender Matcha. Hibiscus and Lemonade. The usual spring drinks.

"Where'd it go?" I rested my hand on the side of the register. The electronics buzzed, but none of the energy felt magical. No spells were cast on this machine.

Isa gave up. She stepped around me to grab a large plastic cup. Perhaps inspired by the specials menu, she made herself a strawberry lemonade with half the ice and twice the strawberry syrup the recipe called for. "Does it matter? The customer got what she wanted."

I leaned back on the counter, watching the other barista. If there wasn't anything wrong with the machine, it must have come from her. "I guess not. Just would be super convenient if they left that button there all year round."

She shrugged, sucking down her pink lemonade.

"You should probably ring that in as a partner drink in case Mark comes back out." Unlike her croissant, a straight-up theft, she could get away with one beverage per shift if she logged it.

"Yeah, okay." She plopped it on the counter next to her register and logged back in. This time, I watched more closely. As soon as the system opened, the button for strawberry lemonade appeared mid-screen. She didn't even have to open the specials menu or apply any modifications, despite the fact that the drink wasn't technically a standard option. The button flashed when she tapped it. "Done. Happy now?"

"You found that quick. How long have you been working here again?" I pulled my water back out and sipped. The headache faded, replaced by a more metaphorical pain. *Is she a witch or isn't she?*

"I don't know, a couple weeks? It's not that hard. The system's pretty intuitive."

Especially when the buttons you need just pop up on-screen whenever you think of them.

I tried to keep an eye on Isa's screen during the rest of our shift, but most of the orders came from the standard menu, and once the evening rush came in, I had to stay behind the espresso bar.

So, she doesn't have any magical energy on her own. I would have sensed it at Noemi's. A witch's Gift doesn't just go away when you enter another witch's home. Although that would be super beneficial for some of the families back home. The odds of her being bound then and free now were slim to none. She'd had so many opportunities to out herself. How dedicated to the covenant would a teenage witch have to be to successfully pass as a mundane in front of other witches?

But if she really was mundane, how could I explain the phantom buttons on her register? Those drinks never showed up for me. I had to weed through the menus and add the components individually.

It had to be magic.

25

By the time the store closed, I'd seen Isa call up buttons for two other off-season drinks, apply a discount that should have required a supervisor's approval, and print receipts from a machine that had run out of ink three hours ago. I didn't know how she was doing it. This wasn't an elemental Gift. Somehow, the kid had an affinity for tech. Mundane magic…

Mark finally reappeared after we'd done the trash run and finished cleaning out the machines. "You ladies have rides home?"

A car horn beeped in the alley, and headlights briefly flashed through the plate glass door.

"That's my stepmom," Isa said. She threw up a peace sign and headed out, not waiting to see if anyone locked the door behind her. "Laters!"

"What about you?" Mark shrugged on a hoodie over his store polo.

"I'm good. The walk's not far."

He nodded. He knew this. Asking probably met some kind of liability requirement before we left the café. "Well, then. See you next shift. Don't be late."

He held the door for me and then followed me out to the sidewalk.

I'd expected a much more involved lecture, honestly. "I'm sorry about today, I—"

He waved my excuse away before it fully formed. "Things happen. At least you showed up. Not like your friend. You tell him I can't have no-call-no-shows. This happens again, we're going to have to have a conversation about how we move forward. If this job is right for either of you."

There it is. The loosely veiled threat. Wait. "Either of you"? I'd been so caught up in Isa's potential as some kind of a techno mage I hadn't stopped to think about why we were so understaffed tonight. Brian hadn't shown up for his shift.

Shit. He was fine when I left him at the library yesterday. Totally busted Nyla's Covid quarantine theory. *Unless Jasmine really is sick? He could be taking care of her. But wouldn't he call off work, then?*

Maybe hunters got them. Or they joined the hunters.

Since yesterday?

Probably not.

Then why wasn't he here now?

Mark locked the door and pocketed his key ring. "You understand?"

Not at all. You think you know people. "Yes. I'll let him know. We'll be paragons of punctuality." I grinned, hopefully.

"Yeah, well. Just get to work on time from now on. Have a good night."

"Good night."

Mark walked past me to his car, an old Toyota with inexplicably yellow hubcaps parked behind the dumpster. I waved as he pulled away. He didn't look back.

Conscious of the safety concerns associated with standing alone in a dark alley, I rounded the corner and started down the sidewalk, speeding up between the streetlights. I shoved my hands in my pockets, wrapping my fingers around my keys just in case. Slipping into a space between a group of my peers going out for the night and an older couple holding hands, I kept pace, walking in the wake of the group.

Before long, the couple lagged behind. At the next corner, the group stopped, arguing amongst themselves about whether or not the illuminated Don't Walk sign really meant it. One guy, strongly in favor of dancing across the street, grabbed a girl and pulled her into a waltz. She laughed, but when a cab rushed through the intersection, she shoved him back on the sidewalk, switching sides immediately to back their friends on the letter-of-the-law side of the argument.

"They're going to get themselves killed."

The voice was too close. Breath on my neck close.

I spun around, sharp keys sticking out between the fingers of my fist.

Brian jumped back, hands raised. "I'm sorry. I didn't mean to scare you. I thought you heard me coming."

I shoved my hands back in my pockets but didn't drop my only weapon. "You missed your shift."

He matched my stance, fists in the pockets of his hoodie. "I'm sorry."

The light changed, and the group moved on. I should have followed them. My dorm was just a few blocks away. Instead, I stepped closer to the bus stop with its cold metal bench, glass surround, and bright overhead lighting.

I can't believe I'm saying this. "I think we need to talk."

Brian sat on the bench, gesturing to the space beside him.

I ignored it. "Where were you? Mark was on the bar when I came in."

Brian grimaced. "How bad was it?"

I smirked. "He forgot to empty the filter basket, and then he couldn't figure out why the shots were coming out all thin and watery."

"Clogged?" Brian shook his head.

"Yeah." I chewed my lip. *How to bring up a secret he doesn't know I know...*

He did it for me. "Jasmine's at my apartment."

I forced my face into the appropriate responses. *Shock. Dismay. Horror.* "How long has she been there?"

"A few days. I should have told you. But after what happened, I didn't know how you'd react." He tilted his head, analyzing me like an unstable chemical compound.

"How should I react to the fact that you moved in with the girl who almost got you killed?" *Deja vu. I have to do this differently this time.*

"She's not like you think." He looked down at his hands. Maybe he recognized the hollowness of the cliche.

"She tried to kill Nora." *I said it before, but it bore repeating.*

He looked up as if there was any room for doubt. "She wouldn't have gone through with it."

I raised an eyebrow. "She seemed pretty confident."

"She was confused." His face begged me to understand, but I couldn't. This went way beyond sympathy. Some kind of reverse Stockholm Syndrome.

"She's not the only one." I straightened my glasses and tucked a loose hair back under my hat, using the fidget to avoid eye contact.

"That's fair." His voice dropped.

A few more groups of college students walked by, talking amongst themselves, oblivious to our drama. The light changed, and they waited at the corner.

I sighed and sat on the bench, leaving some space between us. "So explain it to me."

He turned, leaning toward me. "I want to tell you everything, but I need you to promise not to panic."

A guy wearing a utility kilt hung back as his friends crossed the street. "Oh girl, that's red flag talk, right there.

You want to walk away? We'll keep you company."

This stranger might have a better read on the situation than I do. I met Brian's eyes. "Is he wrong?"

He raised his chin, tilting his head back like he couldn't believe I would doubt him. I could hardly believe it either. "You know me, Cate." *I thought I did.*

When I didn't answer right away, the guy stepped closer.

Brian looked pained. He reached across the space between us but didn't touch me.

I had to trust him. I waved the guy away. "No thanks, I'm good."

"You sure, honey?" asked the guy. Across the street, his friends beckoned him. He waved them on.

"Yeah."

"Can we go somewhere?" Brian stood, guiding me away from the bus stop and my unexpected rescuer.

The guy looked at me with exaggerated surprise. "You gonna let him take you to a second location?"

"Why don't you mind your own business?" Brian stepped toward him.

My eyes widened. The guy was big, and his friends were still close.

He crossed his arms and shifted his weight. "Yours is more interesting."

Another step. "I'll bet."

I put a hand on Brian's arm. Before the hunters, I'd never imagined him starting a fight, but the tension in his neck ran all the way down his arms. "Let's just walk, okay?"

"Yeah." Brian turned his back on the guy.

"Your funeral." The guy stood there for a minute, exuding disappointment, and then jogged after his friends. They made some gestures and then laughed. The guy clearly thought I'd made the wrong decision.

Maybe I did.

We turned the corner, going up a block and over to avoid following the group. Once they were out of sight, I prompted Brian. "Start from the beginning."

He shot me a look but kept walking. "Not sure we've got time for that."

"We do." *Don't make me explain that. Not after everything you've seen.*

He huffed. "Yeah. I guess you're right."

When he didn't continue, I pressed on. Something had been bothering me since I first outed myself to him. "You weren't surprised when you saw me use magic."

He stopped short. "In that tech rehearsal? Are you kidding? That was amazing. I've never seen anything like that."

"But you already knew there was magic in the world."

He shook his head, stuffing his hands in his pockets. "Everybody knows that. Some people just don't want to see it."

"Why were you ready to see it? Who are you, Brian?"

He looked away, focused on something beyond the end of the block. Behind his eyes, some serious mathematical equations were tallied and evaluated. He started walking again. "My family tells stories. They go all the way back. There have always been people who were different. And some people don't like that."

"And your people? Which were they?" I meant in terms of witchcraft, but immediately wondered if he meant something else. *All the way back.* I'd never thought of myself as privileged, but as a Black man, Brian's family history probably looked a lot different than mine.

"A little of both." He turned the corner one more time, coming to a stop under the streetlight. It caught the shine in his dark curls. And the determination in his eyes.

I stopped. The dorm windows glowed across the street. I

couldn't invite him in. This conversation shouldn't happen in front of Nyla. I needed to preserve at least one mundane friend's magical innocence. It sounded like Brian had never been as ignorant of our ways as I'd thought. He didn't have magic. I'd have sensed the energy. And he was so fascinated by mine that there was no way he'd experienced it before. But he knew. Had he known about me?

When I'd asked the card about Brian, it showed me the Moon. *Things are not as they seem. Fear of the unknown. Danger lurking in the darkness.* I could be letting my imagination run wild, but I didn't think so. He was still hiding something.

Just ask. No more vague answers. No room for inferences. "Do you come from hunters? Is that how you and Jasmine know each other?"

He didn't look at me. "You think there's some kind of club where monster hunters hang out?"

"Maybe. Is there?"

"I don't know. I'm not one." *That doesn't exactly answer my question.*

I stepped around him so he'd have to look me in the eye. "But you know about magic. You know about witches, even though you aren't one. You're dating a hunter. Explain how that works. How are you in this world but not of this world?"

His lips tightened, and he exhaled through his nose. "I'm a scion."

Shit.

26

I knew Brian's family. They didn't match any of the things I'd learned about scions. They had a comfortable home but none of the trappings of wealth. They were kind, even when they had no reason to be.

They had welcomed me into their home as a poor out-of-state freshman with nowhere to go for the holidays. Their apartment was up three flights of stairs, next to an L track, but somehow, the noise inside drowned out the street sounds. His little sister was learning to play a flute, his baby brother played video games, and the TV was always on. Brian once suggested they could get Nick some headphones, but his parents liked being able to monitor what he was playing from anywhere in the apartment. When he apologized for the noise, I told him about the sounds that came with sharing two bedrooms with four brothers back in Queen's Creek. We might not have had cable, but our games were far from quiet.

I spent two weeks on their couch while the dorm closed between semesters.

I couldn't imagine them sending a killer after Tori's sister.

But someone had. Or near enough. A scion had burned down her apartment building, trapping her and others inside.

Had Brian's family known the girl they hosted came from a family of witches?

I stepped back, nearly colliding with someone walking by.

"Hey, watch it!" The complaint flew over his shoulder as he hustled down the sidewalk.

"Sorry…" I mumbled, regaining my balance.

Brian reached out to steady me. "I'm not going to hurt you."

"Said every serial killer ever." I pulled away, this time more conscious of the space around me. The sidewalk was empty now. *Because, of course, it was.*

"Come on! How long have we known each other? If I wanted you dead, why would I have tried to save you from the hunter? How many times have I had your back at the café? Or the theater? Do you know how close you've been to killing yourself over there? Without any magic or hunters involved?"

The stage was a dangerous place. That was why we had so many superstitions. A fall from the catwalk, an unbalanced stage weight, a simple accident with a power tool, any number of things could have ended me without the presence of a crew-mate with malicious intent. I tried not to think about it.

"So, what, you're saying you're my guardian angel or something? That's not what I heard about scions."

He took a step toward me.

Against my better judgement, I let him.

"What did you hear?" He lowered his voice.

I took a breath. "Their ancestors were the accusers in the Trials. They've always had power. Not like ours, not magic. But real power in the mundane world. Influence, money, social status, that kind of thing."

"That part's true."

I threw my hands up. "So you can see why I have concerns

about our friendship."

"I'm not responsible for what my ancestors did," he said, thumping his chest.

Neither am I. "I'm not blaming you for them. But I don't see how I can trust you now."

"Why not? What do you really think scions do?" He went still, looking into my eyes.

The contact was uncomfortable, but I didn't look away. "They send the hunters. They are hunters. With more resources."

He stepped closer, his hand rubbing circles on his chest. "I don't. I'm not. I would never."

"Prove it."

He frowned. "You can't prove a negative."

Then what are we doing here? "What do you want from me?"

"I need your help."

Why did everybody need my help all of a sudden? I wanted to go back to the good old days before Spring Break when no one called me Chosen One or asked me to help with anything more dangerous than fixing broken set pieces between acts.

"Please," he said.

"What could a scion possibly need from a witch?"

"It's not for me. It's for Jasmine."

"Even better."

"She's broken, Cate. They broke her."

"Who?"

"The hunters," he said, like it was obvious.

"Oh. Your people. The ones who somehow land on both sides of the *we're different* and the *we don't like people who are different* scale? They broke one of their own murderers? What a shame."

"You don't understand."

"No, I think I get it. You grew up being indoctrinated

against people born with the Gift. You're scared of us. So, of course, you're dating someone who was trained to actively destroy us. But now that she's actually been in the field and seen what can happen, she's having a crisis of conscience. Maybe even some kind of mental break because of the guilt." I glared up at him. "She should feel guilty. She tried to kill somebody."

"Cate—"

"The only part I don't get is what you think I can do about it. Or why you think I should." *Someday, somebody's going to ask for my help who hasn't already tried to hurt me. Those are the people I should be helping.*

His eyebrows tilted down to the outside corners of his eyes. "Are you telling me you won't use your Gift to help someone who needs you? You won't even consider it?"

"Not even a little." *Because that would be insane. Not remotely in my best interest. Probably get me killed.*

He scuffed the sidewalk with the toe of his sneaker. "Maybe I don't know you as well as I thought I did."

Are you kidding me? "I don't know you at all."

His hands disappeared back into his pockets, and he stared at his feet. We stood in silence, an immobile roadside feature, no more alive than the cement planters that edged the sidewalk.

Finally, Brian said, "That's fair."

"I know."

But I didn't walk away. I wanted to trust him. Even knowing what I did. When I asked Nora's tarot card about Brian, it showed me the Moon. *Things are not what they seem.* They seemed pretty hexing sketchy.

I looked up at the sky. The real moon shone on the city, illuminating the buildings on either side of the street like the towers on the card. *Only your intuition can guide you.* On the card, a wolf sits to one side, representing the unconscious and the untamed forces of nature. Adam at the Creek, wearing the mask of the Guardian, waiting for me to open my heart. The dog on the other side stands for civilization and the conscious mind. Lalo, sitting on his bed in a suburban bungalow, waiting for us to figure out a way to bring him back to himself. The road between them is complex. No telling what you'll find.

Brian waited for me to process everything we'd said. The only sign of his impatience was a brief glance over his shoulder after some noise down the street.

Do I follow my heart or my mind? I can just go home. Is that the safe thing to do? If Jasmine is as unstable as Brian makes it sound, can I just leave her to the consequences of her own actions? Or is she more dangerous than ever?

Maybe Jasmine really did want to change. She'd fought Wesson to protect Brian. That had to mean something. What if we could make her an ally instead of an enemy? We could find out what the hunters knew, what their plans were, maybe how to stop them.

If I didn't try to help her, could I live with what she might do?

Consequences again. They would get me in the end.

I took my glasses off and cleaned them on my shirt. "What is it, exactly, that you want me to do?"

Brian's eyebrows shot up. "You looked ahead in the scene shop, right? When the hunter had the gun on us? You knew what would happen. You saw the bullet…"

"It was going to go through your brain." I straightened my frames with one finger on the nosepiece.

Brian winced. "But it didn't. You changed that."

I closed my eyes. Opened them again. *Longest day ever.* "You want to change her future? Send her down a different path?"

"What's wrong with that?"

I don't have the energy. A dangerous grimoire is missing. Adam's already mad at me. Lalo's still a dog. I never found my father. "Not everything can be changed. It doesn't always work. People still have free will, and you can't always count on them to—"

"Show her what happens if she follows Wesson. She needs to see that it ends badly." His eyes were intense.

"Are you sure it does?" I could already feel the headache coming. Maybe Wesson finally saw the light, regretted what he'd done, and would guide her to a safer path. Maybe Tori's parents had taken him out of the picture permanently, and there was no Wesson to follow. *Fingers crossed, and Hecate help me.*

"How could it not?"

This is stupid. This is so stupid. I should have listened to that guy at the bus stop.

But I didn't, and here I was in the back of an Uber on my way to a second location with a guy whose family tree practically bent under the weight of ancestors who'd spent their lives trying to chop down mine.

What if this whole thing was a trap? They could be working together, luring me to my death. Or worse, maybe they'd use me to find others. The hunters knew Queen's Creek existed, but had they found its location?

The car pulled up in front of an old brick townhouse. Behind a tall iron fence, a narrow walkway led up to a long staircase. The main entrance was on the second floor.

Don't get out of the car. Tell the driver to take you home.

But Brian knew where I lived. If he wanted to, he could find me. Better to face the danger now. Nerves brought energy to my fingertips, and I shoved them into my pockets to hide the sparks. I might be alone, but I was not unarmed.

Brian paid the driver and led me down the sidewalk. When he got to the stairs, he veered left, following a secondary sidewalk around the side of the building. The entrance to the garden apartment lay behind another iron fence that encircled the small outdoor space behind the building. Every step brought me closer to consequences I didn't feel ready to face. So, I stalled.

"You don't have a front door?"

He tapped the gate. "Safer this way. Only one point of vulnerability."

"Only one exit."

"Nobody gets trapped inside." He swung it open.

"Exactly what a serial killer would say."

"Look, I doubt anybody could stop you from going wherever you wanted to go, but if it makes you feel better, there's an interior stairwell that leads up to that door." He pointed to the main entrance at the top of the stairs we'd just walked around. "It's not like any contractor in the city is going to pass inspection without a fire exit."

No. I guess not. Flashbacks of my escape from Thomas's apartment above the magic shop blurred my vision.

I shuffled forward. "Does Jasmine know you're bringing me home?"

"I told her where I was going when I left."

"And you're sure she's still in there?" *What's stopping her from using the fire exit?*

"She wants your help, too. All of this, what happened. It messed her up. She wants to know what's coming just as much as I do."

This is a trap. I've been led into a trap, and I'm just going to walk in there and—

Brian waited inside the gate. "I get why you wouldn't want to do this, okay? I'm grateful you came this far. If you want me to, I'll call you an Uber to take you back to your dorm. Or doesn't your brother live in the city now? If you want to call him…"

I should have called him. What was wrong with me? I should definitely have brought Thomas over here with me. At least left a message, telling him where I was. This was exactly why Adam had gone back to the Creek. My insistence on independence had separated me from everyone who cared about me. Praise-the-goddess-in-all-her-forms, no one knew where I was. Even a mundane college student would have texted her roommate before going out after work. Nyla was going to kill me.

If I survived.

27

He's not going to murder me in his own home.

At least four documentaries and two fictional television series said otherwise. My energy rose with my heart rate, sending tingles up and down my arms. I balled my hands into fists. Coming in blazing wouldn't help me convince Jasmine I meant no harm. I took a breath, pushing the energy down.

Our fear makes us dangerous.

Don't be afraid. Be prepared.

Brian locked the gate behind me and disappeared around the corner of the building.

I sent Thomas my location with the words: 15 min. Adam would have blinked in immediately. But the cavalry could cool it. I wasn't ready for a rescue. Not yet, anyway. My brother might give me some lead time. As soon as it delivered, I considered recalling it and telling him to come now. But Thomas's distrust of mundanes might keep us from finding out what was really going on with Jasmine. At the very least, I doubted he'd want to listen to anything the hunter had to say. If we had any chance of making her an ally, I had to hear her out.

The door to the garden apartment swung in, letting out a warm glow and soft jazz.

I raised an eyebrow. Brian's music usually had more bass.

"It soothes her."

"Whatever you say." I tried to picture Jasmine soothed. She always struck me as kind of high-strung. Perfect hair, nails done, above all the mundanity of day-to-day life. Even when I thought she was mundane.

Inside, the main living area opened to a small kitchen. A narrow hallway ran farther into the building along one side. Jasmine sat on a couch facing the door, wearing gray yoga pants and a pink t-shirt. A pink and green head wrap hid her usually roller-set curls. Almost invisible eyebrows jumped. "You came."

Brian closed the door behind me. "I told you she would."

"I'm just as surprised as you are." I didn't think I'd ever seen her without makeup before. Still pretty, but not in the usual practiced way. More vulnerable.

Brian slid onto the couch beside her and put his arm around her. She melted into him, wrapping her fingers through his. If this was a trap, she was playing a very strange long game. No wonder she'd cancelled dance practice. The girl couldn't even sit upright on her own.

"I'd say I'm sorry, but it doesn't seem like enough." Her voice cracked.

"Say it anyway." It sounded rough, but I wanted to hear it.

She sniffled, dabbing the corners of her eyes with her long middle fingers even though there was no mascara to mess. "I am sorry."

Brian rubbed her back, all of his attention on her, even when he spoke to me. "See? I told you—"

"Say it again." I wasn't jealous, exactly. But she'd nearly taken my best friend from me, and I'd be damned if she succeeded this time. My intuition said she didn't mean it.

There was something in her voice…I just needed him to hear it, too.

She stood, wobbling a little, like she wasn't used to being on her feet.

Good move. Separating herself from him.

She stepped closer to me. Her dark eyes grew wide and puppy-like. "I am so, so sorry. The things I did…you don't even know all of them. I hope you never know. I don't want to be that person anymore."

I could really use an empath right now. Elsbeth would know how she really felt.

She seemed sincere, but I didn't trust it.

Adam would know if she were telling the truth.

Thomas could read her desires.

Where was my lie-detector ability? Could you read someone's spirit?

Not the time to be practicing new tricks.

Would have been useful to know, though.

If she really walked away…how useful would it be to have a former hunter on our side?

I considered her. "Who are you going to be now?"

A tear rolled down her face. "I don't know."

I couldn't know what she wanted, but my Gift could show us what she would do. If we wanted to know the kind of person she'd become, her future actions would tell us.

"Let's find out." I looked past her to Brian. "Lock that door, and make sure no one is going to come in the secret entrance."

He turned the lock and jogged down the hall.

I pulled off the baseball cap I wore to work in the café and tucked it under my arm while I took down the sweaty ponytail I'd been wearing since my shift started. Then I put it right back up, tucking in the loose hairs. I twisted the cap between my hands. It gave me an excuse to delay talking to

Jasmine a minute longer.

She waited.

"We're not going to be friends," I said.

She hugged her waist, staring at the floor a few feet in front of her. "I know."

"Brian was my friend." *You took him from me before any magic was involved.*

She looked up, focused on something two feet past my ear. "He always will be."

"Nyla is my friend." But she'd known Jasmine longer. *Goddess, don't let me question everything I know about everyone I've ever met.*

"She is." Jasmine rubbed her arm.

"You tried to kill me." *Since we're putting things out there…*

Brian's girlfriend met my eyes. "Yes."

I stepped back. "Wow. Just. Okay. Wow. I did not think you were going to admit to it."

She shrugged. "There's no point in denying it. We both know what happened."

I didn't know what to do with her direct response, but I was so sick of talking in code. "Why should I forgive something like that?"

"You probably shouldn't." She dropped one hand, letting her arm dangle like something on a string.

Whose puppet are you?

"You're not making this easy." I dropped my hat on a chair by the door.

"It's not an easy thing," Brian said, returning from the as-yet unseen second entrance. "But we need to see where this goes."

Adam's going to kill me when he finds out I did magic in front of, and on behalf of, mundanes. But it's not like they don't know. They've both seen what I can do. I had to agree with Lily on the covenant. Secrecy wasn't going to be possible much longer.

"Alright then." I crossed my legs and sat on the floor, inviting them to join me with my best fortune-teller voice. "Let us peek into the future and see what it holds for us."

Brian and Jasmine sat in front of me, forming a triangle, our knees almost touching.

"What do we do now?" Jasmine asked.

"That is the question, isn't it?" I laid my hands on my knees.

"Should we have candles or something?" Brian craned his neck, looking toward the kitchen.

I snapped my fingers. The energy hadn't gone far, and it returned at my call, multiplying until my fingers glowed.

Jasmine put her hand on Brian's knee, and he turned back. "I guess not."

"Shhh." I held a glowing fingertip to my lips. Baby steps. Walk, don't run. Without Tori here to diffuse my Gift, I needed to concentrate to avoid jumping ahead. It might actually be lucky that I'd knocked myself out trying to turn back time for Noemi and Lalo last night. My energy was still low.

I let my eyes unfocus. Brian and Jasmine shifted slightly, probably unaccustomed to sitting this way. The edges of things slipped, tiny movements overlapping their present positions. The shadow forms of things. *How far does a lamp move every time you turn it on?*

My skin buzzed with magical energy. A hum, not a choir. I pushed it into the vision. *Forward.* Ghostly forms of the three of us stood up. The vision overlapped our present. No time travel, just a little preview. Vision Brian said something to Jasmine, then left, slamming the door behind him. Jasmine ran after him, but I stopped her. *I will stop her.*

Faster. Minutes passed.

The vision accelerated. Jasmine and I talked. I left the same way Brian had, maybe a little softer on the door. Jasmine collapsed, crying on the floor. She pulled out her phone.

Faster. An hour. Maybe more.

She jumped up. Someone came down the hall from the secret front stairwell. Wesson.

So he is free. Or will be, by the time she calls. Is he waiting by the phone?

He didn't like whatever she said to him. They argued.

The door we left through opened again. Brian came back.

This time, I wasn't there to slow time. I *wouldn't* be there when it happened.

Wesson should have been a gunslinger.

Brian fell back against the door.

I gasped.

Somebody screamed.

And I was so proud of myself for not getting a headache this time…

The blackout lasted only the length of a blink. When I opened my eyes, the vision from the time walk faded. Jasmine and Brian stood up.

His face flushed. "You're really going to call him? After everything?"

This peek into the future might not have been for her after all. Maybe Brian had wanted evidence that she had lied to him.

She grabbed his arm. "He's the only family I have."

Family? I'd thought she was an apprentice. A colleague.

"He's not your family. He killed your family." Brian pulled away.

I jumped up. The conversation moved too fast. I couldn't process what I was hearing. "Whoa! What?"

She clung to the front of his shirt, her head tilted back to look at him. "They were evil! Don't you get it? I come from evil. I am evil. I thought I could make up for it, but I can't."

Okay, so when he said they broke her, he meant it. What in the gaslighting hell was this?

Brian pulled her hands away, pushing her back. "I can't do this anymore."

"What?" Tears streamed from her eyes.

He backed away. "I thought we wanted the same thing, but you're always going to go back to him."

She stepped toward him again but didn't try to touch him. "I won't. I promise."

He shook his head, dislodging the tears he'd been holding back. "You will. We just saw you do it. And look what happened."

Jasmine flung an arm behind her, gesturing to the place where he'd fallen in the vision. "It's not going to happen that way. I'll change it. I'll change…"

His hand wrapped around the doorknob, throwing the lock and swinging it open in one movement. "Loving you is going to get me killed. I'm not going to wait around for my time to run out."

Brian slammed the door, an echo of my vision. Jasmine ran after him, but I stepped in front of her before she could make it to the door. She crumpled to the floor as if he'd cut her strings.

My heart raced. This was not my territory to protect. *But she's so broken.*

I knelt in front of her. "Okay. So. Clearly, I can't leave you alone."

"What?" Her eyes were red and puffy. They didn't focus.

"Give me your phone." I kept my voice calm, even though my mind was reeling as I tried to make sense of the argument I'd just observed. One step at a time. Practical action.

"My…" She rubbed her face with both hands.

"You're not going to be needing it anytime soon." The whole point of this was to change things. He wanted to show her there was a different path. It didn't have to end the way it did in the vision, even if Brian hadn't deviated from it.

She dragged the phone out of a pocket in the belt seam of her yoga pants. "What are you going to do to me?"

"To you?" I stood, dropping her phone into my back pocket. I reached out my hand, and she took it without thinking. I pulled her to her feet.

Once she was standing, she backed away from me.

"You're a witch. I'm a hunter. I tried to kill you. It's your turn, isn't it?" Jasmine sank into the couch and pulled her knees up to her chest.

I crossed my arms and leaned back against the door. There, a whole room of space between us. "I think it's a little more complicated than that."

"It's not."

Everything about this girl drives me insane. Like, legitimately, bat-shit crazy. I probably should kill her and put both of us out of our misery.

But I'm the Chosen One, and the good guys don't do things like that.

Plus, imagine the guilt. I'm still waking up with night sweats because I forgot to give Nyla the message about the changing time for tryouts last year. She's only on the team because of Jasmine.

Ugh.

Don't do it. Don't say it. Say something else. "We need to talk."

"Kill me now." Jasmine buried her face in her hands.

My thoughts exactly.

I rolled my head against the door, looking for answers on the ceiling. "Okay, look. We can't go back to your place because, apparently, your roommate spills secrets like Tom Holland. And we can't go back to mine because I don't want Nyla mixed up in this."

Jasmine's watery eyes rounded. "No. She can't know. No one. No one else can find out—"

I sucked in a breath. "Right. So. It's not that I don't trust you, but even if I did know someplace else we could go… well, I don't trust you."

"Fair," she said, the mirror of Brian's response on the street.

I checked my phone. Only ten minutes passed since I texted Thomas. We still had time before my backup arrived. If this went well, I could call off the rescue altogether.

"We just need a few minutes." I slid the lock on the door. "Here's what's going to happen. I'm going to put this room in a time bubble. So, for us, time won't pass. If anybody else comes, they're going to be on a different timeline. So they won't see us. We'll be gone by the time they get here."

"We will?"

"Yeah." *I hope.*

I drew in my energy until my skin sparkled like the reflection of will-o'-the-wisps on the Creek. Then I pushed it out, feeling the bubble expand. Soon, it reached the walls. I tacked it around the door, stopping time on this side. Anyone who opened it from the other side should be able to enter the room in their own time.

My eyes closed, visualizing an analog clock. This bubble exists in the space between this minute and the next. When we leave, the bubble will pop, and we'll return to the regular time stream. Whatever time that was. Hopefully not long enough for anyone to come looking for us. *That's all I need. To have some concerned friend or vengeful hunter waiting when we walk out.*

My breath slowed. I pushed the part of my brain that was concentrating on the bubble to the back. *Watch me multitask.*

I sat on the other side of the couch, breathing slowly.

"That's it?" Jasmine squinted at the room, but I didn't think she could see the bubble. I only registered a faint twinkle around the edges.

"What were you expecting?" Not that this was a spectacle of enchantment, but I would have thought it would inspire a little awe in someone so deeply afraid of witches. Between this dud of a reaction and Brian's, maybe we didn't need to be so concerned about how mundanes would react when magic went mainstream. Most workings just weren't flashy enough to live up to the reputations of centuries of fictional witches and wizards.

"I don't know. Something...bigger." She fanned out her hands.

I rubbed the back of my neck. "This room is on pause until I hit play again. But it can't stay that way forever. Talk."

She pursed her lips. "What do you want me to say?"

I kicked off my shoes and tucked my feet under me. "Let's start with why you think Wesson is your family, but Brian says he killed your family. No offense, but y'all don't look related, and I can't see you hanging with Madison and Morgan."

Her lower lip trembled. "He saved me."

"From what?" Did he have a side gig as a firefighter when he wasn't striking the match?

"My mother."

"Was she abusive? Neglectful?" I couldn't imagine hunters made great parents in general.

"She was a witch."

28

oly Hera.

For once, she continued without prompting. "My father was a scion. She hid what she was from him. He wouldn't have married her otherwise."

"Of course not." *Why would she want to marry him?*

She drew circles on the arm of the couch with her finger. "I don't remember them. There was a fire."

Of course there was.

"Daniel Wesson pulled me out of it."

He probably set it.

"I should have died." She pulled down the collar of her shirt, revealing a burn scar on her shoulder. "I should have died with my witch mother, but Daniel rescued me. He couldn't save my father."

Mother-maiden-crone. The level of brain-washing this guy had done. Did Brian know what he was getting me into? How did he expect me to undo all those years of grooming?

Jasmine's circles turned into suns as she drew lines radiating out against the grain. "Daniel adopted me. He brought me to the League and got them to train me so I could help them keep us safe."

I blinked. It was too ridiculous. "The hunters have a league? Like they have for baseball?"

She flattened her design. "It's more like a legion, but they're not allowed to call it that."

Imagine the confusion. "No. I guess not."

She fell silent again. I wondered if telling the story made her question any of it.

I picked at a stain on the hem of my work shirt. "So, what? He raised you to hate your mother and murder anyone like her in the name of…patriotism?"

"Witches are dangerous." It sounded like a recording.

"Says the murderer." I shouldn't have said it, but we were past all the pretenses now.

"I haven't killed anyone." She sounded like she meant it, but I didn't see how it could be true.

"Why? Because witches don't count?"

Jasmine let her knees fall to one side. She took a breath. "The professor was supposed to be my first."

"Failed that initiation, didn't you?"

"Because of you."

"And Brian."

"I could never hurt Brian," she said.

"I bet your father told your mother the same thing."

"Brian's not a witch."

Are we sure about that? Five minutes ago, I would have said there was zero chance Jasmine was a witch, but now…

"But he's not exactly a card-carrying member of the League either, is he? What were you supposed to do, bring him back over to the Dark Side?"

"He wasn't part of my assignment." She looked down at her legs and ran a hand down the fabric of her yoga pants, smoothing invisible wrinkles.

I didn't buy it. "You just happened to meet another scion on campus."

"There are more of us than you might think."

My stomach flipped. "How many?"

She chuckled. "Wouldn't be much of a secret society if I told you."

I rolled my eyes. "Oh, I think we're past that, aren't we?"

"Brian was…an accident. Daniel would say a mistake, but I won't. We met through Nyla, and it took ages for us to figure out what we had in common."

"You guys don't have a secret handshake or something? Didn't you see each other at meetings?" Witches stayed isolated because of the covenant of secrecy, but these hunters had a formal organization. She expected me to believe they never crossed paths in service to the League?

Her head tilted back. *Here she goes, looking down her nose at me again.* "His family has been inactive for generations. They don't participate in the League's efforts. They barely keep up to date with our events."

"What does that mean? They're not showing up for mixers? Or they're not supporting genocide?" The time bubble pushed on the edge of my consciousness. This conversation had gone on long enough.

She straightened. "Do you want to hear this? Because it sounds like you already have your mind made up."

I concentrated on my breathing, pushed the time bubble back again. I had to know the truth. "No. Keep going."

She cleared her throat. "Brian's family is descended from the original accusers. The League isn't going to let them just walk away. They've been trying to recruit him for years. But his mom wasn't having it."

Mrs. Fowler had always been kind to me. Something in me felt vindication that I had trusted her.

Jasmine sounded disappointed in her. "She told them to back off. She wasn't raised for the call, and she wasn't going to let her babies be called up either. I'm not sure she understood what she was getting into with Brian's dad. Maybe she did. Maybe she's the reason he stepped out."

They were out. "So Brian knows…"

"He didn't know much when we met. He knew his dad was in the League, but it might as well have been fantasy football. He'd show up for the quarterly meeting, but they weren't tithing, and they weren't putting in hours. The League doesn't like to lose people. Especially not now, when the witches are making themselves known. It was one thing when the accursed stayed in the shadows, but now…"

The accursed. "Your mother was a witch. Don't you wonder what that means about you? Did she have a Gift?"

She drew a new design on the couch. "If she did, she didn't pass it on."

It was never that simple. "Are you sure? How can you be part of a group that hunts your own kind?"

She looked up, her eyes hard. "I am not tainted by my mother's blood."

I wasn't sure if I felt sorry for her or scared of her. "Is that what they told you?"

"If I'd shown any kind of magical aptitude, they would have trained me to use it in service of the League." She sank deeper into the couch as if this was one failure too many.

I couldn't breathe. Witches existing outside of Queen's Creek had been a surprise. Witches being hunted by descendants of their ancestors' accusers had been painful. But this? My throat burned. "Wait. Are you saying there are witches in the League?"

She tilted her head and spoke slowly. "Pairings like my parents and Brian's have happened before. It's forbidden. But there will always be exceptions. Mistakes. Children who never should have been born. But the League has uses for them."

It's a cult. This is how cults work. "You hear yourself, right?"

She crossed her legs and let the top one bounce. Her fingers drummed the arm of the couch. "What am I supposed to do? Daniel was there for me when I had nothing. I owe him my life. The least I can give him is my service."

"Is that what you're going to do? In the vision, when you called him…you saw what would happen. Is that what you want?" Jasmine wasn't dumb. How did they get her to work against her own self-interests for so long?

Her eyes welled with tears. "I saved him before. I'll do it again. Calling Daniel from here was a terrible idea. I don't know why I even considered it. I was just so overwhelmed. I don't know what to do."

I shifted closer to her. "He's not the only one you can ask for help. Brian brought you here to protect you. He brought me here…He wanted to show you what will happen if you keep going down this path."

"It's the only path I know. I can't walk away now. They won't let me."

"Do you want to walk away?" I reached out my hand to touch her arm, but she moved too quickly.

She stood, spinning to face me. "I don't know! You don't know what you're asking. How do I choose to walk away from the only home I've ever known?"

"Trust me, it can be done. You'll have help if you want it, but you have to be the one to take the first step." My situation had been different. I thought I'd walked away forever, but I found my way back. Jasmine wouldn't have the luxury of changing her mind.

"I'm not strong enough."

I had never liked this girl, but I would never have considered her weak. "Are you kidding me? Aren't you president of your sorority?"

"Secretary."

"Still." I struggled to remember something Nyla had

praised about her. "And you're the captain of the dance team. You have never once backed down from getting what you want. So tell me. What do you want now?"

"I just want Brian. If I can have him…nothing else matters. I can be whatever I have to be to get him back."

That ship sailed out the front door ten minutes ago. I hated her. I hated them together. But I didn't know if I could deprogram her without him. *Try anyway.*

I leaned forward. "Besides Brian. You can't make a major life decision based on a guy."

"My mother did." She moved her head from side to side like this was some kind of win.

"And look where that got her." Honestly. Did this girl have no positive role models?

"Ouch."

"No. This is my time, and we're not going to waste it sitting around bemoaning your lost love." I stood, walking towards the door. "If Brian doesn't come back, and honestly, I hope he doesn't, what do you want your life to be? Are you going to call Daniel Wesson as soon as I leave? Or are you going to walk away and make your own choices about how you want to live? Are you a killer or a coed? I don't think you can be both." Even Buffy died a few times in the attempt.

Her hands shook, and she crossed her arms to still them. Giving up, she held them out to me. "I haven't slept since it happened. Look at me. I'm a wreck. Every time I close my eyes, I see the gun pointed at us. I see Brian fall. There's so much blood."

There was no blood. The bullet missed. I should hold the only memories of Brian's death. I stopped it from happening…*Did Jasmine see the flash forward? She couldn't have. They were frozen…*

I shook my head. "Stop making it about him."

"I'm not. This is about me. Don't you get it? I'm a failure.

I'm no good at hunting. I don't have the nerve for it. I didn't even really poison your professor's food. I just told you that to piss you off."

It worked.

She stepped toward me. "You were supposed to be scared of me. You were supposed to run out of that theater before Daniel got there."

Nothing about her was physically imposing. Although the crazy eyes did give one pause.

When I didn't back away, she stopped approaching. She sniffled. "I don't want to be a killer. I want to leave the League."

My intuition said *true*.

"I'll help you."

She closed her eyes. "Thank you."

I released the time bubble and peeked through the small rectangular window at the top of the door. Still night, dark and empty. Nothing had changed. How much time had passed out there?

"Does Daniel know you're here, or was that what that phone call was going to be?" I looked back at her over my shoulder.

She patted the hidden pocket where her phone should be before remembering I'd confiscated it. "I haven't checked in with him in days. But that doesn't mean he won't find me. He's a hunter. That's kind of what they do."

A knock at the door made us both jump. My fingers ignited.

Thomas smiled through the window.

Twisting the lock, I flung the door open. "You scared the sparks out of me. Get in here."

He stepped past me. "I'm sorry. My sister, who never asks for help, sent me her location and a cryptic time reference. I didn't know if you'd been kidnapped or finally got invited to a frat party."

"What's that for?" Jasmine pointed to the large bottle of cheap wine in Thomas's hand.

He grinned. "Depends. Are we here to party or…"

Thomas flipped the bottle and held it like a baseball bat.

I held up my hands. "Whoa, whoa. Wine is not a weapon."

The bottle spun in his fingers, and he dropped it back to his side. He surveyed the empty room. "So if it's not a party, and you don't need a rescue, why I am here?"

I looked from Thomas to Jasmine. "Turns out we might need a rescue after all. But not for me. For her."

Thomas frowned at her. "Hey, aren't you—"

"This is Jasmine," I said. *Please ignore the fact that she tried to kill us that one time. The enemy of my enemy and all that…* "She's on the run from the hunters, and she needs a place to stay."

"But I—" she started.

"Do you want to stay here?" It didn't feel like an option after the way Brian had left.

She looked down, hugging herself again. "No, I guess not."

"You're not bringing her to the magic shop." Thomas set the bottle on a table by the door and crossed his arms.

"Oh, come on. You've warded that place from here to doomsday. Name someplace safer."

"Anywhere the hunters haven't already been." He dropped his arms. "Seriously, Cate. Did you really think I wouldn't recognize her? She was working with the guy who burned down my shop. I don't know why we're making friends with the enemy all of a sudden, but we're not going to give them a reason to take a second shot. She is not welcome. Find somewhere else."

He blinked out.

A second later, he reappeared, grabbed the wine bottle, and blinked out again.

I sighed. I could only think of one place where Jasmine

would be less likely to be found.

29

Tori pushed the door closed on me. "No, no, no. Absolutely hexing not. I am on probation."

Jasmine hung back in the dorm hallway, hugging her duffle bag and trying to ignore the curious eyes of Tori's hallmates.

I wedged my foot in the doorway to keep her from shutting me out. "I'm not asking you to brew her a potion. She just needs a place to stay. Temporarily."

Tori's dark-rimmed eye appeared in the crack of the door. She dropped her voice to a stage whisper. "She's a murdering psycho. What is wrong with you?"

A couple of girls in the room across the hall looked up from their study session. If they'd really wanted to get work done, they'd have closed the door. Nosy neighbors came with the college experience, but my new knowledge of secret societies made me wonder if they had more than entertainment as a motive.

I smiled and waved. One girl waved back, not hiding her interest in our conversation.

Using an actual whisper, I hissed, "Are you kidding me right now? With your record? She's no more a murderer than you are. Weren't you the one preaching forgiveness?"

Tori opened the door.

"For me," she said, poking her breastbone with her index finger. "I wanted forgiveness for me. What I did wasn't nearly as bad."

I looked from Tori to Jasmine and back. "I don't think you want to start making comparisons here."

"What am I supposed to tell my roommate?" She crossed her arms and stepped back, leaving the door open so I could see into the room.

The perfectly made bed on the far side of the desk, where every knickknack sat at right angles, lay half-covered in Tori's discarded black clothes. Her mess had expanded beyond her own side of the room since the last time I came over. "Are you sure she actually lives here? Seriously. When was the last time you saw her?"

Tori put one hand on the door, ready to slam it back in my face. "Why can't she stay with you? Isn't your roommate her bestie or whatever?"

I pushed a little farther into the doorway. "That's exactly why she can't. They'll be watching all of her friends. She has to go where they'd never think to look for her. Where she'd never be welcomed or protected."

"You got that right." Tori sighed. "Alright. Fine. She can have Quinn's bed. She moved out weeks ago."

She abandoned the door, turning away to dive onto the pile of clothes on her bed.

"Wait, what?" I stepped all the way into the room. Jasmine hovered behind me.

Tori stretched out on the bed and propped herself up on her elbows. "She moved in with her boyfriend, but she doesn't want her parents to know. They're fundies or something. I don't know. But I'm not going to report her because they'll just stick someone else in here. I've been enjoying my privacy."

She directed that last bit to the someone else I was sticking her with.

Jasmine gave her a withering queen bee glare, momentarily annoyed or offended out of her fear.

Tori rolled her eyes.

I led Jasmine into the room far enough that I could shut the door behind her, but she stayed as close to the exit as she could without actually going back out into the hall. She surveyed the room with an expression that suggested it smelled of something worse than incense.

"You don't need all this space," I said, grabbing a black tank top from the pile on Quinn's bed and tossing it back to her.

"Hey, she's not using it." Tori let the shirt fall between her bed and the window.

"Yeah, well, Jasmine's going to need a little space, so…" I threw Tori a chunky knit sweater, two pairs of stockings, and a scoop neck t-shirt, all back. Underneath, I discovered several flower-shaped pillows in varying pastels and a grass green coverlet edged in pink ribbon. I smoothed it out and waved a hand across the bed like a game show presenter. "Look, it's even your colors! Meant to be."

Jasmine ignored my dramatic reveal. "How long do you want me to stay here?"

Tori raised a hand. "Same question."

I faced the sorority girl with my hands on my hips, half wondering why I didn't just let the hunters take her back. *Because it will hurt Brian. Because she might tell them things we don't want them to know. Because I don't need any more enemies.* "I don't know…until we're sure the League isn't going to drag you back? Until I'm confident you won't run back to them on your own?"

Tori sat up. "Wait. I thought I was her landlord, not her

keeper. Am I expected to monitor the prisoner, or is she on her own recognizance?"

Jasmine glared at Tori again. "This is supposed to be better? At least Daniel let me have my own place."

"You had a roommate in the sorority house, too," I said.

"She's a sister, not a spy." Jasmine gave Tori an unequivocal side-eye.

"Are you sure about that?" I asked.

Jasmine's lips tightened into a thin line. She adjusted the strap of her bag across her shoulder.

I dropped my arms. "Look, this is the best I can do, alright? None of us is happy with the way things are going lately."

"I was happy yesterday," Tori grumbled. "I was on probation, but I was happy."

"I'm sorry," I said, and I meant it. If I had any better idea, I'd take it. We were all facing enough challenges on our own without becoming problems for each other.

Tori flicked at a fuzz ball on her blanket.

Jasmine leaned back on the door and stared at the ceiling.

I sat on the edge of Quinn's newly unearthed bed and fought the urge to fall over and take a nap.

Tori sat up, swinging her legs over the side of her bed to face me. "Oh, hey. Did you fix that other little problem? At Noemi's?"

Oh, bell-book-and-candle, that feels like weeks ago. How many hours have I actually lived since then? What was I going to say to Noemi? *Lalo may be stuck in dog form forever, but at least he's not a vampire?* More apologies. Another problem I couldn't fix.

I rubbed the back of my neck. Something popped. "I tried."

"So, is the kid still…" She glanced at Jasmine. "Giving everybody puppy eyes?"

"Yeah." That was one way to put it.

Tori laughed so hard she fell back into the pillows.

"What's so funny?" I asked when she recovered.

"So you didn't help the adorable witchling, who's probably over there peeing on the floor and chewing up library books, but you're going to risk it all on this mundane...murderer." She waved at Jasmine.

The world's most problematic witch hunter slid to the floor, muttering about how she'd never actually killed anyone.

Tori ignored her. At least they weren't fighting.

Quinn's pillows beckoned me. *If I take a nap right now, no one can ask me for help anymore. I'm tired of feeling like a failure for being incapable of performing miracles. That Chosen One thing was a one-time service.* "I tried to help Lalo, but my Gift doesn't work like that. Not yet, anyway. I wasn't there when he turned, so I couldn't track the time backwards. I used all the energy I had trying. You know when the last time I felt that way was?"

Tori winced. "Speaking of things I thought we were past..."

"Past, but not forgotten." I'd never forget. The nightmares wouldn't let me.

Jasmine yawned, dropping her head to her knees.

My eyes drooped. Tori and I yawned at the same time.

No sociopaths here.

I pulled out my phone. The clock read 9:22pm, but it felt so much later.

The café closed at 8pm. Clean-up and closing duties got us out around 8:30pm. It took maybe twenty minutes to argue with Brian on the sidewalk and get in the Uber. Five or ten minutes to get to his apartment. Fifteen minutes or so of confrontations and time-walking before Brian left. Jasmine spilled her tragic life story over what had felt like hours, but the time bubble locked it into a matter of minutes. We'd caught another quick cab to Tori's dorm. *Thank you, Jasmine's Hunters' League allowance.*

I pushed myself off the bed. "It's been the longest day. Let's get some rest and regroup in the morning."

"You're really going to leave her here with me?" Tori's tone implied a threat, but her toe tapped against the floor, giving away her nerves.

I gave Jasmine my hand and pulled her off the floor again. *Look at me showing support. Definitely not just trying to get you out of the way of my exit.* "Try not to kill each other, okay?"

She raised two fingers. "On my honor as a Kappa."

Tori groaned.

"Chill. You're going to be fine. That's chamomile, right?" I pointed to one of the potted plants on Tori's windowsill. Her electric kettle rested on her mini fridge nearby. "Maybe you can make peace over a cup of tea or something."

Tori watched Jasmine drop her duffle on the opposite bed. "You want some tea, killer?"

"I'm good. You do you." Jasmine's Kappa pride—or maybe it was just her old queen bee attitude—took over. She pulled a pair of pajamas, a toiletry bag, and an oversized water bottle out of her duffle. Straightening to her full five feet, she wiped her eyes and smoothed her head wrap. Opening the door and peering back the way we'd come, she asked, "Bathroom's this way? Never mind, I'll find it."

The door clicked shut behind her.

I crossed my arms, watching Tori set up her tea. "You want to maybe lay off a little? She's been through some stuff—"

Tori pulled a bottle of water from the fridge and poured it into the kettle. "We've all been through stuff. Her trauma doesn't excuse the choices she's made."

"I'm just saying, you could be a little more understanding. You might have more in common than you think."

"Doubtful."

30

I walked back to my dorm with a little more caution than usual. Just because I'd unexpectedly survived a clandestine meeting with a scion and a deserter from the Hunters' League didn't mean that their former associates would be so easy to escape.

Shouldn't have given Thomas his compass back after I went to Noemi's. I would have felt much better if I could have checked Adam's map for enemies before heading across campus in the dark.

I hesitated next to a blue emergency light.

Call him.

One of the last things Adam had said to me before Tori begged me to come over and help de-dog-ify Lalo. He'd wanted me to call Brian and have the hard conversation about his allegiance. I'd avoided it, but that conversation had happened anyway. Brian definitely wasn't working with the hunters.

Call him.

I should have called Adam before I went into Brian's apartment. As soon as Brian turned up on the sidewalk outside the café. When I woke up on Thomas's futon after wiping out at Noemi's, and Adam wasn't there waiting for me because I'd already broken his trust.

But I'd been doing things on my own for the past three years. Blaming my minimal contact with people back home on their lack of cell service and slow post offices.

Maybe this was one more thing I needed to change. Stop avoiding things. Admit my vulnerabilities. Open up. I released magic out into the world. Why was it so much harder to let someone in?

Start small. Go slow.

It was too late to go back. We couldn't start over. But if we could just slow down…maybe go on an actual date when we weren't facing any magical crises. Would it be enough?

My phone buzzed in my back pocket, and my heart sped up.

I'd just left Tori. She couldn't have gotten into another emergency situation already, even with Jasmine hiding out in her room.

It had to be Adam this time.

Could he sense my massive overwhelm all the way from home? We were all connected now. Everyone from Queen's Creek. I hadn't put much thought into what that meant. I closed my eyes, reaching out with my senses. There was something there. Something I'd been ignoring since my last trip home. A net stretching out in all directions. What would happen if I tugged on it?

I opened my eyes, afraid of what I might find.

Adam's concern had overcome his anger: Are you okay?

No. Yes. Maybe. My thumb hovered over the keyboard. If I said I was okay, he would know I was lying. The blinking cursor in the response box mocked me. Adam probably saw those three dots that indicated someone typing on the other side. He'd always been pretty patient, but those dots set an expectation.

If I told him I wasn't okay, he'd come right over to try and fix me. I didn't want to be fixed. Not until I'd had time to explore the broken pieces. But I'd put it off too long already. No more avoiding hard conversations.

Okay. One more time. Ugh.

I typed: We need to talk.

Send.

Immediate regret. *I'm not ready.*

A shimmer in the air in front of me was the only warning before Adam appeared, his eyes alert and scanning the area for danger. "Are you okay?"

When would he stop asking me that?

"Can we walk for a minute?"

He looked past me, made a judgement on our threat level, then stepped back, giving me space. "Alright."

I led him down the sidewalk to the courtyard behind my dorm, still processing what I needed to say. The post lights at the four corners of the brick island lit the space, bouncing leafy shadows like ivy on the walls where the light pushed between the tree branches. An empty set of picnic tables waited. More luck, since this spot attracted the smokers who chose not to stand by a window and burn incense to cover it inside.

I sat on the poured cement bench and leaned my elbows on the heavy table, crossing my forearms and tucking my cold fingers under them. Adam hesitated for a second before settling across from me, mirroring my position.

"What's going on?" he asked. "Did something happen with your roommate? Did Tori do something?"

He looked ready to fight her for me, and that was our problem. Ever since I came home from my Wakening, since my memories started to come back, he'd been trying to protect me. Just like everyone else. And I was sick of it. I didn't need a Guardian anymore.

"It's not about her," I said, even though it was. Kind of. Facing Tori had shown me something about myself. I'd already told Thomas I could handle myself, but now I knew it for sure. Something had unlocked inside me when we defeated the hunter. We'd stood up to the boogeyman that kept our community in hiding for so many years and found he was just a man. Standing up to Tori and being direct with her about what I needed from her had been practice for this conversation. Even if I hadn't realized that until now.

Talking could be scarier than fighting.

"What is it about, then?" Adam asked. Still leaning his elbows on the table, he flipped his palms up.

I didn't reach for them.

He frowned. "Did I do something wrong?"

"No" *Yes.* "It's nothing like that." *It's everything.*

Just say it.

"I think we need to slow down." I stared at a point on the table just in front of his open hands. *Coward.*

His hands drew back. "I don't understand. I thought… with your memories back…"

"It's my fault." *It's not you, it's me. Ugh. I'm disgusting.*

"What changed?" A crease deepened between his eyebrows. His pursed lips opened.

I couldn't look at him. It might change my mind, and now that I was pretty sure what I needed, I didn't want to back down. It would be a lie. I couldn't do that to him. His kind eyes, always looking for the truth. He had to know I was giving it to him without his Gift pulling it from me. I owed him that.

"We can't pick up where we left off. I'm not the person I was three years ago." When my magic was bound, and I wanted to run away from everything that reminded me of what a failure I was. When he'd been the only one who hadn't judged me or tried to make accommodations for me.

He'd supported me, when…*goddess, what am I doing?*

This isn't what I want.

But it is what I need.

Too late to take it back.

I looked up.

Adam rubbed his upper arm. The runic tattoo was hidden under his shirt sleeve, but I knew what he must be thinking. And then he said it. "None of us is who we were then. The things we've been through, what we've done…No one comes out of it the same."

He understands. "Then you have to see—"

"But that's just life, Cate. We evolve, and we become something new. We can do that together." His hand inched across the table.

I sucked in my lips and shook my head. My eyes burned. "I can't. I barely know who I am. As me. I'm not ready to lose myself in us."

For once, the thought came out of my mouth more clearly than it had ever formed in my head.

"Is that how you feel? That you're losing yourself?" He sat back, his hands gripping the edge of the table.

Jasmine had been willing to redefine herself for Brian. To leave behind the girl the hunters built and remake herself into someone worthy of him. But I'd told her not to make him the center of her new identity, even though he'd been a pillar of support. Could I follow my own counsel?

I wasn't leaving a murderous cult, but the Cate who'd taken down the Gate was not the same girl who walked through it for the first time three years ago. I'd tried to fit myself into her mold, but it chafed around the edges.

Adam and I had been tied together as Gatekeeper and Guardian. This relationship wasn't real. It was based on expectations we'd subverted, intentions that we'd broken when we took down the Gate. It might still have been what we'd wanted, but it wasn't what we had. It was time to see who we were to each other without those titles.

His eyes were dry, but they flooded with pain. I caused that. He had no reason to feel guilty. He hadn't done anything wrong. I just wasn't ready.

Say the hard thing. "You've always been there for me. Protecting me. Coming to my rescue. And I appreciate that. I needed it. I needed you..."

He waited for me to continue, but the words wouldn't come. I looked down at my fingers.

Adam released a heavy breath.

Don't make him say it. Old habits were hard to break.

"But you don't need me anymore." His voice cracked as he finished my thought, saving me again.

Why does this hurt so much if it's the right thing?

I shook my head again. "I don't know. I'm sorry. I don't know what I'm doing. I care about you so much."

He leaned forward again but didn't reach for me. "Then let me in. Let me help you figure it out."

I wanted to. But he couldn't help me find myself. We weren't in the same place. We hadn't been in the same place since he'd left on his Wakening, and pretending that we were was more confusing than the days when I'd actually forgotten him because of Thomas's spell. "I just...need some time."

I winced as the words left my mouth.

Adam laughed. The sound echoed against the stone buildings.

He was right to do it. What I said was ridiculous. It didn't mean anything. Even if I couldn't twist time in my fingers. What was wrong with me?

"You take all the time you need, Cate. But I can't promise I'll be here when it runs out."

"Adam, I—"

He shook his head. And then he blinked.

31

I sat in semidarkness alone with my feelings. Hurting Adam had never been my intention, but in avoiding my own guilt, I'd only led him on. Where would he go now? Back to Thomas's? Back to Queen's Creek? What would he tell them when he came back alone? We'd barely been apart since…But that wasn't true. We'd been apart more than we'd been together. First, his Wakening. Then mine. I'd come back to school alone when the Gate fell. But he'd come for me when I needed him.

And I couldn't give him what he needed. It wasn't fair.

I pulled Nora's card from my back pocket and set it on the table. If ever I needed guidance…But I didn't know what to ask.

A tear dripped down my nose and splashed the back of my hand where it covered the card. I didn't want to see the moon right now. Uncertainty. Illusion.

I closed my eyes. *Get it together. Breathe. Set an intention. What do you want to know?*

Adam's eyes and the hurt behind them. The anger I put there.

I pressed my hand over the card, visualizing him sitting

across from me. Wishing he hadn't left, but knowing he had to. Hoping he'd come back. My question coalesced, taking form across my vision. Bold.

Did I do the right thing?

The card nearly burned my hand. I pulled back, blowing across my palm and shaking it out.

On the table, the card sparked. A flash and then the image cleared. A woman sat on a throne surrounded by sunflowers. A scepter, no, a wand in her right hand sprouted with green leaves. A black cat curled at her feet. The Queen of Wands.

Whatever source controlled Nora's card had left no doubt this was the message I needed, but its meaning wasn't as clear. Wands are the fire suit. Passion, spirituality…they're unpredictable. Queens, though. They are mature. Creators, divine and confident. The Queen of Wands is optimistic and determined. She speaks her mind.

It's a *yes*. An enthusiastic *yes* in response to my question. I should feel confident in my actions, in my clear communication, in my ability to build relationships. *That's who the Queen of Wands is. That's who I am.*

I tried again to take a steadying breath, but it snagged. The image on the card blurred as my eyes filled with tears.

Why does it still hurt?

The card shimmered, and I slammed my hand down over it. *Don't answer that.*

I chewed my lip.

Be optimistic. It will all work out.

I let out my breath, counting back from five. The tension in my neck eased, letting the tears flow.

When they slowed, I didn't feel better, but I sensed that I would eventually.

And then my brain betrayed me, forcing another fear to the front.

What about Brian? He wasn't working with the hunters,

but could we trust him? He'd stormed out on Jasmine. And I couldn't blame him. But would he be an ally if things got bad?

The cards could never answer that. Not the way I used them. I had no Gift for divination. For me, the tarot guided my own reflection. *Ask about yourself.* I covered the card again.

How should I handle what I know about my friend?

This time, the card shifted slowly. The heat of its energy rose, warming my hand, but nothing like the sudden flash and burn when I asked about Adam. I pulled my hand away.

Wands.

Unpredictable wands.

A figure on a hill, both hands on a staff, fighting off six more wands rising from below.

The seven of wands.

The message was unmistakable.

Protect yourself.

I couldn't know where Brian had gone or what he would do. But I could prepare and take steps to limit the damage if he turned out to be an enemy.

Not exactly the encouragement I was hoping for, but the figure stood on the high ground. I just had to find a way to keep it.

I stared up at the stars, almost invisible beyond the city lights.

The day's magical experiments had expended more energy than I'd thought I could access in my entire life. But I was still here. Still upright. As my Gift grew stronger, I felt the energy in the air around me. Lily was right. Releasing the magic of Queen's Creek had changed the ecosystem. How many other communities like ours waited to release more?

I had to prepare myself. It wasn't just about protection from hunters. If I couldn't control my Gift, I was as dangerous as they were. We'd worried about what Tori might do in the name of vengeance for her sister, but her whole vibe changed after she and Grace linked their Gifts to protect the residents of Queen's Creek.

Grace had spoken to me through the veil when I unlocked my mind palace. *Ick.* I needed some other name for the place I went to recharge. My imaginary Gatehouse. The memory space. That place where I connected to the Time Stream. My super secret spirit spot. The clubhouse where I'm the only member. Hecate's Hideout.

My laugh echoed through the courtyard, and I clasped a hand over my mouth. All I needed was to attract the attention of some academic night owl or drunk dorm mate stumbling in from a frat party. I sniffled, wiping my eyes. They must look huge behind my glasses, all red and watery from crying over my own choices.

I shifted, pulling my legs up and crossing them in front of me, balanced sideways on the picnic bench. Shook out my hands, cleared my throat, rolled my head to loosen my neck. My eyes drifted shut as I pulled a slow breath through my nose and out my mouth. I sent myself back to the Gatehouse. The small main room came into focus. Sun filtered through the thin curtains, dancing on the rag rug where I'd sat with Elspeth and later where we'd formed the circle to open the Gate. The space felt warm and inviting, no longer the prison I'd expected it to be. I went to the external door and opened it. The forest outside sparkled with fireflies and will-o'-the-wisps, mundane and magical creatures learning to coexist. The air smelled like rain and lightning, as though a storm had just passed through. But the glistening droplets clinging to the leaves were the only sign of its influence. Leaving the door open, I crossed to the interior door, the one that led to Queen's Creek. The sun shone on this side, too. I stepped out on the Gatehouse's small stone porch.

On this side, the effects of what we'd done were more

evident. There was a footbridge here before. A narrow strip of wooden planks, so slick when they got wet, used to connect the Gatehouse to the rest of the community. It had been invisible when I came home from my Wakening, and I'd fallen into the water. More recently, I'd faced the former Speaker of our community there, trying to keep her from encapsulating the town in a magical barrier. Elspeth had fallen in that time.

Now, the creaky wooden footbridge was gone. In its place stood a wide stone pathway with protective side walls lined with a smooth wooden railing. I leaned over the side and couldn't see how far down the supports went. Did the Creek even have a bottom?

I wondered if this was what the real Gatehouse looked like now. They'd rebuilt the house before I left, but the old bridge had still been in place. I had to remind myself that I wasn't actually home now. I couldn't travel the way Adam did. Physically, my body was grounded on the concrete bench in a college courtyard. I'd only projected my consciousness to this place. This alternate reality, otherworldly dimension, whatever it was, where I connected to my Gift and to the Gatekeepers who'd come before me. I thought I'd lost that connection when I released the mantle of Gatekeeper. But after Grace used this place to guide me, I'd discovered my Gatehouse might still be a conduit that worked both ways, allowing passage to other times and places. I just didn't know how it worked or why. Studying with Brian was supposed to help with that. The science behind my magic.

Now, I might have to learn it without his help. I went back inside and closed the door behind me. A wooden lock slid into place. Across the room, a breeze from the external door ruffled the curtains. I closed that one too, setting the lock.

Sinking to the floor, I spread my hands in front of me. The spongy rag rug welcomed me. I lay on my back and stared at the ceiling. Sleep had evaded me the last few weeks, but here, the peace of the place enveloped me. I closed my eyes and let my spirit soak in the rejuvenating energy of my home.

Time passed, and didn't.

When I opened my eyes in the courtyard, the sky was still dark and the lanterns glowed around the ancient tree. Nora's card lay on the table where I'd left it. I started to reach for it and nearly lost my balance. My foot had gone to sleep against the concrete. I tapped it until the pins and needles went away. The sharp pinches grounded me back in the physical world. As I became more aware of my body, I sensed the effects of my meditation. The magical energy I'd expended had returned to me. It tingled in my fingers, stronger than the pins poking my foot. Maybe I didn't need to know how it worked as long as I knew that it did.

I yawned until my ears popped. Magically and spiritually restored, but emotionally exhausted. My conversation with Adam ran behind my eyes, backwards and forwards, close-ups on everything I said or did. I'd done it all wrong. He'd gone away broken. But any new line I tested in my mind ended in the same result. I hurt him, and I was alone.

It had to be done. Some consolation. The Queen of Wands was a bitch.

My eyes felt dry and sandy. I still needed sleep. How had this day gotten so far away from me? One more question, and then to bed. Only one more problem would keep me up tonight. Tori and her vegan vampire, and the book club from Hell.

This one was easy: *How can I resolve the problem of the missing grimoire?*

Hoping for something simple, like *it fell under Noemi's bed*, and not something terrifying like *that scary revolutionary green witch stole it and she's going to use it to bring about the first-ever magical civil war*, I covered the card with both hands. *Really think about it, okay? I need an answer I can work with. Something that won't get us all killed.*

The card warmed, slow but steady and climbing. When I almost couldn't stand it anymore, I pulled my hand away.

Goddess-be-blessed. Wands again.

I picked up the card between two fingers and shook it. *Maybe something's stuck there.* But the image didn't change. A knight in shining armor, his horse rearing, armed with a long pole instead of a sword. The plume of his helmet, the horse's mane, and the tassels on his armor all flashed orange and red, like flames.

Great. Awesome. More unpredictable passion. But knights are men of action. The card was calling me out. Practically yelling at me to do something.

Is this still about the book? I was only kidding about the magical war thing. How serious was this going to get if the book fell into the wrong hands?

Ugh. Choice is an illusion. It's the moon all over again.

If I had to take action, I knew where to direct it.

32

In the morning, my phone pinged.
Thomas: What did you do to Adam?
Me: Not ready to talk about it.
Thomas:…
Me: Is he okay?
Thomas: Not sure.
Me: What does that mean?!?
Thomas: Showed up. Drank all my wine. Disappeared.
Me: Disappeared where?
Thomas: IDK. QC?
Me:…
Thomas: Ready to talk yet?
Me: We're going to need some time.
Thomas: <eyeroll emoji>
Me: You know what I mean.
Thomas: call me later.
Me: <thumbs-up emoji>

Yay. Another fun conversation to look forward to.

Meanwhile, I texted Tori to make sure both she and Jasmine had survived the night. Her response required some parsing because of the sheer number of emojis. As near as I could tell, she didn't appreciate having an unexpected guest. She understood the assignment but wanted her complaint registered.

I thanked her for her service.

After some back and forth with Jasmine, we agreed on a plan to explain Jasmine's absence from class for a few days that incorporated Nyla's theory. Jasmine emailed her professors, informing them she would be out of school for the mandatory ten days after a positive Covid test. She had access to most of the lectures online and would follow along from quarantine at her parents'. In reality, she'd stay behind Tori's wards at the dorm. Thomas gave Tori the kynigolabe so she could track anyone who might be tracking her, and managed not to pressure me to talk about Adam. All in all, the next few days passed quickly and relatively peacefully if you ignored the constant buzz of anxiety insisting something was about to go terribly wrong.

"Hey, come in, I was just on my way out." Jasmine actually smiled at me when I arrived for an after-class check-in. She wore a pink satin sleep bonnet with a soft bow at her hairline. It matched the pink lemons on her bright yellow pajamas. Her bathroom basket hung over her arm, weighed down by cosmetics and hair products. A white dress draped over her elbow.

"Where's she going?" I asked Tori as Jasmine flitted down the hall.

Tori rolled her eyes. "Got to do up her face before her gentleman calls."

"Brian's coming over?" I hadn't heard from him since he walked out of his apartment. Should I be disgusted that he came crawling back or impressed that he'd stand by her after all her mistakes?

Tori's black lips twitched. "Nah. He won't be in the same room with her. But he's agreed to periodic Zoom calls. I think he's going to counseling. Sometimes, he sounds like he's reading a script."

"You're eavesdropping on their calls?" *Totally offended on their behalf, not jealous at all.* When was he going to come back to the café? I couldn't take too many more shifts with Mark, and I'd made no progress on the physics front since our study session went bust.

"What else am I supposed to do? Go hang out in the lounge with the losers like she hung a sock on the door?" Tori crossed her arms, daring me to defend the privacy of the roommate I'd forced on her.

I looked down the hall to the open lounge, where guys from the next hall over watched a football game while a couple of girls competed for their attention. Not exactly Tori's scene.

Closing the door behind me, I sacked out on a beanbag Jasmine must have found under Tori's mess. She'd really made herself at home. Tori's dorm looked like two functional students lived there. No more Goth explosion. The opposite sides of the room still bore dramatically different styles, but for the most part, the clothes were all in drawers, and the kitchen garden had been tidied. Maybe Thomas needed a refugee hunter to come and stay with him for a while.

I had just settled in when one of our fears caught up with us.

Tori's phone pinged. Then it pinged again.

"Who is it?" I asked, struggling to sit up in the marshmallow of a seat. There might be something to be said about too much comfort.

"It's Noemi. She wants to know if we're coming to book club. No, wait." Tori tapped a new message. "She's telling us to come to book club. Special emphasis on my bringing you with me."

"She's still doing that?" Was she just going to pretend her

mundane guests hadn't had a family breakdown and her magical ones hadn't accused each other of theft?

"Apparently." Tori stirred honey into a mug of tea, tapping the side with the spoon.

"How? What for?"

Tori scrolled through the messages. "I don't know. She just said: Can't wait to see you and Cate at book club!!!"

Her impression implied the presence of at least three exclamation points.

"Now?" My eyebrows jumped to my hairline. The skin on my forehead actually ached from the stretch. Noemi had a positive attitude, but to think book club could continue…

Tori shrugged, leaning back against the windowsill with her tea. "I would think the usual time. You want me to ask?"

I tilted my head, waiting for her to show any sign of the incredulity I felt. "We're just going to go over there like nothing happened? Just us? I mean, there's no way Isa and Emily are coming back, is there? Has she been talking to Lily?"

Tori tilted her head to the opposite side, mocking my expression. "I don't know. I've been busy babysitting the enemy. Did Isa say anything? You work together, right?"

Fair point. "Yeah, umm. Things have been weird at the café."

Tori pursed her lips. "Weird, like the teenager is embarrassed to admit she knows you, or weird like someone randomly turned into a German Shepherd, and now we're all acting like that's normal?"

May as well tell her. Secrets never saved anyone. "Something in between. I think Isa's a witch."

Tori dropped her spoon into the mug, splashing tea across her black tank top. "Who isn't these days?"

I smirked. "Well, I don't think Emily is. And I don't think Isa knows she is."

"How is it you know she's a witch if she doesn't?" Tori set the mug on top of the mini fridge and grabbed a paper towel from a roll on her new gardening stand.

Why doesn't she know? She was interested enough in magic. Maybe she wasn't ready to recognize it outside of fiction. "She seems to think she's just...I don't know, lucky? Really tech savvy? But when she's at the register..."

Tori dabbed at her shirt. "She's using magic to lower the prices?"

"No—"

"She's overcharging assholes?" She crumpled the towel and tossed it at a waste can across the room. She missed.

"No..." *But she totally should.* I waited for Tori to pick up the paper towel ball, but she left it in its new home by the baseboards.

She took a long inhale of the steam, her eyes fluttering. "Are you sure she's a witch? Magic and tech don't usually mix, and if it did, and I was working minimum wage, I would definitely—"

"She's manipulating energy, but I think she's doing it subconsciously." I explained what I'd seen with the out-of-season holiday drinks.

Tori hummed. "Maybe they didn't clear the registers' memory last season. There's probably a new button somewhere you missed."

Ordinarily, I'd be inclined to agree, but I'd seen more and more examples over the week. "She went out the security door without setting it off. She popped her cash drawer to change over the money without using the key. She's on her phone twenty-four-seven and never has to charge it."

That last one got Tori's attention. "She doesn't have a battery pack?"

I shook my head. "And she's posting videos all day."

"Without charging it?" Tori's black nails clicked around the mug.

I shook my head. "Not once. I thought maybe she had a burner, and she was swapping them out or something. But that's not it. I put a little coffee sticker on the case to be sure. It's the same phone. All day."

"Wow." Tori lowered the mug, letting it rest on her belt buckle, fingers still tapping the sides.

I pulled my legs up under me for more stability and leaned forward. "Right? She's a techno mage with mundane parents. I've never met one before. Have you?"

Tori stirred her tea slowly, watching the spoon trail a path around her mug. "No, but…things are changing, you know? If all the witches got a boost when your Gate came down, what happened to the mundanes? Especially the ones who might have already been a little…special? Sensitive? The energy is out there for everyone. The only thing that sets us apart is our ability to sense and manipulate it."

33

Are you saying I made her a witch?" My stomach twisted. I did not need more guilt.

Tori let out an exasperated breath. "Goddess, Cate. Step down from that pedestal. You did a thing. Yeah, there are consequences. But there would have been consequences if you didn't. Just because you set the ball rolling down the hill doesn't make you responsible for the path it takes."

I smiled. "Look at you getting all philosophical."

She shrugged. "I had a meeting with Nora yesterday. Maybe she's still in my head."

Nora's meeting with students again? I should probably check in. Did I miss an invite?

My phone showed no new messages, nothing on the calendar. I checked the time. If book club happened at the same time as last week, we had about an hour to get there. Two buses. One train. *Ugh. I just got comfortable.*

Pushing myself out of the beanbag, I shoved the phone into my back pocket. "If they do show up…"

Tori squinted. "I don't think that was the family bonding experience Emily thought it would be."

Their family therapist must have been so disappointed. "I wonder what they'll do instead?"

Tori ran a finger over the leaves of her mint plant. "Maybe Zaze will go over and give Emily some gardening tips. One grower to another."

"The demon boyfriend?" I asked.

Tori rolled her eyes. "He's not as bad as Emily made out. I think the guyliner makes her nervous. He looks like he spends a lot of time in the garage with his dad's My Chemical Romance albums. But he smells like there's a grow room in there."

Eww. "When did you smell him?"

She pulled the leaf off the plant and rolled it between her fingers. "I needed a ride home. But the stink wave rolling out of his car almost knocked me out."

"You don't think that's the reason Emily doesn't like him?"

Tori held the crushed leaf under her nose. "Nah. Momma has a habit. She's not as straight-edge as she looks."

"Really?" Emily had felt more like a Karen than a Mary Jane to me.

"Trust me." She dropped the leaf into a small stone mortar.

Everybody's surprising me lately. Maybe I'm not such a good judge of character after all.

I picked up the paper towel Tori had thrown and dropped it in the trash. A pink and green striped notebook lay on the floor beside it. I set it next to Jasmine's rose-gold laptop on her bed. She was going to have to miss that Zoom date.

Leaving her alone for an hour or two while Tori went to class was one thing. But leaving her behind while we went all the way out in the suburbs felt wrong. What if the hunters came for her while we were gone and we weren't here when she needed us?

What if she called them? Just because she hadn't so far didn't mean we'd permanently circumvented what I'd seen in the vision at Brian's.

"How do you think Noemi will react if we bring a new member to book club?"

The door creaked open.

Tori blinked. "How do I think our vegan vampire friend would feel about us bringing a witch hunter's apprentice into the home where she's raising her nephew, the dog?"

Jasmine stepped back into the room, now wearing a white babydoll dress and a full face of makeup, her barrel curls bouncing against her shoulders. The pink bonnet peeked out of her bathroom basket, and her pjs hung over her arm. No more teary-eyed coed in last season's athleisure. This was the girl who'd picked up Brian from work every week and driven him home with his music blaring from her speakers. If she'd heard what Tori said, she didn't show it.

"Hey! You didn't call her the killer this time! Progress." Witch hunter's apprentice was a much more accurate description, anyway.

"Jasmine and I have come to an understanding," Tori said.

Jasmine tucked her bathroom supplies under her bed, then turned to clarify. "She won't call me killer anymore, and I won't kill her in her sleep."

She's kidding, right? "You know when you say things like that…"

"God. It was a joke." She clapped on each word. "When can I go back to Kappa House? Are all witches as tense as you guys?"

"Excuse me?" I wasn't tense. And if I was, well, didn't I have enough reasons to be? My stomach tightened at the memory of Lily's power. The way she'd pulled an answer from me and the way the room had darkened when we accused her of taking the book.

Jasmine put her hands on her hips. "What? Did you give up your sense of humor when you made your pact with the devil?"

I raised my eyebrows at Tori. "An understanding, huh?"

She looked up from the mortar, tapping the pestle on the side. "It's more of a loose interpretation, I guess."

Jasmine tucked some pillows behind her and sat on the bed. "She gets me. She's just not ready to admit it."

I took another look around the room. It wasn't just neater. The space felt more in harmony. Sure, Tori's side remained shrouded in darkness, while Jasmine's literally sparkled with fairy lights tucked around the headboard. But a bejeweled skull sat on the shelf of Jasmine's study carrel, and three pink roses stuck out of a mason jar among Tori's green herbs.

"Must have been some week," I said.

Tori scraped the mashed mint into a jar and poured a clear liquid over it from a bottle with a crescent moon cork. She tucked the jar into the mini fridge and grabbed her boots. "So, are we going to this thing then?"

"I think we have to." *Goddess, protect us from whatever we find there.*

"What about my new best friend?" She looked up from tying her laces.

I sighed. Tori was right. Noemi wasn't going to like it. But what other choice did we have? It was painful to admit it, but Jasmine had conflict training that the rest of us didn't. *What if we need her?* I'd feel a lot better if we could turn our protectee into a protector, at least for a little while. "She's coming with us."

"Ooh! Field trip! It's about time." Jasmine swung her legs over the side of the bed, narrowly missing her laptop. Straightening it, she interrupted herself. "Oh! Wait! I can't. I have a date."

"You're going to have to miss it," I said.

"Says who?" Jasmine crossed her arms, setting her stance as if preparing to be physically dragged from the room.

Tori stood, the chunky heels of her boots adding several inches to her stature.

Jasmine didn't flinch.

I shoved my hands in my pockets. Not ready to admit we might need her skillset. Not interested in reminding her that calling Wesson was an option for her. "You can stay here, but we have to go. You'll be on your own."

"I've been on my own all day. Every day." She glared at Tori.

Tori rolled her eyes. "This is a safe house, not an Air B&B. Entertainment services are not provided."

I tried appealing to her frustrated extrovert side. "Hey, if you're lonely…we're about to go to a book club. There'll be other people there…"

Tori nodded, plastering on a fake smile. The result was equally patronizing and off-putting. "And a dog. You like dogs, right? Everybody likes dogs."

Jasmine arched an eyebrow. "You're ditching security detail to go to a book club? I thought you were going to protect me?"

"The people in the club might need protecting from you," Tori grumbled.

Jasmine's eyes sparkled. "Wait. Is it a witches' book club?"

"Well, now you definitely can't come." I stepped toward the door.

Jasmine's arms fell to her sides. "Oh, come on. A minute ago, you were begging me to come with you."

"I don't think we were begging," Tori said.

"Definitely not."

Jasmine glanced back at her laptop. I could almost see the same thought process I'd been working through cross through her mind. Ultimately, I'd never know if it was fear of the hunters or excitement about meeting more witches that changed her mind. She grabbed a sweater from the back of her desk chair. "I'm coming."

Tori and I exchanged a look, agreeing to nothing.

"If you come with us, there are rules," I said.

"No killing our friends," Tori said.

"No killing anyone," I corrected.

Tori frowned, "But what if…"

"No killing." Jasmine pulled on her sweater. "Anything else?"

"You can't tell anyone about anything you see or hear at this meeting," I said.

"Or on the way to the meeting. Or on the way back," Tori said. "No telling your hunter friends where to find witches."

"Are you going to blindfold me?" Jasmine asked.

Tori looked up at the ceiling.

"Maybe you should just stay here and talk to Brian." I gestured to the computer on the bed, no longer quite as motivated to protect her from possible invasion. Who was to say the hunters wouldn't welcome her back with open arms? If they found her, and Tori's wards failed. Maybe it wasn't such a risk, after all, leaving her here. Not as much as taking her with us would be.

"I'll put up the wards again. Just like when I go to class. You'll be fine. Probably," Tori said.

"What do you mean, probably?" Jasmine asked.

"I don't know." Tori shrugged. "Nobody's actually tested my wards, have they? You used to have an amulet that negated magic. Doesn't your partner have one of those, too? Does it work against wards, or did it just protect you from direct attacks?"

The conference room had dropped twenty degrees when Wesson walked into Tori's hearing with that sigil around his neck. It had leached energy from all of us, made him immune to my Gift. I never considered what it might do to a ward.

"I don't know…" Jasmine rubbed her wrist, where her

charm bracelet had rested.

"You don't know?" Tori asked. "You went into battle against people who can manipulate the energy in the world around you, and you didn't know if your enchanted charm bracelet worked as a weapon?"

"It was defensive. It was just supposed to protect me from you," Jasmine said.

As if the hunters ever needed protection from the prey.

"See, 'cause they didn't need magic to destroy us, did they?" I asked. "Not when fire worked just as well."

Tori leaned back against the cinderblock wall. "Probably don't need to worry about that here, though. It'd take a lot to burn through cement blocks and sixteen coats of latex paint."

"Probably," Jasmine whispered.

Her laptop rang. Brian calling for their virtual date.

She turned it off.

34

Jasmine consulted the kynigolabe from the first bus stop, the second bus, the train platform, and the bottom of the stairs once we made it safely down to street level from the elevated tracks. No signs of an enemy tracking us. A single tool had never been the source of so much anxiety and relief all at once. I almost wished we'd left it behind.

We heard Lalo barking as we turned up the sidewalk at Noemi's.

Something inside the house crashed, setting off another round of barks. We walked up to the porch a little more slowly than we'd come the rest of the way from the bus stop.

"Noemi knows we're coming, right?" I glanced at Tori, nodding my head to Jasmine.

Tori nodded, holding up her phone with the text chain. "I let her know we had a guest. She seemed fine with it, but you know she has other things on her mind. She's still calling this book club, but I don't see how she expects anybody else to show up after what happened last time."

"What happened last time?" Jasmine asked, raising her voice to be heard over the dog.

"Oh, you know. The usual book club drama," Tori said.

"Not everybody read the book."

Jasmine nodded solemnly, leaving me wondering what was on the sorority's reading list.

Bet none of it's written in Latin on fairy-wing parchment.

I stepped up onto the porch. "Any word on Lily?"

Tori looked down the street. "I don't think we're going to see her around. Not after you accused her of theft."

"Some book club," Jasmine said. "Why are we here again?"

Tori and I exchanged a look. There had been too many mundanes on the CTA to fill her in on the way, but she was going to find out soon enough. I had no idea how to prepare her for vampires and shapeshifters. Maybe the hunters already knew. Just because I'd grown up in isolation didn't mean others were ignorant of the apparent diversity of the magical world.

Lalo howled inside.

Jasmine side-eyed the door.

"Our friend needs our help," I said.

"And we look out for our friends," Tori added, ringing the doorbell. She probably meant it as a warning, but it almost sounded like a promise.

Jasmine nodded.

The door swung open and a half-grown German Shepherd barreled out, nearly wiping us off the porch. Jasmine shrieked, plastering herself to the wall. The dog ran in a tight circle between us, sniffing anything he could reach.

"Whoa, Lalo! Down, boy." Tori put out a hand to block his jump. He left it dripping with happy puppy kisses. She knelt in front of him, scratching the thick scruff around his neck and running her hands over his huge ears. "Who's a good boy?"

I laughed, which only drew the attention of the affectionate animal. Bending down, I gave him a few scritches under the chin. We hadn't gotten to see much of Lalo-the-little-boy since he was so often hidden behind a tablet, but Lalo-the-puppy had the same playful attitude as the kid who welcomed the book club by inviting them to join the brujas in the kitchen.

The screened door swung out again. "Blessed Be. I'm so glad you're here!" Noemi hugged me quickly before circling around to prevent her nephew's escape. "Help me get him back in the house."

Tori, Noemi, and I corralled the enthusiastic puppy back through the door while Jasmine stood behind it, holding it open. Once I was in, she let it swing shut. Turning, I faced her through the screen. "What are you doing? Get in here."

"I'm not going in there with that." Her voice trembled.

I looked over my shoulder. Lalo had flopped on his back and submitted himself to Tori for tummy rubs. His tongue hung out the side of his mouth, and his eyes rolled back in his head. He couldn't have been less intimidating at half the size.

"He's not going to hurt you. Come on." I guided her inside, keeping myself between her and the dog. In human form, Lalo might come up to Jasmine's shoulder. If he wanted, the dog could probably knock her over.

"Is this the…classmate you told me about?" Noemi asked.

I wondered what Tori had told her to explain why we needed to bring Jasmine along. "Sorry, Noemi. This is Jasmine. She's staying with Tori for a while," I explained.

"It's nice to meet you. Please excuse the mess." Noemi gestured to her home, which had suffered a little from the presence of the new animal since we last visited. Couch pillows leaked fluff, fresh scratches marred the floor, and a lamp lay in pieces (that must have been the crash we heard).

Jasmine hung back, keeping space between herself and the dog. Her mumbled response managed to be as polite as it was inaudible. "Pleasure-to-meet-you-you-have-a-lovely-home."

"Can I get you anything? I have water or pop in the

kitchen. I could make some tea…" Noemi twisted her hands, trying to play host while her nephew rolled on the floor, making vague rumbling sounds.

Lalo twisted over to his belly and scrambled to get his big paws under him. He popped up and put his front paws on Tori's shoulders, where she knelt on the floor. She laughed and pushed him back down.

Jasmine jumped. Without taking her eyes off Lalo, she answered, "No, thank you."

"Honey, you don't look well. You sure you're okay?"

Jasmine's wide eyes rose to Noemi's face. "What did you do to him?"

"Did you tell her about Lalo?" I asked Tori.

"Yeah, you know, I figured the covenant is a bust. Might as well just start telling the hunters everything directly—cut out the need for them to spy on us," Tori snapped.

"Your friend is a hunter?" Noemi backed away from Jasmine, spreading her arms to keep Lalo behind her. Her eyes flashed red.

"What is he?" Jasmine pointed at Lalo.

"He's a fluffy cuddle muffin," Tori said, burying her face in his fur, oblivious to the change in Noemi's tone.

"He's my nephew," Noemi said at the same time. "I won't let you hurt him."

Her nails extended, and her lips pulled back, exposing larger-than-average incisors.

"She won't." My fingers buzzed, ready to hit pause on this meeting if I had to.

Jasmine stepped forward, squinting past Noemi. Whatever she saw made her step immediately back again, more shocked by the dog than the vampire. She covered her mouth. "I'm not…what happened to him? This isn't natural. That's not his body. What did you do?"

"What do you mean?" I asked. "What do you see?"

All of us turned to give Lalo our full attention. The puppy sat up like a show dog, unfurling his tongue and wagging his tail. If a dog could smile, this one did. One of his giant ears flopped over. He really was a cute puppy.

Jasmine looked from Lalo to each of us. "You don't see him? Can't you tell how wrong he is? That body doesn't fit him."

"I thought you said she was a hunter," Noemi said, still keeping herself between Jasmine and Lalo, though her nails retracted. "Does she have the sight?"

I thought about what Jasmine had told me. She'd seen Brian's blood in my vision at the theater, even though he never actually spilled it. I couldn't think of any other workings she'd been present to witness. Could she see magic? "It's possible."

"What? No. I'm not. I don't have any sight. I've never had. Do you know how useful I would have been if I could—" Jasmine backed up against the wall.

"They thought her mother was a witch. It's why the hunters raised her. They wanted to train her so they could use her," I said.

Noemi sucked in her breath. Her lips pulled together. "They killed her parents. Didn't they?"

 I nodded.

Noemi's eyes faded back to brown. Empathy overtook her fear.

"Honey..." Noemi approached Jasmine as if she were standing on a ledge. "Can you tell me what you see when you look at Lalo? What did you mean about his body not being right? How can you tell?"

Jasmine blinked, her lashes flashing up and down. "None of you can see it?"

"He just looks like a dog," I said. We hadn't been there to see the transformation, and now that it was complete, it was as if he'd always been this way. There was nothing to see anymore.

"The softest, fluffiest, cutest dog." Tori scratched between his ears, and he turned his head against her hand.

"But you're witches." Jasmine looked at each of us in turn. She stopped at Noemi. "And you're…"

"We know," I said. Was this really the first time her sight had activated? She wouldn't have needed it to see magic happening right in front of her—like when I froze time—but to see the effects of magic that had already happened was a Gift.

Nora was supposed to be her first assignment, and the professor had been so far in the broom closet I hadn't known she was a witch until she told me. Maybe Jasmine really hadn't seen much magic before. Or what she had seen was so small that she assumed everyone else could see it. The idea that the hunters trained her to destroy witches out of the fear of what they might do without ever actually seeing what they could do shortened my breath. They didn't know what they were afraid of. I swallowed. *But they will.*

Noemi took a half step forward. "Just tell us what you see?"

She tilted her head one way and then the other. "It's like I have double vision. There's the dog, but there's also a little boy. He's skinny. He's got dark hair and long eyelashes." While she spoke, she stepped closer.

Lalo turned his head, listening to her description of him. The dog's tail dusted the floor, swinging back and forth where he sat.

"Is he okay?" Noemi asked.

Jasmine reached out a hand, hovering just out of his reach. "He's smiling. I think he thinks it's a game? He was laughing when he was lying on the floor."

"That's because he loves scritches," Tori said, applying a

few under his arms.

Lalo twisted in her arms, trying to lick her face.

Jasmine stepped back. "He's just a little boy. Why would you do this to him?"

"We didn't do anything to him," I said.

She straightened. "He's not supposed to be a dog."

"We know."

Tori untangled herself from the puppy, but he kept jumping to reach her hands. She flattened her palms to keep him out of her face. "Tell him that."

"What?" Jasmine asked.

Tori gave up fending him off and resumed petting the dog. "He did this to himself. So, he's probably the only one who can undo it."

"But you're *witches*. Why don't you turn him back?" It was like I could see the gears turning in her head but couldn't do anything to speed them up

Tori looked like she might strangle her.

"We can't," I said. "He's stuck that way. The caster is the only one who can reverse it."

"But the caster is a dog…" Jasmine watched Lalo curl into a ball and lie down at Tori's feet, fascination and disgust at war on her face.

"Yeah."

Noemi looked up from her nephew. "But that's not why I called you."

35

Noemi led us to the den. She and I shared the couch while Tori settled on the rug with Lalo. Jasmine kept her distance, pretending to prefer the brick fireplace to Noemi's overstuffed armchair.

Noemi squeezed her hands in her lap. "Thank you for coming. I don't know what to do."

"What happened?" I asked.

"Did you find the book?" Tori grabbed Lalo's big furry head and looked him in the eyes as if he might answer.

Noemi shook her head. "Last night, I was locking up, and there was a knock at the door. When I opened it, there was no one there, but this…" Noemi held up a ragged sheet of stationery.

A note, written in loopy script read, "Remind the girls it's my turn this week. I'll be expecting you all at the usual time. See you at book club!"

I passed it to Tori, who scanned it quickly.

"It's from Lily," she said.

I took the paper back, turning it to see if I'd missed anything. "This doesn't make any sense. She thinks we're still going to sit around and talk about that book?"

"Emily didn't even read it," Tori said.

"Not the point."

"Kind of the point. It's a book club." She shrugged, turning her attention back to Lalo.

"Not after last week, it's not." I handed her back the note, gesturing to share it with Jasmine.

Jasmine read the note. "What is this? I thought you said your friend needed help."

Lost for words, I performed a frantic series of gestures to indicate the whole situation. Should have filmed it in case I ever tried out for the dance team.

"But what is this about?" Jasmine asked.

Tori shook her head. I tilted mine to the side. She raised her eyebrows. I pursed my lips. We both looked at Noemi, who shrugged.

I sighed. "Okay, look, we brought her along. We might as well read her in at this point."

"But she's—"

I cut Tori off before she could accidentally destroy the "understanding" she'd developed with Jasmine. "She's with us now. So, unless you want to lock her in Lalo's room…"

Jasmine stood. "Nobody is locking me in anywhere. I swear you guys are worse than the League. I should just take my chances with—"

At the mention of the League, Noemi bit her lip. The empathy Jasmine had won with lost parents might not extend to a card-carrying member of a hostile organization.

Tori rolled her eyes. "Chill Buffy. You're in the Scooby gang now."

"Then tell me what's going on." Her hands went back to her hips.

"First, tell me why I should trust you." Noemi's hand tightened on the arm of the couch, her nails extending slightly. Maybe Lalo wasn't responsible for all of the new scratches. It had been a stressful few days for both of them.

Jasmine swallowed. "I—I don't know. You probably shouldn't. I've made a lot of mistakes. But I'm trying to make up for them. I don't want to hurt anyone."

"But you might," Noemi said.

The former hunter's apprentice took a steadying breath and puffed out her chest. "Anyone might, don't you think? You're witches. You're much more dangerous than I am. You might hurt me. But you haven't."

Her eyes flicked to each of us before going back to Noemi and resting on her claw-like nails. "And I don't think you will. But even with all that magic, you're still human like me. And humans sometimes make mistakes. So I can't promise not to hurt you. But I'll try not to. Will you make the same effort?"

A contract worthy of her business degree or maybe a lesson from the League. What did Jasmine see when she looked at Noemi? I wasn't as certain as she was about our host's humanity.

But Noemi's nails drew back and a faint blush colored her cheeks. "You are safe in my home as long as you mean us no harm."

Jasmine nodded.

We filled her in on most of the last secrets we'd been keeping from her: the grimoire, its possible contents, its recent disappearance, and the book club meeting that ended with Lily blinking out with a burst bulb like some kind of stage magician.

"And now she wants you to come over to her house and pretend to be normal?" Jasmine asked.

Tori snorted. "She wants us to come over there. I don't know if any of us is going to pass for normal."

"Mundane." I waited for Jasmine to take offense.

Her eyes narrowed, but she didn't say anything.

"That either," said Tori.

Jasmine shifted her weight from on guard to at ease. "You know, this kind of thing happens at Kappa sometimes. People get into fights, but when the House puts on an event, everyone puts all of that aside for the good of the—"

"This isn't like some catty disagreement between sorority sisters," Tori said. "This is a witch who stole a powerful text for reasons she didn't want to tell us. We can't just ignore the fact that she's armed herself and go over there for a casual book talk."

"But you will go over with me, won't you?" asked Noemi.

I'm so tired of doing dangerous things because the alternative is worse. Of course we were going over there. But I didn't have to like it. "Is it safe? If she has the grimoire…"

Noemi sucked in her lips, then covered her mouth with her hand. I could swear she almost laughed. "It's definitely not safe. Even without the book. She'll be in her own home. Who knows what kind of defenses she's built up over the years."

"So we're not going then." Jasmine checked with each of us for confirmation.

She didn't get it.

"No, we have to go," I said.

"If there's any chance of getting the book back, we have to try," Tori said, stroking Lalo's back.

I picked up the note from where Jasmine had dropped it, reviewing the details. "And the usual time is…"

"Sunset," Noemi said.

"Of course it is." Outside, the already pink sky cast a warm glow over the house.

Noemi picked at a piece of fluff leaking from the couch cushion. "It's just more convenient for all of us, you know? Isa's home from school. Lalo and I don't have to bundle up as much."

"You can go out in the sun?" I asked. It was a stupid realization. She worked outside the house. There had to be a safe way for her to get to and from the library. At some point, I was going to need her to sit down with me and explain which, if any, of the movies had gotten anything right about vampires.

"If I put on enough sunscreen. Wear a big hat. Long sleeves."

Jasmine's eyebrows pinched together.

This is where we find out what the League knows about other supernatural beings.

She didn't say anything, so I asked a follow-up. "You're not going to start steaming or turn to dust or something?"

Jasmine sat back down, leaning forward as if her academic future depended on understanding this lecture.

Noemi pushed the fluff back into the cushion, pinching it closed. When she released it, it popped back out again. "No. It's more like an allergy. Photosensitivity. Really bad sunburns. The doctors call it Erythropoietic Protoporphyria."

"But that's not it," Jasmine said. "You're a vampire."

"They don't know that."

Jasmine straightened at the confirmation.

To me, Noemi looked completely normal. Most mundanes would assume she had nothing to hide. *Still.* "You convinced a doctor you have both a sun allergy and sickle cell?"

She shrugged. "What else is it going to be? These are men of science. They're not going to consider supernatural causes when the symptoms line up so well with known natural ones, even if the odds are against them."

What did they say on that hospital show? *When you hear hoofbeats, look for horses, not zebras.* How many times had I depended on Occam's razor to keep me from spiraling into panic? *It's usually horses. But sometimes the animal has stripes.*

Noemi stood, straightening her blouse and running her hands down her jeans. "Anyway. Sunset works better for everybody."

The light from her window drew an orange line down the middle of the room, glinting off Lalo's fur. Time to go.

"Is there a plan?" Jasmine asked.

"What are you going to do about Lalo?" Tori stood, leaving the dog staring up at her.

Noemi addressed the dog. "He's going to stay here. I'll put him in his room with a water bowl."

He tilted his head, listening, but I couldn't tell how much he understood.

Noemi walked to the side table and lifted a shopping bag. She pulled out a couple of dog toys. "I picked up some of these chewy things. Hopefully, he won't wreck the furniture in there."

He continued watching her but didn't get up from the sunny spot on the rug.

"Have you been able to communicate with him at all?" I asked.

She pulled her eyes away from him with effort. "What do you mean?"

I gestured to the dog. "Like...he can't talk. But have you figured out a way to tell if he's still in control in there? Or is he all dog?"

Noemi's eyes watered but didn't change color. "I don't know."

"He's still in there," Jasmine insisted.

"Does he understand what happened to him?" Noemi asked.

Jasmine squinted at Lalo like he was out of focus. "He's listening. It's like...he knows something is wrong, but he can't fight his instincts. And his instincts are more dog than boy right now."

"What happens if we can't change him back? He goes all dog?" Tori asked. She looked like she might be good with that. Girl needed a pet of her own.

Jasmine threw up her hands. "How would I know?"

Noemi took a strengthening breath. How was she keeping it together? She'd probably been considering that possibility ever since she found him in this form. "Lily might know."

"Because she has the book, or because she's been around longer than we have? Do you think she's seen something like this before?" I asked.

"She's a green witch. She senses life. Maybe she can separate the boy threads from the dog ones." Noemi held out one of the chew toys for her nephew. "Come on, Lalo."

He jumped up and followed her down the hall to his room.

"Let's hold off on asking her for favors until we find out what she wants," Tori said as Noemi closed the bedroom door.

"Maybe there's something in the book," I said.

"Any chance she's going to admit she took it, much less let us see it?" Jasmine asked.

Noemi picked up the note from the couch and set it on the side table. "Maybe? It is book club, after all."

"So we're doing this?" Tori asked.

I watched the sky outside fade from orange to purple. "Let's go."

36

Lily lived in a bungalow like the rest of the houses on the street, but hers nearly disappeared behind a garden of wildflowers. They climbed the iron fence at the sidewalk, encircled the two oak trees in her small front yard, and trailed from baskets hanging in the archway of her porch. The bricks of the house had been painted white, but her front door and the fish scale shingles on her gabled dormer window were purple. The setting sun made everything glow.

"And she thinks people can't tell a witch lives here?" Jasmine asked.

"Not helping," Tori said.

"Maybe she's forgotten we accused her of stealing the grimoire and honestly just wants to go back to the way things were?" Noemi said, staring up at the door from the narrow path. Where Noemi's house had a cracking cement sidewalk, Lily's entry felt more like something carved out of a meadow over years of tracing her own steps.

"Maybe she feels guilty for stealing it, and she wants to apologize," I offered.

Tori put an arm around Noemi's shoulders. "Maybe she

already found the recipe for the elixir of life and wants to surprise you."

"Maybe she wants to sacrifice us to Hell for the continued bounty of her poison garden," grumbled Jasmine as Noemi reached her hand toward a purple-blue flower. "I wouldn't touch that if I were you."

Noemi pulled back her hand.

"She's not going to—wait. What do you see?" I stopped short behind Noemi, and Jasmine almost bumped into me.

Jasmine pointed to the flowers growing under Lily's wide bay window. "Does your coven not teach you herbalism? Basic garden safety? That's foxglove, monkshood, hellebore… and over there…that's belladonna."

Cool. Cool, cool. Remind me not to drink the tea.

Before we could discuss Lily's garden further, the front door swung inward. A mat on the floor inside read *Welcome*. Golden flickering light spilled out onto the shadowed porch and rolled down the white stone stairs.

"No turning back now," Tori said. One arm still around Noemi, she climbed up to the porch.

I turned to Jasmine. "If you see anything strange in there, I want you to tell me. Even if you think I can see it, too."

"Okay. Then you should probably know there's some kind of trip line across that doorway," she said, just as Tori and Noemi crossed into the house.

Nothing happened. I climbed the steps. I didn't see anything unusual about the doorway. "You're sure?"

She pointed at something I couldn't see, about a foot off the floor. "It's kind of like when Tori sets the wards at the dorm. I think it's an alarm system."

"But it's not meant to hurt us?"

Jasmine sighed. "It's witchcraft. I doubt it's there to help us."

But she lifted her foot and stepped over the invisible line, following the others.

Maiden, mother, and crone, what have we gotten ourselves into?

Lily's voice drifted through the house. "Welcome! Come in. Come in. Join us."

"Join us? Who else is here?" Tori whispered.

"Just this way. Yes, yes. Come along, now. We're waiting for you," came Lily's voice again.

We followed the sounds of soft conversation through the house, finding the layout very similar to Noemi's. But while Noemi kept her heavy curtains drawn, all of Lily's windows shimmered with nearly translucent shades. Rugs woven of natural fibers defined the edges of the living space and green leaves sprouted from every surface. Turning the corner into the kitchen, we faced a room that didn't exist at Noemi's: a three-season space with floor-to-ceiling screens and a tile floor. Giant planters in each corner held broad-leaved trees that brushed the ceiling. Smaller pots on an eclectic mix of plant stands dotted the room. A lattice of small cups bearing green herbs hung on the wall against the house. The furniture was woven from what looked like bamboo and covered in colorful pillows. In a bigger house, I would have called it the conservatory.

"Welcome to my home," said Lily, standing in the middle of it all with her arms raised. Her long dress brushed the tiles and a fringed shawl dripped from her elbows. A breeze drifted through the screens, carrying the scents of flowers and magic. The air tingled with untapped energy, lifting the hair on my arms.

Behind her, Isa and Emily sat on a wicker sofa, ignoring each other. Isa tapped on her phone without looking up, apparently as oblivious as her stepmother to the rising energy.

Emily stood as we came in, raising a glass of wine in place of her usual iced coffee cup in salute. "Hello again! So good to see you. I thought we might have scared you off. Who's your friend?"

"Umm…hey. This is Jasmine." I cleared my throat. "I didn't expect to see you…here…"

Emily smiled and sipped her wine. "I know, right? We brought the drama for book club last week, huh? But we decided to give it another go. The therapist really wants this to work out for us."

She sat back down and patted Isa's knee.

Without looking up from her phone, Isa said, "She promised to actually read the book this time."

Emily's shoulders rose in a show of embarrassment. "I will! I said I would, and I will. That's why we're here. We're picking the next book today, aren't we?"

Lily stepped back, folding herself into a large wicker egg chair that I'd mistaken for another plant frame. She gestured for us to join them in the sitting area. "Yes. That's it, exactly. After our last selection, I think something has become clear to all of us."

Noemi, Tori, Jasmine, and I found seats among the plants: a couple of stools, an armchair, and a loveseat that should never have fit into the space. Absolutely nothing had become clear to me, so I waited for Lily to elaborate. The others apparently felt the same.

Lily crossed her legs, pulling both feet under her skirt. "We need to go more in-depth with our study. Back to the basics."

Isa dropped her phone face down in her lap. "What study? I thought we were picking things we liked?"

Lily smiled. The expression of a teacher whose student has asked what the assignment is for the fourth time that day. "But why do we like them? The last four books have all had one thing in common."

"Romance?" suggested Emily. She stretched the vowels in an attempted French accent.

"Five-star reviews on Goodreads?" said Isa.

"Endorsements from talk show hosts?" Tori said, picking at a hole in her black jeans.

Jasmine's fingernails clicked against the wicker chair.

Lily shook her head, making the crystals dangling from her ears jingle. "Magic."

Noemi exchanged a look with Tori, who nodded in confirmation. "Oh, yeah…I guess they did."

"Wait, all of them?" Emily frowned. "What about Garden Spells? Wasn't that mostly family drama? I thought it was chick lit."

Isa groaned. "It's literally in the title, Emily."

"I thought that was metaphorical." Emily sipped her wine.

Isa shifted sideways to watch her more carefully. "Are you trying at all?"

The sconces on the wall lit automatically, bathing the room in simulated candlelight. Isa and Emily jumped, then covered their laughs. Jasmine's leg started to bounce.

"Ladies." Lily's hands rested on her knees, her large rings catching the light.

"Sorry," said Isa.

Lily straightened in her chair and looked at each of us in turn. "I think it's important for us to build our base knowledge of the subject if we're going to continue reading these types of books. It will make our discussions so much richer."

"You're giving us homework?" asked Isa.

"Not at all." Lily stepped from the chair in a fluid motion and rested her hand on a cloth draping the small table beside it. "In fact, I don't think this book should leave the meeting. But perhaps we could look at it together and see what we learn."

We all leaned forward as if drawn by invisible strings. Even Jasmine.

Lily smiled and then dragged the cloth off the table, letting it slide to the floor. Tiny dust motes sparkled in the candlelight, floating into the air before vanishing back into the shadows. Underneath, on a painted iron garden table, lay the book we'd been searching for all this time. Its dark purple binding looked like leather, but I knew the material came from a much rarer source. Gold threads picked out the shapes of arcane sigils on the cover, and a deep umber ribbon bookmark draped down from between the pages.

"Cooooool," Isa murmured, half rising from her seat. Her phone lay forgotten beside her.

My breath caught more audibly than I intended. Knowing Lily had stolen the book and seeing a powerful, ancient grimoire this close were two separate things. The symbols on the book were as familiar as my father's handwriting. For a second, I imagined them lifting off the cover, rotating in the air, three-dimensional, like origami. Like the folded papers on Thomas's coffee table. Waves. The branches of a tree. I blinked, and the floating shapes dissolved.

Tori gripped my hand. Was she seeing what I saw?

Jasmine's eyes darted between us, clearly attempting to honor her promise to tell me if she saw anything strange without alerting the others. We should have come up with a signal. Not that it mattered. Everyone in the room could tell this book was special.

Emily tilted her head, frowning. "What is it?"

Noemi stood so quickly her chair scraped the tile floor. "You said you didn't take it."

I told you so. But she hadn't wanted to believe it.

Lily stroked the book, tracing the wave symbol with one long finger. "It's a library book. I borrowed it."

The librarian's voice deepened. "You know that's not how this works. It's not in circulation." She stepped forward, reaching for it.

Lily stepped between Noemi and the book, crossing her arms with a flourish that set the fringe of her shawl fluttering. "I have it now, and I'm not ready to give it back. Fine me."

Noemi frowned, apparently caught between deference to her elder and dedication to her job. Only the darkness shadowing her eyes hinted at the real reason she wanted the book back so badly. "The library—"

Lily lowered her voice to barely above a whisper. "Would be disappointed to learn that you removed it from the building, wouldn't they?"

"Are you going to turn us in?" asked Tori, still clutching my fingers.

I didn't want her to lose her job now that she'd finally found a place where she felt safe and useful, but her employment did not top my current list of concerns. What did Lily intend to do with the book? Why finally admit that she had it? What did she need the rest of us for?

My curiosity warred with the instinct to grab it and run. A push in the back of my mind said *wait. You'll want to hear this.* I blinked it away but couldn't convince my legs to move. The pressure I'd felt in our first meeting returned.

The older woman turned in a half circle, addressing everyone in the room. "I don't see why any of us needs to be hostile. You want to study the book. I want to study the book. Why not make this the focus for a little group study? And then you can put it back before anyone notices. That was your plan anyway, wasn't it, mija?"

"Is that a real grimoire?" Isa stepped up to the table as if the book might bite her.

"It is. One of the oldest known collections of magic and its history. Would you like to see it?" Lily guided Isa closer. The whole scene had vibes of gingerbread and wood-burning ovens.

Noemi stepped closer, though I couldn't tell if she meant to protect Isa or the book.

"Wait. A real one? Like with spells and things?" Emily asked. She crossed her legs and leaned back into the couch. "You girls are taking this witch thing a little too seriously, don't you think? I mean, we are just reading these books for fun. Right?"

37

agic is all around us. In everything and everyone. I don't think you can take it too seriously," Lily said. The breeze caught a tendril of gray hair escaping from her braid. She closed her eyes to let the air wash over her. The energy tightened around her. I half-expected her to glow.

"Are you messing with me?" Emily squinted at her over her wine glass. Then her legs uncrossed, and her feet hit the floor, tapping hard on the tile. "I know what this is! This is an RPG. That's what they call it, right, honey? When they pretend like they're knights fighting dragons and whatever? It's like acting in a play they're making up. Improv. Roleplay, but not the sexy kind."

Isa spun around, her face red. "Em-i-ly!"

Lily's eyes fluttered open and in the split second it took for them to focus, I thought I saw something dark behind them. Something powerful.

"What? Is this what you want to do together? I can do this." Emily put her empty glass on the floor and threw one arm across her face. "Oh, no! Please, do not eat me, you evil witch! I am a princess and not meant for such an end!"

Tori laughed so hard she had to let go of my hand. Her fingers wound around the necklace at her throat, gripping the ankh like a security blanket.

Jasmine melted back into her chair, pulling her legs up and wrapping her arms around them. Of all of us, her response seemed the most appropriate.

"It's not a game," I said.

"What?" Emily dropped her arms. "Well, then, I don't get it. What are we doing here? That doesn't look like any kind of book club pick. Can you imagine Reese dragging that on stage? Oprah would never."

"No, she is correct. As are you." Lily smiled that syrupy smile again. "This is not a game, and it is unlike any of the other selections we've made. But if you will indulge an old woman, this book may change your life."

Notice how she didn't say for the better. *My life's been through kind of a lot of change lately. Enough unprecedented times. I could use some status quo, thank-you-very-much.*

"Can I touch it?" Isa asked. She looked like a kid at a carnival, about to have her first-ever pony ride.

Lily looked to Noemi, for once letting the librarian determine the fate of the book.

Noemi's mouth tightened in a firm line. But she nodded.

Isa ran the tips of her fingers along the edges of the book.

I waited for sparks to fly, an energy wave, some kind of magical response to her touch. There was no reason such things should happen. The grimoire had no reaction to Lily, and in my time walks, Tori and Noemi had both handled it without issue. But the energy in the room had risen when we entered, and I sensed tension building between all of the magic users present.

The teenager tucked her fingers around the edges of the cover and gently eased it back. Her hands shook. Everyone moved closer to get a better look at the pages inside, though

Jasmine kept me between her and the book.

"Is that Latin?" asked Emily.

"Some of it is." Tori pointed to a few lines surrounding an illustration of a rosemary bush.

Emily sighed. "I'm going to need more wine."

Lily's eyebrows dipped. "The bottle is in the kitchen, dear. Feel free to bring it back here."

"Bless you," Emily said, scooping up her glass and heading back into the house.

Isa frowned over the book, completely ignoring her stepmother's exit. "I'm taking Latin at school, but the letters are hard to read. Is this cursive?"

"It's script," Lily said. "This was how everything worth writing was written. Until everyone got a home computer and forgot how to form the letters."

She said it with such nostalgia that I wondered how old she really was. I grew up without the internet, but we still used word processors, and even my father's scribbles looked more like printed words than the elaborate script in this book.

The lettering reminded me of the grimoire in Queen's Creek, where I found the prophecy about the Gatekeepers. Not the same author, but a similar style, written around the same time. My brother Jonathan, the librarian back home, spent a lot of his time with our book. Adam, Thomas, and I hoped he could find something the ancestors recorded when they created the boundary. Anything to guide our study of Dad's work.

I reached past Isa without thinking. Would this book have the information we needed? Who wrote it, and what, if anything, did they know about the hidden communities that were now rejoining the world?

Lily blocked my hand with hers. "Before we all take our turns leaving our marks on the book, maybe we should discuss how we plan to use it."

If I could have grabbed it and blinked out of there, I would have. Lily wants to do magic in the presence of a mundane? *Let's go all in.*

She looked at Noemi again. "We should set some ground rules so that everyone is comfortable."

I doubted Noemi would be comfortable until the book was back in the library and her nephew was back in his original form. But she nodded again, agreeing to Lily's terms.

To the idea of setting terms, anyway.

The pressure in my mind intensified. Could the others feel it, too? That tension pressing against my will, telling me to be patient, to listen, to wait. The sensation didn't soothe the way Noemi's influence had. It was chains and commands instead of cotton and comfort.

We stepped back, each of us dragging our feet against the pull of the book.

"What did you have in mind?" Noemi asked.

Lily closed the book and replaced the cloth over it, shaking off the dust before settling it in place. "Oh, I think our needs may align quite well. I, too, would like to discover the recipe for the elixir of life."

Of course, she would. We should have known. Witches tended to live longer than average lives, but none of us were immortal. I didn't think. I'd have to ask Noemi more about the whole vegan vampire thing.

What unfinished business kept Lily from accepting her age? Was it just fear of death? Or did she have bigger plans?

"How did you know…" Tori asked.

"That you sought the elixir?" Lily arched an eyebrow. "For what other reason would you risk removing this from the security of the library? The wards on that building could keep out an army of hunters, but you brought it here."

Well, not here exactly.

Wait. The library is warded? It made a certain sense. Noemi and Tori couldn't be the first witches to find employment there. And this wasn't the only book of power in their collection.

Tori turned her head, silently imploring Noemi. Maybe she hadn't known about the library wards either.

Noemi avoided her eyes, twisting her hands in front of her. She looked up at Lily. "You understand why I did it, though. Don't you, Mama Lily? It wasn't for me."

Lily put a hand on her arm. "My dear one. You may tell yourself you did it for the child, but you did it for yourself as well. There is nothing wrong with acting in your own self-interest. You must be strong for him. And how can you be in your present condition?"

Noemi winced against the truth but didn't pull away. "Do you know what happened to him, Mama? Is there anything in the book to bring him back to us?"

Lily's hand slid up and down Noemi's arm. "There will be *time* for that."

She winked at me.

My stomach dropped. I hadn't used my Gift, although I should have frozen the room as soon as I saw the book. Why hadn't I? *The pressure. The little pushes. She's influencing us. She knows things she has no business knowing. And she has plans. How long had she been looking for the book before Noemi brought it out past the wards?*

Goosebumps rose on my skin despite the warmth of the evening.

Lily looked into Noemi's eyes. "Once we have the elixir of life—"

"I've got it!" Emily called, returning with her refilled glass in one hand and the wine bottle in her other. "Elixir of life for everyone of legal drinking age. Should I get more glasses?"

Noemi and I looked at each other.

"No, thanks," I said.

Jasmine raised her hand. "I'll take one."

Emily set her glass and the bottle on the shelf of one of Lily's plant stands. She wiggled a finger past each of us, starting with me. "None for the nerd, then. Sorry Isa, Tori, you're too young. Noe?"

Noemi shook her head.

"Lily?"

"I'll abstain tonight, but you go ahead. I believe you need one more glass." She looked at Jasmine as though she might taste delicious with gumdrop buttons.

"Be right back." Emily grinned and went back to the kitchen.

"Mama Lily, if there's anything you can do for Lalo…You know how much you mean to him…" Noemi tried again.

"We will come to that. But don't you think he's better off as he is until we have the elixir? What good would it do him to return him to a state of such…disability before we have the cure?" Lily said.

Isa sat back on the couch, a look of genuine concern on her face. "What's wrong with Lalo?"

"Nothing. Just some…health problems. He'll be fine," Noemi said.

Lily laughed. "Is that what you tell people? I think vampirism is a bit more than a health problem."

"Oooh, are we doing vampires now?" Emily returned with a wine glass for Jasmine and poured a heavy draught. "Is this going to be the sparkly kind or more…Nosferatu? Have you seen that new one on AMC? Where the vampire is a rock star? So hot."

"Emily! Shut up! You don't know what we're talking about," Isa said. She turned to Noemi, her eyes wide. "Are you really? And Lalo, too?"

Noemi couldn't backpedal fast enough. "What? No? What are you—she…"

I knew Lily wanted out of the closet, but I had no idea she intended to drag us all out with her.

"Sit down, dear. Gather your pride. The time for subterfuge has passed." A low vibration rippled out under her voice, carrying energy and intention. The push in my mind lost its subtlety.

Noemi sat.

The rest of us followed her lead.

Jasmine sniffed the wine Emily handed her.

"I think I missed something," Emily said. "Has the game started already?"

Isa smacked the cushions on either side of her. "Oh. My. God. Emily. Are you blind? This isn't some game. They're all witches!"

Jasmine raised her glass. "I'm not."

Emily sipped her wine. "Witches? Like…tarot and pagan gods and all that?"

My shoulders rose, and I turned up my hands. *You got me.*

"And I think Lalo's a vampire," Isa continued.

Emily choked. "Lalo? Noemi's nephew? The kid with the tablet addiction? You're saying that kid drinks blood? I couldn't get you to eat your greens at that age. At least he's getting his iron."

"This isn't a joke, Emily."

"Sure, hon. Alright. They're vampires." She lifted her glass to salute us.

Isa waved at us. "They're witches. Lalo's the only one who's a vampire."

"Well, that's not completely true. Is it, Noemi?" Lily said.

Emily crossed her legs and leaned forward. "Noemi, what is going on? I thought this was a book club. Have I accidentally joined some kind of cult?"

Noemi closed her eyes and took a deep breath. When she opened them, they glistened. "I'm sorry, Emily. I should have told you. It's just…this has been such a difficult year."

Emily looked around the room. She set her glass on the floor and held up her hands, pressing her back against the chair. "This is insane. You are all insane."

"Emily," Isa said.

"No, girl. Let her process," Jasmine said, setting her wine glass on the floor, undrunk. "This whole thing is insane. Doesn't make them not what they say they are, though."

Emily leaned toward her, cocking an eyebrow. "You're saying they're really witches?"

Jasmine nodded. "They are. And that one's a vampire."

She pointed at Noemi.

Emily pulled back. "And what are you?"

"Dance captain. Sisterhood chair. Business major." Jasmine's leg bounced as she spoke.

"Witch Hunter," Tori said.

Lily's tongue traced her lips. She released a long breath through her nose. *She already knew we brought a hunter into her home. And it doesn't scare her.*

A witch who didn't fear the hunters would have to be almost as insane as Emily believed us to be. Or more powerful than any witch I'd ever known. I bit my lip, unsure which scared me more.

Emily blinked. "I need to sit down."

"You are sitting, Emily." Isa tapped her stepmother's knee.

Emily rubbed her face. "This is not happening."

Lily ignored her and sank back into her egg chair, assuming the lotus position with a straight back and once more tucking her skirt over her legs. "It will take all of our skills to achieve what we desire."

"How do you know what we desire?" Tori asked.

"You desire what all women do," Lily said.

"And what's that?" I asked.

"Justice."

38

She's not wrong about that." Emily grinned, waving her wine glass in the air.

"Emily." Isa's eyes darted around the room. She gripped her phone in both hands, rubbing circles on the lock screen.

Who was she going to call? If a mundane who didn't know anything about the supernatural world suddenly knew four witches, a vampire and a witch hunter, who did she call first? A friend? The police?

Emily chuckled into her wine. "Don't think it never occurred to me to hex your mother. Maybe then she'd stop harassing your father."

"It's not..." Noemi started.

"Why didn't you tell me, Noe? Do you know how to make voodoo dolls? Oh! Should we put her in a jar? That's a thing you do, right? Put people in jars in the freezer?" She smiled at Isa. "I saw that on Instagram."

Isa jumped up. "Emily, are you serious right now? These people can do real magic."

"So can you," I said. Maybe I was a little defensive, but she looked ready to throw stones, and I wanted to remind her of her very glass house.

"What are you talking about? I'm not a witch." Isa's phone disappeared inside one of her bell sleeves. The fingers on her other hand poked through the lace trim.

Tori snickered. "The lady doth protest too much, methinks."

So, she has been going to class. English 203, at least. Probation suited her.

"I'm not!" Isa flapped her arms once, the sleeves trailing through the air.

"Let's just see, shall we?" Lily held out her hand.

Isa looked at it as if she expected it to sprout extra fingers. "See what?"

"Will you let me read your palm?" Lily asked.

"Why?"

"It's something I picked up in my travels. In India, they once believed you could read your whole life in your hand. Let's see what yours can tell us." Lily beckoned her closer.

"Oh, go on," Emily said, pushing her stepdaughter away from the couch. "It'll be fun. Like a gypsy fortune teller at a carnival."

"Emily. You can not say that."

"What?"

"Gypsy is offensive to the Roma people."

Emily ducked her head. "Oops. Sorry. Is someone here…"

She looked around, trying to identify Roma lineage in our faces.

"Oh, my god. Stop," Isa said. She strode to where Lily was sitting and offered her palm. "Here. Please. Before she says something else, and I have to move to another country out of sheer embarrassment."

The electric candles flickered.

Lily licked her lips. She took Isa's hand and turned her palm up. The witch's long finger traced the lines on the girl's hand. She peered more closely, frowning, and then threw Isa's hand back at her. "Disappointing."

"What?" Isa rubbed her palm with her thumb. "What's disappointing? What did you see?"

"Nothing," spat Lily. "Not a speck of talent. You have no Gift. You are no witch."

Isa's shoulders fell. "Didn't I say I wasn't?"

But she looked like she might cry.

"She can do magic," I said. "I've seen it."

Way to put the kid in danger, Cate. She almost had an out. She and Emily might have walked right out of there if they didn't have anything Lily wanted. Who knew what she had planned? She said she needed all of us, but she couldn't have meant them.

Then why were they here at all? The memory of girls passed out on the beach flashed behind my eyes. Would Lily use these mundanes the way Tori had?

"Explain yourself," Lily said.

Emily reached for the bottle and refilled her glass. At this rate, we might not have to worry about what she saw or heard. She wasn't going to remember it tomorrow anyway.

"It was probably nothing. I mean, if you didn't see anything in her palm, I must have made a mistake." *Definitely a mistake.*

"What did you mean, you've seen it?" Isa asked. "I've never done magic."

And, now, everyone's looking at me. Cool. Let's see where this goes. "When was the last time you charged your phone?"

Isa slid her thumb across the screen, unlocking it. "What?"

"Are you getting service right now? Because the signal is crap in this area. I always lose all my bars as soon as I come down from the L." The neighborhood had a higher-than-average magical energy level...probably because of all the magic being done in this house and the one across the street.

Are there others on this block? It would make sense. Adam once told me witches tended to gather, even subconsciously. That was how he'd ended up in the same apartment building as Tori's sister when he came to the city for his Wakening.

"Maybe my phone is just better than yours." Isa turned to her stepmom. "What plan are we on?"

"It's not your carrier," I said before Emily could answer.

Tori's eyes widened. She stood, pointing at Emily. "Oh! What if she's a carrier?"

"What?" Emily looked offended.

"Like, she's mundane, right? For sure."

Emily smacked her lips and grumbled something into the edge of her glass.

Isa smirked.

Tori continued. "But what if she's a carrier for the witch gene or whatever, and she passed it down to Isa? But like… it's latent or recessive or whatever, so her magic is hard to read."

"She's my stepmother," Isa said. "I didn't get anything from her."

"Ouch." Emily mumbled something about this being why they were in therapy.

"Anyway, there is no witch gene," I said.

Noemi shifted in her seat.

I tilted my head in her direction. "Wait. There isn't. Is there?"

She looked down at her hands. "We don't really know. There haven't been a lot of studies into why we can manipulate energy. Most people are more interested in how we do it. And in how to stop us from doing it."

Everyone looked at Jasmine this time.

She held up her hands. "Hey. No. I don't know. The League has scientists who…but I'm not. It's like she said. We're not meant to understand you. Just to stop you."

"We can discuss the logical fallacies in the hunters' ideology another time," Lily said. "At the moment, I'm more interested in why you believe this child has any measurable magical abilities."

"Nope." Emily stood so quickly that she had to put one hand to her head to steady herself. She set her nearly empty wine glass next to the bottle. "No, I think that's it for us. Isa, grab your bag. We'll find some other way to spend time together."

"What? We can't leave now. It just got interesting." Isa sat down, prepared to hold the space. "I want to hear more about why Cate thinks I can do magic."

Emily shouldered her tote bag. "There's no such thing as magic. I'm sorry, honey. I thought this would be a fun little bit of escapism, but these people are clearly—" She whispered the last word, "Crazy."

Jasmine snorted.

"Tell her," Isa said. "You're not making it up, are you?"

Maybe we could still get them out of this. "If she wants to leave right now…"

"Let her." Tori waved. "Bye-bye."

"Isa. Let's go." Emily took a step toward the door and banged her hip against a plant stand. The pot wobbled.

"Are you alright?" Noemi asked. "How are you getting home?"

"I'm fine," she said, but her words ran together. *Mmmmfinnn.*

How much wine had she drunk before we arrived? The bottle on the table had maybe a glass left in it. I didn't recognize the label, but the vines decorating it looked familiar. The same leaves twisted through the trellis on Lily's wall. The plant names Jasmine gave us outside all blended together. I nudged Tori and looked pointedly from her to the bottle.

"What? Ohhh." She sucked in her lips. "Hey, Lily. Is that a home blend? I've been wanting to try winemaking, but you know, underage. It'd break my probation."

Lily smiled. "It is."

Jasmine leaned over and tucked her full wine glass behind the leg of her chair. She wiped her fingers on her jeans.

Ignoring her reaction, Lily waved a hand in the direction of the tree in the corner of the room. "In fact, I grow the fruit right here. Next time you come over, I'll walk you through my process. The final product takes time to mature, but once it does, the flavor is…intoxicating."

Emily put the back of her hand to her head. "It really is. So delicious. But I think I might have had a teeny bit too much…"

She backed into the planter again, and this time, the pot overturned.

"Ohh!" Jasmine pulled her fist to her mouth, her knee bouncing in her seat.

Without thinking, I threw up my hands, intending to prevent both Emily and the plant from falling on the hard tile. The pot froze in midair.

Emily didn't.

She landed in a heap, hitting her knee and elbow hard. Noemi rushed to her side, shielding the hovering plant from view. Tori stepped around them and placed her hands on the ceramic planter. She caught my eye and nodded. When I released the energy, she shifted her weight to catch it and eased it back on the stand.

I blew out a breath.

Jasmine chewed her lip, apparently still uncomfortable with magical displays.

Isa stared at me. "That was awesome."

On the floor, Emily rolled off her knee and sat up. She rubbed the red marks and winced. "Not awesome."

Noemi put an arm around her and helped her up. "Let's go to the kitchen and get you some ice."

Emily's head bobbed, and she allowed her friend to lead her from the room.

When she was gone, Isa got up and moved to examine the planter. "That was so cool. How did you do that? Is there some kind of string…"

She waved her hands through the space around the plant.

"Thank you for protecting my plant," said Lily, apparently unconcerned about the fate of her mundane guest.

"What happened?" Tori stepped back from the plant stand so Isa could continue her investigation. She shoved her hands in her pockets and rocked back on the chunky heels of her boots. "I mean, Emily's not my favorite, but you didn't have to let her wipeout like that."

The hair on my arms stood up. "I don't know. I tried. The time bubble was supposed to enclose both of them."

"Magic is a sensitive thing, isn't it?" Lily said. "It will not respond to nonbelievers."

"I believe." How could I not, after what I'd seen and done?

"But Emily doesn't." Isa turned from the planter. "You heard her. She thinks it's some kind of hoax. A trick for page views."

Tori's eyebrows jumped. "You're saying our magic has no effect on people who don't believe?"

Curses aren't real. Not if you don't believe in them. Where had I learned that? I'd always known it. But my magic worked on the students in the theater when the drop fell and on the others studying in the library when I reversed time to erase Brian's confession. No way all of those people believed.

Lily chuckled. "Belief is such a fickle thing. So easy to poke a hole. To plant doubt. Isn't unbelief the same? Occasionally, just a spark of hope breaks through."

The leaves of the rescued plant shivered.

What hope allowed my magic to take effect on people who would never have admitted to believing in magic? Were the actors hoping not to die? And the students in the library… hoping for more time to study? And I just happened to be there helpfully granting their wishes?

The electric lights flickered again.

"Are you doing that?" I asked Isa.

"I can't," she said, but her eyes flicked from one sconce to the other.

Jasmine shifted in her seat. It only gained her an inch or two of distance from Isa. She glanced at the door but didn't get up.

Lily twisted the ring on her middle finger. "Even the atheist will pray for relief in times of darkness."

Tori smiled. "You're going to have to believe in yourself, kid. Just a little."

Isa frowned at her. "What can you do?"

"I can transfer energy." Tori looked around the room for a suitable demonstration.

"I've struggled with that one," Lily said, pointing to a small pot that sat against the screen on the far side of the room. "It refuses to respond to sunlight, doesn't absorb fresh water, and retains no nutrients from fertilizer."

A stubby brown stem poked out of the dirt. I couldn't tell what it was meant to be. It looked pretty dead.

Tori nodded. She lifted the small pot and set it beside the planter that had fallen. Huge waxy green leaves stuck out in all directions, apparently undamaged by the excitement. Tori brushed one leaf with a gentle finger. She pinched the brown stem of the smaller plant with her other hand. Her eyes drifted closed.

The effect took a moment to become visible, but soon, the leaf on the larger plant turned brown, crackling like dry paper in a fire. The stem of the smaller plant expanded, growing up and out, ever greener as it climbed out of the dirt. By the time the big leaf crumbled, a tiny green shoot branched out from the smaller stem.

Tori opened her eyes.

39

Thank you. I think that will do for now. You've given it a fresh start." Lily gestured for Tori to return the now-healthy plant to its spot by the screen.

As she stepped past Jasmine, the hunter pulled her legs up, avoiding any accidental brush with magic.

"That was amazing!" Isa hooked her fingers over the side of the larger planter, poking at the crumbled leaf dust. "You're actual, for real witches. This is so cool. Zaze is never going to believe it."

"It would be better if you didn't share this with him," Lily said. "He might not understand."

Isa kept talking, stepping away from the plant and getting out her phone. "Oh, he'll understand. Totally. You don't know him, but he's way into occult stuff. He's got this following online, who—"

"Cate, if you would…" Lily opened her hands wide, mimicking the move I'd done when the plant fell. Her eyes were still on Isa, whose fingers raced over the screen.

I stood and stepped toward the girl. Behind me, Jasmine nearly melted into her chair. The legs creaked as she pushed back.

"Hold on a sec," Tori said, reaching for the phone.

Isa spun a full circle, giggling as she danced away. "Seriously, you guys. I have to tell him. He'll be so jealous he isn't here right now. I wish I had that on video. Can you do it again? Oh, my god. Can I invite him over?"

The lights flickered with Isa's excitement. They buzzed, about to pop. What would it take for Isa to acknowledge her own power?

"Cate!" The old woman's voice refused any disobedience.

I froze the room. A reflex. A panic response that happened to align with the intentions of the pressure in my mind. Tension gripped my brain.

Sparks from the electric candles hung in the air. Isa stood in the middle of the indoor garden, half-turned, with her phone held above her head. Tori's immobilized body reached for it, towering over Isa. She'd have had it if I hadn't stopped time.

Behind me, Jasmine gasped.

I turned, keeping as much of my focus as I could on the time bubble. "What's wrong?"

She'd seen me use my Gift before. She hadn't reacted to Tori's demonstration beyond widened eyes and avoiding her legs. Sitting so far behind me had kept her from feeling the active energy I controlled.

"Everything alright, dear?" Lily folded her hands in her lap, thumb tracing the stone on one of her rings.

Why wasn't Lily frozen? The bubble in front of me encompassed most of the room. No air ruffled the fringe on Lily's shawl, though the breeze whispered its way through the screens behind me.

"That sigil," Jasmine said. "On her chair. It's not just basket weave."

"What?" The egg chair stood almost as tall as Tori, and elaborate shapes were woven into the backing. When Lily sat straight, she obscured a lot of it. But she'd leaned forward to get a better look at the frozen figures in the middle of the room. From Jasmine's angle, the whitewashed chair back must have stood out against the darkness outside.

Jasmine stepped beside me. "Look for yourself. Tell me I'm not seeing what I see."

Lily smiled. She leaned sideways in the chair, draping one arm along the edge and letting her legs fall from their bind. The intertwined branches behind her formed six overlapping circles.

A hexenfoil.

The sigil the hunters used to protect themselves from magic. The one they needed a witch to make.

"That's…why do you have that?" I asked.

"What, this old thing?" Lily laughed. "For protection, of course. Why does anyone keep a security system?"

"But that symbol is from the League," Jasmine said.

I swallowed hard. "Are you working with the witch hunters?"

Lily ran her hand along the twisting wood. "This symbol existed long before the witch hunters. They coopted it. Defiled it for their own purposes. But it is witchcraft, and it belongs to witches. We will take it back. We'll take back everything they stole from us."

Sounds great, but I'm not sure if any amount of rebranding is going to make me forget the fact that that sigil was used against us. If she wasn't working for the League, what made her think they'd give anything back willingly? She's not planning to ask nicely.

"Is that why you want the book? You think the elixir will protect you from the League?"

"It will do much more than that." Her voice deepened with each word.

Sweat formed at my hairline, the effort of holding the time

bubble starting to take a toll on my energy. "What, then? What is it that you want to do?"

"It's not what I want. It's what the world needs. Don't you see what's coming? Or haven't you looked that far into the future?" Disdain dripped from her lips, and her eyes darkened to black.

Not terrifying at all. And calling me out on my Gift? Okay, ouch. "I've been a little busy. My dad disappeared. My hometown almost imploded. We were attacked by hunters. Noemi's nephew is a dog…"

A rumbling laugh broke through her. "Insignificant irritants. I told you the world is changing. Magic will not be contained. It will flow through the world and over it. And we must be ready to control it."

"We must…?" *Happy to be included, just not sure what kind of cult I'm signing up for. Emily might have been right.*

She stepped out of the chair, pulling herself up to her full height. Even in bare feet, she rivaled Tori. "Witches are the rightful rulers of the magical world. Not these mundane pretenders."

"I'm not pretending anything. Told you I wasn't a witch," Jasmine muttered, keeping me between her and Lily.

The older witch stepped closer to Isa and Tori's frozen forms. She reached between them and plucked Isa's phone from her hands. I still didn't understand what Isa and her stepmother were doing here in the first place. I shook my hands, releasing the energy that held Isa and Tori. But the connection didn't break. The time bubble remained intact, still linked to me, pulling energy from my body. *Oh fun, a scary new problem.*

"Why did you invite them if you hate mundanes so much?" I asked, stalling while I tried to figure out what had gone wrong.

Lily's eyes cleared and her voice returned to its normal

pitch. "He needs them."

"Who? For what?" *My head.* I should have released the bubble immediately. Let Isa fight Lily for the phone. But something pushed me to maintain it. My arms grew heavier as the bubble drew energy.

Lily watched my struggle with mild interest. She dropped the phone into a tall vase. It made no noise as it struck the bottom. "His ways are not ours to know. But he will bring the change we have awaited for so long."

Oh, right. Him. An unknown figure of mysterious ways. I feel so much better.

"Is he here now?" Jasmine asked. "If he wants to do all that, maybe we should sit down and discuss—"

"Enough!" The voice came from Lily's throat, but it didn't belong to her. My head pounded with its echo. "There is nothing to discuss with you. Your line is tarnished."

"Excuse me?" Jasmine stepped out of my shadow.

I fought for breath, my chest tightening against the pull of the energy that maintained the time bubble. *Let go.*

Lily waved a dismissive hand. The voice that wasn't hers said, "You have a purpose to serve, but it will not require your approval or acceptance."

Jasmine planted her feet. "What in God's name—"

"Do not call Him here," the voice boomed.

Some of the smaller pots shivered with the vibration. My heart raced. I still couldn't let go. I may as well have been as frozen as Isa and Tori.

"What should we call you?" I asked. Because this definitely wasn't Lily. I wanted to see the man behind the curtain.

Her dark eyes glistened, all color leeched from the irises.

My skin broke out in fresh goosebumps, reacting to the rising energy in the room. Fresh sparks tingled at my fingertips.

"Hello? Hey, umm...is Isa here?" A young male voice

called from inside the house.

Jasmine looked at me. "Who's that?"

As if I knew. We were about to face off with whoever—whatever—had taken control of Lily's body. I had no idea if she'd given it over willingly or been possessed by some kind of malevolent spirit. I couldn't exactly turn my back on it (much less the time bubble that still held Isa and Tori) to go and greet an unexpected guest.

Someone knocked on the doorway to the conservatory. "Sorry. Is anyone home? The door was open…"

Shit.

Isa stood frozen in front of me, but she must have hit Send before I cast the bubble.

Her boyfriend had come to get her.

"Whoa! Whoa, hey, what the hell? What's going on in here?"

Jasmine disappeared behind me again, this time approaching what sounded like a very concerned young man. "Hey…you…you must be Zaze, right? Isa's told us so much about you. We're just finishing up things here. Nothing you want to see. Why don't you come with me to the kitchen and—"

"The hell, girl! We're not going to the kitchen." Some shuffling sounds implied his efforts to get around Jasmine.

Lily tucked away the scary voice and answered with her own. "Oh, let him in. I want to meet him anyway."

40

Lily blinked, her eyes returning to normal. She shrank a little, every inch the nonthreatening little old lady. She inhaled, and when she exhaled, the energy attaching me to the time bubble finally released.

I staggered backward. Tori's momentum carried her into Isa, and they fumbled to regain their balance.

"Ouch!"

"Hey, watch it!"

"What are you—"

"Where's my phone?"

The young man pushed past Jasmine, knocking me sideways in his rush to get to his girlfriend. Tori backed into a chair and sat, pulling her feet up to get out of his way. She held her head and blinked like she'd just gotten off a roller coaster.

The guy rested a hand on Isa's back, steadying her. "Isa? Are you alright?"

"Zaze?" She spun to face him, her short red dress twirling like a dancer's.

He clasped her shoulders in his hands, inspecting her for spell-related injuries.

Isa's boyfriend was shorter than me, maybe an inch over her. His pitch-black hair hung straight down, brushing the collar of his black canvas trench coat. Dark plaid pants were scrunched into combat boots with loose laces.

"She's fine," said Lily. "And you are?"

Isa bounced on her toes, bumping her nose against her boyfriend's. "Oh my god. How did you get here so fast? I just texted you. You're never going to believe it…"

He cupped her face in his hands. "Babe. What's going on in here? I walked in and you were…it looked like…"

"They're witches!" Isa announced.

Zaze pulled her closer, eying the rest of us over her shoulder. "What did you do to her?"

Lily smiled. "As I've said, Isa has not been harmed. Nor will she be. You, however, have entered my home uninvited."

"I invited him!" Isa said, pushing back from Zaze's chest. She straightened her dress and took his hand. "Zaze, I want you to meet my coven."

Zaze frowned, turning almost a full circle to see all of us, ending with his back against Isa's. "You're witches."

"Duh." Jasmine crossed her arms and dropped into the loveseat. "Tried to warn you."

Tori chewed her lip, looking back and forth between Jasmine and Zaze. I wondered if she was as nervous as I was about letting another stranger in on what was quickly becoming the worst-kept secret in the city.

Lily's eyes flicked black, then green. "Introduce yourself properly."

"Erm. Hi. I'm Azazel. People call me Zaze." He held out his hand to Lily.

But the old woman had ceded her body back to the owner of the frightening voice. She glared at Zaze with blackened eyes. "You dare claim that name? You are not him."

"What? Nah, man. I'm not…it's just a name, you know?

But it's way cooler than the one my mother gave me." He stopped speaking suddenly and stepped back, bumping Isa's shoulder. He seemed surprised to have said so much.

"And by what name does she know you?" the voice prodded. She pointed a long finger at his chest, and the nail grew like a claw. No, like a thorn.

Zaze shook his head.

Good for him. I wished I'd never told her mine. Fae weren't the only ones who found power in naming.

"You will tell me." Lily stepped toward him, but he stepped back again, dragging Isa with him. The candles flickered.

"Why do you need to know?" Isa asked. "Just call him Zaze. Everybody does."

Brave girl. Possibly stupid girl. Did she not feel the power emanating from the older woman? Where was the line between witch and mundane who can do magic?

Lily pushed forward, forcing them against the trellis. Her hair broke free of the thin braid that encircled it and unfurled down her back, a wild gray stream. "I will have your name."

Isa stepped in front of him. "What is your deal? I wanted to show him how awesome you are, and it's like you're trying to scare him on purpose."

The leaves along the trellis trembled, but I didn't feel a breeze. Zaze didn't notice.

Lily leaned forward, puckered her cracked lips and blew like she was putting out birthday candles. The electric candles in the sconces didn't respond, but the vines did. They stretched, reaching out from the trellis to embrace Zaze. They wrapped around the leather cuffs he wore on his wrists and over his legs.

"Holy Hell." Jasmine gripped the armrest, scrambling to get her feet back underneath her. Tori held out a hand, keeping Jasmine behind her. I called the energy for another time bubble, but none came.

"Tell me..." Lily whispered, and the vines wrapped around his throat. Her face took on a greenish tint, the veins in her neck and arms stood out as the skin shriveled around her bones. Every second brought her closer to embodying a fairytale witch.

I snapped my fingers, waiting for the sparks. My head throbbed. Whatever had held the bubble in place still controlled the energy in the room. I couldn't access it.

Zaze's eyes bulged and a tear ran down his cheek, marring the black eyeliner Emily hated so much.

"My name is Justin!" His voice sounded raw and dry.

"Thank you." Lily flicked her wrist, her nails flashing in the candlelight.

The vines retreated.

So did Zaze.

He nearly tripped over Isa in his hurry to escape.

"Hey! Wait!" she called, rushing after him. Before she reached the doorway, a vine wrapped around her ankle, and she fell to the ground.

In the distance, the front door slammed.

Isa rolled off her knees to sit facing the garden room. She pulled at the vine in vain. None of us was close enough to help her. Not without crossing Lily. And whoever shared her body. I'd never seen a real possession before, but several late-night bonding events sponsored by college RAs informed me that we were going to need a priest or some holy water or something in here.

I'd felt an otherworldly presence on the hill back in Queen's Creek when the veil was thin, and a shadow nearly swallowed the library when Elspeth and I studied the town's grimoire. This was darker. Scarier.

Lily stood still, watching the doorway as if there was any chance Zaze might return. When she was sure he was gone, she returned to her seat under the sigil.

Tori looked up at me, still curled up in the chair. "Did she just try to murder that kid?"

"See?" Jasmine said, advancing on Tori and waving at Lily. "That was an actual attempted murder. I hope you were paying attention."

I grabbed her arm. "Shut up!"

Lily sighed. Her eyes fluttered closed. Asleep or in meditation? How much energy did it take to host a demon?

If that's what it is. A malevolent spirit? An old god? If vampires existed, how many other urban legends might come true?

I fought the urge to follow Zaze out of there. *No sudden moves.*

"Isa? Honey? I think it's time for us to go home." Emily stepped back into the room, bracing herself on the doorframe with one hand.

"I really think you should lie down," Noemi said, coming in behind her.

Lily's eyes opened, still colorless. The air in the room swirled, lifting the branches of the trees and sending loose leaves dancing in circles. A pair of large iron doors that I had assumed were decorative swung shut behind Noemi, trapping us in the conservatory.

Noemi pushed against the doors. They rattled uselessly.

This might be a good time for some vampire super strength. So far, Noemi's monster side was less impressive than I might have hoped.

"Isa? What's going on?" Emily knelt beside her stepdaughter. The vine that wrapped Isa's ankle sprouted a secondary branch that caught Emily's wrist when she tried to free her. Emily shook it off, and it fell to the floor, no more animated than any other house plant. The vine around Isa's leg, however, clung tight.

On the next breath, Lily's coloring returned to normal. The dark shadows pulled back from her eyes, revealing soft brown irises. Her nails retreated to a more natural length. She wound her hair back into a bun and wrapped the narrow braid to secure it. "Please, take a seat. Stay a while longer. Book club isn't over yet."

"What are you doing? Who's controlling you? Do you even know?" I faced her with Jasmine beside me. Tori came to stand at my other side. Their presence strengthened me. I sensed my energy returning.

Lily smiled. She reached to the table beside her and slid the cloth-covered book into her lap as if it didn't weigh as much as a box of bowling balls. She pulled the cloth away and lifted the cover, turning to the table of contents. Her finger trailed a line down the list. "We haven't done what we came here to do. Let's discuss the book. I'm sure that you'll find it fascinating. So many useful spells. One recipe in particular might be of interest—"

"The hell are you talking about?" Jasmine interrupted. "You really going to sit there in your wicker throne and pretend you didn't just use some kind of dark magic to torture that guy?"

Tori stepped towards the older witch. "You've made some kind of pact, haven't you? A deal between you and another entity? It's not too late to break the connection. Let us help you."

Lily pulled her shawl tighter over her shoulders, balancing the book across her knees. "The only help I need from you, Salemite, is translation. Noemi told me about your work at the library. You've already begun to transcribe this book, haven't you?"

"There's a reason it was kept in the restricted section," Noemi said, stepping forward now that it was clear the doors would not open for her. "It's dangerous."

"Indeed," said Lily. "And I thank you for releasing it. Those library wards, preventing anyone but a librarian from accessing it…very powerful. I'd never have gotten my turn without you. If you help me, I'll share the elixir with you. I know why you want it. But if you oppose me, well. I don't actually need your help anymore."

She waved a hand and the wind pressed Noemi back against the door.

41

S top it!" Tori yelled. "She's your friend. You've protected her family for years. How can you turn on her now, when she needs you?"

Lily's fingers slid over the page, petting it like a familiar. "I do this so that I can go on protecting her. You wouldn't understand. So young. So naive. All of you. Babies. You don't know what it's like to grow old. To have everything that mattered slowly stripped away from you. Your government, your community, even your body betrays you."

Jasmine crossed her arms. "You allowed a demon to possess you because you can't get health insurance?"

"No one appreciates the crone stage," Lily muttered. "It should be my finest hour. The culmination of my life's work, mastery of my Gift, and a place of honor among my people. They should call me Matriarch. But I am left alone to rot."

The plants nearest her shivered, their leaves turning yellow and cracking along the edges.

"It's not true!" Noemi shouted, pulling against invisible restraints that kept her at the door. "Whatever entity you've accepted, it's lying to you. You've never been alone. You've always had us. Lalo and me."

"Then prove it," Lily said. "Help me. We'll make the elixir together. You know what it can do."

"What can it do?" Jasmine asked me, turning her head and threading her fingers under her curls. *Sidebar.*

Tori rolled her eyes. "It's called the elixir of life. What do you think it does?"

Lily rolled her head along her shoulders. "It will restore me to the full strength of my youth. It may undo the damage Noemi and her nephew suffered at the hands of those monsters and bring them back to their natural state."

Jasmine nodded. "Uh-huh. Okay. So you want to form a study group to make some kind of magic Botox that might also unvamp the librarian over here? That's your evil plan?"

"Maybe don't call the possessed witch who's holding us hostage evil to her face," I whispered.

"Umm, excuse me?" Emily called from her place on the floor. "Look, I don't want to interrupt this really impressive performance. But we didn't sign up for this. Isa and I were just looking for a nice neighborhood book club so we could sit around and talk—away from the stressors of school and work…this is all just a little much. You know what I mean? So if you could…do you have, like, some pruning shears or something? Your plant got a bit tangled around her leg. If you'll let me trim it back a bit, we'll be on our way."

"Damn, her denial's working overtime, huh?" Jasmine patted her hair.

Why do mundanes always work so hard to avoid seeing what lies right in front of them?

"You can let them go," I said. "What do you need them for, anyway? Like you said, they're mundane. How are they going to help you get the elixir?"

Lily's mouth moved, but the other voice answered my question. "There must be seven. Seven of wisdom, seven spirits, seven truths, seven cups."

"Cool. Umm. Okay. Good to know." *Feels a little more like a Seven of Swords moment—betrayal, deception, lies…but sure. Let's go with cups. Illusions. Choices.* This back-and-forth was getting on my nerves. I addressed the thing possessing Lily. "Hey, look, I get you don't want to tell us who you are. And I'm trying to respect your privacy or whatever. But you've got to give us something to work with here. What are we supposed to call you?"

"You do well to understand the power in naming. What is a spell but words of power said with intention? I will not give you mine. But you may call me Azazel. That boy was unworthy of such a name."

Isa whimpered.

"Is she talking about Zaze? When was he here?" Emily asked.

Her stepdaughter dropped her head to her knees, hugging them to her chest.

"I'm sure he's fine, honey. Lily would never hurt anyone." Noemi's voice wrapped around me. Warm, soft, and safe. My heart rate slowed, and air filled my lungs. When I exhaled, the muscles in my shoulders relaxed.

Everything's going to be fine.

I almost believed it.

"I'm glad you understand," Lily said. "I have no desire to harm you. What use would you be then?"

"That's not as comforting as you might think," Emily said. "You want to explain what's going on here?"

As Noemi's peace settled over me, my head cleared. I ignored Lily's response to Emily. It would be full of lies anyway. While she rambled about women supporting women, the damages of old age, and the hope she held for our book club as some kind of beacon of the feminine mystique, I considered our options. *It's amazing how much better your brain works when it's not flooded with panic.*

I closed my eyes. Something—probably Azazel—had blocked my energy before, but it was still there. If Lily could use it, so could I. I just needed to get past the barrier. A bypass to another source. The Gatehouse of my visions rose behind my eyes. Stepping through the door, I turned to face the sun streaming in through the far window. I soaked in the energy of my spirit home. When I looked back through the window that faced away from the community, the usual scene faded. Instead of the dense trees that surrounded Queen's Creek, I saw Lily's conservatory, all of us trapped, listening to the complaints of a woman in pain. A woman who would use her pain to destroy the world that caused it.

We had to get out of this room. Ideally, with the book. But Lily didn't seem likely to give us up until we'd helped her get what she wanted. What her body snatcher wanted too, I guessed. Probably something less wholesome than eternal health and well-being. It named itself after a demon, so I couldn't imagine its motivations were pure.

No magic we used against her (them?) would take effect while she sat under that sigil. So we needed to get her out of the chair without drawing her demon back to stop us. Or we needed a mundane escape plan.

She was a green witch. Her magic was probably aligned with the earth. She seemed to have significant control over her plants, but while they grew with unnatural strength and speed, they didn't seem to be independently sentient or anything. Still just plants.

But Azazel was stronger. He had telekinetic abilities capable of holding a teenage boy against the wall and squeezing the truth out of him. Powerful enough to throw Noemi across the room.

What did we have?

Tori's energy boosts.

Noemi's calming presence.

Isa's tech support.

My time management skills.

A witch hunter who could see magic.

And a mundane who denied its existence.

No plans immediately came to mind. And we couldn't exactly call a time out to discuss one.

Wait.

Nothing comes to mind.

Except when someone reached out. Like my brother, Caleb could.

I was no telepath, but Tori had once spoken in my mind. An energetic link of some kind back when she'd used the lives of sorority girls to power a spell on the beach. She'd been trying to call her sister back from beyond the veil but called down lightning instead. Could she draw enough strength from the energy in the garden to do it again?

And wasn't I basically the queen of timeouts? If I could form a bubble like the one I used for my chat with Jasmine at Brian's apartment, maybe Tori could create an energetic field of protection long enough for us to huddle up.

I stepped through the Gatehouse door, exiting my vision and settling back into my body. My skin tingled with renewed energy. Taking a deep breath, I reached for Tori's hand, where it lay on my shoulder, and squeezed. *Remember our connection at Noemi's.*

She squeezed back.

Going to need more than moral support here. I squeezed again, turning my head to make hopefully meaningful eye contact.

Her eyebrow quirked, but I didn't hear her thoughts in my head.

Come on. I squeezed her hand, raising my eyebrows and tilting my head to give her my ear. My ridiculous movements would have already drawn Lily's attention if she weren't so enamored of her own voice. The longer she spoke, the more I started to hear the reverberations of Azazel's voice underneath.

What are you doing, wacko? Tori's voice cut through my own thoughts.

Finally.

I visualized my idea for her. A time bubble encased in energy. A fortress of solitude. A cone of silence. Our own secret base within enemy territory.

You're crazy. She shook her head, smiling as she stepped in front of me.

"You got a better idea?" I said aloud. My fingers tingled as I called the energy I would need to create a bubble around most of the room.

If Lily noticed, she didn't show it. Or maybe she didn't consider me a threat.

"Nah. I like crazy." She winked over her shoulder. Sparks zipped between her fingers.

"Jasmine, stay close," I said, backing up closer to Isa, Emily, and Noemi.

Jasmine took one look at the energy forming around Tori and followed me.

"Where do you think you're going?" called Lily.

"We just need a minute," I said.

42

I pushed the energy from my fingers, blowing a bubble of time that enclosed most of the room. It pressed into the plants behind Isa and Emily and flattened against the door behind Noemi. Freed of the constraints of physics and separated from the force applied by Lily's magic, Noemi slid down the door and sat on the floor. She took several deep breaths, no doubt replacing the energy she'd expended in keeping everyone calm.

Tori's hands rose in front of her, drawing energy from the plants inside the bubble. She released it as an electric field in front of her. A shield of lightning between us and Lily. The energy expanded until it surrounded the bubble.

Outside, Lily glared at us. I wondered if she was more mad about the wilting plants or our refusal to obey orders she hadn't yet given. I'd never tested a time bubble against an outside attack, but I hoped it would hold.

"Okay, y'all. In theory, she saw the time bubble go up, but from the outside everything in here is frozen. No time is going to pass for us. When I drop the bubble, it will seem to her that it only lasted a few seconds, not long enough for her to react." My forehead warmed from the effort of maintaining the space. I took a breath, remembering the sense of calm Noemi had given me. No need to panic and burn up more energy on fear.

"What was in the wine?" Emily mumbled.

"It's not the wine, Emily." Isa pulled at the vine on her ankle, and it finally came free.

"Noemi, what happened when you tried to open the door?" I asked.

She stood, pressing her hand against it. "It repelled me. Like someone was pushing from the other side."

"Do you think she locked it?"

Noemi shook her head. "It doesn't have a lock. It's meant to be ornamental. She's holding it closed…he is. That thing inside her is holding it closed with magic."

Emily frowned. "There's no such thing as magic."

Tori shot me a look that said she understood where I was going. "You just keep believing that."

"What?"

I ignored her and spoke to Noemi. "It's very important that nobody panic right now."

Noemi looked from me to Emily. "Hey, Em? Come here for a minute, would you? I need some help to stand."

"Oh no! Are you okay?" Emily pulled herself, shaking, to her feet and stumbled to Noemi's aid. When she grasped Noemi's hand to help her up, Noemi whispered something to her. "What?"

Emily knelt beside her.

"It's your turn to rest now," Noemi said.

Emily sat on the floor, leaning against the door, and closed her eyes. She must have really been exhausted to let Noemi's magic soothe her. *She might have been right about that wine.*

"Thanks," I said.

Noemi pulled herself up and went to Isa. "Are you okay?"

"What did you do to Emily?" Isa stood with Noemi's help

and started toward the door, but Noemi held her arm.

"She's alright." A warm touch on my skin assured me that what Noemi said was true.

"Okay," Isa agreed. She looked around as if seeing the room for the first time. "How are we going to get out of here?"

"Emily's going to open the door for us," I said. "But we've got to distract Lily if we're going to get through it. Any ideas?"

Outside, the sun had set. The electric candles in the wall sconces cast more shadows than light across the space. From our perspective, none of it moved. The clouds stopped drifting across the sky. No breeze disturbed the plants along the porch screen. The candles didn't flicker. Lily remained seated in her woven chair.

"Can't you just freeze her?" Isa said, gesturing to the bubble in which we stood.

"Not while she's sitting in that chair."

"There's a sigil on it that stops magic," Jasmine explained.

"How do I get one of those?" Isa asked.

"You're not going to need it because you're going to use your own magic to help us escape," Tori said through gritted teeth. It sounded like maintaining our security blanket was taking as much out of her as holding the bubble drained from me.

"What do you think I can do?"

"Remember how I said you've got to believe in yourself? Now's the time. You're going to overload those electric candles." Tori released the energy from one arm and shook it out, quickly replacing it before the shield could drop.

"I'm what?"

"That could work," I said. "Do you think you could get them sparking enough to catch the chair?"

"You want me to set her chair on fire?"

"I mean, that would get her out of it," I said.

Jasmine shrugged. "And you know, if she doesn't get out of it, problem still solved."

Noemi's eyes went wide.

Thanks, Jasmine. Way to kick the killer rep. "She's going to get out of it."

"Why can't you do it?" Isa asked Tori.

Tori groaned, shifting her position to maintain the shield. "Kinda busy at the moment."

Sweat dripped from my hairline. "Look, you're not going to hurt anybody. You're just going to concentrate on those candles. Think about how great it would be if they were brighter. How warm and cozy the room would feel if they weren't made of glass. Think about the electricity that flows through them. Call it to you."

"You want me to call electricity?"

"Can she do that?" Noemi asked.

"Maybe? She's some kind of techno mage. Mundane magic? I don't know how it works. If anybody else has a better idea, speak now because we're running out of time." My head throbbed in agreement.

"What are we going to do after I set her chair on fire? Isn't that just going to piss her off?" Isa asked.

A reasonable concern. "Hopefully, Noemi's going to get her to chill out long enough for me to freeze her."

"And then we grab the book and run like Hermes," Tori said.

"You mean, run like hell?" Jasmine snarked.

"Nah, Hel's not known for her speed."

Noemi crossed herself. "May we never meet her."

"Everybody ready?" My neck cracked when I tried to look around me. All of the muscles above my ribcage tensed from the pressure of holding time in place.

Affirmative noises responded.

"Who's gonna tell her the plan?" Jasmine gestured at the unconscious mundane on whom our entire escape depended.

I chewed my lip. "You are."

"What?"

"I'm sorry. Did you have something better to do than protect the only true mundane in this room? Isn't that your whole life's work?" Tori said.

"Jasmine, you've got to time this right. Wait until Tori drops the shield before you wake her. Then get her up and get her to open the door. Try to keep her back to us. We can't risk her seeing something that'll break through that wall of denial. The door might open after I freeze her, but if it doesn't…Emily's the only one who doesn't believe Lily can keep us here." *This is insane. I sound insane.*

"This is nuts. You know that, right?" Jasmine shook her head but knelt beside Emily.

Magic isn't logical. It's intuitive.

I dropped the bubble.

Tori's shield dissolved. She stepped back and put a hand on my shoulder.

I hoped the shuffling sound behind me meant Jasmine was doing her part.

"Well," said Lily, as if our sidebar had never happened. "I suppose I could give you one minute. How do you intend to use it?"

Stall. Tori's voice whispered in my head again.

How long would Isa need? We basically asked her to master a Gift she hadn't known she had and use it against a witch with decades—centuries?—more experience.

I sighed. "Can we just talk? Like, just as women and witches who want the same thing?"

"Do we?" she asked.

You said we did. How much of what the demon said and did was she aware of? Did they communicate inside her head? "I think we do. We just want to feel safe again. Don't you? Things have changed so quickly recently. It's been hard to keep up. Hard to prepare for the next challenge. But you've seen this all before, haven't you? This can't have been the first time a community like mine—"

"Not the first. Not the second. But every time we push forward, every time we make just a little headway, they push us back. I don't intend to go back this time." Lily scooted forward to the edge of her seat.

Just a little farther.

Did I imagine the lights warming as we talked?

"How will you stop them?" I asked. "How will you protect yourself from the witch hunters and the scions of the accusers? There are so many more of them than I ever thought there could be."

Maybe don't draw attention to Jasmine right now? Tori's voice said in the back of my mind.

Shit. Sorry.

Lily crossed her legs, bracing her elbow on the book that still lay in her lap and gesturing with the opposite hand. A wave of the obvious. "The same way that I always have. By being stronger. Smarter. Better than they are. You know it's true."

"Is there more in the book than the elixir?" I asked, stepping closer. "Something to guide us and keep us safe?"

"More things in heaven and earth, child." She snickered.

Tiny sparks like fireflies hovered just beyond my peripheral vision. *Keep going, Isa.*

"Will you show me? I'd love to learn. Noemi told me you've been such a wonderful mentor..." I stepped closer, with Tori still right behind me. Just out of reach of the book, I held out my hands.

Something popped, and the lights went out. Sparks sputtered and flew from the sconces, catching on the wooden trellis against the wall. Blue flames erupted from the electric candles. More sparks broke off, fluttering and dying in the air before they reached the across the garden.

"What is this? What are you doing?" Lily stood, gripping the heavy book to her chest.

Now, Cate! Tori screamed in my mind.

My hands had already flown up in front of me, but my energy lagged. Too much used up in the team meeting. Tori's hand on my shoulder warmed as she fed energy into me to fill the deficit. Around us, the plants wilted, flowers dropping over the sides of the pots. Leaves shriveled and cracked. My heart raced. The energy flowed from the plants through Tori into my spell. Sparks flew from my fingers as I set a new intention.

Stop.

She froze in place like a statue. Lily's hands clutched the book. No ring-twisting, hand-waving, long-fingered direction this time. She had only her eyes to manifest her wishes.

They turned black.

Could I hold a demon in place? I had no idea how strong Lily's new friend might be. Tori increased the energy. My head buzzed with it, unable to keep up. The excess energy made every nerve in my body come to agonizing ecstatic life. It couldn't last. I'd burn myself out.

In front of me, Lily's arm reached out, her nails extending into claws. Her face hollowed out as the demon took over, gaining speed as it fought against my Gift.

"Run!" I yelled.

43

We left Lily and her body's new driver behind us, racing from the garden of dried-out plants as sparks lit their corpses and caught fire. Stumbling through the bungalow, we called out to each other, grabbing arms, shoulders, and waists as we made sharp turns and tripped over oddly placed furniture. We slammed into the front door so hard it fell against the side of the front stoop, ripped from its hinges. We didn't stop until we collapsed in Noemi's front room, ducking below the bay window as she reinforced the protective wards.

In his bedroom, Lalo growled and scratched at the door.

I lay panting on the hardwood, my eyes closed. The reflections of the fires we'd left behind burned after images into my eyelids. Had Lily gotten out? Would her demon protect her?

Would she come after us?

In the distance, sirens rang out.

Around me, the others checked for injuries in mumbled whispers.

I peeked above the window sill. Across the street, smoke rose from the back of Lily's house. It almost looked like chimney smoke, except that another plume appeared when the wind shifted. Then another. Then orange flames dotted the roofline.

A firetruck careened down the street, bringing curious neighbors to their porches and front yards. A firefighter jumped down from the truck, holding his hands out in front of him to remind people to stay back, but none of them stepped beyond their own gates.

"I don't think we can stay here," I said.

After minimal discussion and a little bit of scrambling, we made our way out the back door, leading Lalo on a makeshift leash.

"He was never going to use that jump rope anyway," Noemi said.

Spending some time in his room had apparently given the puppy time to think. He became much calmer once we let him out and assured him that despite all the noise of our arrival, we were not enemy invaders. Maybe the little boy was still in there after all. As we walked through the alley behind his house, he stopped to sniff a few things but managed to mostly stay close to his aunt.

We convinced the first bus driver that Lalo was a service animal, and she let us board. He lay down quietly at Noemi's feet, all but invisible to most of the passengers. The next driver was less accommodating.

"Has to fit in a carrier," he insisted. "No room for an animal like that."

"But we just got off a bus, and he was fine," Isa argued. "He'll be really good. Promise. You won't even know he's there."

"I'll know." The guy reached for the lever that closed the door.

Tori nudged Noemi, "Tell this guy to relax. It's all good."

"No dogs." The driver pulled the door closed and the bus

left us behind.

"Hex it all, Noemi!" Tori turned on her friend. "Why didn't you whammy him so we could get a ride?"

Noemi shook her head. "He was already calm. We were never going to change his mind."

Emily pulled up a CTA map on her phone. "There's an L stop two blocks that way."

She held it up for us to see.

"That's a purple line," Tori said, scrunching up her nose. "We need red."

By the time we climbed down from the train station closest to the magic shop, we'd run out of energy for panic or planning. We trudged down the sidewalk in silence.

The bell over the door tinkled to herald our arrival. Six times. Six and a half, really, if you factored in the chimes that shook when Noemi maneuvered Lalo into the building.

"Come on in, please, and stop playing with the door," Thomas called from the back of the shop. "Are you trying to bring back Tinker Bell or arm a whole fleet of angels?"

"Thomas, do you have any customers right now?" I called.

He stuck his head out from between a couple of bookshelves. "Cate?"

"Is there anyone else in the shop?" I asked.

"Not just now, but I'm sure—"

I flipped the sign in the window and threw the lock on the door. "Set your wards, please."

My brother walked directly to the door, pulled a piece of chalk from above the door frame, and drew a couple of sigils on the metal. Replacing the chalk, he turned. "What's going on?"

"Can we talk upstairs? We really need to sit down."

He sucked in his lips, taking in my ragtag entourage. "Yup. Let's go. This way, ladies…"

Thomas held the beaded curtain aside while we climbed

the stairs. Lalo sniffed the beads, jumping back when they swung against his nose. Noemi whispered reassurances, petting the top of his head and giving a gentle tug on the jump rope leash. I led the others up to Thomas's apartment.

I'd just reached the top when he called out, "Oh! Hey, you should know—"

"Cate!" Adam stood up from the futon, dropping a handful of papers.

I stopped short, nearly causing a pileup in the stairwell. "Umm, hi. I thought…Thomas said…I thought you went back at the Creek."

"I was going to, but…after what you told Thomas about Brian…"

"Brian?" Jasmine pushed past me.

Adam stepped to the side, revealing my former friend and coworker seated on the futon.

My brain struggled to accept the unexpected appearance of two guys I'd last seen separately walking away from me waiting in my brother's apartment. I watched dumbly as Jasmine threw herself on the floor in front of Brian, putting her hands on his knees and looking up at him with tears in her eyes. "Baby, I'm so sorry I missed your call. There's so much I want to tell you. To explain…but then they came—"

She pointed at Tori and me, still at the entrance to the apartment. Emily and Isa stepped in behind us, Noemi, Lalo, and Thomas making slower headway on the stairs as Lalo snuffled the corners all the way up.

"And they dragged me to this book club where this possessed witch tried to kill us with her plants, and—"

"Whoa!" Brian put his hands on her arms. "Whoa, slow down. Witch did what?"

"We're okay," I said, despite all indications otherwise. "I just…there's a lot. I need a minute."

I braced myself against the back of Thomas's recliner.

"I need tea." Tori strode into Thomas's kitchen, pulled the kettle from the cabinet and set it in the sink to fill.

"Oh, God, yes. Anything with caffeine." Emily sighed. She pulled one of Thomas's stools out of the way and stood across the counter from Tori like she was ordering from a bar. Isa followed, her eyes darting around the room, landing briefly on Thomas's goddess statues, the mortar and pestle on the counter, the candles and crystals in his altar on the bookshelf.

"Here we go. Come right on in," Thomas said, guiding Noemi and Lalo the last few steps.

"Nice dog," Adam said. He crouched, holding out a hand for Lalo.

Noemi hesitated.

"It's alright," I said. "Nobody here is going to hurt him."

She untied the jump rope, allowing Lalo to explore on his own. He sniffed the floor, turned a circle and approached Adam.

The former Guardian waited, still as a statue, until the dog bumped his hand with his nose. "Good dog."

Lalo stepped closer, allowing Adam to scratch between his ears. The dog turned his head, looking up at him.

Adam's fingers stilled. "What's…who are you, then?"

He looked up at Noemi. "He's not himself, is he? What happened?"

She looked at me.

"Long story," I said. "Noemi, this is Adam. You can trust him. He used to be the Guardian of our community. And that's my brother, Thomas, who brought us upstairs."

Thomas saluted on his way to help Tori in the kitchen.

Worlds collide. I'd never have imagined these people in the same room. Basically, the entire spectrum of magical abilities represented. What was the protocol for this? You were supposed to start with the highest rank, right? Or the eldest? *I should just make them all stand in a circle.*

I felt Adam's eyes on me. He'd been so angry when he'd left, but now he just seemed sad. Resigned, maybe. I couldn't take the expression on his face. Even if I hadn't meant to cause it. I cleared my throat. "Adam, you've met Tori—"

She waved, her back to the room as she pulled mugs down from the cabinet. Adam nodded.

"And this is Emily and Isa…"

"From the café," Brian said. "Hey, Isa, is this your mom?"

Isa side-eyed Emily's stance, leaning her elbow on the counter, one hip popped to the side. "That's my stepmother."

"You can call me Em," she said with a smile.

Isa gagged.

Brian coughed to cover the teen's disgust.

Jasmine backed up against the futon and leaned against his legs.

"And that's Brian," I told Noemi, unsure how else to define him. Very unsure we could trust him or his girlfriend despite our new common enemy.

"Everybody, this is Noemi and her nephew, Lalo."

"Hi." Noemi's hands twisted around the jump rope.

"Nephew?" Adam stopped petting the dog, causing Lalo to jump up to lick his face.

"Lalo, get down!" Noemi hissed.

"So." Thomas clapped his hands. "Full house, huh? No, no. It's great. Like a party. Timing could be better…"

"I'm sorry to disrupt your very busy work day with our life-threatening emergency," I said.

"Maybe you should sit down," Adam said, still examining Lalo like he expected him to talk.

"Yes," Thomas said, pressing his hands into the kitchen counter. "Everyone find a seat. Get comfortable. I have a feeling we have a lot to catch up on."

Lalo sat, show dog style, in front of Adam.

"Good boy," Adam said.

As it turned out, Thomas's apartment was not quite furnished enough to provide seats for such a crowd. Tori and I gave Noemi the recliner and went out on Thomas's fire escape to drag in the folding lawn chairs he'd been using as deck seating. My brother disappeared into his room, returning with an oversized bean bag chair. By the time we'd all found seats, Lalo had fallen asleep on the floor at Adam's feet and Emily had gone back to scrolling her phone. Isa looked like she might pass out. Blowing up those candles took a lot of energy for a new magic user.

"So, y'all look like you've had a day," Thomas said after throwing himself into the beanbag and shifting it around to his liking.

"Okay, so you remember we told you the book went missing?" Tori started.

44

Time passed quickly as we took turns explaining everything from Lalo's unexpected dog form to Lily's new guest.

"Wait, wait, wait..." Brian said. "So this lady's possessed?"

"I think so. Has the League ever dealt with something like that?"

Brian and Jasmine looked at each other.

"There are stories," Jasmine said. "But they're in the history lessons. It's not like we're getting Exorcism 101."

Tori sipped her tea. "Nah, 'cause that kind of training would be useful."

Jasmine pulled herself up straight. "I just want to remind you that it wasn't the hunter who set that house on fire."

Adam jumped. "You set a house on fire?!"

Isa raised a hand, keeping it close to her chest. "That was me, actually."

Brian shifted in his seat so that he faced me directly. "Why didn't you, you know..."

I'm going to need people to stop trying to do impressions of my Gift. "It didn't work on her."

Jasmine patted his knee to draw his attention back. "She had a hexenfoil. The witch. It was woven into her chair."

"Was she from the League?" Brian asked.

Tori laughed. "No way. You should hear the way that woman talks about mundanes. Or about men, for that matter. Zero chance she's aligned herself with a bunch of dudes who made it their life's mission to control powerful women."

Jasmine started to argue. "That's not what—"

"Girl, look at you." Tori sniffed. "Sitting at his feet."

I could see what she was saying. The optics weren't great, but…"Brian's not—"

"You don't know what you're talking about," Jasmine said, but she stood up.

"Are you sure you do?" Tori asked. "What have you been hiding from in my room if the League is so great? Wesson's locked up—"

"Actually—"

They all looked at me.

I bit my lip, not sure how much of the vision I'd seen at Brian's was my story to tell.

Brian sighed, leaning his head on his hand. Thomas may have talked him into helping us, but it didn't look like he'd completely forgiven Jasmine.

Jasmine pursed her lips.

I turned up my hands. *You can tell them, or I will.*

"Daniel's not incarcerated," she said.

Thomas straightened. "What?"

Adam turned to Tori. "I thought your parents…took care of him."

His eyes darted to Jasmine.

Tori pulled out her phone and started scrolling her messages. "I thought so, too."

"Like the League would let that happen," Jasmine said, turning to Brian for support.

Brian rubbed his face. "Wesson is one of their best. They would have sent someone after him."

"Excuse me a minute." Tori took her phone to the fire escape.

"You better hope her parents are okay," Thomas said.

Jasmine crossed her arms and stared at her feet.

One by one, we all let our eyes drift to the glass door separating Tori from us. She stood at the rail, one foot propped on the bottom guard. Her head dipped in a nod, and she dropped her phone into her back pocket. Her shoulders rose and fell in a heavy sigh. She came back inside, acknowledging our attention with a wave.

"Are they…" I almost didn't want to know.

"They're alive," Tori said. "Banged up and bruised. Mom has a broken arm."

A collective wave of relief circled the room.

"But she's right. He's out there." Tori glared at Jasmine from across the room. "Someday, we're going to have a talk about how and when you knew that."

Jasmine met her eyes. "I'm sorry. I didn't—"

Tori brought down her fist on Thomas's bookcase. "What? You didn't mean for anyone to get hurt? Because you absolutely did."

Jasmine flinched. "I didn't know you…"

"That shouldn't matter! Goddess, they really screwed you up." Tori shook her head. "It shouldn't matter whether or not you know somebody. *Thou shalt not kill*! Isn't that what your book says?"

Thomas held up a hand from the beanbag chair. "It also says *Thou shalt not suffer a witch to live*, so maybe—"

"Is he going to come for you?" I asked Jasmine.

"I don't know," she whispered.

"Do you want him to?" Tori crossed her arms and leaned back against the wall.

At first, Jasmine didn't answer. When she looked up, her eyes were wet. "He was everything I had, alright? The League isn't some kind of country club. They don't have mixers to introduce the next generation. I had Daniel and no one else. Until I came to school."

No wonder she pledged Kappa. Joined the dance team. She was lonely.

"That's what happens when you join a cult," Tori said.

Jasmine looked like she wanted to slap her, but she was too far away.

Brian held up a hand, blocking Jasmine as much as warning Tori. "Hey, can you not? She's been through—"

I'd said the same thing, but I was done making excuses. For any of us. "We've all been through it, Brian. But if we don't do something, we're not all going to come out the other side."

Brian took a beat. He looked out the window to the fire escape. "Look, I'm not saying we aren't on your side here. We fully endorse Team Save the World From the Evil Witch, okay? But this is a little bigger than anything we've ever faced before, and y'all aren't exactly making it easier for us."

"You think any of this is easy for us?" Tori walked closer and put her hands on the back of the futon. "You want us to trust you, but you're a direct descendent of the people who killed our ancestors, and she's an active member of the group who's still carrying out their plans! It's systemic genocide, and you both are answerable for it."

"Oh, shit," Thomas mumbled.

Isa's eyes flicked from one person to another, absorbing everything we said as if there'd be a test later. Her mother was oblivious. As usual.

Adam rubbed a hand over his chin.

When Brian spoke, his voice was low. "You really want to talk about whose ancestors murdered whose?"

Tori's cheeks pinked, embarrassment flooding her pale skin.

Adam's face was an apology. "I'm not saying we shouldn't all be doing the work. But is this really the time for it? We're not going to dismantle—"

"When is the time?" Jasmine shifted her weight away from the group.

I put my hands up.

Everyone turned.

My face burned. "No. It's not like that. I'm not…This is an important conversation. We shouldn't rush it."

Jasmine huffed. "Gee, it's too bad we don't know anybody who can stop the clock for us. Or do we only get timeouts when you need them?"

I rubbed my head. The dull ache that followed me from Lily's house spread along my hairline, wrapping all the way across my forehead, down behind my ears, and across the base of my skull. "I can't. I'm sorry. Just. Not right now. I don't have the energy…"

Jasmine looked down at Brian. "She doesn't have the energy."

He looked from her to me and back. "We can wait…"

"I hate waiting." Jasmine stormed to the back door and stepped out onto the empty fire escape. Her back to us, she gripped the railing and stared out into the alley.

"Jasmine—" Brian followed her, sliding the glass door closed behind him.

"That's going to be a fun conversation," Thomas said.

"Goddess, bless it, Thomas," I said. "Just shut up."

"We can't pretend that there aren't things about each of us that make us dangerous to each other," Adam said. "But we also can't let our own fears stop us from doing what's right. From protecting each other and anyone else who can't protect themselves."

"Not everybody wants to be protected," I said.

He dropped his head.

I sighed. "But maybe we can keep from making it harder for them to protect themselves."

"How do we do that?" Isa asked.

"We start by correcting our own mistakes," Tori said. "The pain we caused. The trouble we started. And by not making any new ones. If we can help it."

"Is that one of Nora's lines?" Maybe our advisor should have gotten her degree in psychology instead of theater.

Tori shrugged. "She's not wrong."

Thomas rubbed his hands together. The movement attracted the dog, who lifted his head from Adam's foot and wagged his tail. Adam reached down to scratch his ear.

"So," Thomas said, "which one of our mistakes should we tackle first?"

Noemi rocked forward in the recliner. "Mama Lily has the grimoire. The elixir of life isn't the only powerful spell in that book. We have to get it back before she decides she wants more than health and longevity. That voice is whispering in her ear."

Noemi's voice cracked, and she covered her mouth, shaking.

Isa nudged Emily's phone. The blond blinked. Maybe she was still coming out of the effects of Lily's wine. But she was lucid enough to see her friend near tears. She slid down from the bar stool and went to Noemi's side, sitting on the wide arm of the chair and rubbing Noemi's back.

Noemi wiped her eyes. "I'm telling you, she wasn't like this before. She was kind. She helped me when Lalo first came to live with me. She brought him gifts from her travels."

What else did she pick up on her travels? Who else?

Adam leaned back in the futon. "Do you think she survived?"

No one answered right away.

I looked at Noemi. "I hope so."

Tori cocked an eyebrow.

I took a breath. "Because otherwise, that book is probably ash by now."

Thomas leaned back in his beanbag and crossed his arms under his head, staring at the ceiling. "Tell us more about this book. Did it have any distinguishing features?"

He knows something. Or he thinks he does. I recognized the performative nonchalance. He was waiting for confirmation before he got excited.

"Only Tori and Noemi ever got a good look at it." I turned to Tori. "You did the translations. What did you find?"

Tori twisted her ankh on its chain. "So, there's definitely something there. Most of the beginning is just the usual stuff: records of births and marriages, plots for an herb garden, a planting schedule aligned with the moon. Journal entries about rituals and poetry for spellcasting. Then, it gets into basic potions and curatives. But the second half is different. Written in Latin like the rest, but with some kind of code laid over it. Literally two layers of writing on top of each other. Symbols that might have been sigils or wards. I was working on the key when…anyway, I was close."

Adam and Thomas exchanged a look. They both sat up. Thomas leaned towards Tori. "What did they look like?"

"The sigils?" Tori said. "Umm…different things. But two kept repeating. Like a tree. And some wavy lines. Water, maybe?"

"I knew it!" Thomas shot up from the floor and shuffled through the papers that had covered his coffee table for weeks.

Adam pulled a clipboard from the pile and flipped the pages. Notes in his own handwriting. He held it out to Tori. "Did it say anything about the Ichoriad?"

She grabbed the clipboard from him.

Noemi's eyes widened.

"Wasn't that what you said your book was?" I said. "The book that held the recipe for the elixir was called the Ichoriad."

She nodded.

Thomas shoved some papers into Tori's hands. The folded sheets with the sigils Dad had drawn.

"They're the same," she said, laying them down in front of her and shifting from the sigils to the clipboard. "These are the sigils in the book, but this…is this right?"

She pointed to something in Adam's notes.

He clasped his hands together, leaning his elbows on his knees. Hanging on her next word. "You tell me."

"What?" I asked.

"It's what we thought," Tori said to Noemi.

"Are you sure?" Noemi got up from her chair to look over Tori's shoulder. Emily slid off the arm into the recliner.

"What is it?" Isa asked. She joined us, kneeling on the floor by the coffee table and lifting a few of the papers.

"The Ichoriad," Tori said. "The text that holds the secrets of the elixir of life. It's not just one book. It's two."

45

There are two potentially life-altering, world-changing books out there?" I asked.

"More than two…Eat, Pray Love changed my life…" mumbled Emily. "What a funny book club."

I lowered my voice in case we needed to preserve Emily's mundane immunity to magic for later. "There are two books that hold the magical secret recipe to eternal life?"

Noemi nodded, holding the papers with the tree sigil on them. "The elixir was too dangerous to put it all in one place. The ancestors separated the ingredients from the instructions. You can't make it unless you have both."

"So, which do we have?" I asked.

Tori put the papers down. "Our book explains what the elixir is for and why it might be dangerous, but doesn't give the instructions for making it. I think we have the ingredient list, but it's behind all that code."

Isa pulled the pages Tori dropped closer to her. "Does it say how to find the other book? Maybe you need both of them to unlock the code."

The glass door to the fire escape slid open.

"Any chance it's still in the library?" I asked Noemi.

"Ooh, another field trip?" Jasmine smiled, but it didn't feel as enthusiastic as when we'd left Tori's dorm.

"I don't think it's going to be there," Adam said. "If they went to the trouble of separating them…wouldn't they want to keep them apart?"

Isa's eyes widened. "It could be anywhere."

"A quest," said Jasmine. "Even better than a field trip."

"But where do we start?" Tori put her hands on her hips, glowering at the pile of papers spilling over onto the floor.

"I still think we should start with the library. Maybe there's a clue in one of the other books from the collection where you found this one," I said.

"Tori and I could maybe each bring one of you into the restricted section," Noemi said. "We'll say you have special approval for a grant or something. But if we try to walk this whole crowd in there, it's going to raise some eyebrows."

"Y'all go on without me." Thomas stood up, stretching. "Searching the library catalog doesn't seem like a team sport anyway."

"Thomas, this is important," I said.

He held up a hand. "And I get that. I do. But I've got the shop to think of. It's one thing to close up for an extra long lunch, but there are appointments in the afternoon. My regulars have expectations."

"Your priorities—"

"Look, somebody has to stay behind. Library Vampire said so, right? You're not going to take the dog, and I don't know what you did to your mundane friend, but she doesn't look ready for action…"

Emily punctuated his argument with a snore.

"Is she going to be okay?" Isa squinted at her stepmother and tapped her toe against Emily's foot. Emily pulled her leg back but stayed asleep in the chair.

"Maybe we should put her feet up and let her sleep it off,"

Tori said. "Lily definitely spiked the wine, but if she'd meant to kill her, she'd be dead by now."

"Not comforting," I said.

"Wasn't meant to be." Tori shrugged. "Sorry, kid, but that garden room was full of stuff that could knock her out for a while. No way to tell what she went with. But that tea I gave her should help balance things out."

"Umm…thanks?" Isa said.

"Okay, so Emily and Lalo will stay here. Thomas will check in on them…" I waited for him to nod his consent.

He glanced at the clock on the microwave. "Yeah, sure. Of course. But I've got to get downstairs. Mrs. Jones is coming in for her reading any minute."

"Mrs. Jones?" asked Adam.

Thomas held up his hands as he backed toward the stairs. "Look, she pays in cash, and I don't have to log it for the Holloways. She's the one who gets to ask questions, not me."

He ducked down the stairs, and a minute later, the bell rang at the shop door.

"How do you want to split the party, Cate?" Brian asked. "We have two books to bring back here."

The prospect of going back to Lily's or sending any of the others there tied my stomach in knots. But we had to get the grimoire away from her, and we needed it for our own purposes. We needed Noemi and Tori to go to the library. Isa's emerging Gift could help us search the digital catalog, in case the missing book had been entered into the system. It would be a safer mission than sending her back to the bungalow, and she'd already thrown the fuses. There might not be much more for her to do there. That left Adam, Brian, Jasmine, and me to face the angry crone.

I wasn't ready. It hadn't been a lie when I told Jasmine my energy was sapped.

Adam stood, straightening his jacket. "It's alright. You

don't have to come with us."

"You're sure?" I could argue my usefulness, my determination to take the more dangerous mission. Test the limits of my spirit palace and see if it had anything left to give. But maybe I'd let him protect me this time. I didn't want to go back there. *Goddess, Jasmine was right about me. Such a hypocrite.*

Adam closed his eyes, dipping his head in a short nod. I imagined him back in his wolf mask, accepting my role as Gatekeeper.

"Please be safe," I said, uselessly. "We don't even know if she's still at the house. The firefighters—"

"We can handle the first responders," Jasmine said.

Of course.

"But can you handle Lily?" Tori asked.

"I guess we'll see," said Brian. As a scion, he had more knowledge of magic than most mundanes. But he hadn't trained as a hunter, so I wasn't sure how prepared he'd be when he needed to defend himself.

"Don't worry about us," Adam said. "Focus on finding the other one. Who knows what kind of wards they've got in the library. There might be dragons."

A joke intended to lighten the mood. Make me forget he was walking into another burning building for me. My stomach twisted.

He winked.

Jasmine rolled her eyes. "There's no such thing as dragons. God, for a witch, you really don't know very much about the supernatural, do you?"

Brian smirked.

I raised my eyebrows, seeking confirmation from the academic.

He shook his head. *Nah, no dragons.* Then he looked up at the ceiling, considering. He raised his shoulders, pulling down the corners of his mouth, the living embodiment of the IDK emoji.

If it turns out that dragons are real…

Noemi knelt in front of Lalo and tried to explain why he needed to stay there and watch over Miss Emily while she slept. The puppy licked her hand and sniffed behind her ear when she hugged him goodbye.

Tori turned to Isa. "Alright, if anybody asks, you're my shadow. A potential student checking out the college for next year."

"Are shadows allowed in the restricted section?" Isa asked.

They are in Queen's Creek. Well, not allowed exactly, but they certainly held the space. Last time I'd been in the library back home, Jonathan pulled down our grimoire for me. As I studied it, a shadow crossed the veil between our world and the next and slowly flooded the entire space, swallowing everything in its path. Elspeth and I barely escaped. According to Jonathan, sending it back where it came from had required the coven elders to call a quorum and knit the punctured veil back together.

"Let's just hope nobody asks that question," Tori said.

We all walked to the L station together but had to split up once we arrived. Adam, Brian and Jasmine would take the train north, then catch the two buses to the suburbs. The rest of us headed downtown to the library.

On the train, we crowded into the last row, where two sets of seats faced each other. One was busted, so Noemi stood in the aisle, holding the bar on the back of my seat. The first three stops rolled by. As the train pulled away from the fourth, Isa broke the silence.

"What does the elixir of life do, exactly?"

I raised my head from a half-doze. Maybe the library would have coffee. *Focus. She asked about the elixir, not your caffeine addiction.* "It grants the drinker immortality."

Isa's eyes flicked up to Noemi. She lowered her voice just above the rumble of the train. "Aren't vampires already immortal?"

I deferred to Tori, who'd been friends with a vampire longer than I'd known they existed.

"Not exactly," Tori said. "They're dead."

Isa frowned. "So the elixir could make them live again? Like a human?"

"Maybe?" Tori picked at her black nails. She glanced up at Noemi and sighed. "We're talking about a recipe that's older than this country. I don't know if we can even find the ingredients anymore."

Isa thought for a minute. I could almost see the light bulb explode above her head when the idea came to her. "Time Travel shopping trip!"

After my utter failure to turn back the time in Noemi's house without backtracking my entire trip, I didn't hold out much hope for a plan that involved time hopping by decades or centuries. Maybe, if I were still connected to the time stream back home, I could ride it up and down the timeline, but here? Unlikely at best.

"I don't know," I said.

Isa pursed her lips. "But what about the kid?"

Tori raised an eyebrow. "He's not dead. Or dying."

"He's a dog," Isa said, in case we'd forgotten.

"It's temporary." Tori flicked the polish off her thumb, revealing a purple-stained nail with ragged edges.

Isa scooted forward on her seat, gripping the plastic under her legs. "Sure, but for how long? He's a dog, and they don't have as long a lifespan as we do. What if it takes us ten years to turn him back?"

Tori looked up as if she hadn't considered that particular consequence. To be fair, it hadn't occurred to me either.

I chewed my lip. "Once we find the recipe, we'll get the

ingredients. Extra ingredients. We're going to need to make enough for two."

Tori nodded. For a moment, we all stared into space.

Find the recipe. Get the ingredients. It was two-step process, but it could never be that simple.

"So he drinks the elixir and then what?" Isa asked. "He's the world's first immortal dog?"

46

The library was the most beautiful building I'd ever seen. Belle would have cried. The granite facade reached out the full length of the block and up four stories with the arched windows of a cathedral. The style changed a little on each floor, growing more intricate and complex on the way up to the copper cornices along the roofline.

Noemi led us in through the triple-arched main entrance and past the grand staircase to a smaller door set deep into the wall. She swiped her key card, and we followed her down the narrow hallway. The reading room at the end of the hall glowed with natural light from the large windows on that side of the building. A couple of cataloguers sat at tables with books piled in front of them.

"This way," Noemi called.

I hadn't realized I'd stopped, gawking at the rows of books in this gorgeous space.

At the end of the room, she keyed us into another doorway. This one led downstairs to the basement. Another card swipe at the bottom, and we were in the restricted section.

It was nothing like I'd expected.

The basement space, unlike the architectural marvels upstairs, had been thoroughly modernized with a drop ceiling and fluorescent lights. A high-tread carpet deadened our footsteps as we crossed to a bank of computers.

"Where are the books?" Isa asked.

Same, girl.

"The next room is climate-controlled. Before we go in there, we need to get a better idea of where to look, or we could be searching for hours," Noemi said.

"Won't it just be…like…next to where you found the other one?" Isa asked. "I mean, it's basically a sequel, right?"

"That's just it," Tori said. "The other one wasn't where it should have been. It just turned up one day in the reading room. It wasn't listed with the other books that came in from the estate."

"So, how are we going to find it?" I asked. "This place is huge. We can't just wander around and ask to see what people are reading."

"No, we can't do that," Noemi agreed. "But I thought maybe Isa could help us out with this one."

"But I've never been here before. How would I…" Isa trailed off, wandering around the space.

Noemi looked at me. "What you told us about how her magic worked at the café. You said she could pull things up in the system that weren't on the menu. What if she can do the same thing here?"

"You want her to call the book up in the digital catalog?" I asked. "But weren't you still processing the collection? Would it even show up?"

"It shouldn't," said Tori. "But that's exactly why it might. If she's the one who calls it."

"I think I've got it," Isa called from across the room.

"Already?" Tori smiled and went to look over Isa's shoulder.

Noemi and I followed.

"What search criteria did you use?" Noemi asked.

Isa chewed her lip. "Umm, I said *Magic Book of Spells Elixir of Life.*"

"Makes sense," Noemi said. "What did it give you?"

"Well, there are a few things here that are definitely not right." She scrolled through the list, showing us. "They're like, spelling lists, I guess? You know, those old grammar books they used to give kids to teach them to read or whatever? But like, really, really old. Grandma's grandma's homework."

"Don't bury the lede, kid." Tori put her hand over Isa's on the mouse, making the list scroll faster.

"Wait, wait! You're going to go too far." Isa shook Tori's hand away. "I think it's this one."

She highlighted an entry labeled *Book of Magical Charms - 17th Century - Ashley Grimoire.*

"That does look promising," I said.

"Where is it shelved?" asked Tori.

"See, that's the problem," said Isa. "It isn't here."

I peered around her to get a better look at the listing. "Where is it?"

"It's at another library." She drew her finger across the screen to another column. "See? Right here. It says QC in the library code. And I tried to request a transfer, but it says it's not eligible. You have to go to that library to read it."

"It's in the reference stacks," Noemi said. "Just like this one. We weren't supposed to take ours out either."

"What's QC?" Isa mumbled to herself. She tapped a few keys, bringing up a different database. "Hold on, I can look up the address."

"You don't have to." Tori leaned on the computer desk, crossing her arms. Glaring at me. "We know where it is."

"I didn't know." I held up my hands. "How could I? We

didn't even know this book existed—"

"We didn't know," Tori agreed. "But we didn't grow up in a gated community that apparently hoarded the magical world's most valuable resources."

"We did not hoard—"

"I guess I just imagined the massive wave of power that exploded out of there when you finally opened the Gate. You don't think energy like that would have been a useful resource for the rest of us living out here without the benefit of a border guard?"

"Girls, can we not…" Noemi watched the door, but we were still alone.

"Seriously, Cate," Tori continued. "What else are you hiding back there?"

"What's going on?" Isa turned away from the computer. "What's QC?"

"Queen's Creek," I said. "The book we need is in the library in my hometown."

"But that's great!" Isa said. "Call them up. Tell them to—"

"They don't have phones."

"What?"

"There was this boundary…It blocked everything. No satellites. No cell service. So nobody has phones."

"But the boundary is down now," Tori said.

"And a lot's changed. But it's only been since Spring Break. Plus, my brother's never really been interested in anything outside the Creek."

Isa frowned. "But he lives here."

"No. Not Thomas. My brother, Jonathan, is the librarian in Queen's Creek. He can get us in, but we're going to have to go there. I don't have any way to reach him."

The computer behind Isa dinged.

"What's that?"

Isa scanned the popup. "It's a response to my request for

the interlibrary loan. I don't know, I think your brother has been doing some updates. He's online."

"What?"

"Says he's sorry. The book I've requested is not available. Please call this number for more information." Isa held out her hand. "I need a phone."

Whose number was that? When did...what? I should have kept better contact with my family back home. I spent so much time reacting to the ways we'd affected the world outside, and I never stopped to consider how the world affected Queen's Creek.

I gave her my phone, and she typed in the number.

Isa put the call on speaker. It rang three times.

"Hello? Queen's Creek Community Library. Jonathan speaking." My brother's voice sounded so close. I couldn't believe he had service.

"Can I?" I held out my hand for the phone, but as soon as Isa let it go, the connection dropped.

Ding. Ding. Ding. We're sorry, the call cannot be completed as dialed. We're sorry...

"Shit. Call him back," I pushed my phone back into Isa's hand.

She hit redial.

My brother answered immediately. "Hello? Is anyone there?"

"Jonathan? It's Cate."

"Hey! I didn't recognize the number. What do you think of this, Kitty? Just had a couple of phone lines put in. They've been installing power lines all week. They go right out to the substation on Waller Mill Rd. We're still not getting many calls—"

"That's, that's great. Umm...actually the reason I called..."

"Sorry. Yeah. You called me. From outside the Creek. This is so cool. What's up?"

"There's a lot to explain, but I need you to trust me."

"Always."

"I'm looking for a book. I think Dad might have been looking for it too. For his research on the elixir."

"I know. Matthew and Gabe have been in here a lot. We're all trying, Cate. But I haven't found anything like what he was researching."

"I think it might be warded. We just pulled it up in the digital catalog, but it's saying unavailable."

"Oh, wait. Was that you with the transfer request? I just got that system up and running yesterday. It shouldn't be accessible. I haven't had time to update the catalog. I don't know what that book is or why your system would say it's here. We haven't entered anything yet. Our catalog is still on cards."

"Could you check the cards?"

A drawer creaked and the sound of cards shuffling interrupted Jonathan's response. "I'm doing it now, but I'm not seeing anything for an Ashley grimoire. And sorry, but Book of Magical Charms is pretty vague for our collection. That could be anything."

Noemi leaned in. "It would be 17th century. Maybe associated with the Ichoriad."

The shuffling sound stopped. "Who's that?"

"Sorry. Jonathan, I'm working with some friends here. That was Noemi. She's a librarian, too."

"Ah. Wonderful. Lovely to meet you. But sorry, no. I'm not seeing anything like that between 1500 and 1700. Are you sure of the provenance? Does someone else possibly have custody?"

I looked at Isa.

She tapped into the catalog again. "It definitely says it's there."

"I don't want to question your system, but I've got a friend here who's pulled it up in the library catalog, and she's kind of got a Gift for these things."

"A Gift for catalogs?"

"Sort of. It's a long story. But I don't think she's wrong."

"I can check the stacks, but nothing's turning up in the cards. Sorry, Cate. I'll let you know if I find it."

"Thanks."

"Take care of yourself, okay?"

"You too."

Isa gave me the phone back. "I'm telling you, that book is in his library."

"He's going to look for it," I said.

"Meanwhile," Tori said. "What are we going to do?"

I pulled my phone out of my back pocket and texted a quick check-in to Adam. He and Thomas were the only ones I trusted to blink us back to Queen's Creek. But first, we needed an update on the Lily situation. His answer took longer than it should have. Waiting for the three little dots to resolve into his response, I said, "I think we're going to have to have another book club meeting."

47

According to Adam, the bungalow survived the fire, with the damage mostly contained to the back of the house. No first responders remained on site when they arrived. The neighbors had gone back to minding their own business. Adam, Brian, and Jasmine found a spot at the park down the street to watch the house for signs of its occupant. The recon phase of their mission hadn't turned up any immediate red flags, but neither had they made any solid plans for action. So far, they'd managed to keep a low profile, although Adam thought a nanny had her eye on them from the playground.

I texted: We're on our way. Don't act suspicious.

Adam: Doing our best.

When we arrived, Adam, Jasmine, and Brian sat around a stone table with a built-in chess board, playing some kind of card game.

"Who's winning?" I asked.

"I think she is." Adam tilted his head to indicate a young woman waiting for a small child at the bottom of the slide. We definitely had more of her attention than the kid did.

"You think she's with the League?" I asked Jasmine.

Jasmine looked past her cards. "Not sure. Like I told you, they keep us pretty separated. It's supposed to be for our safety. Can't give someone up if you don't know who they are."

"How comforting," said Tori.

"What did you find out?" I asked Brian, who had his back to the babysitter and had the best view of the house.

He rearranged the cards in his hand. "Pretty sure she's in there. Heard some stuff slamming around inside. Some cursing in three or four different languages."

"Grandma is well-traveled," Jasmine said.

"What about the other voice?" I asked.

Jasmine shook her head. "Not sure what the demon's up to, but I don't think he's helping her with the cleanup."

"Any ideas on how to keep him out of it when we go in?" I asked.

"Are we going back in?" Isa fidgeted with her skirt.

"We can't let her keep the book," Adam said.

"Do you really think she's going to use it for something awful?" Noemi asked. "She said she just wanted the elixir for her health. Maybe—"

Jasmine scoffed. "There's no way the demon she summoned is going to be content with acting as a health insurance adjuster. She promised it something."

"Are we sure it's a demon, though? I mean…"

Tori shook her head. "I don't know what it is, but if it walks like a demon and talks like a demon…"

"I'm comfortable using that label until we get more information," Brian said, laying down a card.

Six of spades. Corresponding to the Six of Swords. A transition. Leaving something behind. As far as I knew, Brian didn't practice divination, but I'd been taught to read playing cards in place of tarot years ago. You never knew what you would have available.

"Whatever it is, I think we need to get moving if we're going to stop it," I said.

They dropped their cards on the table, and Adam swept them up.

The nanny lifted the kid into his stroller and fastened the straps. She pushed him in the opposite direction. Either we'd become less interesting now that we weren't staying, or she'd gathered as much intel as she needed.

"What's the plan?" Adam asked as we walked down the sidewalk.

"Maybe we can talk to her," Noemi said, stopping at the edge of Lily's garden path. "She said she wanted to study the book together, right?"

"That was before she tried to strangle Isa's boyfriend," Tori said.

"I'm just...she's always been good to us. I don't want her to get hurt because she made a mistake. There's something really wrong with her."

"Yeah. There's something wrong with her, for sure. She's possessed," Isa said. "I'm not saying that she's asking for whatever comes to her, but I've never seen a movie where the possessed person didn't have to invite the demon in. She did this to herself."

"There are a lot of things the media gets wrong," Noemi said.

"Don't vampires also have to be invited in?" Jasmine said.

Noemi sighed. "Doesn't everybody? I mean, it's just good manners."

"So, you could go in if you wanted to?" Brian asked.

"She came in with us before," Tori said.

Jasmine frowned. "But didn't Lily invite us? She sent over a note and anyway, when we got there, she called out from the back..."

"We were already inside when she called out," I said.

"Are you sure?" Jasmine said.

"I think so."

"She has a mat," Noemi said.

Isa looked at her. "What?"

"There was a welcome mat inside the door. Once the door opened, and I could see it…that's an invitation. Even if she hadn't sent the note first."

"So, if she's moved the mat," Adam asked. "Are you going to be stuck outside?"

"I don't know. I've never tested it."

"Never?"

"It's not polite!"

"Good lord," Jasmine muttered. "We have a vampire on our side, but she might not be able to help us fight the demon because she was raised right."

"I think we might be past manners at this point," Tori said. "Even if she is an elder."

At the other end of the path, the front door opened. Lily stood in the doorway, adjusting her shawl over her shoulders. She looked up, feigning surprise at the crowd standing at the end of her walk. It seemed like she was faking it, anyway. Her reaction was a fraction too slow, and I thought I caught a mischievous smile between her startled expression and the welcoming one she settled into.

"Well, hello, you all. Back again? And you've brought new friends this time. Lovely. Won't you come in? I was just going out, but my errands can wait." She backed into the house, leaving the door open. Her voice trailing behind her. "Come in. Come in."

"Said the spider to the fly," Tori mumbled.

"So, I guess we don't have to worry about the invite," said Brian.

"This is too easy. There's no way she's just going to hand us the book and let us walk out of there," Jasmine said.

"But what if she does?" Noemi asked.

Everybody stared at her.

She sighed. "Yeah. I hear myself. I'm sorry. Can we just not have murdering my godmother be our first plan of action?"

"I think we can agree to that," Adam said. He looked at each of us in turn. "We don't strike first. Agreed?"

"Agreed," I said.

Brian and Isa nodded.

Jasmine and Tori hesitated.

Great time for them to start seeing things the same way.

"Guys. Come on," I said. "*No Murder* should be a pretty easy rule to abide by."

Tori looked back at the house. "But what if—"

"Fine." Jasmine dug a toe into the dirt of Lily's yard.

Brian looked up at the house. "So if violence is off the table, what's our plan? Cate freezes the house, and we just walk in and take it?"

I shook my head. "Last time I tried to freeze her, the demon fought it. I don't know if it will work again. She'll be expecting it."

"Then we'll have to distract her," Adam said.

"Can we go in now?" Isa rubbed her arms. "It's getting cold. And I think it's going to rain."

The wind had kicked up while we debated the use of lethal force, and it was starting to become one of those days where the Windy City earned its name. Low clouds hung in the sky as the temperature shifted. Shadows danced along the path to Lily's porch, and the wildflowers leaned in.

"This is…not natural," Adam said. He bent to the ground, laying his hand flat in the dirt.

"What is it?" Brian asked.

"The energy is rising," Adam said. He looked at me. "Don't you feel it?"

I turned my face up to the darkening sky and closed my

eyes, reaching out with my other senses. It felt familiar, this disturbance.

Thunder rolled in the distance.

"Get inside!" I yelled, just as a passing cloud that should have coasted right past us stopped and poured down sheets of rain.

We ran for the porch, slipping on the wet stones. Lightning lit the sky in a way the hidden sun could not. The smell of ozone burned my nose. We scrambled up the stone steps to get under the overhang that protected Lily's front door.

The sky cleared immediately.

"I said, 'Come in,' didn't I?" Lily called from down the hall, chuckling.

"Oh, we are so dead." Isa hugged herself, staring across the street, where the homes looked completely dry.

Jasmine peeked through the door and turned back. "Yeah, I'm not going back in there."

"Okay," Brian said, his hand on her back. "Maybe we can wait out here. We'll be lookouts."

"Look out for what?" Tori said. "The book is in there. The scary witch who stole it is in there. There's nothing to look out for out here."

Jasmine held up both hands. "I can't. I'm not doing it. I'm sorry."

She stepped down from the porch.

The ivy that ran along the foundation stretched across her path. It wound around her ankle and up her leg. She cried out as she fell into a bed of thorn bushes that almost definitely hadn't been big enough to hold her when we first climbed the stairs.

"Jasmine!" Brian jumped from the porch to help her, but another vine twisted around his arm.

"Stay here," Adam said before stepping down. As soon as

his feet touched the earth, the plants attacked him, too. Adam took a breath, grounding himself. He knelt to the ground again. This time, placing both hands in the dirt.

"Get out of there!" I yelled, watching flowers overtake him.

Noemi pulled me back before I could step off the porch. "He's got this. It's okay."

The soil in front of Adam started to churn, pulling the ivy under. The leaves disappeared under the rolling earth as if tilled by a plow. I remembered the way he'd lifted the ground to catch me when I'd fallen back in Queen's Creek. His affinity with the earth sometimes had more practical uses than sensing what lay beneath the surface of things.

The plants loosened around Jasmine and Brian. They dragged each other back toward the porch. When they came close enough, Adam released the earth and grabbed their hands, pulling them up the steps with him.

They collapsed on their hands and knees, breathing hard.

"Maybe wait on the porch," Tori said.

"She wants us to come in," Noemi said. Her curls stuck to the side of her face, dripping rainwater down her neck.

"Isn't that all the more reason to get the hell out of here?" Isa said, taking off her velvet ballet flats and shaking them out over the stairs.

Tori pulled at the hem of her drenched tank top. "I don't think that's an option anymore."

"Time for that distraction," Adam said.

48

ily waited for us in the garden room again. I had expected roasted vegetables and crispy herbs, maybe with a side of burned-up siding or blackened roof panels. But she'd managed to strip away anything with so much as a singe, leaving behind an open space with hearty, fresh growth. Without the screens, the three-season room felt bigger.

It glowed with soft candlelight. Pillar candles stood on the floor in a circle around her. A tall candelabra with five arms stood on a plant stand behind her, short flames flickering from stubby white candles. The breeze floated through the room unchecked, though much less brutal than the winds that blew us up the front steps. Her flowers bloomed almost as big as they had before.

Her chair was gone.

All of the furniture was gone, actually, except for a single stand in the middle of the room where the book lay under its cloth. It couldn't all have burned. Some of it had iron frames. But now, there was nothing to impede her plants.

"Nice," I said. "Love what you've done with the place."

"I'm so glad to see you again." She interlaced her fingers in front of her, standing at ease, ready. Like a restaurant hostess. "Are we all prepared to begin our study? The gentlemen can wait inside."

The gentle breeze became a tornado directed at Adam and Brian. They pushed against it, but there was nothing to hold onto.

"No!" I called the energy for my Gift. My fingers sparked, but it felt like trying to light a match underwater. The pressure held me back.

The guys stretched out their arms, and Jasmine and Tori reached for them, but the air kept them apart. It pushed Brian and Adam back through the iron gates. A heavy curtain dropped into place in front of the gate, silencing any noise from the rest of the house. The tornado dissipated. I nearly fell over when the pressure released me.

"That's better, isn't it?" Lily said. "Men can be such a distraction."

I swallowed. My head ached. Pins and needles pricked my fingers. If I used my Gift again now, it might wipe me out. Besides, we needed to know what she had learned. If she'd already worked out the key...well, that would be both extremely helpful and terribly dangerous.

We needed the book, which she had. But she needed to be able to read it, which we might.

But we also had to somehow keep her from completing any of the spells she might have learned. It was impossible. I could scream.

Just as my heart started to beat faster and my nerves threatened to remove any filter that remained between my mind and my mouth, Noemi squeezed my elbow. A warm touch wrapped around me. I was enveloped in comfort, a sense of peace slowing my breaths.

She stepped forward. "Mama Lily, I'm so glad you're okay. I was worried about you."

Because of the fire? Or because of the possession? Either way, I was grateful. This might not be the distraction Adam had in mind, but the good cop approach might buy me time to recover. Empathy as a shield. Noemi should have been a hostage negotiator instead of a librarian.

"Thank you, my dear. I think we all got a little heated at our last meeting." She smiled, waiting for the dad joke to land.

With an incredible show of willpower, not a single one of us rolled our eyes. Jasmine even managed an awkward chuckle.

"Why don't you all come a little closer, and I'll show you some of the amazing things this book has to teach us." She beckoned us with both hands, stepping behind the plant stand.

It was a terrible idea, but what else were we going to do? We came here to get the book, and it was right there. We approached with all the caution of a firefly who's already lost friends to the flame. A faint rustling behind the curtain gave the only hint about what Brian and Adam were doing on the other side of the gate. How long could she hold them out?

Lily pulled back the cloth, revealing the grimoire. It lay open to a page near the middle. "First, you should know that I haven't done this alone. I've had the support of the ancestors. They want us to stop hiding, to reverse these past centuries of oppression. They are disappointed that we have fallen so low, living in fear of those who are weaker than us in every way."

She eyed Jasmine and Isa, making it clear that whatever magic we'd seen them do, she didn't consider them her equals. She exhaled sharply.

"But there is room for those who join us. Those special few who show their loyalty. Especially if they have already proven themselves ready to learn our ways. To adapt to the new world we will create." Her eyelids fluttered as she made the concession.

Tori leaned forward, her lips moving as she translated the text. "It's a summoning spell. It draws energy…beings composed of energy…from beyond the veil."

Lily nodded. "The witches who went before us have shuffled off this mortal coil. They are not burdened by the physical. They exist as pure energy and light."

Jasmine nudged Tori aside so that she could get a better look. She pointed to a sketch near the bottom of the page. "What's this? Lucerna…that's lantern, isn't it?"

"Indeed," said Lily. She seemed both surprised and displeased that the mundane could identify the illustration.

Isa frowned and squinted, trying to see what Jasmine had pointed out.

Maybe it was like when Jasmine looked at Lalo and could see the boy inside. Somehow, she saw through magic to the truth beneath it. Isa, on the other hand, might recognize the presence of magic but couldn't see what it was doing. Unlike her stepmother, who didn't seem to see magic at all. The dividing line between mundane and magical experiences might not be as solid as we'd always thought.

Lily ran her fingers over the page. "The author of this spell wanted to bring forth the essence of someone who'd passed. She developed the spell to draw the energy from beyond and place it into a special lantern to sustain it."

"Cooooool," Isa breathed. "Like a ghost light."

Jasmine and Tori exchanged a look that said neither of them particularly liked the idea of trapping their ancestors in a lamp.

"You said you…you've done this spell?" Noemi asked. Her eyes roamed the room. I didn't see anything like the pictured lantern in the garden.

"I improved it," Lily said.

"How?" I asked.

"It was not enough to host an ancestor in so small a space. They should not be caged. And the original spell does not provide for adequate communication. I needed more than 'blink once for yes, twice for no.'" She paused for dramatic effect.

We glanced at each other, making vague sounds of agreement. *Oh, yes. The ancestors deserve more. Definitely need more…*Until Lily cleared her throat.

"So I became the lantern myself." She held up her hands, candlelight flashing off her rings.

I recognized a call for applause. She should have been on the stage.

"Wow," I said.

"But what does that mean, exactly?" asked Tori. "You're the lantern?"

Lily pursed her lips, annoyed at the underwhelming response. She placed her hands back on the book, closing her eyes reverently. "I've accepted the energy within my own body. The ancestor resides within, sharing my breath and his wisdom."

"His?" Jasmine said.

Lily's eyes popped open. "Excuse me?"

Jasmine glanced back at the door, hidden behind the curtain. "You said *his*. The ancestor you've summoned is male? I thought you said witches should only be women."

Lily frowned. "The energy has no body and is therefore neither masculine nor feminine. But, yes, the being who answered my call formerly identified as male. He was a great leader among our people in the old days."

While Jasmine focused on Lily's hypocrisy, I considered the other detail of her story. Her possession was not a spirit but a being of energy. A creature with no body and no spirit of its own. That didn't sound like a benevolent force.

It did sound like something we might be able to handle. All of us had proven capable of manipulating energy to a certain extent. Even Jasmine's sight was a form of it.

But pulling an energy source from the unwilling body of another witch…this had Tori's name written all over it. I hoped she was up to it. We just had to choose the right moment.

"Has your guest helped you?" I asked. "You were seeking the elixir of life."

Lily smiled at Noemi. "I believe I am close. Let's finish this together, and then we can restore you to your former strength."

This woman had clearly never found herself on Noemi's bad side if she thought vampirism weakened her in any way. The dark circles under her eyes didn't come from lack of sleep.

"Thank you," Noemi said.

Lily's head bobbed a response as she flipped through the pages, moving past the sheets of recipes into a section that looked more like something from my dad's notes. Tori's description that it looked like a code of overlaid text proved true. Two different colors overlapped across the pages. The writing covered the open spread from one side to the other instead of stopping at the edges of the pages. There were no margins in the middle, and Lily had to press down the pages to show writing continuing through the binding as if the pages had been written across both before the book was bound.

A border of blue runes framed the outside edges. Although I didn't know what they said, I'd seen those runes before. And I knew their purpose.

We had to find the other book if we held out any hope of reading this one.

Across the book, Lily's eyes met mine. They twinkled.

"What do you see?"

Shit. My stupid face showed every emotion. She knew I recognized something. And I'd already felt what she could do when she thought I was holding out on her.

I shouldn't have done it, but I panicked. My hands flew up on their own. Sparks flew from my fingertips. Before I even thought to call the energy, the magic of my Gift flowed out of me. Lily froze with both hands still pressing on the book. My head pounded. How long did we have before the demon worked its way to the surface?

Tori turned on me. "What did you do?"

"She was just about to tell us about the elixir!" Jasmine said.

Isa reached out and poked Lily's arm.

"Don't..." The word pushed its way free of my gritted teeth.

She pulled her hand back. "Sorry! But this is so cool. Do you think she can hear us when she's like that?"

Noemi put a calming hand on my back. "Are you alright? What's happening?"

"I understand the code," I said. "We have to get this book back to Queen's Creek. The only way we're going to be able to read it is if we have both of them together."

"Great!" said Jasmine. "So let's grab this thing and get out of here."

She reached for the book, but it didn't move.

49

Cate, let go of the book." Jasmine tugged at the grimoire.

"I can't," I said. "She's touching it. I'm holding her there, but she's holding the book. I can't release it without releasing her." And I wasn't sure I wanted it in Jasmine's hands, either.

Behind me, something crashed. I jumped but held Lily in place. "What was that?"

"I think the guys got tired of waiting," Tori said.

Another crash, and heavy footsteps raced across the room.

"Are you okay?"

"What's going on?"

Adam and Brian pulled up sharply just at the edge of my vision.

Jasmine let go of the book and grinned at them. "Hey, guys. Good news. We know how to read the book now…"

Tori took over. "Bad news. Cate's trapped the book on that table."

"She's also trapped Mama Lily there…which is probably for the best," Noemi admitted.

Brian circled the table, examining it from different angles.

"I think we can get it out. I've moved stuff that was frozen before. It's hard to get started, but then…"

He made a motion to imply the thing would slide right out.

That was not how I remembered our experience on stage. He'd pushed several cast members and one large set piece out of the way of a falling drop while I held it all in place. But he'd been exhausted afterwards and nearly hadn't done it in time.

"We can't risk ripping the pages," Adam said. He ran a finger over the runes and caught my eye.

I was right.

But we had to get it out of here to prove it.

Sweat tickled behind my ear. "If you guys have a plan, I'd love to hear it."

"She doesn't look so scary," Brian said.

Jasmine put a hand to her forehead. "Boy, you better…"

"Nah, nah. I get it. Evil plants. Kind of Poison Ivy's grandma vibes, but like…" He pointed to each of us. "Vampire. Time travel. Earth bender. Goth Magneto—"

Tori balked at the description. "That's not—"

"And what does she do again?" Brian pointed at Isa.

"Techno mage," said the teen.

"Respect."

"Yes. Everyone is very special and powerful in their own way," Noemi said. "How do we get out of here with the book? Without killing anyone?"

She looked pointedly at Tori and Jasmine.

"So, I think Lily's friend is the bigger problem anyway," Tori said.

"Her friend?" asked Adam.

"She's possessed," Isa reminded everyone.

"But it's not a spirit. It's energy," I said. "Tori—"

She nodded. "Yeah. Okay."

"Wait, wait, wait. If she's going to pull it out of her, where is she going to put it? I don't like the idea of sentient energy just loose…" Brian said.

Tori bounced on her toes like a fighter.

"Find a lantern," Noemi said.

"But she said she didn't make one for the spell, remember? She improved it." Jasmine put air quotes around the word *improved*.

"It doesn't need to last forever. Just long enough for us to get away." She paced the room, looking behind planters and along the wall.

"Here's one!" Isa lifted a large decorative lantern from the floor near where the screen door used to be.

"Okay, when I release her, somebody grab the book. Then I'll try and freeze her again while Tori ejects her visitor." Emphasis on *try*. I didn't know if I would have enough energy left to do this again. Especially if she saw it coming and fought against me. "Is the door open?"

"I don't think we need it." Adam waved a hand through the opening where the screens used to be. "Jump down and run for the alley. Her backyard looks smaller than the front. Fewer plants trying to make compost out of us,"

"Ready?" I tried to make eye contact with each of them.

Tori stepped up next to me, still bouncing and rolling her head.

Brian set the lantern on the table beside the book and opened its little glass door.

Adam stood by the edge of the porch, preparing to help with the escape.

Jasmine stepped beside Lily and grabbed the book again.

I bit my lip and glanced at Noemi. She seemed to understand my concern. Coming up beside Jasmine, Noemi put a hand on her arm. "Let me get that, mija. You help Adam get everyone out when the time comes."

Jasmine hesitated.

Lily blinked.

"Uh, guys? Can we go now?" Isa backed away from the waking witch.

Noemi squeezed Jasmine's arm. "It's alright. I've got it. Go on."

"Fine." Jasmine huffed and let go of the book. She put an arm around Isa and guided her to the edge of the porch, watching the backyard plants for movement.

Noemi gave a nod.

I released the energy.

Tori's fingers glowed with white light.

Lily's hands came up reflexively to protect herself, and Noemi slid the book out from under her. She ran for the backyard.

I pulled more energy and directed it at Lily, willing her to freeze again, but it wasn't enough. I could barely stand. The witch slowed, like moving through sand. I called out to Tori, even though it was obvious. "Hurry!"

She drew more and more energy from Lily, pulling a string of light from her chest and pushing it toward the lantern. It doubled back, trying to get to her instead. Tori's hands rolled over each other as if she were wrapping a ball of yarn. The string of light caught and tangled. She pushed it back toward the lantern but overshot it, and the ball unraveled across the room, one end still connected to Lily's chest. Jasmine shoved Isa behind her as the ball rolled toward them, and Tori groaned as she pulled it back. The evil sentient ball of energy lunged one more time, trying to get to Noemi, but just as it got within inches of the vampire, its light sputtered. It spun in place and rolled backward as if it had hit a wall. Tori pulled back on the string, and this time, it fell into the lantern. It pooled around the candle inside.

Lily pushed against my Gift but couldn't break through.

She shrieked in defiance, her will against mine. My hair clung to my face, wet from the storm and my sweat. I held my breath. Any energy I had left faded. I forced it all through my hands, sending sparks flying. Lily deflected them, pushing me back. My spell collapsed, and I pitched forward, knocking into the table. It slammed into Lily, breaking her concentration and throwing her off her balance.

Brian caught the lantern just before it hit the floor.

Tori growled, making one last effort and pulling the end of the thread free. It swirled into the lantern, and Brian slammed it shut. Tori took off down the stairs into the backyard.

Releasing Lily, I set a time bubble over the lantern, locking it temporarily. There was no way to tell how long the makeshift demon trap would hold or what would happen when it broke free.

We ran.

Brian launched himself off the porch and hit the ground running, the lantern swinging in his hand.

At the edge of the porch, Adam took my hand and helped me jump down. I wobbled, but he braced his arm around me, and we chased Tori through the yard toward the alley.

Behind us, Lily screamed. Shoots exploded between the weeds. They reached for our feet, but the energy behind them didn't compare to the attack when we'd first arrived. With the demon trapped in the lantern and her own magical energy nearly exhausted from resisting mine, Lily didn't have enough left to do much more than trip us. Still, if Adam hadn't been there, the next wild chamomile might have taken me out.

He held out his free hand ahead of us and the soil flattened into a dirt path that smoothed the way from our feet to the paved alley. The others waited for us behind a bank of garages. Isa sat on the cement ramp, leaning against the wide garage door. Beside her, Jasmine stood with one hand on the wall. Brian rounded the corner and wrapped his arms around her, pulling her farther from Lily's garden. Tori bent at her waist, hands on her knees, breathing hard. Noemi kept her back to the wall, clutching the book with her eyes closed.

Adam rubbed my back. "Everyone okay?"

"I can't believe that worked," Isa said, her eyes wide.

"It's not going to last." I didn't mean to be the bearer of bad news, but I'd only done a time lock spell like the one I put on the lantern once before. When I bound Tori's power to protect her from the hunter who tracked it, the spell dissolved after an hour. I doubted this one would hold as long.

"But we have the book now, so…" Jasmine gestured to the leather cover in Noemi's arms.

"So we need to get it somewhere safe. Somewhere she won't be able to get it back." I looked at the librarian. "I know the library wards are strong, but—"

"But it's the first place she'll look," Tori said.

"I know." Noemi looked back toward the house. "It's not safe there anymore. She's changed so much…I'm not even sure how much of it was the demon or whatever that thing was. She let it in."

"I'm good with *demon*," said Jasmine. "It's evil, and it possesses people. That's a demon as far as I'm concerned."

"It promised her the elixir of life when she felt weak and powerless. That's a pretty big temptation," Tori said.

Noemi knelt, balancing the heavy book on her knees. "But even the…demon…couldn't read the book. It was a false promise." She rubbed her eyes. She'd been let down by her mentor and had the chance to unvamp herself and Lalo ripped out from under her.

We were so close. The recipe hid on those pages. Under the code.

My father's notes flashed in front of my eyes. The way the

words formed shapes. The overlapping text, just like the text in the book.

Blue runes circling the pages.

I turned to Adam, pulling up his sleeve.

He brushed my fingers away and pulled the sleeve up to his shoulder.

Tori and Jasmine stepped closer.

"They're the same, right? Or am I imagining it?" *I may be imagining it.* I could barely stand. My heart raced, my head pounded. Hallucinations might not be far behind.

"You're not imagining it," he said.

Tori looked from Adam's tattoo to the book. "Those are the same runes that border the pages about the elixir."

Noemi nodded.

"These runes," I said. "You told us they were part of the spell to protect you and Duncan during your Wakening. How did it work again?"

He rubbed the tattoo. "As long as one is hidden, the other can't be found. But neither of us is hiding anymore."

"What does it mean?" Isa asked. "We know where the other book is."

"Knowing where it is and being able to find it, being able to read it, are not the same thing," Noemi said.

I knelt beside Noemi, as much to rest my legs as to get a closer look at the book. "I think this book is the key to the other one. I don't think you can read one without the other."

"They're twins," Tori realized.

"You ready to go home?" Adam asked.

"I think we need to make a stop first."

50

Back at the magic shop, I informed my twin that he might have to close indefinitely. "This could be the answer to everything. Stopping Lily, helping Noemi and Lalo, finding Dad. It all comes back to the elixir of life."

Thomas took one look at the book and put a new sign in the window. "Closed for the apocalypse."

"I don't think it's going be that bad," Jasmine said.

"Why do you even have a sign that says that?" Adam asked.

Thomas raised an eyebrow. "Have you been paying attention to recent events? If this isn't it, it's going to be the next thing."

Noemi set the book on Thomas's coffee table with our notes and wrapped her arms around Lalo, assuring herself that nothing had changed since we left him behind. The puppy licked her cheek, wagging his tail.

Emily snored on the futon.

"Why is she still asleep?" I asked a roomful of people who knew as much as I did.

Isa stood over her, concern breaking through her teenage

attempts at apathy. "What do you think Lily put in the wine? Is she just going to stay like this?"

I looked at Tori, whose potion experience far exceeded anything I'd ever tried.

She pursed her lips. "I have a few ideas, but none of them is good. The effects should have worn off by now. If the tea didn't cut through it…she's going to need a healer."

Thomas looked my way. "Elspeth?"

I nodded. "She might be able to help with Lalo, too. They both have water Gifts."

Adam made eye contact with Thomas. "I'll take Cate, Isa, and Emily. You handle Noemi and the dog?"

"Why do I get the dog?" Thomas whined.

"What about us?" Brian held up the lantern. It gave off a pulsing light that made me nervous. We had to find a more secure way to trap it. Soon.

"We're not witches," Jasmine said. "They're trying to leave us here."

Too late, I saw her eyes go to the book. She grabbed it, hugging it to her chest.

"Not that you haven't been an excellent houseguest…" Tori reached for the grimoire. "But I think we got this from here."

Jasmine backed away from her. "You think you're just going to ditch out of here and leave us? Where do you think Lily's going to go once she gets her energy back? I'll be lucky if the League finds me first."

Brian's eyes widened. "You can't let that happen. When they figure out she's been helping you…"

Tori scoffed. "Helping us? She's—"

"I'd be dead if she hadn't knocked the gun out of Wesson's hand," Brian said. He pointed at Thomas. "And so would you."

Thomas held up his hands. "Whoa, whoa…I didn't write

the guest list for this party."

Brian turned to Adam. "You're some kind of security guard back there, right? How secure do you think your town is going to be if we get captured? Cause I'll tell you right now, I will not hold up well under torture."

"We've got to take the whole class," I said. "Are you up for it?"

I couldn't know if he'd used his Gift to test Brian and Jasmine's honesty, and I might have broken his trust too many times in the last week to justify asking him for anything. But I hoped he'd see this was our only chance. We had to go home, and he was the only one strong enough to get us there. No shade to Thomas, but I couldn't afford a crash landing with that lantern. We might need the Guardian to save us, after all.

Adam rubbed the back of his neck. His eyes tracked something invisible back and forth on the floor. Mental calculus to see how much energy it would take to transport ten people halfway across the country. "Might take more than one trip."

Thomas chewed his thumbnail. "Hey, Wednesday, you been practicing?"

Tori stared at him for a second, then closed her eyes. She disappeared, popping back into view behind my brother. She tapped his shoulder, and he jumped.

"Cool," Isa whispered.

Thomas nodded. He looked at Noemi. "Vegan vamps turn into fruit bats or anything?"

Noemi sighed.

Tori put a hand on her arm. "No worries. I've got you and Lalo."

Thomas rubbed his hands together. He turned to Adam. "Okay. I'll take Sleeping Beauty and the witchling. You bring my sister and the walking red flags."

Adam nodded. "See you at the Gatehouse."

Thomas gave an uneven salute and took Isa's hand. As he reached for Emily, Adam added, "Try not to break anything. We just got the place rebuilt."

Thomas disappeared, taking Isa and her stepmother with him.

Adam pulled up a map on his phone, the old one I'd given him the last time I left Queen's Creek. He held it out to Tori, enlarging the image. "The Gatehouse is here, past the power plant, behind this copse of trees. Focus on the energy of the Creek. You can't miss it."

"I think I've got it," Tori said, twisting her fingers into Lalo's fur. "See you there!"

"Thanks," Noemi added. She put a hand on Tori's shoulder. And then they were gone.

Adam touched my arm. "Bringing them back with us is a huge risk."

"I know."

"You're asking me to bring hunters into our home." His eyes searched mine.

Brian raised his hand. "Still not a hunter."

"Me either," Jasmine mumbled. "Not anymore."

I didn't look away. After everything we'd been through and all the ways allegiances had shifted, I had to trust my own intuition. If that wasn't enough for Adam, he could use his own Gift to make himself feel better. Although I hoped he wouldn't waste the energy. "We can trust them."

"I trust you," Adam said.

"Take us home."

When we arrived at the Gatehouse in Queen's Creek, Thomas had already left to take Noemi, Lalo, and Emily to meet Elspeth at the healer's cottage. Isa and Tori waited for us at the bridge.

"Ready for another library adventure?" Tori asked.

Jasmine hugged the heavy book, carrying it like a shield in front of her.

"You sure you don't want me to carry that for a while?" Brian asked.

"I've got it," she said.

"And I've got that." I took the lantern from Brian and tucked it into Alice's bedroom. Even without the boundary spell, the Gatehouse was the safest place for it, except maybe the Watch Tower. But I didn't want to bring any more danger into town than absolutely necessary. The former hunter's apprentice carrying the grimoire was a big enough risk without dragging an angry energy creature through the town square.

We crossed the Creek more quickly than I'd ever imagined possible. No tests of the Guardian or protectors of the boundary to keep us out. I tapped the new stone walls that ran along the side of the bridge. Cool and strong.

On the other side, the beaten path carved a straight line through tall grass and wildflowers until we reached the tree line. Daisies and yarrow bent in the breeze, greeting the butterflies and wisps that flitted between them. They weren't as showy as Lily's garden, but they welcomed us all and let us pass unharmed.

Under the trees, the path wound in expanding circles. We passed Elspeth's cottage but couldn't stop. She'd hung a curtain across her open doorway, and soft conversation floated through it. Tori squeezed Isa's hand. "They'll take good care of her."

Isa nodded but hung back a little until we rounded the next corner.

Soon enough, we arrived at the cottage library, set back from the path and draped in ivy. My older brother greeted me with a warm hug, ruffling my hair.

"Tell me more about this book you're looking for," he said. "I've been all through the stacks, but I haven't found anything matching your description."

"It probably looks like this one…" I stepped out of the way to reveal the heavy grimoire in Jasmine's hands.

Jonathan's eyebrows jumped. "That is quite a specimen. Do you mind if I…"

Jasmine held tighter. "I need assurances."

"What kind?" Jonathan shifted his weight back and tucked his hands into the pockets of his trousers.

"That I, that we," she elbowed Brian beside her, "Will not be…harmed or turned into frogs or anything once I give this to you."

Jonathan looked genuinely confused. He looked to me and Adam for an explanation. I shook my head. Adam turned his hands up. Jonathan turned back to Jasmine. "I can honestly say the thought never crossed my mind."

Jasmine eyed the rest of us.

"I wouldn't know how to turn you into a frog if I wanted to," Isa said.

Tori smirked. "There are way more interesting ways to—"

"Tori," I said.

She shrugged, then held up two fingers, "On my honor, I promise not to turn you into a frog."

Jonathan held out his hand. "May I see the book now?"

Jasmine sucked in her lips.

Brian rubbed her back. "You can't hold onto that thing for the rest of your life."

She took a deep breath, passing the book to the librarian as if she were giving him her entire life.

"Thank you," Jonathan said. He took the book to his desk and opened it. Turning the pages with care, he nodded. "Yes, I can see what you were saying. There's a ward over many of the spells here. You'll need to find the key."

"Cate thinks it's in the other book," Adam said.

"She thinks it is the other book," Tori clarified.

"Is that so?" Jonathan's nose was so close to the page he might have inhaled the ink.

I tapped the runes bordering the page. "*As long as one is hidden, the other can't be found.* You couldn't find the other book before because this one had been hidden in the restricted section in Chicago. Once it was removed from the library, the other one started to leave clues. It appeared for Isa in the digital catalog. Maybe it will appear for us now that we've brought this one home. And once the other is found, we'll be able to read this one. It's a double lock."

"Maybe." Jonathan straightened. "But I've been all through that card catalog, and there is no reference to—"

"Can I take a look?" Isa asked.

"There's no wires or electricity in this thing," Tori said, knocking on the wooden cabinet that contained cards for all of the books in the library. "Not sure this is the job for a techno mage."

Isa smiled. "It's still a system. I don't know how my Gift works, but I think this is still tech. It's just analog."

"What can it hurt?" I asked.

Jonathan waved his assent. "Be my guest."

"While she's testing the limits of her brand-new powers, can we take a look for ourselves?" Tori asked, throwing a thumb in the direction of the shelves.

"Certainly, just promise me that nothing leaves the library." My brother gave me a very stern look that told me he remembered I'd removed our grimoire without permission on my last visit. In my defense, it was that or leave it to be absorbed by the shadow.

I crossed my heart with my index finger.

"Got it!" Isa called.

"What?" Jonathan frowned. He hurried back to the front of the library and plucked the card from Isa's hand. "This wasn't here before. Where did it come from?"

"Guess you were right," Tori said. "Now that we brought the grimoire home, its twin wants to be found."

"Where does it say it's shelved?" I asked Jonathan.

"This way." He strode past us down the narrow hallway. Shelves shifted around him. We struggled to keep up but somehow managed to make each turn before the books fell back to their original positions. He stopped at a heavy door and pulled out his keyring. A large brass key slipped into the lock, and when he turned it, the door to the restricted section disappeared, revealing a dark entryway. "Just through here…"

Jonathan stepped behind a curtain I'd never seen before. Turning back to hold it open, he waved us in. "Well, come in, come in. Let's see what we can find."

The dark room beyond the curtain gave off distinctly unwelcoming vibes. As soon as I entered, I felt a strong urge to go back to the warmly lit front room.

"Are you sure it's in here?" Jasmine asked. She took Brian's hand.

Jonathan flicked the card. "This is what the card indicates. If the book is to be found, it will be found in here."

"This doesn't feel right," Adam said. "Are you sure?"

Jonathan smiled, enjoying the challenge. "Just because it can be found now that you've returned the one that was missing doesn't mean it's going to make it easy for us."

51

The farther we stepped into the room, the more uneasy I became. The whole room felt heavy, like swimming in deep water. Nausea nearly overcame me. Something buzzed in my ears. The noise grew until I was sure the library had an infestation. Adam had understated things when he said it didn't feel right. Something wanted us out of there.

Tori groaned. "Ugh. That book does not want to be found."

"Excuse me," Isa covered her mouth and pushed past us back to the main library space.

Jasmine coughed. "I'm just going to go…check on her."

She ducked out of the room and heaved a deep breath as soon as she crossed the threshold from the restricted area. Brian held out a minute longer and then followed her.

Taking shallow breaths, in through my nose and out through my mouth, I tried to push past it.

Jonathan let out a long, slow breath.

I braced myself on a bookcase, concentrating on keeping my lunch down. "Hey, you maybe want to turn down the library's defenses? I know this section is restricted access, but we have permission, right?"

My brother shook his head. "This isn't me. Trust me. I feel it, too."

"He's right," Tori said. "It's the book. It's that whole *as long as one is hidden* thing."

"But it isn't hidden. It's on Jonathan's desk." I looked back through the door, but there were too many stacks between us and the circulation desk to see it.

Adam frowned. "I mean, technically, all of Queen's Creek is hidden."

"What? No, we took down the boundary and…"

Adam rubbed his neck. "And we couldn't leave the town undefended. The elders called a quorum and decided to reinstate the glamour. You can still come and go as you please, but nobody's going to wander into the Gatehouse that isn't looking for it."

That explained why the hunters hadn't barreled in as soon as we released the energy. The glamour might have them wandering in the woods for days, unable to recognize the Creek or the Gatehouse, even if they walked right up to it. The ever-present will-o'-the-wisps would have distracted a few of them even without the disguise.

I leaned my forehead against the cool wooden frame of the bookcase. "So these books have to be together to work. The missing one is definitely here. But the protection spell won't let us find it so that we can bring them together as long as the other book is in Queen's Creek?"

Adam frowned, staring at the shelves as if he could force the book to reveal itself. Then, he nodded. "I have to take the other one out past the Gatehouse."

"You what?" Tori asked.

"If the first book is outside the glamour, it's not hidden anymore. The ward on the missing one should relax."

"Should being the operative word." Tori's face looked paler than usual.

"We have to try something," I said. None of us was going to be able to stay in that room much longer.

Jonathan swallowed. "It's our best bet. That spell isn't going to let us get any farther unless we break it."

I looked at Adam, hoping he was right. Praying to the goddess he'd be safe outside the glamour. I caught his eye. "Be careful."

He nodded again and hurried back to the front of the library, where we'd left the book at the circulation desk.

A moment later, my ears popped. The air in the room cleared, suddenly lighter and fresher. I could breathe without my stomach turning over.

Tori gasped. She must have been holding her breath. She slid to the floor and leaned against the wall.

Jonathan staggered and braced himself against a shelf, blinking at the shift in air pressure.

Jasmine and Brian ran back to the restricted section, stopping short in the doorway. Isa followed a step behind.

"What's going on?" Jasmine asked. "Your boyfriend just grabbed the book and disappeared."

"You can come back in now," I called.

The others stepped cautiously into the room.

"You're sure it's safe?" Jasmine asked.

Tori waved her in. "See for yourself."

"When did Adam go?" Brian asked.

"He took the book to Gatehouse," Jonathan explained. "Testing a theory."

Isa stepped farther into the room and turned in place. "Must have worked. I don't feel like vomiting anymore."

"Don't say *vomit*," Jasmine said.

"Are you still feeling nauseous? The spell should have been neutralized for everyone. Unless the book suspected Jasmine had negative intent..."

"I'm fine. I just don't like that word. It's gross. Like *moist*."

She shivered.

Tori rolled her eyes.

Jonathan clapped his hands. "So, back to work then, huh? Let's find this thing before the one Adam took attracts unwanted attention."

We each took a section of the room and scanned the spines for the Book of Magical Charms or the Ashley Grimoire. Jonathan's organizational system probably made perfect sense to him, but there was no way of knowing how the original librarian had chosen to categorize it. There was no doubt in my mind that the book had been hidden here in the earliest days of Queen's Creek. It was certainly old enough.

I ran my fingers over the dusty spines, chewing my lip. Every minute wasted left Adam and the other book unprotected outside the Gate. I was tempted to ask Tori to check the kynigolabe for hunters, but I didn't want anyone to panic more than they already were.

I pulled Nora's card out of my back pocket. Facing the shelves to block my detour from the others, I covered it with my hand and set my intention. My mind whirled with distractions—fear for Adam's safety, for the trapped energy we'd left in the lantern at the Gate, for the hunters who must have noticed Jasmine's absence by now, for Lily back in her poison garden. It was too much. I couldn't focus. *Where should I concentrate my attention?*

The card warmed in my hand. I squinted, afraid to look. A man carrying swords, looking back over his shoulder. The Seven of Swords. The card that had come to mind when Lily's guest started rambling about sevens. Theft. Deception. Trickery. But the card also suggests strategy and using shortcuts to resolve problems quickly.

It calls you out on trying to escape your problems instead of facing them.

Alright, card. I opened my eyes wide. *Let's find the thing that's hiding. But let's be smart about it.* I pushed the card back into my pocket and stepped back from the stacks, watching the others pull books from the shelves and pile them on the floor, feeling around inside the cabinets in case anything lurked where we couldn't see it.

"Everybody stop," I said.

One by one, they stepped back from the shelves.

I looked at each of them. *Six of us here. Adam makes seven. It can't be a coincidence.* "We're not going to get anywhere like this. We need to be more strategic, use all of our skills. Isa found the listing that got us here. Jonathan unlocked the restricted section. Adam is holding the other book outside the Gate. We can't just rifle through the stacks and expect a book that's been hidden for decades to appear because we want it to. But one of us can see things she shouldn't."

Tori smiled at Jasmine. "Ready to earn your keep, roomie?"

Brian tilted his head. "What? What do you want her to do?"

"You didn't know? Your girl's got skills!" Tori said. "Might be useful after all."

Isa explained Jasmine's newfound sight to Brian and Jonathan.

Ignoring them, Jasmine tapped her lips with her fingers. She stood in the middle of the room and turned slowly, taking in each set of shelves, one at a time. After two passes, she paused, stepping closer to a bookshelf in the back of the room.

"Jasmine?" I asked. "What do you see?"

<h1 style="text-align:center">52</h1>

J asmine stared at a row of shelves. Books packed it from floor to ceiling, just like all the others. "It's here."

"Where?" I asked. All of us joined her in the back of the restricted section, scanning the shelves for anything that looked *extra* magical.

She stepped back, squinting. "I don't know, but can't you see how this section shimmers? There's something hidden here."

We went book by book, pulling them out one at a time, each of us checking a shelf in the bookcase and then rechecking each other's. Even with Jasmine's ability to see magic, we couldn't find it.

A tiny bell rang in the distance.

"Hello?" A soft voice came from the front of the library.

"Keep looking," Jonathan said. He walked purposefully back to the entrance, making the shelves dance out of the way with every step.

Something scuffled, and a dog barked. Moments later, Lalo barreled past the books we'd stacked on the floor and pounced on Tori. She laughed, scratching his furry head.

"Hey there, boy. Whoa. Whoa, slow down." She pushed his

head away from her face.

A tiny voice somewhere far away called out, "Hi! Hi!"

I turned but couldn't find the source.

Noemi and Jonathan caught up, panting in their efforts to keep up with a four-legged child. Noemi braced herself on a bookshelf. "So, I guess he's already told you his big news."

"What? What news?" I put down the stack of books I'd been checking.

Someone giggled.

"I guess Elspeth couldn't help him?" Isa asked.

Noemi sucked in a breath and straightened. "No. She did. It's just that he's…"

"He's not ready to turn back just yet." Tori smiled, scratching the dog between his eyes.

"He's what?" Jasmine frowned at the dog.

"Too haaaarrrrrd…" The voice was louder now.

"No way." I could swear the dog smiled at me.

"Yes way, José," said Lalo's voice in my head. He dissolved into giggles, and his puppy body rolled onto his back, wriggling and wagging his tail.

Isa laughed. "He speaks!"

Jasmine narrowed her eyes. "But he's still a dog."

Noemi nodded. "She helped him find his voice, but she said if he wants to return to his true form, he has to do it himself."

"Then why hasn't he?" Isa asked.

"He doesn't think he can do it himself." Noemi sighed. "He wanted her to fix him."

She may want that more than he does.

"But we can hear him now," I said. "That's a massive improvement."

"We thought he might be all dog," said Noemi, her voice shaking. "But he's in there. That little boy is still in there."

"I told you he was," Jasmine muttered.

Noemi took her hand. "I'm sorry we doubted you. I was afraid to hope."

Jasmine lowered her head. "It's okay. I'm getting used to not being trusted."

"Give me a break," Tori said. "You were telling the truth this time, but can you blame us for wanting to prove it?"

Lalo snuffled at the books next to Tori, bored now that the conversation had moved on from his new skill.

"I made mistakes. How long are you going to hold them against me?" Jasmine said.

"Mistakes like trying to get us killed? You're going to have to give us some time on those. Don't hold your breath." Tori pulled another book down and flipped it open.

The dog pushed past her, his nose following a path along the floor to the pile of books at Jasmine's feet. He blew out through his nose and started snuffling again.

Noemi tilted her head. "What are you after, mijo?"

The kid's voice grew stronger every time he used it. "Something smells funny."

"What do you mean by funny?" Brian asked, watching the dog go from one stack of books to another. "Funny how?"

Lalo sneezed. "Like the big book."

"What big book, Lalo?" Tori asked. "The one you found in Noemi's room?"

"Sí. Yes. That one. The big, ugly book. It's super stinky." He nosed along the bottom of the bookcase.

"Did you all bring it back here?" Noemi asked.

Jonathan shook his head. "Adam has it. He had to take it outside the Gate."

Noemi's eyes went wide. "Unprotected?"

"It was the only way to find the second book," I said. "Adam will keep it safe."

Her eyebrows jumped. "You found it?"

"We're close," Tori said, watching Jasmine pull books away

from Lalo's wet nose.

"But outside...won't it lead them here? The hunters... Lily...they'll have both books." Noemi's voice trembled, her usually calm facade starting to crack.

"Every book in the library is safe here," Jonathan said. "No one can take them without checking them out."

"I did," I said, thinking of the grimoire I'd saved before.

"That was different," Jonathan said. "Thanks for leaving me that mess to clean up, by the way. Do you know how hard it is to get sentient shadows out of the corners?"

"I'm sorry?"

"I'm just saying, a warning would have been nice."

Lalo barked. He pawed at a book from Jasmine's pile. It didn't look any different than the others, large, covered in dark cloth, metal corners protecting the edges.

"Here! This one. This is what you want, right? Smells just like the other one." Lalo's voice in my head bubbled with excitement. He sneezed again.

If he found the missing grimoire, I'm going to buy so many puppy treats. Maybe Mom had some peanut butter back at the house.

Isa picked it up. "There's something strange about the cover. It's like a dust jacket, but it won't come off."

We crowded around her. She was right. Some kind of translucent cloth lay over the book like a protective film. I scratched gently around the edges, trying to find an opening. There was none.

"Let's take it back to the front and call Adam," I said. "He should be able to bring the other book back now. Maybe that will unlock this one. They're supposed to work together."

I took one step and almost tripped over a book on the floor. We'd nearly emptied the bookcase by the time Lalo arrived. "I'm sorry about the mess. We'll come back afterward and..."

Jonathan sighed a deep librarian sigh that was not unlike

the many older brother sighs I'd heard in my lifetime. "Don't worry about it. Go on."

Jasmine, Isa, and Tori ran for the front of the library. Lalo loped after them with Noemi just behind. Brian offered to help reshelve the books.

Jonathan turned his palm toward the ceiling and all of the books lifted from the floor. With another twist of his wrist, they moved closer to the shelves. "I've got it."

We joined the others at the circulation desk. I sent Adam a quick text, and he appeared beside me almost instantly.

"All clear out there?" Brian asked.

Adam's mouth tightened. "We need to hurry. That lantern's not going to hold much longer. I could feel the energy pulsing, even from outside the Gatehouse."

He set the book on the desk.

I held my breath as Isa placed the new book down next to the original.

An explosion of light shattered over both books. The translucent cover on the new book peeled back like paint chips, revealing a leather binding identical to the first one.

"Good boy, Lalo," I said.

He wagged his tail.

A small crash behind the desk heralded Thomas's arrival. "Oh good, you found it!"

Jonathan followed the sound, abandoning the mess in the restricted section. When he saw Thomas behind his desk, he huffed and shoved his hands in his pockets. "Impeccable landing, as always," he muttered. He spared our brother the lecture but stood beside him to prevent any further damage.

Thomas ignored him, running a hand down the letters on the spine. "So this is it, huh? The grimoire that holds the secrets Dad spent his life looking for?"

"The elixir of life might be in those pages," I said. The recipe he'd promised our Speaker in exchange for postponing my initiation as Gatekeeper. It was too late for it to extend Alice's life. The last Gatekeeper had already gone to better lands. But it might be the secret to surviving the time stream long enough to rescue my father. And the cure for Noemi's half-life.

"Then what are we waiting for?" Thomas asked, his hand ready to lift the cover.

I tucked my fingers under the cover of the original book. "Together."

We opened the books at the same time. Something snapped. Whether it was inside me, the books, or the universe, I couldn't tell. Everything was loud and bright and free. Pages lifted untethered from both books, floating into the air and shuffling like a deck of cards. Above them, the sigils appeared, a great tree rising from a swirling wave. The images blended to make a new sigil, branches flowing like a fountain, curling in all directions as they grew. Life out of change. Chaos and creation. Another flash of light and the books combined, the pages settling down into the binding as if they had always been there. One book. The title shimmered on the cover, letters rearranging, coming into focus, shining in gold leaf. *The Ichoriad.*

Jonathan's eyes glistened. It was the kind of book librarians dreamed of, never daring to hope they might someday encounter it.

"Wow," said Isa.

Tori dropped a hand on her shoulder. "Yeah, wow."

A red light blinked in Tori's bag.

"Uh, Tori…is that what I think it is?" Thomas asked.

"Hex-it-all." Tori pulled the kynigolabe out and popped it open. "Yeah, we're definitely being hunted. They know where we are, and they're on their way."

"It's the book," I said. "We broke the ward that was hiding it. Now anyone who was looking for it can find it. They might have been close before, but now they know exactly where we are."

A chill ran down my spine."You mean Mama Lily?" Noemi said. "Lily can find us here because she still wants the book."

Tori twisted some dials on the kynigolabe. "That would be my guess, yeah. This thing tracks anybody who might be hunting us, and she was the last person to trap us. I don't think she's got us pinpointed yet, or she would have blinked in like we did. But I don't know how much time we have. And I don't want to alarm anybody, but if these readings are right, she's not the only one."

Hunters. Had they sensed its power as soon as Adam took it past the Gate? Or only since we joined the two books together? Did we have any kind of head start?

Did it matter?

53

Jonathan went to the door, pulled a piece of chalk from the frame, and drew a series of sigils like the ones Thomas had drawn at the magic shop. Stepping back, he drew more sigils on the floor. Facing us with the chalk still in his hand, he said, "Stay here. I'm going to ward the windows and the back door. The library is one of the safest buildings in Queen's Creek, but it doesn't hurt to lock it down when danger's coming."

He strode out of the room.

"While we're sharing terrible news and trying not to panic…" Thomas looked at Isa.

"What?"

"Elspeth thinks Emily was poisoned. She's trying to work up an antidote now, but she's kind of stuck with herbal remedies because, you know, magic doesn't work if you don't believe in it, and Emily's been unconscious for all the fun stuff, so…" Thomas trailed off.

"Did she find a remedy, though? An antidote to whatever Lily gave her?" Isa asked. She grabbed Tori's hand on her shoulder.

He frowned. "She's having a hard time figuring out which

poison it was, and if she chooses the wrong one, sometimes the antidote is as bad as the poison."

The poison sounded like it might kill her. What antidote was worse than death?

Isa's lower lip trembled.

Thomas looked away, his eyes landing on mine. My brother was finally starting to develop empathy for mundanes. It might not be much, but it gave me hope. Maybe Lily wouldn't have as much support as she thought.

Isa heaved in a breath and looked at the book. "What about this, though? If we make the elixir of life, that's got to cure anything, doesn't it?"

Thomas squeezed his eyes shut and opened them again. "I don't know. I'm sorry, kid. But she doesn't believe…"

"I believe!" Isa yelled. She stepped closer to the desk, letting Tori's hand fall from her shoulder. "I believe it will work."

"That might not be enough," Tori said.

"It will." Isa pulled the book toward her and lifted it closed, nearly losing her balance from the weight of it. "Take me to my mom."

Tori and Thomas locked eyes across the table. She put one hand back on Isa's shoulder and reached for Thomas's with the other. He blinked, and they all disappeared.

Jonathan's going to be so mad.

"Anybody else concerned at all that they just took the book everyone wants out of the library wards again?" Jasmine asked.

"How well protected is the healer's cottage?" Brian asked.

Well, it doesn't have a door anymore.

"It could be stronger," Adam admitted. "Want to help me shore it up?"

"Let's go be bodyguards," Jasmine said.

Adam took their hands and blinked them away.

Alone with Noemi and Lalo for the first time, I realized I had questions no one had ever answered. I wanted to sit down and talk while we recovered from the emotional rollercoaster of escaping a possessed witch, coming back home, and finding the book that could potentially solve all of our world's problems. But I couldn't. We'd left an energy bomb at the Gatehouse, and our Guardian had just gone to protect the book.

Plus, I didn't want to be the last one here when Jonathan realized we'd all ignored his safety lesson.

"You up for another walk?" I asked Noemi.

Lalo stood and ran to the door, his tongue hanging out. His paws scuffed the chalk on the floor.

"He's ready," Noemi said. She cast a quick glance in the direction Jonathan had gone and followed. "Back to the Gatehouse, then?"

"Yeah, I don't know how we're going to contain that demon thing if it gets out of the lantern, but we have to keep it as far away from that book as possible." Maybe we could ask the wisps for help. They'd nearly destroyed the boundary spell all by themselves, consuming its energy along the Creek. But the demon might be too big a meal, even for an army of will-o'-the-wisps.

I put my fingers inside the bell on the door to keep it from ringing and set it on the floor. We were out before Jonathan returned from warding the rest of the library. He'd be safe anyway. Nothing our enemies wanted was here anymore.

As we walked, I turned over the possibilities but didn't come up with a solution. Magic was energy plus intention, so was that what this demon was? A creature of pure magic? Energy with its own intentions? Bad intentions. Negative energy. There'd been something about that in Brian's notes. A quantum field…gravitational potential energy…something that pulled you in. It reminded me of a few people I knew.

Of all the ways my friends and family could influence people, only one had a condition that predisposed people to feel safe around a predator. To feel calm in the company of someone who might eat them for breakfast. And she didn't do it by expending her own energy but by inviting yours in.

"Noemi, I need to know more about this whole vampire thing," I said.

Lalo loped along beside us, bouncing off and on the path to inspect whatever caught his nose.

She didn't look surprised. "What do you want to know?"

"You said something before about not having enough energy because of your condition. What did you mean? What's the connection between vamps and energy?"

"Vampires are not capable of sustaining their own energy," she said. "We don't breathe, so we don't take in oxygen. Without oxygen, we can't convert food to energy. That's why vampires drink blood. We can't metabolize energy from regular food the way humans do. We need blood that is already rich in energy sources."

"You can't produce energy."

"Not really, that's why we go in for our treatments. We get topped off, and that keeps us going for a while, but the transfusions aren't enough. We're still low on iron and protein. And our white blood cells are…"

"But that's why the demon couldn't use you," I said.

"What?"

"Back at Lily's. When Tori pulled it from Lily and put it into the lantern. The energy fought her. It tried to go anywhere else. But when it came to you, it stopped. You didn't have enough energy to feed it."

Noemi stopped walking as we came out of the trees. Ahead of us, the Creek sparkled, colored by the setting sun. Tiny flashes on the banks revealed the presence of wisps, still drawn to the Gatehouse, even without the boundary spell.

"Does it always look like that?" she asked.

"Like what?" The Gatehouse looked the same as always, small but cozy, strong but welcoming. The new stone bridge made it seem a little more modern than the wooden footbridge had. Less a relic of where we'd been and more a reminder of how far we'd come.

"Bright." Noemi shaded her eyes as the sun dipped behind the building. She'd avoided daylight by blinking straight to Elspeth's from the Gatehouse, and the trees had blocked most of the direct light during our walk.

"Do you want to wait here?" I didn't want to see what would happen if I dragged the vampire into the sun, even after what she'd told me about the effects being exaggerated by the media. But I also couldn't risk the demon escaping while we waited for the sun to set.

Noemi looked embarrassed. "I'm sorry—"

"Save your energy," I said. "We don't know what's going to happen in there. We might need your influence if Lily finds us."

She nodded.

"I'll be fine," I said as much to myself as to reassure her.

Her nephew started to follow me. She called him back, but he trotted closer. Lalo nudged my hand, and his little boy voice spoke in my mind. "If you need us, just call out. I have really good hearing now. You prolly only need to whisper."

I scratched between his ears. "Thanks, kiddo. I'll see you soon."

Like I'm ever going to call this sweetheart into battle against a dangerous energy creature. But he didn't have to know that.

He turned his head into the scratches and then ducked to turn back to Noemi. She leaned against a shady tree, and he curled up at her feet.

I stepped onto the bridge and crossed the Creek.

It was strange to stand inside the Gatehouse—the real

Gatehouse—on my own. This would have been my destiny if things had gone to plan. But they so rarely do. I'd grown up the prophesied Chosen One, seventh child of a seventh child. But even with Alice's foresight and the elders' years of study, no one had predicted the way my prophecy manifested.

The Last Gatekeeper.

I ran my hand along the narrow mantel over what I still thought of as Alice's fireplace and turned to face her bedroom. My bedroom. Where I'd left the lantern with the demon trapped inside.

How is this my life?

I took a deep breath and called the energy of this sacred space. It came to me from the air around me, the water outside, the earth below. Directing some of that energy to the logs in the fireplace, I snapped my fingers and lit the fire. A month ago, I'd been jealous that my mom could light a candle that way. Now, I drew energy from the flames that I created. An endless loop. My fingers sparked. How long could I hold the demon in its cage before I burned out?

No way to know but to walk through that door.

I reached for the doorknob just as the wooden door exploded into the room.

54

My hands flew up in front of me, reflexively calling my Gift to stop the door fragments. Chunks of wood hung in the air, some of it only inches from my face. I avoided being impaled by the shrapnel, but the energy behind it refused to obey. On the other side of the explosion a bright light pulsed. I blinked away the dust, and my eyes teared up.

I closed my eyes and dropped to the floor, releasing the energy. Bits of the door flew over my head and dug into the wall behind me.

"Cate?" Noemi called from somewhere outside. She and Lalo both must have heard the explosion. The demon couldn't take control of Noemi, but I couldn't put them at risk if it kept blowing stuff up.

"Don't come in!" I yelled. "It's free! Get help!"

She didn't answer, and I hoped she'd run back into town for reinforcements.

I squeezed my eyes shut against the light. My eyelids burned red. I sucked in a breath, drawing my energy back. *I am the Last Gatekeeper. I will not let this thing into my home.*

We brought it here. But this is as far as it goes. This place.

This liminal space where the veil is thin and the time stream connects us to our history. This is where we send it back to wherever it came from.

Pushing back to my feet, I shielded my eyes with my arm and addressed the creature. "What do you want? There's nothing here for you. No one here is going to invite you in. You are not welcome here."

A cackle behind me drew my attention to the Gatehouse door. Lily stood on the threshold, frowning. "Rude."

I gasped as the light in Alice's room intensified, sensing the presence of its latest host.

She folded her hands in front of her and smiled. "Luckily, I'm not a vampire, not that even they would need an invitation. You left the door open."

No. It had been closed. Adam stood out there with the book —*he stood out there with the book. Who else had sensed it?* And then he came back through the Gatehouse and blinked to the library. No way did the Guardian leave the door open behind him.

But there was no ward up to lock it. We'd taken down the protection spell. The glamour the Watch put up in its place wasn't enough. She'd already found us. Was there anything left to keep her out?

Lily stepped through the door.

Shit.

I threw my hands up again, calling my Gift to stop her, but the light moved faster than I could. It enveloped her, lifting her off the floor. As the light suffused her skin, the energy creature that created it lowered her back down. Her head rolled along her shoulders, and her neck cracked. Looking up, she smiled. "That's better."

My fingers tingled with unspent energy. If I froze her now, the demon would only work itself free again. If I reversed time, could I get it back to the lantern? I felt strong, but I doubted I was strong enough to hold it there indefinitely. "The book isn't here," I said.

"But it was," said Lily. "Very recently. It must still be nearby."

She closed her eyes. Her hands turned slowly upward, rolling at the wrists, reaching for something unseen.

Something slammed against the door on the Creek side of the Gatehouse. It swung open and Lalo bounded in with Noemi and Jonathan. My brother skidded to a stop.

"Who's that? What's she doing?" he asked, his voice barely audible over Lalo's barking.

The boy inside yelled some very hurtful things at his Mama Lily. Noemi tried to hush him, but he was gripped by the opportunity to act out the hero from his games. Noemi wrapped her arms around his neck, whispering in his ear. Even so, she struggled to keep him from launching himself at the older woman. *Which one of them is she protecting?*

Lily might have been meditating. She stood mostly still with her hands out at her sides, head tilted upward, eyes still closed. The barking dog may as well have been on a different continent. If I hadn't seen a living star incorporate itself into her body a moment ago, I might have considered her vulnerable.

I stepped back toward the bedroom in an effort to keep both doors in view. "I think she's trying to figure out where we took the book."

Jonathan put his hands on his hips, shaking his head. "You assholes cannot follow directions."

The crass words surprised me coming from my most staid brother. Any other time I would have laughed. I made a joke to keep from panicking. "Hey, language."

He looked at Lalo, then Noemi, and flinched.

"Sorry. But Cate. You promised." Jonathan used his stern, I'm-not-angry-just-disappointed voice.

"Yeah, sorry. Maybe tell Mom to ground me after we defeat the demon?"

"Defeat the…what now?" Jonathan asked.

"This is my dear friend, Lily Vallaria." Noemi gestured with a nod, but the green witch didn't acknowledge her. "I'd introduce you, but at the moment, she's been possessed by some kind of energy creature that wants the elixir of life. It's promised to cure all the ravages of her old age, but I think we all know it wants more than that. Calling it a demon is kind of shorthand."

"Interesting…" said the rumbling voice in Lily's body. She didn't move, but her eyes rolled behind the lids.

"I was thinking terrifying," said Jonathan. "But I suppose it could be interesting as well, from an academic standpoint."

"I don't think she's talking to you," I said.

"I don't think we want to know what she finds interesting," Noemi said.

"Such great power. So much energy. And all in one place," murmured the voice.

Jonathan looked from Lily to Noemi and back to me. "Kitty. What have you done?"

Before I could answer, Lily's eyes popped open, black as night. Cold energy rolled off her, sending shivers down my back. She stepped farther into the room.

Jonathan moved between us. He held up a hand. "Stay right there if you would, ma'am. I don't want to hurt you."

She stepped forward, pushing her breastbone against his hand. "You will not stop me."

He set his feet, this man who could lift bookcases with one hand. Whose Gift of Strength could have made him a bully, but who had chosen to use it to build the library. His workmanship was all over the renovated Gatehouse. And now he used it to hold back an old woman.

It wasn't enough.

The demon roared in his face, Lily's features contorting, exposing the true face of the creature she'd aligned herself with—the monster she'd chosen over her own people.

Jonathan's eyes widened, but he held his ground.

The energy creature pushed out under her skin, making it glow with a burning light. A flash blinded me.

When I opened my eyes, she stood inches from my face. It should have taken four or five steps, but she did it in one. Her hand shot out, closing around my neck, pushing me into the bedroom. The door slammed shut behind her, pulling its broken pieces from all over the room, reincorporating them before it disappeared into the blank wall as if it had never existed.

Noemi and Jonathan yelled, but the sound was dull and distant.

The demon's voice echoed in my mind. "Timeweaver. Veil crosser. Gatekeeper. You will show me the way."

"What way? Where?" I squeaked. Darkness closed around me until all I saw was Lily's face. Too bright. Too wild. Too angry.

The gravelly voice rumbled, making the image of her face vibrate around the edges. "You alone can give me what I need."

I stiffed my spine, fighting for the air to speak. "You can't have the elixir. I won't help you find the book. No one should live forever."

The voice laughed, deep and low. "I have no need of recipes anymore. Not now that you've led me here. What a lovely home you've made for yourself, right atop the Source of magic."

What was she talking about? The Source was the people. Magic existed because we called forth the energy and directed it to our will. The magic had always come from us.

"A place where the veil thins and time slows. Where past

and present flow side by side with the future. This is a place where the multiverse meets…"

"Have you been spying on Brian? You sound like one of his sci-fi shows." Did the words come out of my mouth? I couldn't breathe. Speech felt impossible. But I heard the demon's voice inside my head. Louder and clearer than Tori's or Caleb's had ever been.

"You know…" the voice insisted. "You have been there. Through the stream of time."

A vision of the Creek rose behind my eyes. I couldn't block the memories. A childhood of sneaking out to watch the sparks fly over the Creek. The fireflies that were actually ancient will-o'-the-wisps feeding off the energy of the boundary spell. The cracks in the spell when the energy inside exceeded its capacity. The storm of purple lightning. The explosion from within me when I accepted the mantle of the Gatekeeper. The release when I let it go. The fire.

"The energy is gone," I said. "We let it go. The boundary spell…there's nothing to hold the magic here anymore."

"We'll see about that."

Darkness overcame me.

When the light returned, it was filtered through the water of the Creek. I opened my mouth to scream. Stupid. Cold water poured into my mouth.

"Take me to the time stream," the voice said.

Where was Lily? I couldn't sense anyone else around me. Not even fish to witness me drowning. I was going to die. There was no time stream here anymore. I'd let it go when I let go of the mantle of Gatekeeper.

"You waste your life," said the voice. "I could save it."

What?

"Invite me in, and I will stop the water from entering your lungs. You are stronger than the others. We could do so much together."

Yeah, I bet. You can't do much of anything on your own. Can you? You're just energy.

A jolt, like electricity, shot up my back. I cried out from the shock more than the pain, gulping water in the process. It burned in my chest. The water pressed in on all sides. I struggled against it but couldn't find the air. Which way was up?

"You're drowning, Hecate Corey. Let me save you."

You are the one who's killing me.

"I am energy. I am life. I can save you. I can help you find your father."

The thing was in my head now. I couldn't believe anything it said. *Why would you do that?*

The voice sighed, a deep breath I couldn't take. "I need you. To access the energy of the time stream. To make myself whole again. You are the key."

I'm what?

"You are the key. But you are mortal, and you are dying."

No.

The voice laughed, thunder in my mind. "Help me and live. Join me, and you will have the power to protect everyone you love. You fear the hunters, but you could be so much stronger than them. You are so much stronger already. Take what you want."

I want to breathe.

"Then let me in. Take me into the time stream, and I will no longer need the elixir to sustain me. The energy of the time stream is infinite. I will never need another host."

How many people had this creature destroyed in its quest for power, for the immortality promised by the elixir of life? If it was willing to give that up now, the energy of the time stream must still be there, waiting beyond my senses. But I'd lost the connection. Even if I'd wanted to…

I can't.

The voice growled. "Why do you fight me? You will not win. All you are doing is delaying my victory and ensuring your own death. You are dying, Gatekeeper. And when you do, I shall choose another host. The elixir of life is almost within my grasp. Once I have it, I will have centuries to discover the secrets of the time stream. Centuries in which I will gorge myself on the energy of your friends and their descendants. I will burn through them all if I have to, but I will find a way in. Or you can open yourself to me, unlock the time stream, and give me its energy now. This is your crossroads, Hecate. Save yourself. Save them all. Or die and let me have them. I will get what I want in the end. Will you be there with me?"

I needed air. My head felt like it would explode. Dots crowded my vision.

Freeze.

55

I blinked, and when my eyes opened, I sat on the floor of the Gatehouse. Not the real one, the Mind Palace I'd created for myself. How long could I stay here before the demon found me?

I pushed myself up to standing and coughed. Water splashed from my mouth onto the floor. That couldn't be good. I'd never brought anything here from the physical world before. I retched again, forcing the water out of my lungs. My breath escaped in broken pieces. A high-pitched tone rose and fell in my ears, knocking off my equilibrium.

Staggering, I dragged myself to the window on the Creek side of the house. Outside, a figure of glowing light rose above the water. The demon, freed and growing, drawing energy from the time stream. On the far bank, my brothers—all six of them—worked together, building something I couldn't see. Adam's father, Giles, stood beside Mrs. Kirk, shoulder to shoulder with other elders from Queen's Creek. They all lifted their arms, raising a shield between them and the demon, a wall of water like the one Mrs. Kirk had used to trap me in the Gatehouse a few weeks ago. I clung to the windowsill, struggling for breath.

Was it only weeks? How time flies when your world is ending.

The demon grew brighter, even as more witches, my friends and neighbors, poured out of the trees and joined the elders at the barrier. The light was too intense, reflected by the shimmering wall of water. It dazzled my eyes.

It's not real. It's only a vision.

But was it the future or just a hallucination of my oxygen-deprived mind?

On the other side of the Gatehouse, someone screamed. I rubbed my eyes and turned. Across the empty room, the door opened to the forest outside. Jasmine, Brian, and Adam stood with their backs to me, facing shadows in the trees. No. Not shadows. Hunters. Men and women in dark clothing used our forest for cover. A broad-shouldered man with bowlegs stepped out onto the path, his cowboy boots scuffling the loose gravel. *Wesson.*

Jasmine said something to him, but I couldn't hear the words through the ringing in my ears. She raised her hands above her head. Adam's staff fell to the ground.

No!

I called my Gift, but the energy didn't respond. My hands tightened into fists, my nails biting my palms. My head throbbed, and I gasped, but nothing came.

Was this what would happen if I refused the demon? I coughed, choking on water I couldn't see. Because I wasn't really there. Whether my friends and family stood ready to fight outside the Gatehouse or not, I wasn't there. I wouldn't be there if I didn't let it in. I would drown. Another sacrifice lost to the Creek.

My mind whirled. There had to be another way. I reached for the energy of this place, my Spirit Palace, the seat of my power…and came up empty. I tried to sense the time stream, my ancestors, the Gatekeepers who'd guided me before. But all I heard was the incessant whine of the tone in my ears.

Louder now.

I fell against the wall, chest heaving, eyes burning. I had to get out.

They're counting on me.

My eyes went to the open door.

The veil is thin here. Where would that door take me? I gasped for breath, preparing to run. A new voice stopped me before I took the first step. A voice I knew better than my heart.

"Slow down."

Tears ran from the corners of my eyes.

Turning, I found my father standing in the center of the room. I ran to him, melting into his embrace. "It's going to be alright. You've got this."

"I've got nothing, Dad," I sobbed. "I'm drowning, and that monster is going to keep taking bodies until it gets what it wants. It's going to destroy people's lives."

"One thing at a time," he whispered. "Focus on just one thing."

"But how can I choose? Everything I do ends in someone getting hurt. If I let go, sacrifice myself to protect the time stream, it will choose someone else. It will get the elixir of life and live forever, getting stronger all the time. If I let it in to save myself, I let it into the time stream. I don't know what it will do with that kind of power. I don't know what will happen to the time stream. To you."

He pulled back to look at my face.

My eyes burned from the water of the Creek and the salt of my tears.

Dad straightened my glasses and pushed my hair behind my ears. "Everything doesn't have to get solved all at once. And you don't have to do this alone."

"But I—" I was going to say *was chosen*, falling back on the responsibilities I thought I'd escaped. But he'd never wanted that for me. He'd fought against it so hard he'd ended up here, lost in time to keep me from being tied to my destiny.

He smiled as though he knew what I'd held back. He didn't argue. Instead, he said, "It's not the job of the Chosen One to save everyone all the time. It was a one-time gig, which you executed admirably. From here on out things only get better if everyone makes the choice to do what they can to fix what they can. Concentrate on the things you can control and trust others to do the same. Saving the world is an everybody, every day, all day job."

The room flickered, everything disappearing for a second, replaced with the water rushing over my head. I thrashed against it, and my father caught my hand, pulling me back into the Gatehouse dream space.

"I don't know what to do," I cried. "Everything feels out of control. What do I do? How do I— "

The room faded again, but as he melted into the dappled light on the water, I heard my father's voice again.

"You're not going to win every fight, but you only lose if you stop fighting. Not every fight is for survival. Not every battle is against an enemy you can see. Choose yourself."

Everything went black.

My body convulsed in the water, searching for air where there was none.

The voice in the darkness asked, "Have you made your choice?"

I want to live.

56

Energy rushed into my body, air filling my lungs despite the cold creek water still surrounding me. I rose through the water, cresting it and more. My feet tickled the surface. I felt stronger and more connected than I ever had. The energy of the world buzzed at my fingertips. I knew that I could do anything I wanted. Have anything I wanted.

"Yes," said the voice. "But there is more. So much more to be had."

Jonathan and Noemi ran out of the Gatehouse and across the bridge. Lalo stopped halfway, growling his deepest puppy growl from the slippery stones. His human voice yelled something I couldn't hear. Inside my head, the demon roared back.

Noemi called to her nephew from the far bank, struggling against my brother, who held her back.

The creature's energy flooded my veins. I held up my hands to show them that I didn't intend to harm anyone. My fingers glowed. The light rippled up my arms and across my chest. It reflected off the water below me.

"Shhh, Lalo. It's okay." My voice reverberated with power.

The dog cowered, his tail tucked low and ran to Noemi. Jonathan released her, and she wrapped her arms around the lanky puppy.

"It's okay. It's all going to be okay." I pulled the energy in, hoping to dim the light that frightened him. But it only got brighter.

"You cannot hide your strength," said the voice in my head. "Embrace our power. Show them what we can do."

I smiled. *Yes.*

They looked so scared. They didn't need to be. My brother yelled something, but his voice seemed very far away, dulled by the buzz of energy in my ears.

"Don't be afraid. I can help you." I floated closer to the bank, still hovering above the clear water of the Creek.

Noemi shaded her eyes with her arm, pushing Lalo behind her. The puppy lay down at her feet, shaking.

I had to show them there was nothing to fear. My fingers tingled. The energy was right there. I could change them both back, give them their humanity.

"Show them," whispered the voice.

Jonathan stepped in front of Noemi, squinting against my light. He held up his hands, and I felt his Gift work against me, pushing me back.

"What are you doing? Don't you understand? I have it now. I'm in control. I can do all the things I was meant to. I can help…"

He strained against me. His face turned up to meet my eyes and his lips formed a single word. "Stop!"

I pulled back, and he staggered.

"No!" cried the voice in my mind. "Use your power."

But they don't want me to.

"They don't believe you can do it. Give them no reason to doubt you."

I could do it. I could show them how much I'd changed. I

didn't need protecting anymore. I could protect them. With each breath, I grew stronger. The light expanded around me, making everything glisten. The demon's energy hugged me close, and its voice started to sound more like my own. *Show them our strength.*

I turned up my palms, drawing the energy into glowing orbs of light. Visualizing my intentions, I pictured Lalo as he was when I first met him, an excited young boy, silly and funny and full of mischief.

Bring him back.

Jonathan backed up, spreading his arms to shield Noemi and Lalo. They ducked their heads against the light.

"Don't be afraid." I turned my hands out.

My brother raised his head, his eyes sparkling in my sunshine.

And then he blinked.

All three of them disappeared from the bank of the Creek.

"No!"

The energy I'd called had nowhere to go. It burned my hands.

Redirect it.

I'd redirected Tori's energy on the beach to protect those girls. Where did it go? Into the fire. Back to the elements.

My hands shook. The energy raced up and down my arms, burning tracks into my skin. It rolled up my neck. My muscles tensed. Any thoughts of Jonathan and the others burned away. All that was left was the pain. I had to release it. My body couldn't contain it. The energy needed direction.

Open the Gate.

The demon's voice came from somewhere in the back of my mind, almost an afterthought. It wanted to go into the time stream. I knew I shouldn't let it in, but I couldn't remember why.

Flashes of memory forced their way to the surface. The

time stream was dangerous. I'd almost gotten lost last time. I had lost someone.

Bring him back.

Yes. That was why I was here, wasn't it? To bring someone back. It was my fault he was gone. But now I was stronger. I could find him.

My own light blinded me.

Release the energy. Open the Gate.

Yes. I was the Gatekeeper. That was my purpose. I closed my eyes.

I visualized a door opening to eternity. The flowing waves of time reaching out in all directions. I stepped through.

Into the time stream.

The energy dissipated, and I could breathe again.

"Thank you," said the voice in my head.

The demon loosened its hold. The fog lifted from my mind, slowly releasing me back to myself.

"Wait!" As hot as the energy had been, its absence left me shivering. We were supposed to do this together. Wasn't that what it promised? Stronger together. More capable. But now it wanted to leave me alone. I'd be back where I started, incapable of controlling my own Gift, lost in the time stream.

I clutched at the creature. It glowed with the energy it drew from the time stream.

"Your help is no longer required," said the voice. "You've given me my own source of energy, and I will never need another. This is where we part. My goals are no longer your concern. You have your own goals here. Don't waste your time."

Don't waste your time. My time. The Seven of Swords reversed. We had everything backwards. I'd been deceiving myself. Convinced myself I wasn't enough. Hexing imposter syndrome.

I am the seventh child of a seventh child. I was Chosen. *I choose myself.*

My father's face appeared in my mind. Emily's eyes, glazed from the poison. Noemi and Lalo, trying over and over to change themselves back to the human witches they used to be. Jasmine and Brian facing the hunters outside the Gatehouse. Adam at their side. Somehow, I was the key to it all.

My skin thrummed as the energy of the time stream washed over me, warm and welcoming. It tickled. I smiled. "My Gift is the manipulation of time. All of the energy of the time stream is mine. All of it. Even the energy you've taken. It's mine. You are mine now."

I twisted my fingers, and the light danced around me. The voice screamed at me, but I ignored it until it was lost in the whirlpool of energy I created. I held out my hands and drew the energy back into my skin. Nothing could hurt me here. I absorbed the energy of the creature and let its voice settle into the back of my mind, no louder than my conscience.

57

I rode the current of the time stream, floating along eddies and surfing the waves as they crested the years. My muscles warmed and I breathed deeply, taking in energy with all of my senses. For once, there was no rush. I had all of the time in the world.

Bubbles passed me by, sparkling with movement. I caught one and brought it close. Inside, a scene played out. On the banks of the Creek, a young girl spread out a blanket. A friend joined her, and they sat together, watching the sunset over the water. The sky turned pink and purple, and it glowed on their skin. On Elspeth's and my skin. We laughed together, sharing secrets. I released the bubble, letting it float away.

Another bubble brushed my fingers, a window to another time. Inside, a young Cate ran through the woods, chasing a fairy. But it wasn't a fairy after all. The wisp led me astray. Lost and alone in the darkness, I fell, crying out. A new light twinkled between the trees. Three lights held in glass globes. My brothers' star torches. They found me and brought me home, their enchanted lanterns lighting the way.

The voice in the back of my mind whispered, its tone so

low I had to strain to hear it. "They don't understand you. You don't need their protection."

In the next scene, I lay in my bed. My parents on either side. Something tightened over my eyes. The voice tried again, fighting its way back from the deep subconscious where I'd buried it. "See how they held you back?"

The betrayal felt new again. My face burned. I would show them.

I peered into the next bubble, something closer to the present. Lily sat in Noemi's living room, twisting the rings on her fingers. My fingers sparked, and the bubble popped. I grasped for another. The green witch in her garden. Her thumb twisted the ring on her index finger. It was silver, antique with a small hinge on the side. The bubble popped.

This time, I knew it wasn't my own reflexes. I pulled the demon closer, lifting it from the depths of my mind. If it was going to try to influence me, it could do so in the open. "What don't you want me to see?"

"She is not your concern. She is nothing. An old woman whose time has passed."

My hands shook. The hypocrisy. That attitude was the whole reason Lily had accepted the demon in the first place. She'd felt unappreciated and undervalued until it told her she was better than those who belittled her. And now, this creature would try to make me feel the same way by tearing her down. "I will decide who is and is not my concern."

"Of course." The voice gave in too easily.

I reached for another bubble. Just before it brushed against my fingers, the demon spoke again. "It's only…I thought you wanted to protect your friends. She is no longer a danger to you. But there are others…"

She's not a danger to me because I allowed the real threat into my mind. I am the danger now. But I knew what it meant. External threats loomed outside of Queen's Creek. The vision I'd seen in my Spirit Palace showed hunters at the Gate. Had they arrived already?

"Show me," I said.

A time bubble grew in front of me. The path that led to the Gatehouse was shadowed by the swaying branches of large trees. Another storm hovered nearby. Darkness between the trees solidified into human figures. Wesson stepped onto the path.

"You can stop them."

I can. I knew it as well as I knew the demon's intentions. The longer it lay curled in the back of my mind, the more its consciousness merged with mine. It had read my thoughts and my memories, but now the connection opened in both directions.

This thing thinks I'll leave it here to gorge itself on the energy of the time stream while I go to battle against an unknown number of witch hunters carrying who-knows-what kind of enchanted weapons.

I could defeat the mundanes. It would be easy. But how would the demon have evolved by the time I got back? What did it want with all of that energy?

"Let's do it together," I said.

The creature complained, throwing out a hundred arguments, but I pushed it back down again.

I visualized the door we'd come through. Leaving the time stream was easier this time. I rose above the Creek, blinking in the sunlight. No, the sun had set. My own light lit the sky. I floated like a star above the Gatehouse. On the far side, Adam, Brian, and Jasmine faced the intruders. They shielded their eyes.

The energy I held begged for release. Thunder cracked in the distance, and I could not say for sure I hadn't caused it. My light erased the shadows below me, and I could see everything clearly. Seven hunters hid beneath the boughs, clutching weapons that ranged from mundane handguns to something that looked like a fantasy staff with a glowing jewel embedded in it.

Fewer than I'd expected. Maybe the League wasn't as informed as we'd feared. They found Queen's Creek, but they had no idea how many witches lived inside.

Or how powerful we are.

I smiled. This time, I didn't need the creature's encouragement to show them what we could do.

Someone was yelling, but between the thunder and the energy buzzing in my ears, I couldn't make out what they were saying. It didn't matter.

"Stop." I spoke softly, directing my intention with barely a flick of my fingers. Everything in the woods became still. The tiny sounds of life among the trees went silent. Even the wisps by the creek bed stopped flickering.

The hunters froze in their places.

This was how I should have felt in that memory from my childhood. Not lost in the woods—I was in control of everything. But I hadn't understood my Gift back then, and it had frightened me.

I took a deep breath, feeling my lungs expand. My senses awakened, flooded with energy.

Below me, Adam, Jasmine, and Brian approached the frozen hunters. Brian waved his hand in front of Wesson's face. Jasmine's eyes widened. She touched her mentor's arm, but he didn't react.

Adam stepped back to face me. He ducked his head until his eyes adjusted to the light.

Thunder crashed, and the clouds rolled in, blocking out the other stars.

His mouth moved, but I couldn't hear him.

Dampening the energy around me, I lowered myself to the ground. The buzzing became a soft hum.

Adam kept his distance. "Cate, what's happened to you? What are you doing?"

"I'm protecting Queen's Creek."

I looked at Wesson, standing frozen on the path to Gatehouse. He would never reach it. My hand drifted up from my side, fingers twisting of their own accord. I felt the edges of the time bubble around him, pulled them tighter. Energy sparked.

Jasmine and Brian jumped back.

A clock ticked in the back of my mind. I focused it on Wesson, letting his time unravel. Inside the bubble, he grew older as his years passed. At first, the changes were hardly noticeable—dark spots on his cheeks, creases under his eyes. His brown hair had already been streaked with gray, but after a few seconds, he'd never get away with passing them off as highlights again.

Jasmine screamed.

What did it look like from her perspective? Could she see the magic working on him?

Brian put an arm around her and pulled her back toward the Gatehouse, but that brought them closer to me. She broke away and disappeared into the trees.

Maybe she belonged with the hunters after all. "They shouldn't have come. I won't let them into our home."

Adam stepped between me and Wesson. The hunter's time continued to wind down behind him. Adam raised one hand as if to hold me back and gestured to Wesson with the other. "They came because they're afraid of us. This is not going to make them fear us less."

"They're here because they feared us without reason. I'm giving them a reason."

He inhaled. "You think this will keep them away? They'll just come back. They'll bring more hunters next time."

I glared at him. The Guardian at the Gate telling me to go

easy on these invaders. "And I'll stop them, too."

He dropped his arms to his sides. "How? Are you going to stay here in the Gatehouse? Go back to being the Gatekeeper after everything?"

Gatekeeper. The voice echoed deep in my mind. That was who I was. Why fight it?

I rolled my head, releasing some of the tension in my neck. "If I must. It's what I was meant for. You know that as well as I do. The prophecy was right. I will be the last Gatekeeper. This is my place. Eternally."

Adam shook his head. "This is not self-sacrifice. It's not noble. It's guilt."

It's both.

"I can't keep letting people down. I can't keep saving people who won't stay saved. How am I supposed to walk away?"

"You have to trust us, Cate," Brian said. "You have to believe in us the way that we've believed in you."

Belief makes it real.

Jasmine stepped back out of the tree line, holding a crossbow.

Was that an antique? How long had the hunters been waiting to use that?

"Trust you, huh?"

She raised her weapon. "If you don't end this, I will. Trust that."

"I thought you weren't a killer," I said.

She shrugged and adjusted her line of sight. "You told me I didn't have to be. Maybe you were wrong."

"Do you even know how to use that?"

The door behind me creaked open.

The arrow shot from Jasmine's bow.

I lifted myself up into the sky again as she reloaded from a quiver on her back. *Okay, Katniss.*

At the Gatehouse, an elderly woman pulled at the arrow where it punctured her shawl, pinning her to the entrance. She mumbled something at it and then threw her hands down and stepped forward, unharmed. The shawl remained attached to the building.

Lily looked up at me, shading her eyes. "It's lying to you, you know."

58

O*bviously.*
I didn't trust the creature any more than I trusted the hunters, my friends, or myself. None of us had managed to do all the things we'd said we would. The demon had made me strong, but it tried to desert me at every opportunity to pursue more energy. Wesson's entire methodology revolved around his cover as a concerned uncle and youth mentor. Jasmine had never liked me, even before she knew I was a witch. Brian turned out to be a scion, hiding his true identity for our entire friendship. Adam disappeared when the conversation got hard.

"Look what it's doing to you," Lily said. "It's using you. It's already absorbed more energy from you than I could give it."

She looked so small, standing on the ground beneath me. What had the demon ever seen in her? She couldn't offer it what I could. No wonder it had abandoned her. "You're wrong. I'm in control. The energy is mine to wield."

"For how long? You've overfed it." Lily made a face like I'd let my dog poop in her yard.

Brian stepped closer. "She's right, Cate. The human body

wasn't designed to support that much energy. Your body won't be able to contain it much longer."

He's wrong.

"What will happen to her if she doesn't release it?" Adam asked.

Nothing. Everything. I'll be invulnerable. Unstoppable.

Lily licked her dry lips and squinted up at me before facing Adam. "She'll become one of them. That's where these creatures come from. They burn off their physical form and evolve into pure energy. Energy with the memories of an angry spirit."

I'll show them angry. Several options for resolving the hunter threat flashed behind my eyes. How would they like living in the seventeenth century? Maybe further back. Could I get them eaten by dinosaurs? The light around me flickered as I ticked off ideas one by one, only half listening to the people on the ground.

Adam rubbed his head. "Why would you…why would anyone summon something like that in the first place? Why take the risk?"

Lily's eyebrows dropped until they nearly met in the middle. "I had it under control, boy. I knew how to limit its influence. I kept my goals reasonable."

Jasmine rolled her eyes, nocking the next arrow into place. Its tip shimmered in the light. "And you would have gotten away with it if it weren't for us meddling kids, right? Give me a break, lady. You're no better than the League. We almost died in your backyard. Emily still might. What did you put in her wine?"

Lily looked as if she didn't know what Jasmine was talking about.

"Yeah, you were in control." Jasmine shook her head and pointed the crossbow at me again. "Release the hunters. They won't come back. They've learned their lesson."

I raised an eyebrow. "Oh really? Do you promise?"

"Let them go, Cate," Brian said.

"I knew you were on their side."

He held up his hands. "I'm on your side. But this isn't you. This is going to destroy you. Don't let it."

Adam stepped back. One more step, and he'd cross into the time bubble that held Wesson.

"Stop." I reached for him, and he froze. *Safe.*

"The hell?" Jasmine stomped her foot. "Come on, Cate. You are making it so hard not to shoot you. Don't make me break my promise to Tori."

"I'm protecting him," I said. "It's my turn."

Brian blew out a breath. "That does not look like protection."

"He's fine." The light around me flashed.

"If you say so," Brian said, still holding up his hands.

"I'm not going to hurt you," I said.

"Of course not." But he didn't move, even though I wasn't stopping him.

The voice in the back of my mind chuckled.

What are you laughing about?

"Your strength is delicious. I knew you had potential."

My potential had never been in question. My potential was the reason I was Chosen. The hope of my people. The safety of our community. It all rested on my potential.

The light brightened. No star in the sky could compete. My eyes burned. I lifted myself higher, well out of range of Jasmine's weapon. Across the Creek, the watch tower peeked out of the trees, still mostly hidden from view. Broad branches shaded the rest of the buildings. But the hunters had found it. They knew exactly where to look. I imagined a dome over it—a bubble of time to separate Queen's Creek from the rest of the world. Safe forever.

Was this how Mary had felt when she first set the

boundary? My spell would be stronger. Filtering our energy through the time stream instead of letting it build up. No more fear of potential destruction from within. My potential realized.

My parents would be so proud.

My skin itched with unreleased energy. I could do it. Even if Lily was right, and the energy burned everything away, I could direct it one last time. Let this be my legacy.

A lone figure stepped out from the concealed community, following the path toward the Gatehouse with a star torch in one hand. When she broke through the trees, my mother lowered the torch. The open area that led to the Creek shimmered in the light cast by my energy.

I hadn't seen her since spring break. She walked slowly, her face drawn. We'd argued the last time I came home. I told her to let me go.

She let him go. When we were in the time stream, closing down the boundary spell, meeting with each of the past Gatekeepers in their own times. She'd been Dad's anchor. I trusted her to bring him back while I held the time stream open. But somehow, he'd fallen back. Her anguished scream as she lost him rang in my ears.

I'd failed so many times to bring him back. I could have tried harder. Should have come home sooner. Should have known.

I could still save him.

She looked up at me, and her eyes watered. Was she crying or just dazzled by the light?

On the other side of the Gatehouse, Adam and the hunters remained frozen in place, Wesson's aging temporarily arrested. Where had the others gone? I didn't see Lily, Brian, or Jasmine in front of the building.

Mom called out to me. "Don't do this for us. Don't do this for him."

"You don't know what I'm doing. I can fix everything."

"Not like this." She put the star torch down at her feet.

I drifted lower, watching for Jasmine and her crossbow. "This is the only way. I'm strong enough now. I can bring Dad back. I protect us like I was supposed to."

"This isn't what he wanted. You know it isn't. Don't lay this on him." Her tone stung.

"Are you mad at me right now? I'm fulfilling the prophecy. Meeting my destiny. What more do you want?"

She sighed. "What do you want?"

When has what I want ever mattered? I didn't say it. It wasn't true. But it felt true.

A tear made of starlight twinkled in the corner of my eye and ran down my cheek. "I just miss him, Mom."

"Oh, honey." She wrapped her arms around herself. "So do I. But he wouldn't want you to burn yourself out like this. Not for anything."

"What do I do?" I pushed down the voice in my mind. It's opinion didn't matter anymore.

"You're the only one who can decide what you'll do next." She sucked in a breath. "But I'll tell you, I would hate to lose you, too."

The sparkling tear caught at the corner of my mouth. I nodded. "I'm sorry. I love you."

Her eyes widened, and she called my name, but I'd already risen over the Gatehouse.

On the far side, I blew the hunters a kiss, making a wish as I released them from their time bubbles. Wesson staggered backwards, falling to the ground.

No! You cannot let them go. Think of what they might do. Think of the energy wasted.

That was the truth, finally. The demon didn't care if the people of Queen's Creek survived. It only wanted the energy it could take from anyone who threatened me. Once I'd burned through all of our enemies, what opponent would it turn to? Who would it turn me against?

Pressure built in my mind. The creature pushed its will against my own.

I almost laughed. "You think you can control me, demon? Weren't you the one who told me how strong I was? I thought I needed you. But maybe you were right. The time has come for us to part ways."

I forced it back down and faced the hunters. My fingers twitched. The hunters stood in their places, frozen by fear instead of magic.

"Leave this place." My voice thundered, the energy rattling the branches.

The remaining hunters looked at each other for a split second before coming to the unanimous decision to retreat.

Wiping my eyes, I drifted down to face Adam. I snapped my fingers. He stepped back, carried by the momentum from before I stopped him.

My eyes burned into his, and I wished for Elspeth's Gift. To understand his feelings without words. Because what words would make things right between us? "I'm sorry."

He reached for me.

I blinked.

59

I opened my eyes in the time stream. My breathing slowed. The burning in my skin faded to a low vibration. I released the energy I'd taken.

The creature complained, but every time I pushed it back, its voice became softer.

With all of time stretching out around me, I turned, looking to the future. The stream branched in three directions. Each of those broke off into more and then more. Too many possible outcomes. But in one of them, things would work out.

The energy of the time stream nipped at my skin. I hadn't noticed it when I'd let the demon draw it in. But now it stung. Maybe Lily was right about the effect of that much energy. How long could I stay before it destroyed me?

Was that what had happened to my father? Why, lately, I'd only heard his voice?

I chose a direction and pushed forward. Time passed on all sides. Bubbles caught in my hair, popped on the corners of my glasses. I caught edges of conversations, flashes of moments. No sign of my father.

Elspeth held a vial of purple liquid. I backtracked downstream to watch her make it.

A stone. A purple crystal with streaks of red. The philosopher's stone. She pulled it from a drawer, but how did it get there?

The current dragged me away. The demon whined.

Lalo stood in the moonlight, a human child in his red hoodie. He held something in his hands, a faint red glow emanating from between them.

Whatever it was interested the demon. I pushed the creature's consciousness down, visualizing a door closing between us.

A garden of roses. Lily plucked a lavender bud and held it out to me.

As I reached for it, time passed again, taking the bubbles with it.

The last one flickered it as it passed. A scene not set, but on its way. Caleb sat in an antique chair. It looked brand new. There was gray in his hair and a small child playing at his feet. Across the room, Elspeth smiled from behind a large book.

I drifted back the way I'd come. The bubbles here all held moments I'd recently lived through. My mother's star torch bobbing through the woods. The strange glimmer on the tips of Jasmine's arrows.

I smiled as the pieces fit together. Images from the visions slotted into each other, forming a single idea. And then another, bigger one. Solutions without sacrifice. Almost showtime. Just have to get the props in place.

My fingers tingled, itching for the return of the energy I'd released.

Alright. Just a little.

Just this once. And then maybe once more.

I visualized the things that we'd need until they became as real as my memories. Folding them tightly, I dropped them back into the current, messages in a bottle directed by my intentions. They would reach their destinations.

The demon pushed at my makeshift door, sensing the energy. It threatened, then begged me to release it as the energy ebbed away.

Not yet. You'll have to wait.

Closing my eyes, I settled into the flow of the time stream, letting it carry me back to the present. Perhaps a little farther. Give them time.

A week and a day. That should do. Now, for my last dramatic entrance.

I pulled in the energy I would need to escape the time stream at the point of my choosing, forcing my way against the current. My skin began to glow.

Pushing back to the surface, I crested the water, shooting out like a star.

Screams from the bank heralded my return. Half of the town must have been there. Jonathan led my brothers forward, carrying a large glass globe. The grandmother of the star torches they'd used to find me.

People shielded their eyes. The light washed them all out. I was lost in a black-and-white landscape. The energy I'd brought with me pushed out at my skin, seeking out places to escape. It was too much for this world.

Behind my brothers, the people of Queen's Creek lifted their arms, linking their magic to form a shield. Protecting themselves from me. Giles and Mrs. Kirk shouted instructions, but the buzzing had returned to my ears. Their words weren't for me anyway.

The water of the Creek rose between me and the bank.

"They will never understand you," said the voice in my head. "Not like I do."

You wanted to abandon me in the time stream.

"Only to get out of your way. To let you step into your own power. There is still so much more you could have."

See? This is your problem, demon. You'll never be satisfied. No matter how much you take.

"You want your father back, don't you? Take me back into the time stream, and we'll find him together."

I'll find him.

"You need me."

I don't think that I do, actually.

"You're a fool. You can't do this alone."

I'm not alone. I have them.

On the banks of the Creek, Brian stood with Adam and Tori. He held a large silver frame.

"You think that will hold me? Have you learned nothing?"

I've learned a lot, actually. But mostly, I've learned to trust the people who know more than I do.

My brothers carried the globe to Brian and carefully fit it together.

The demon twitched, looking for an escape, but the shield my elders had created gave it nowhere to go. It had already admitted it couldn't get back into the time stream without me.

Brian and Adam lifted the new lantern. Tori stood ready beside them.

"Ready?" called Jonathan.

I lowered myself to the bridge. Mrs. Kirk called out another command and an opening appeared in the boundary, just as wide as the bridge. I walked to the shore.

Jasmine stepped up beside Tori and raised her crossbow. A shining silver cord ran from the end of the arrow to the frame of the lantern.

"You see!" screamed the voice in my head. "They mean to destroy you!"

She's not here for me. Those arrows are silver-tipped. I've been wrong about a lot of supernatural lore, but this is just science. Brian was a good tutor before I let my fears get in the way. Silver has the highest electrical conductivity of all metals. If you don't follow Tori's directions, Jasmine will be sure you get where you're going.

I met Tori's eyes. "Now."

Her magic surrounded me, holding me in place. It tugged at my chest.

I forced a long, slow breath, relaxing my muscles.

The golden thread she'd pulled from Lily unraveled in front of me. The voice in my head grew softer. The cord of energy thrashed in the air, tangling and knotting in its efforts to avoid the iron cage.

I gasped as the last of it pulled free.

My hands flew up instinctively, but Jonathan's strength and Tori's Gift were enough to force the creature into its new home, even without Jasmine's encouragement.

Adam slammed the door shut after the last of the threads crossed into the frame.

Jasmine mumbled something about not getting to use a perfectly good weapon. Then she pulled the silver cord loose from her arrow and tied it around the lantern, weaving between the bars. She tied it off and handed the end to Adam.

He separated the threads, and a shimmering net—some kind of ward—expanded over the lantern.

Jonathan lifted it over his head, letting the light spread across the bank.

Mrs. Kirk barked a command, and the other elders released their spell. The water sank back into the Creek, splashing the bridge.

My hands shook as I remembered the last time I'd faced her here. But she didn't even look at me. She smiled at Giles and shook his hand. Then she led the elders back toward town, laughing in conversation as if they'd just won at Bingo.

Giles met us at the bridge. He slapped Jonathan on the back, but the lantern didn't waver in his hands. "Well done, kids. That should hold it. Have you given any thought to where we should keep it?"

"We can't take it to the Watch Tower, Dad," Adam said. "It's not a lighthouse. It'll draw too much attention."

"Actually, Isa had an idea." Brian beckoned the girl forward. I hadn't seen her there before, hanging back behind my eldest brothers, Matthew and Gabriel. The ones who'd helped Dad with his experiments.

Gabe put his hand on her shoulder. "It's an excellent idea actually. Wish I'd thought of it."

Isa grinned.

He really was a good teacher, and with his Gift with electricity, she'd probably learned a lot from him while I stalled the demon in the time stream.

"Out with it, then." Giles crossed his arms.

"Well, you know how there's that electrical substation down the road?" Isa twisted a finger in the red strands of her undercut. "Don't you think that would mask the energy pretty well?"

"We've been studying the map," Adam explained. "Watching to make sure the hunters don't come back. Not that we think they would, after you…"

"Went full *Arc of the Covenant* on them!" Tori laughed. "Jasmine told me all about it. Sounds fantastic."

"I didn't melt anybody's face off." I chewed my lip. But I might have if Adam hadn't stepped in the way.

They all stared at me with varying levels of awe and disgust.

Right. So. This was going to be one of those you-have-to-live-through-it-to-get-through-it things. Awkward as fae feasts until everybody got over what I'd done. If they got over it. If I did.

Anyway.

"That sounds like a great idea, Isa," I said.

"Oh, that's not all," Gabe said. "We're going to wire it up to act as a beacon to warn us if anyone's coming."

I tried to picture it. "Like an extra large kynigolabe."

"Exactly." Gabe pointed at me like I'd just earned extra credit.

It was a much better plan than an endless cycle of maiden Gatekeepers.

Isa shifted her weight back and forth from one foot to the other. "Okay, so, umm. We're going to go now, okay?"

I realized I was blocking the exit. "Sorry."

I stepped to the side, and Isa led Gabe and Jonathan across the bridge and into the Gatehouse. I started to follow, but Adam took my hand.

"They've got it from here," he said. "Elspeth wants to see you at the healer's cottage. Your work's not quite done yet, Chosen One."

60

lspeth started talking as soon as I walked in. "So, I don't know how you did it, but this is my handwriting, right?"

She brushed back a stray gray hair and held up the Ichoriad, open to a page near the end. Plain blue ballpoint ink scrawled across the page. Definitely Elspeth's handwriting.

"I can explain…"

She pursed her lips. Lines formed that hadn't been there before spring break. "This wasn't here when you got here. And I've read it, but I have no idea where I got any of this information. So when did I write it? When will I write it?"

The flashback bubbles in the time stream. I'd known it would all come down to her. That I could never have finished this without her. Two girls sitting beside the Creek, making plans and breaking all the rules.

She was almost as tied to the time stream as I was now. She'd lived so much of her life without us, trapped back in the early days of Queen's Creek. We still hadn't had a chance to talk about it.

"You wrote it…umm…when you were. Well, you wrote it in the past."

She frowned, closed her eyes. I felt a tug on the edge of my psyche. Her empathic abilities searching for clues. "Why are you nervous? What did you do?"

I sat down on the recovery bed where she'd treated my concussion. "I'm not sure how long it's going to take for you to catch up. Because you've done it already. But also, I have one more thing I have to do before it's even possible for you to have done it. And I'm not sure I can do it anymore."

She sat in the chair by the bed where she'd waited for me to wake up after I fell in the Creek. "When?"

"About a hundred years ago."

She nodded. "Okay. So, we're going finish all this and then you'll take the book back...and I'll write about it?"

"Not me."

"What? Who?"

I grimaced, not ready to tell her before I told him.

Her eyes widened. "Oh. Your mother's going to kill you."

I leaned forward, bracing my elbows on my knees and covering my eyes. "Probably. Yeah."

"Thank you," Elspeth whispered.

My head leaned to the side. "It's not just for you, you know. He's...he just can't. Without you. You know? And anyway, somebody needs to get the book back to where it'll be safe. I'm leaving you with the hard stuff. Protect it, figure out how to split it in two. Put the wards back on before your descendants drop it in the library donations stack."

Someone in their line was going to have to get to Chicago during their Wakening, but closing that part of the loop was definitely out of my control. *Trust.* They had a few generations to get out of Queen's Creek before we went looking for it.

"My descendants? You really think this is going to work?"

"Three or four really cheesy movies say it's possible."

"I'll take your word for it."

"You don't have to," I sat up. "We could get a DVD player in here. Who knows, Gabe might have us set up for WI-FI in a month or so. Movie nights are coming."

"And as much as I'm looking forward to that, we have more pressing concerns."

I looked around, realizing for the first time that Elspeth didn't have any patients. My stomach knotted. "What happened to Emily?"

"She and Isa are staying with Gosnalls for now. She's taking it slow, but I think she'll recover."

"Lily gave you the antidote?" Maybe Noemi's Mama Lily would return to the woman she'd known now that we'd unpossessed her.

Elspeth wrinkled her nose. "She didn't want to, but between Adam's Gift and mine…"

"Must have been some interrogation." I imagined Lily tied to Elspeth's chair with a star torch casting shadows above her head. Adam pounding the table where Elspeth mixed her herbs.

The healer shook her head. "I don't think she wants Emily to die. But that woman has some unresolved issues with mundanes that she really needs to work through."

Maybe the demon hadn't had to push her as hard as I'd hoped. But if Emily was getting better…"What are the pressing concerns?"

Elspeth frowned. "It's Lalo."

"He's still a puppy?"

"Yes and no. He finally decided to make the change two days ago when the moon was full. He said something about that being a special time. It made him feel stronger." She waited for me to clarify her suspicions.

I tried to remember what his aunt had told me back in Chicago. "Noemi said that they got their transfusions on the full moon. I think their family traditions were built around the lunar cycles. It might remind him of his parents."

Elspeth nodded. "Belief makes it stronger. If he believes that's a special time, and he sets his intentions around it, that belief should be enough."

"What do you mean *should be*? Is he a dog or isn't he?"

She looked out the window at the moonlight. "He's a boy for now. But when the sun comes up…"

"He's a dog in the daylight? Like a werewolf? Wait. That's backwards. Isn't it supposed to be the other way around?"

"He's working through it, but in the meantime…" She stood and went back to the table with the book, flipping pages. "If we still want to make the elixir of life, I think we need to do it soon."

I gripped the edge of the bunk. *No more bad news.* "Is he dying?"

"What?" she looked up. Her eyebrows jumped up when she followed my train of thought. "No! No, it isn't for him. Well, it is for him, but for the vampire thing, not the werewolf thing. And it's not an emergency. He'll be okay. No."

"Then what?"

She put a hand on the book, holding the page open. "We need him to make it. And he needs fingers to be able to do it. So we have to do it while he's a boy. The moon won't be full anymore tomorrow. The cycle only lasts three nights. It's not even really full tonight. He had a harder time making the change than yesterday. I don't know if he'll be able to do it tomorrow. So unless you want to wait a month…"

Dad might not have a month. It might already be too late. If the energy of the time stream had been pulling on him this whole time the way it pulled on me…There might not be much left of him. He might be more like the creature that we'd trapped in the lantern.

"What does the book say?"

"We need the philosopher's stone." She continued to list

ingredients, some more rare than others.

I'd seen the stone in one of my visions. She pulled it from that drawer. I stood, leaning past her to open it. The drawer held a small tray of crystals, as well as a few other esoteric tools, but none of them matched my vision of a purple stone streaked with red. She didn't have it yet.

"Lalo can make it," Elspeth said.

"You're sure?"

"Matthew is. He's been experimenting with different stones since your father first started trying to create the elixir. He said it was beyond him. But Lalo's Gift is just as strong. Matthew thinks that the two of them together could complete the transmutation." She pushed the drawer back into the cabinet.

"So they'll do it tonight," I said, my heart racing.

"Yes, but did you hear me? We also need…"

"A purple flower," I said, remembering the vision of Lily plucking the rose. It had grown in my mother's garden but not from any of the plants I'd ever seen there.

"And bottled time."

"That's easy. There'll be thyme in the garden." Not remotely as rare as purple roses.

She took my hands. "No. Time. From the time stream."

"I can't go back." I pulled my hands away. It was a stupid thing to say. How else was I going to find Dad? It wasn't like I could sit on the bridge and drop a fishing line. But the idea of going back into the time stream without the demon to filter the energy was terrifying. My skin prickled, goosebumps rinsing over the places I'd felt the energy burn me, pulling me apart.

Elspeth leaned back against the table. "No one will make you. But if you want to try, tonight is our best chance. For your dad. And for Noemi and Lalo."

She didn't mean it as a guilt trip, but she may as well have packed my bags. Could I condemn that goofy little boy to a life of vegan vampirism? Noemi tried so hard to hide the things that challenged her, but could I look her in the eye if I'd had the opportunity to get the cure and didn't take it?

"You'll have anchors this time," Elspeth said.

"How?" Last time we'd done a group field trip into the time stream—back when we were contacting the ancestors to help us break the boundary spell—I'd anchored everyone with a partner whose Gift matched their own. Earth with earth and air with air. There was no partner for me. I was the only witch we knew with a Gift aligned to spirit.

Elspeth smirked. "We all have spirit, Cate."

61

I swore to myself that this would be my last dip into the time stream, knowing that it was probably a lie. My family waited on the bank of the Creek. I called on my Gift and visualized the open door. The current carried me away.

This time, it was as if time knew why I'd come. I brought no threat with me, and my intentions were set on the greater good. The bubbles that caught on my fingertips showed me my father's life.

A young boy playing ball with a friend.

An older boy hanging upside down from a tree—a tree I was pretty sure he'd forbidden me to climb.

He brought my mother for a picnic by the Creek.

I saw him in his classroom, teaching children whose children now sat in Gabe's class.

He played with his own children, laughing just as hard as they did.

His head bent over his work at a desk covered in papers.

Was this all that he was now? A collection of his own memories?

Voices called my name in the distance. My brothers. My

mom. Calling back to my own time.

I pulled the vial Elspeth had given me from my pocket. Closing my eyes, I asked the time stream for its help. Time flowed around me, swirling and lifting me up. When I opened my eyes, the vial was full of an iridescent liquid. Gold and silver spinning together. I gave the time stream my thanks and pushed myself up to the surface. As my head broke through the water, I gasped for air. Instead of rising above the Creek as a living star, I found myself treading water. I sputtered, laughing.

Thomas pulled me out, and I smashed into him as I dragged myself up the bank. "You've got to stop doing this. Maybe get some swimming lessons or something."

I gave Elspeth the vial.

She blinked, taking the bottled time with her.

"Done now," I said, lying on my back in the dirt. "When the next apocalypse comes…it's your turn."

I closed my eyes.

When I opened them again, I was back in my own bed. My mother sat in a chair by my side.

"Don't do that again," she said.

I pushed myself up to sitting and crossed my heart with an index finger. "Promise. Where are my glasses?"

She handed them to me, along with a large ring.

"What's this?" I put my glasses on and held up the ring to the light. It looked like one of Lily's.

"Elspeth made it as a thank you after she completed the elixir. She said she got the idea from something in that grimoire you brought with you? There's one for you, one for me, and she's working on more, but she was worried about running out of ingredients. Apparently there's a drop of time in there. And I told her you'd given her as much time as you could. When she's out, that's it."

I tilted the ring sideways. It had a hinge, but she'd welded it shut. Whatever was in there was not coming out.

"How are you feeling?" Mom asked.

"Better, thanks," I mumbled, still puzzling out the ring.

"I'll leave you alone then. I just wanted to be sure…"

I set the ring on the bed and grabbed her hand as she stood up. "I'm sorry, Mom. I'm okay, and I'm sorry that I made you worry."

There were other apologies underneath, but they were too hard to bring to the surface. I hoped she saw them.

She smiled and looked away. "You just rest."

When I was alone, I lifted the ring again, wondering what was inside besides of course, a drop of time. I slid the ring on my index finger, spinning it with my thumb. If nothing else, it made a great fidget.

I should have known better.

The metal warmed under my hand, but my fingers were too cold to draw body heat. It pulled energy from the air. A window opened at the end of my bed. A vision like the ones I'd seen in the time stream. This time, my father stood in the Gatehouse door, waving goodbye. It was the day I'd left for my Wakening. He smiled.

I pulled the ring from my finger and the window closed, taking the vision with it.

Elspeth had given me a piece of the time stream. I could take it with me anywhere. What else could it do?

The next time I saw Elspeth, she was saying goodbye to my brother. Caleb held the Ichoriad, wrapped in cloth and wax paper, under one arm. He made promises he had no way of keeping. She made them back.

"I'll see you soon," she kept saying, a tear running down

her cheek.

I knew she would—or she had. I saw it in the time stream. The two of them together, living in one of the first cottages built after the Gatehouse. In another bubble, they'd had children, a boy and a girl. He taught them to draw. They illustrated the pages of the book where Elspeth recorded the collective knowledge of Queen's Creek's first coven. They grew old together. They would live out their lives in peace.

But I didn't know if this Elspeth—the one I'd pulled from the Creek when we thought she was lost—would ever see him again. So I kept my distance as long as I dared.

Caleb turned. "Send me back to her."

I twisted the ring on my finger. The energy came rushing back, but I held it at bay, pulling only what I needed. I held out my hands and Caleb laid his over them. "Close your eyes."

The door I visualized this time had only one current. It ran straight to 1730. To Mary and the founding of Queen's Creek. When the door opened, I saw the Gatehouse as it had been. The newly built home of every future Gatekeeper was warm and inviting. Inside, Mary rocked in a chair by the fire. Elspeth stood looking out the window. Her dark hair lay braided against her back. I could call out to her, bring her back now, and let her have her youth in her own time. Would the older Elspeth disappear? Too many of Brian's favorite movies warned of the paradox.

Caleb called her name.

She turned from the window, a wide smile breaking across her face.

I opened my eyes, and he was gone.

Elspeth threw her arms around me. She hiccoughed, sobbing into my shoulder. "Thank you."

Elspeth's memories came back, or maybe they changed, over the next few weeks. In an odd reversal of the usual aging process, she started to describe more, clearer memories of her life with Caleb. It was a strange loss, as if he'd only moved somewhere far away and we still received the occasional letter. But his letters came in the form of Elspeth's dreams.

Noemi and Lalo stayed in Queen's Creek, working with Elspeth to develop a cure for vampirism from the elixir of life. Adam and Thomas brought Jasmine, Brian, Isa, and Emily back to the city, where Emily threw herself into yoga, saying something about needing to get her mind right again after her recent illness.

Jasmine and Adam hung out at the café, waiting for Brian and me to get off work. We were all taking it slow, but it felt good to have them around.

I heard a familiar voice at the register.

"She says this one's on you," Isa called. "Should I ring up a partner cup?"

Nyla grinned widely. "You owe me."

After she'd gone all secret spy for me with Jasmine and covered for my sudden disappearance at school, I owed her a lot.

"Yeah," I told Isa, "Use my numbers."

She nodded and keyed it in without asking for details. My code should have been confidential, but it had become obvious that if it had ever been entered into a machine, Isa could find it.

"Thank you…" Nyla sang. "But don't think that's the last one."

While I steamed the milk and pulled the ingredients for Nyla's potion of choice, Brian tried to talk her into buying the last chocolate chip cookie so he wouldn't have to mark it out while he cleaned up the pastry case.

"Nah," she said, "I'm watching my sugar."

Brian turned in time to see me coat the inside of her cup with caramel.

"Yeah," he said, "Me too."

"Hey, balance is important." She swung her hair around and marched to my side of the bar to pick up her drink.

I slid the cup across the counter like a bartender in some old movie. "Iced venti soy matcha latte with caramel drizzle."

"Thanks!" Nyla reached for it and missed.

The cup careened over the side. The lid went flying, splashing caramel-coated whipped cream everywhere. The cup hit the ground with a crunch, sending ice and creamy tea across the tiles.

Nyla grimaced. "Oops. Sorry."

So much for dance team reflexes. Jasmine better get practices going again soon.

I grinned. "Don't worry, I've got it."

I reached a hand over the side of the counter, flexing it above the spill. I called energy from my morning chai and felt it tingle down my arm. My fingertips glowed like fireflies, no sparks this time. Nyla backed up, her eyes wide. Concentrating on the cup, the tea that slowly spread across the floor, and the lid that had somehow rolled under a nearby chair, I imagined time reversing for them and them only. The lid popped up on its edge and rolled back into view. The pale green liquid oozed back toward the cup as if sucked by a straw. The cracked plastic on the side of the cup knit itself back together and the whole thing righted itself. Splattered whipped cream floated back just in time for the lid to pop itself back on. The cup rose through the air, catching the drips that had leaked on the way down. It settled on the edge of the counter and slid back toward my hand. I lifted it and released the magical energy. My fingers dimmed as I placed the cup back on the handover stand where I had meant to put it to begin with. Pristine. As if the spill had never happened.

Because as far as that drink was concerned, it didn't.

Nyla stood still. For a second, I thought I might have misjudged the spell and frozen her too. Then she blinked.

I cleared my throat, wiping my hands on a rag. "There's something you should know."

"Oh yeah?"

"I'm a witch." I waited for her to panic. To scream about how I'd been lying to her for years. This might be the end of our friendship.

Nyla eyed me and the cup. She stared down at the floor. When she looked up again, she raised an eyebrow and tossed her braids over her shoulder. "Uh…cool. Look, that was great and all, but I can't get over it was on the floor. You're going to make me a new one, right?"

I laughed. "Coming right up."

Jenn Lessmann

Thank You!

I hope you enjoyed the final installment of the
Cate Corey's Unmagical Life Trilogy.
Please consider leaving a review if you liked
Unbelievable.
You can help this book find its audience (and
earn my eternal gratitude!) by typing a sentence or
two.

Not ready to leave Queen's Creek?

Subscribe to the *Queen's Creek Chronicle* to get access to bonus
content, author updates, and witchy book recommendations.

You can find the signup link, as well as my shop for magical
merch, at www.JennLessmann.com

Also by Jenn Lessmann

The Cate Corey's Unmagical Life Trilogy
Unmagical: a witchy mystery
Unforgivable: an urban cozy
Unbelievable: a suburban legend

Short Stories
Street Muse

Serials
The Devil in the Details
Sixes

Acknowledgements

This series would not exist without the patience and support of so many people.

George, you are everything, and you make everything seem possible. I'll be thanking you forever.

Thank you to Kat Keenan, who reads everything first and talks me through logic problems on and off the page. You keep me on track. My writing and my business would be a mess without you.

Thank you to Chrishaun Keller for reminding me to celebrate the small wins. Working on our podcast together has forced me to think about my work, goals, and values from a new perspective.

Thank you to Holly MacGregor and Kristen Tassin for sharing your experiences and making the whole writing life a little less lonely.

Thanks to Chelle Honiker, Nicole Schroeder, and the rest of the team at Indie Author Magazine for giving me an opportunity to grow my craft and nurturing an educational environment for indie authors.

Thank you to Karryn Nagel for organizing the community and events for the Cozy the Day Away sale, through which I've found so many new readers.

Most especially, I want to thank my readers for taking a chance on a new author. It means so much to me that you have found Cate relatable. There's a lot of me in her.

About the Author

Jenn Lessmann writes more snark/less dark urban fantasy and apocalyptic cozies. She is the author of the Cate Corey's Unmagical Life trilogy, including Unmagical: a witchy mystery, Unforgivable: an urban cozy, and Unbelievable: a suburban legend.

A former barista, stage manager, and high school English teacher with advanced degrees from impressive colleges, Jenn continues to drink excessive amounts of caffeine, stay up later than is absolutely necessary, and read three or four books at a time. She lives in Virginia with her husband and their two boys and writes snarky paranormal fantasy whenever their dog will allow it.

In her spare time, Jenn runs a podcast about what it means to live a creative life - as a business owner and creator - with bestselling author and game designer Chrishaun Keller. Catch their conversations on Building the Creative Life, now on Spotify.

Follow across social media platforms @JennLessmannAuthor